ANGELTOWN

FIONA CANE

Dear Helen

with loads of love

Fiona xx

Caracol Books

First published in the UK in 2022 by Caracol Books.

ISBN
Cover design by Adrian Newton
Cover image: Krzysztof12 - iStock

For Sam

It is undesirable to believe a proposition when there is no good ground whatever for supposing it true.

Bertrand Russell

Believe in what you see ... If you see me as your God, I'll be your God.

Keep them poor and keep them tired, and they'll never leave.

Jim Jones

Three years earlier

The door slams with a bang, and my teeth start their chitter-chattering again. Why, I don't know because he does that, Elijah. Slams doors. Every single day. No word of a lie. It's a wonder ours is still hanging on its hinges. *Bang*. I'm leaving. *Bang*. I'm home. *Bang*. I'm headed for the yard.

Bang. Bang. Bang.

As if we give a damn.

All the same, the breath I didn't know I was holding leaves my lungs in a satisfying sigh, and my limbs seem to melt like butter in the sun. I wriggle and writhe and shake my arms and legs. Boy, does that feel good. And smile because it's Saturday, which means no more mean-faced Elijah and no more banging doors today. No school, chores, nor meetings neither.

I pull on my bib overalls and tear down the stairs. I can't see my shoes so I dash into the street in case Mom has me searching for them. I've got places to go, people to see, to borrow one of her favourite sayings.

'Lois!'

'What?'

'Your shoes?'

I twirl around and look at Mom in such a way I know she'll believe what I'm about to say. 'They're at Abi's. Headed there right now.'

And before she can say another word, I'm sprinting down the road, my clean white feet kicking up the dust.

• • •

David is sitting in his usual place on the jetty, legs swinging, waiting for Fisherman Cain. Never seems to tire of those ugly, whiskery catfish, does David. Spends all his free time trying to catch 'em.

'Hey, Lois. Fancy joining us?'

I stop to think about it. I'm sore tempted cos they fish on the ginormous river outsidda Edenville, and I like reeling in those monsters with the chicken-liver bait, too. But I like David even more. I mean, who wouldn't? Even I can see he's what Mom would call real handsome. Golden hair. The cutest smile. He's a year older but a whole lot wiser, so I'm thankful he even notices me, let alone wants to hang out. Once he showed me a nest of fluffy grey cygnets he'd found hidden in the reeds. *Our secret,* he said. *You mustn't tell a soul.* Boy oh boy. He could've shown any kid, but he chose me. Yessiree. He's about the bestest boy in the whole of Edenville.

I screw up my nose. 'I promised Abi.'

'Next time, then.'

I nod so hard it hurts.

David laughs. 'It's a deal. Have fun. And Lois?'

'What?'

'Stay out of trouble.'

I grin and wave and set off again, slower now, more ladylike. Sometimes it's important to create the right impression.

The fields around Farmer Samuel's barn seem to be deserted, but I check the area, just in case. It's not that we aren't allowed to play here. It's ... well ... I guess ... better if no one knows we do. It's kinda hard to get any privacy in a town like ours, see.

A couple of swans are swimming on the canal, but nothing and nobody else is about, so I dart inside. It's dark after the white brightness of the sunshine. I blink rapidly, but there's no rushing my eyes.

'*Psst*. Lois.'

I squint and look up to the rafters where Abi's white-blonde hair shines like a halo.

'What you waiting for? C'mon.'

I clamber to the top and dive over the hay bales into the den the three of 'em have built already.

'What kept you, Lois?' Ben and Gideon ask.

I scrunch up my cheeks until their bug-eyes blur. Right away, Abi puts her arm around me, and I know I don't have to say any more. She knows all right. No need to waste any words.

Next thing, Ben is stuffing hay down the back of my T-shirt, and pretty soon we're tumbling about, squealing.

Later, Abi hands us all some lemonade she's thought to bring along, and a loaf of bread which she tears into chunks. She's like that, Abi. What Mom would call real practical. I cram mine into my mouth cos I skipped breakfast, what with avoiding Elijah and all.

'I wish it could be like this always,' I say when I'm done eating.

Ben clicks his tongue. 'Three more years is all we've got.'

Those words seem to suck all the joy from the air. No one speaks for thinking things through. What lies in store? No more free time, that's for sure. I guess I'll be sent to work in The Mill and The Bakery, like Mom. I'm not clever like Abi. I swear she's destined for something special. One of the chosen few. David will be a fisherman, no question. Ben a carpenter, perhaps.

'I'm gonna run away,' Gideon says.

Ben digs him in the ribs. 'Don't joke, Giddy.'

'I'm serious.'

'But it's dangerous, you know ...' I tilt my head, '... out there.'

'Yeah, but I ain't gonna spend the rest of my life being told what to do.'

He's got a point, but running away?

Abi sniffs. 'It's not that bad, and anyway, where will you go?'

'Anywhere but here.'

I have a hundred questions I want to ask, but my thoughts are all tangled, and I don't know where to begin. Not that it matters because the unmistakable thud of footsteps brings our chatter to an end.

Ben puts a finger to his lips, and I peep through a hole expecting to see Farmer Samuel or, at worst, Elijah's mean face. But it isn't. It's half a dozen men dressed all in black. Black shirts, black jeans, shiny black boots, and black scarves wound around their heads covering all but their eyes. Hell, I know what they are even though I've never seen them before. Nobody has, at least none I've met. Us kids think they're fiends made up by our parents to frighten us into behaving. But here they are. The Powers. The faceless, nameless men. Jet-black and menacing with guns in black holsters strapped around their waists.

I gulp down my fear, a solid, prickly ball, and turn to Abi. But that doesn't help me one little bit. Silent tears stream down her cheeks, and from beneath her shorts, a trickle of pee dribbles past her knees.

'It's okay,' I whisper, reaching for her hand. 'They won't find us.'

It's what I'm hoping, but I'm thinking, what will happen if they do?

CHAPTER
ONE

December 1982

I shouldn't be here. It's absolutely forbidden, which makes it kinda exciting. Nobody can see me, though. There's the mother of all storms coming, and I'm talking the hell and fury kind. The sky is bruised. No trace of a moon, no hint of a star. Too dark to see any more than my hand in front of my face. My ears, though, are on high alert. I can hear every little thing. The crunch of a cheese-bush needle underfoot. The flick of a bat's wing. The clickety-clack of my heart. And my mother's hoarse whisper scooting towards me through the still night air.

'Lola. Lola. Where *are* you?'

There's a pause, the long, drawn-out kind. Uh-oh. Here it comes ...

'Lois! Lois!'

I smile. I shouldn't, though, cos it's a serious matter and likely to get her into a heap of trouble. Mom says Lola is for her. Her favourite name of all time, apparently. *So pretty. Like you.* Hmm, debatable. But the syllables do trip off the tongue, light and easy like the first notes of a favourite hymn. Lo-LA.

My given name, Lois, is fairly unusual. Only gets a single mention in The Book. Timothy's grandmother. I mean, who cares? It's not like she features in The Story. She just happened to be an influence. On Timothy's life, that is, nobody else's. Still, it could have been worse. I could have been Eunice. That's Lois' daughter's name. Ew! Eunice. Imagine?

For years I've assumed I'm incidental, unimportant, a nobody. I'm the only Lois in town, which kind of proves my theory. But here's the thing, according to the whispered word, the Divine Protector's been showing an interest in me. Rumour has it I'm about to be summoned. See, it's not like you can simply stroll up to him, unannounced, and say, *Hi, it's me, fancy a chinwag*, or drop in uninvited because you happen to be passing. There's a whole lot of protocol involved. I'm not sure what exactly. But I do know that it's complicated.

I can't tell you how much I want it to be true, but I have my doubts. These rumours have a habit of being way off the mark. Somebody whispers something to someone that no one is supposed to know. That someone passes it on to somebody else, skewing the facts ever so slightly, and telling them to keep schtum. Except that somebody goes right ahead and tells someone else, getting another little detail a teeny bit wrong, and what becomes fact is something so far from the original truth it's split-your-sides funny. I'd hate that to be the case with me. Not now I've got my hopes up. So, before I get all excited and start yelling about my up-and-coming meeting – *as if* – I need to check if my source is reliable. It won't be easy. Edenville is a town tied up in secrets. That's just the way it is.

Hasn't stopped me from being excited, though, which is why I'm hanging around outside Ascension House. Hidden behind a tree, of course. It may be dark, but I'm not totally dumb. If the doors open, my plan is to sneak in, I'm that desperate to get up close to The Divine Protector. Course, I've *seen* him plenty of times. We all have. But only ever from the chest up when he waves at his people through the window of his car. And what a car. Sleek and shiny, with a silver angel on the front. I love that angel. Arms and wings outstretched, she looks fearless, like she's about to dive right into the world no matter what.

The DP wears a white tunic when he's out and about, not the robe he's wearing in the paintings and the photographs. We gotta couple of portraits in our house. They're man-dat-ory, Mom says, which apparently means there's no way round it. And there's one in every classroom at school and in the Meeting Room. That one is colossal. Nobody could be that tall, could they? So, I know what he looks like. Dark shoulder-length hair and matching beard. Brown eyes, smiling mouth. Clean hands with long fingers and neat nails. And around his body a radiant, glowing light. I know what he sounds like, too, from The Meetings and the Tannoy Announcements. But I don't know exactly how tall he is. Or what he smells like. The way he walks. What makes him laugh. Does he laugh? That's another thing I don't know. If the rumours are true, and I sure hope they are, then these are things I ought to know.

My mother taps me on the shoulder, and my bones almost burst through my skin. 'Jesus, Mom.'

'For pity's sake,' she hisses, and an unattractive spray of spittle spews from her mouth onto my chin.

I try not to cringe. It would only make her angrier.

'How many times do I have to tell you not to speak like that?'

'I'm sorry. With the shock of you creeping up on me it fell out of my mouth.' Which is true, it did, although that kinda cussing is a real stress-buster. Boy, does it make you feel good.

'What on earth are you doing? You know you shouldn't be here. What if someone sees you?' Seems she doesn't need an answer because she takes hold of my arm and yanks me backwards. 'Come on.'

'Ouch, that hurts.'

'Good. Now hurry up, before we're seen.'

'Who is going to see us? It's Curfew. Everyone's inside.'

'Everyone but the Powers.'

The words alone make me twitch. Since the day in the barn three years ago, we haven't set eyes on the Powers again. It's got so we're convinced we imagined them. That they're just a silly bogeymen story after all. 'Gee whiz, Mom. When did you get so paranoid?'

'I am not paranoid.'

'You so are.'

'Honestly, Lola—'

'Lois.'

'Ugh! Stop with your talking, will you, and get a move on.' She gives me a gentle shove.

'Well, what's the worst that can happen?'

'My dear sweet child, you have no idea.' She throws up her hands and marches on for a few paces then pulls up short, no warning, and I bump into her.

'Jesus, Ma!'

Quick as a flash, she reaches out to cover my mouth

with her hand and steers me behind a bush. 'Get down,' she whispers. 'Listen.'

She gestures frantically towards Ascension House, the gates whirring as they swing open.

I swear Mom has the hearing of a bat. I squat on my haunches, seconds before two beams of light illuminate the spot we were standing in. The Divine Protector. Who else could it be? But why is he leaving Ascension House at night? I stare at my mother with a *what-the-hell* look, but she frowns and puts a finger to her lips. There are beads of sweat on her forehead, her chest rising and falling, lickety-split.

'It's okay, Mom. No one can see us,' I whisper.

'I hope you're right, otherwise ...' She shakes her head.

We're done for, I think, filling in the gaps. It's how my mother thinks. All doom and gloom. I want to tell her not to worry. The Divine Protector wouldn't harm us, or any of his people for that matter. His agenda is about love, not pain. It's why, these days, he insists we're home after dark.

But for some reason my mother has other ideas. She's a glass-half-empty person. Worries over the slightest thing. The other day she got all fired up when she found the storybook I'd hidden in my room, although she hasn't admitted it yet. I'd come across it quite by chance, peeking out from under some maths papers in Principality Judith's study. I'd been sent there for some trivial matter. Answering back, most likely. Only she wasn't around. While I was waiting, I caught sight of its dog-eared corner. It seemed to be daring me to take a closer look which, of course, I did. I liked the cover, the almost-face with the strange eyes and the red mouth, so I snuck it into my apron pocket. Not a moment too soon, because Principality Judith marched in and dealt out her punishment – no drama, just ten raps with a ruler on the palm of my hand. Couldn't have cared less because I had the book.

It's got a nifty title, too. *The Great Gatsby*. And it's set in the Otherworld, the evil place of the Eternally Damned. And maybe it is evil, but I'm not entirely sure anymore because it sounded far more exciting than dreary old Edenville. I hardly got started, so not a lot of it made sense. The language was strange, and the central character, Gatsby, seemed freakily obsessed with a crazy lady called Daisy and the green light at the end of her pier. I didn't like Daisy all that much but I held out some hope that I might if I got to know her. The parties sounded a lot of fun, though. All that food, the music, and the sparkly lights. Strikes me the Eternally Damned know how to have a good time. I'd like to go to one of their parties. And I'm curious to find out what's so great about champagne. Anyway, I hid it in my bottom drawer wrapped in two T-shirts, but Mom still found it. What the hell? Why was she going through my private things, that's what I'd like to know?

Mom is chewing the inside of her cheek. A sure sign she's nervous. Soon she'll be drumming her fingers or tapping her foot. The ground's so hard, chances are they'll hear us if she does. I hate to see her this worried so I slip my hand in hers, and she squeezes it tight.

The car rolls past us at a snail's pace and, the weirdest thing, it's black. A black car, searching for something in the black night. It draws to a halt a few metres from where we're cowering.

My mother's eyes bulge in their sockets, and her lips tremble.

And now I begin to wonder. What if she's right? What if it is the Powers? What if they *are* real? What if they've heard about the storybook I stole? What if they're looking for me?

My mind is racing. I can barely breathe for trying to think this through. Suddenly I don't feel so good about this situation I've landed us in. Not at all. I close my eyes, clench my fists, and pray.

Don't get out. Please, don't get out, whoever you are.

The silence grows, fatter, taller, stronger, until it takes up all the space around us. I close my eyes and think encouraging thoughts. It'll be over soon. Whoever it is will drive away, and Mom and I will go back to our cosy little house and eat supper, just as we always do.

There's a click. The car door opens. Someone stomps across the stony ground towards us, far too close to where we're crouched.

A black leather boot. Regulation lace-up.

Shit.

My muscles tense, every single one of them as rigid as my bones.

'Hey, you there?' The Power's voice is deep and scratchy like he's got a throat full of razor blades.

My heartbeat thunders in my ears. I hold my breath and wait for the inevitable. He knows. He knows about the storybook. We're done for. My life over before it's really begun.

CHAPTER TWO

'What do you think you're doing?'

Again, the Power's question is left hanging. Mom squeezes my hand even tighter. Dots dance in front of my eyes. I pray I won't pass out. He'll be sure to hear the thud when my body hits the ground if I do. He's that close to us now, if I reached out the teeniest bit I could touch his shiny black boot. What if they find us? Will the Divine Protector banish me like he did Gideon?

'Hey, you. Come out, or we'll shoot!'

I lick my dry-as-old-rope lips. Sounds like he thinks we're imposters. The Enemy. Maybe it would be better to show ourselves after all. Explain what we're doing. How all I wanted was a peep at my beloved Lord. They wouldn't punish us if I owned up to that. Would they?

Stupid question. I may have boxed up the memory, buried it in a deep dark corner of my mind, but I know what really happened to Gideon. Everyone does. He'd done something far worse than steal a storybook. He wasn't banished. He did what he said he was going to do and ran away. Trouble was, he was caught, and his embarrassed parents isolated him in his room for days. Rumour has it he refused all food. His death from starvation was held up as an example to us all.

This is what happens if you break the rules.

A blinding flash of light sends my heart skipping. A sign? A warning?

'Hey. Stop. You cannot do that.'

The boots are on the move again. They're running. Away from our hideout, away from us. A door slams, there's a crunch, a roar, and the car shoots back real fast.

I suck up air and flick the sweat from my brow. I shall grow old after all. 'Gee, that was close.'

My mother fans her flushed cheeks. 'Too close.' She shuts her eyes and breathes in through her nose, out through her mouth.

I'm mighty relieved she isn't shouting at me. After all, this is my fault. Neither of us speak for a bit, we're that busy trying to control our bouncy-ball hearts. I even find time to cross myself and thank the Lord for sending us that light. 'That bolt of lightning sure was timely. Somebody was looking out for us.'

'It wasn't lightning.'

I raise my eyebrows.

'A flashbulb. Someone was taking photographs. Someone from the press, most likely.'

'The Devil's Disciples?'

She frowns. 'A journalist after material for a story. They're curious about us. Our way of life. They want to share it with the world. Hence the camera.'

It always amazes me how much Mom knows about the Otherworld. Silly really because I know full well that, unlike me, she wasn't born in Edenville. Except her version doesn't always tie in with the one we're taught. I know what a camera is even though I've never seen one. They're not allowed, for obvious reasons. Nobody ever told me anything about a flash, though. That has come as a big surprise.

'But how did they get in?' Even in the dark, the giant outline of the mountainous bowl that protects us is visible. And at the other end of town is the wall with the vast gates, guarded day and night.

'I don't know, but the press are persistent. They always find a way.'

'Why don't we just let them in then? Surely the more people from the Otherworld who know about us the better. Plenty more would want to join us.'

My mother sighs, a real whopper, until there's no more breath in her lungs. 'It's not that simple.'

It never is.

'Okay,' she says before I can hurl another question her way. 'I think it's safe to make a dash for it. Quick, the storm is about to hit.'

My part-time father, Noah, is away, thank goodness. He's a Virtue, so he's often away. Sometimes he goes to other countries and stays in a hotel. I've never seen a hotel but, judging by the way Noah's eyes light up when he talks about them, I imagine they tick all the boxes. Anyway, it's an important job, and he's good at it. Last year he recruited twenty-three members, seven more than anyone else. As part-time father's go, he's not bad. I like him a gazillion times more than Elijah – whose meanness, Mom explained, is due to the gigantic chip he lugs around, him being a lowly labourer and all – but still, I'm pleased Noah's not here. One less thing to worry about.

Isabel and Jemima, my pain-in-the-ass younger sisters, are in the other room. Mom has told them supper is going to be late because she wants a word with me. They're supposed to be working on their quilts – ha! Rather them than me – but I can tell from the shrieks and bumps they're playing some dumb game. So, what's new?

We are in the kitchen with the windows closed. It's a good thing – even though, with the stew bubbling away on the stove, it's boiling hot – because Mom is reading me the riot act. It wouldn't do for anyone to hear. And it's okay. I understand. It's just her way of releasing tension. We had a close shave with the Powers. It was my fault. She feels the need to make it clear, at the top of her voice, many times over with several *shits* thrown in for good measure.

'You could have got us into serious trouble,' she says as the thunder rolls.

I'm expecting it, so I don't jump. Nothing can shock me after the fright I've had. The Powers are real. Fact. Though Lord alone knows where they've been hiding these past three years. Thing is, ever since we got back, I've been thinking if the rumour about me is true, it seems unlikely. 'We wouldn't, though, would we? Not if he's asked to see me.'

My mother stalls mid-tirade. And I realise the thought that's been trotting around my head has popped clean out of my mouth. Oops. No going back now. I've said it. Time for the moment of truth.

She gapes at me, eyelids blinking double-quick. Open–shut–open–shut–open. My stomach flips. I wait, but nothing. No words at all. Perhaps, like me, she's in the dark about all this. I sit tight. Thunder claps and lightning flashes, but still no rain.

'Would he?' I prompt.

'Why would you say such a thing?' Her voice is little more than a whisper.

My heart sinks. She doesn't know, which means it can't be true. I hang my head. 'It doesn't matter.'

'It most certainly does, young lady.'

Great, now I've made her cross all over again. What a shit awful day this has turned out to be. 'I'm sorry. I shouldn't have said anything. It's just that ...'

'It's just what?' She grabs my shoulders. 'Speak to me, Lola.'

Lois, I want to say. My name is Lois. But I can't, the fight has deserted me. Instead, I continue staring at my scuffed and dusty shoes, waiting for the next burst of thunder.

'Lola, please. This is important.'

I jut out my chin and look her directly in the eye. 'I just want to know if it's true.'

'Who told you?'

I shrug. Last thing I want is to get someone into trouble.

She lets go of me and smiles. But I can't help noticing it's an odd sort of smile, like she ate something that's made her sick but doesn't like to complain. 'It's okay. I won't tell on them.'

Oh boy. It's as if she can read my mind. No point in lying then. I take a deep breath and pray she means it. 'Well, Abi heard her dad tell her mom, because Joshua mentioned it to him at the meeting last week after Tobias told him a couple of days earlier, that it was big news amongst the Principalities.' It's why I got my hopes up. If the Principalities are talking about it, it must be true.

She clasps her head. 'Shit! Shit! Shit!'

Ta-da. Point proved. Cussing might be wrong, but boy does it bust that stress. I hold fire for a moment, until the dust settles. No point in rushing her.

'Oh, Lola,' she says eventually.

'So, it's true then? He has asked to see me.'

She walks towards me all in a rush and wraps her arm round me. 'Oh, Lola.'

It's a day for repeats, it seems.

'Oh, Lola. I'm sorry.'

Sorry? Why is she sorry? Shouldn't she be pleased? Or is she trying to tell me Tobias was lying? I'm profoundly confused. Gently, I prise her off. She seems vulnerable. It's a bit concerning to say the least. Maybe the DP has heard about the book. Maybe I'm not in favour at all but about to be isolated. My knees go weak. This is not good. Not good at all. 'Mom, what's going on?'

'I've wanted to tell you, really I have, but I couldn't. I promised.'

Like I said, that's Edenville all over. Hundreds of secrets knitted into a tight little web, the truth lost somewhere between the strands.

'You understand, don't you, sweetheart? Michael, made ... I mean, I promised Michael I wouldn't. It was important to him. He didn't want anyone to know.'

Whoa! What's going on here? First-name terms. Promises. 'Know what?' My heart is bouncing again, jiggedy-jig. 'What are you saying, Mom?'

'Sweetheart, I know this must come as a shock, but Michael, the Divine Protector, I mean. There's no easy way to say this ...' She stares at me, eyes wide, as if she doesn't recognise me anymore.

'What about him?'

Only now there's a knocking on the front door. No, more of a battering, as if the door might at any minute be broken off its hinges. Blood pounds my eardrums. I glance at my mother but I don't have a chance to register her expression because my sisters have run into the kitchen and are shrieking in alarm.

'OPEN UP! IN THE NAME OF THE DIVINE PROTECTOR, OPEN THIS DOOR NOW!'

'Stay here,' she says. 'Do not move and do not speak unless I ask you to. Do you hear me, Lola? Not a word.' And with that, she sprints from the room.

I'm shaking all over. This is not what I'd expected when I'd heard the rumours. How wrong could I be? I've not found favour with the Divine Protector at all. He's heard about the storybook. And now the Powers are after me.

Dear Lord and Master of *all* mankind, what is going to happen to me now?

CHAPTER THREE

A magpie. Just the one. A blur of black and white, it swoops past Donna with a fluttering of wings. She ducks, hands in front of her face, and stumbles backwards, stepping on someone's foot in the process. The woman, a stranger, is all smiles and bats Donna's apology away with a casual wave of her hand. Her mood, in harmony with Donna's, and everyone else it seems, is upbeat. And why not? What they're doing is unbelievable.

They laughed when the idea first came to them. It was impossible, they agreed. But they went ahead and tried it anyway. A chain letter. Very casual. Nothing more than a rough-and-ready scribble they photocopied and sent to ten of their friends, inviting them to join them along with breezy instructions to pass it on. Who would have thought it would breathe fire into the imagination of so many women, of all ages, and from every walk of life? They've been arriving by the coach-load from all over the country since first light, some with their children in tow, all of them armed with a gift as instructed. Remarkably, in the absence of any leadership, they all seem to have worked out what to do. Find an empty bit of fence and stand there in the mud.

The rain forecast hasn't materialised, thank goodness, but it's bitter out. Donna wishes she'd remembered her gloves. Despite blowing on her hands all day, her fingers are red raw. Tess, of course, had offered her hers. Dear Tess. The most up and at 'em of her three children, she's been campaigning with her mother since she was a toddler. She should be at university. Term doesn't finish for another week but, even though Donna tried to stop her, Tess insisted on coming. She has a mind of her own, that one.

Donna cranes her neck, but she can't spot her daughter's face amongst the hordes. She was only a couple of metres away a minute ago, but the swelling crowd must have squeezed her along the perimeter. Never mind, it's not as if she's alone. She's brought quite a crowd with her from Nottingham: Lou, Tinks, and Alice, and three or four other girls Donna hadn't recognised.

'Not long now, dear,' says Patricia Seath, a flamboyantly dressed, steel-haired woman from Eastbourne, knitting furiously as always, the many pockets of her beautiful homemade coat full to bursting with balls of wool. One end of a scarf attached to the fence, from time to time her needles cease their clacking as she stops to weave another length through the wire.

There's a screech overhead. The magpie is perched on top of the chain-link fence, its black bead of an eye jerking this way and that as if it's laughing at them. A sudden shaft of sunlight pierces the clouds, accentuating the blue-green iridescence of its tail feathers. Donna shivers. Its plumage may be beautiful, but its presence is unsettling.

One for sorrow.

An omen, perhaps, or a warning?

'You all right, love?' asks Sophie Slater, a young nurse from Taunton who, in a nod to her profession, always has a first-aid kit to hand. *Protesting,* she is fond of saying, *can be a dangerous business at times.*

Donna forces a smile. 'Yes, fine. Excited, actually. All this is beyond my wildest dreams.'

'Who'd have thought it, eh?' Sophie winks and laughs, a proper burst right from the belly, and Donna smiles, for real this time.

Sophie's gift is a green cellular blanket and a photograph of her nine-month-old son, Laurie, today at home with her husband, Sean, one of those modern men in tune with their feminine side. She's not the only one to have brought a picture of her baby. Hardly surprising, because saving their children's futures is the reason they're here. There are cakes – courtesy of the Wetherby WI, according to Patricia – flowers, ribbons, toys, teapots, paintings, soiled nappies, and bloodied sanitary towels; even a wedding dress. Donna glances at her own offering, a stuffed Rupert Bear, its left eye missing, its seams frayed. It used to mean the world to her, an ironic reminder of a man she once loved. But that seems a lifetime ago to her now.

A helicopter thrums in the sky above them, its occupants taking in the scene along the nine-mile fence. More are expected if they achieve what they set out to do. The press, apparently, and the police, Patricia informed her this morning. She's a mine of information, Patricia, her finger well and truly on the pulse. Donna grins, imagining this evening's headlines. They've been dismissed as eccentric. Woolly minds in woolly hats. But this is not a game. It isn't fun. Cruise missiles are not a joke. The politicians have got it wrong. These women, these ordinary, hardworking wives, mothers, sisters, grannies, aunts and daughters, mean business. They are bold. They are tenacious. They are powerful.

'It's time.' Patricia tucks her needles, a section of scarf, and the ball of wool into the largest pocket of her coat, and clasps Donna's hand. 'Oh my God, you're freezing. Why didn't you say?' But before Donna can reply, Patricia has reached inside another of her many pockets and drawn out a pair of red knitted gloves. 'There you are, love, they should do the trick.'

'Thank you, Patricia.' Donna hugs her, but Patricia shrugs her off.

'Get on with you.'

Smiling, Donna turns to Sophie, hand outstretched. 'Ready to Embrace the Base?'

'You bet.'

In the distance, somebody – Mel most likely – starts singing, and they all join in. Donna can sense the unease of the armed American soldiers on the other side of the fence. It's written all over their faces – open mouths, exchanged looks – that they have no idea what to do. Heavy artillery, blood, smoke, and loud explosions they can deal with, but thousands of women singing the 'Spirit Song' at the tops of their voices is way outside their comfort zone. A youth with pock-marked skin, who can't be more than eighteen, raises his machine gun and points it at a buxom woman with dyed red hair who is singing louder than the rest.

Donna holds her breath. He wouldn't, would he?

The woman, Moira, she thinks, brazens it out, raising her arms above her head and rocking side to side as she continues to sing louder, if possible, than before. The youth narrows his eyes, his trigger finger twitching. For an awful moment, Donna is certain she's about to witness a murder. The soldier next to him must think so, too, because he nudges the hothead sharply in the ribs. Grimacing, the man lowers his gun.

For some reason, Donna thinks of Jos. Odd, because the young soldier is nothing like her blond-haired, brown-eyed son. Her eldest, Chrissie, calls him their little angel, but Donna doubts angels, even if there were such things, scowl as much as Jos, or swear, or pierce their ears. And, having morphed into a tall, lanky sixteen-year-old, he can hardly be described as little anymore. This total and utter transformation from funny, bright-eyed child to moody teenager has taken some getting used to. Not that Donna has entirely, although the times she used to mistake him for a stranger when she bumped into him on the stairs have passed.

It began two years ago, shortly after his beloved rescue dog, Rufus, died. For six years they'd been inseparable, but his altered personality wasn't down to Rufus' death. He was being bullied at school, he told Tess. Strange, given he was a popular child who made friends easily. But then Donna had no idea his two closest friends, Billy and Tubs, were mocking him and excluding him from their group – he wrote songs and sang in the choir and, therefore, wasn't cool – because for the first time in his short life, he wouldn't tell her anything. Every time she tried to get close, he clammed up, disappeared inside his shell. It was as if someone had flicked a switch, turning her open, happy-go-lucky son into this mysterious, angst-ridden enigma. A gigantic chasm opened up between them, and their wonderful relationship sank without trace. Not a day passed without her trying to fathom what was going on in his mixed-up, teenage mind. If only she knew, she could help. She probed gently, desperate to know what had happened, but Jos continued to shut her out.

'You wouldn't understand,' he said, no matter how hard she tried to convince him otherwise.

And then the crying started, face down on his bed for hours at a time. Donna wasn't unduly worried the first morning she found him – insecurity and anxiety often came hand in hand with adolescence – but the second time he refused to go to school and, three weeks later, refused to leave his room. He told her he was useless, insignificant and a failure, that the world was a dark, futile place, that there was nothing he could do to make it better, that he had nothing to look forward to. So, she sat on his bed and stroked his back and told him to focus on the good things in his life. How lucky he was to have a family who loved him. That he was a handsome young man, funny, clever, and brave who could turn his hand to anything, if he had a mind to. That when he felt better he might find the strength to change the world in some small way, as she had tried to do.

But nothing she said made any difference. Jos was a shell of the boy he'd once been. He never smiled, hardly spoke.

Donna raises her eyes to the darkening sky and thinks of the magpie again.

One for sorrow.

Is Jos hurt? Has he got himself in trouble? Call it a mother's intuition, but something isn't right. I shouldn't be here. I should hop on a train and go talk to my son; find out the cause of this cataclysmic change, once and for all, before it's too late.

'Non-violent confrontation of power,' Sophie says, leaning across to light Patricia's candle. 'Isn't it wonderful.'

'It's a bloody miracle,' Patricia replies. 'We've done it. They'll have to take notice of us now.'

Donna stares into the distance, at the brilliant chain of flickering flames, stretching as far as the eye can see into tiny pinpricks of light. It's a moving sight. Peaceful. Heart-warming. Completely at odds with her relationship with her son.

Tomorrow, she tells herself, as Sophie links arms with her. One night won't make any difference. I'll take a break from the camp and talk to Jos tomorrow.

CHAPTER FOUR

The Powers burst into our house, the metal heels of their boots clacking on the floorboards. They sound like an army, but it may only be half a dozen. I don't know. I can't see them. I'm in the kitchen, a dumb mute frozen to the spot. By the time Mom returns, with two in pursuit, I'm barely breathing. I steal a peek out of the corner of my eye. Tall dark men. Dark clothes, dark hair, dark eyes. Dark hearts, too, I suspect. My eyes float about the place, at the ceiling, the floor, the windows. Anywhere but at them.

'Sit down, Lois,' Mom says, nudging me towards the table where Jemima and Isabel are already sitting.

The storm must have passed because we wait in petrified silence while these big, bad brutes open the cupboards, the fridge, pulling out pans and bowls, plates and cups, peering into the oven, the small pantry, the drums of flour and rice. When they have searched every square inch, they move next door and then upstairs, banging, slamming, and crashing their way through the four rooms of our house.

For the first time in my life, I remain obediently silent.

We all do, apart from Jemima, my youngest sister, who is making a strange mewling noise. From time to time, Mom nods at us and smiles a watery kind of smile. It's not the least bit reassuring, but I appreciate her efforts. Judging by her whiter-than-white cheeks, she's as terrified as we are. To keep myself from crying out, inside my head I'm praying harder and with more conviction than I can ever remember doing.

Dear Sweet Jesus, please don't let them find the storybook. Please may my mother, who I love above all other human beings, have hidden it somewhere they will not think to look. If you do this for me, I promise I will never ever break any of the Divine Protector's rules again, for as long as I shall live. You have my word as a loyal member of the Guardians of God.

They search our little house from top to bottom. I cannot believe how long it takes them. Longer it seems, as the minutes on the wall clock tick slowly by, than it takes my mother, on her cleaning days, to scour every nook and cranny with her feather duster and broom.

One of the Powers marches back into the room. Coming to a halt with a sharp stamp of his foot, he salutes my mother. 'Thank you, ma'am,' he says in his devilish growl.

I dare myself a peep at him. I can't see his face, but I see the menace in his narrowed eyes, the cruelty in his clenched fist. Shivering, I commit the image to memory.

Let this be a lesson. This is the very least you'll have to deal with if you break the rules.

My mother stands. I'm surprised at how graciously. My legs are shaking so much I doubt I could manage it.

'Thank you,' she says. Hell, she even raises a smile.

The man swivels on his heel, and my mother follows. How she can keep up the pretence that this ransacking of her house is okay with her falls well outside my comprehension.

The front door clicks, and the three of us leap to our feet. Mom reappears, still smiling, her trembling hands the only clue she's not as relaxed as her face would have us think.

Us kids talk all at once. Yackety-yak.

'What the hell is going on?'

'Why were the Powers searching our house?'

'What were they looking for?'

My mother puts a finger to her lips, and we all fall quiet. 'They're looking for two Dominions.'

Never have words sounded so sweet. I want to jump up and down and shout for joy.

'Why?' Isabel asks. 'What have they done?'

'It must be something serious if they've sent out ... the Powers.' Jemima's eyes are as big and round as the windows of the Meeting Room, and I wonder if, like me, she hadn't believed they were real.

'They've gone missing from Ascension House,' Mom says. 'The Divine Protector has warned us to be wary of them. They're mentally unstable, and therefore dangerous. They might even be armed. Hence the Curfew. Hence the Powers.'

Now she tells me. Hmm. What would be worse, I wonder? A close encounter with the Powers or an armed maniac?

'Why did the Dominions leave?' Isabel asks.

'It's complicated.'

Of course, I think with a wry smile. It always is.

This is a true story. When I was five, my mother sat me on her lap and told me the parable of the wheat in the field.

'A man sowed a field of wheat,' she began, 'but when everyone was asleep, his enemy came and sowed weeds among the good seed. When they sprouted, the owner told his servants not to pull up the weeds because they might uproot the wheat. "Let them grow together," he said, "but when it comes to the harvest, I will tell the harvesters to first collect the weeds and tie them in bundles to be burned, then gather the wheat and bring it to the barn." When the disciples asked Jesus to explain the parable, he said, "The sower is the Son of Man, the field is the world, and the good seed, the people of the kingdom. The weeds are the people of the enemy, the Devil. The harvest is the end of the age, and the harvesters are the angels. Just as the weeds are pulled up and burned in the fire, so the Son of Man will send out his angels and weed evil from his kingdom and throw them into the blazing furnace. There will be weeping and gnashing of teeth, then the righteous will shine like the sun in the kingdom of their Father."'

After she finished, I sat in silence, too scared to speak. My mother's expression was as grave as I'd ever seen it, her voice without its usual brightness. I chewed my sleeve and tried to make sense of the story. It seemed important that I should. Up until then I'd been a big fan of angels and everything they stood for. The thought of them suddenly picking people up willy-nilly and hurling them into a blazing furnace was terrifying.

'Will I be thrown into the fire, Momma?'

She leant down and kissed the top of my head. 'No, Lola, of course you won't. You know that. On the day of enlightenment, after the Apocalypse, you, and everyone else in Edenville, will be granted an eternal life in a spiritual realm.'

'But what if they make a mistake? What if they accidentally throw me into the fire, too?'

'They won't.'

'You promise?' Even at that tender age, I needed to know how she could be so sure.

'The Divine Protector will lead us all to salvation.'

Well, that came as a huge relief. 'And all the evil people in the Otherworld will burn?'

'Only if we've been unable to save them.'

'Can we save them?'

'Some, I hope, but sadly, not all.'

'And when will it happen?'

'Thursday the twelfth of May 1983. Ascension Day.'

I adjust my brand-new headscarf for the third, maybe fourth time, but I can't seem to secure it the way Mom showed me, and it slips off my head again. 'Stupid bloody thing,' I mutter, throwing it on the floor. But it's not my inability to tie the scarf that's making me angry. It's knowing there's just over four months until the Apocalypse. In Jesus' name, how am I supposed to get to know the Divine Protector in that time?

It's been two days since the Powers searched our house, but it was only last night, after my sisters were safely tucked up in bed, Mom confirmed the rumours were true. I *was* in favour. The Divine Protector had summoned me.

'He wants you to stay with him for a while,' she said dully. 'What an honour.'

I was beyond excited. Who wouldn't be? My boring little life was about to undergo a humongous change. But I looked at her face, and it was real sad, so I found myself thinking: What's the right answer? This is the Divine

Protector we're talking about here. 'It's the best thing ever.' *Isn't it?*

Her voice wobbled as she hugged me. 'Oh, sweetheart, I'm so proud of you.'

Only now, this morning, my belly is churning. And questions, the heavy-duty kind, are ricocheting around my brain. What if I'm a huge disappointment? What if he doesn't like me? What if he sends me back? Will I be hurled into the fiery furnace? Or will I be isolated and starve to death, like Gideon?

I fling myself face down on the bed and hammer the quilt with my fists. Did I really believe all that stuff about death and damnation, enlightenment, and salvation? Was Satan really all around us, leading us astray? As a five-year-old, I'd been utterly taken in by the terrible tale my mother had told me. My only understanding of the depressing Otherworld and all the ignorant and evil people in it, was what I'd been taught. And I'd accepted it like a sponge accepts water. But a couple of years ago I'd begun to question the doctrine that what Jesus had planned for me was far better than life itself. Why hold back? Why not give it to us now? As good Guardians of God, didn't we deserve it?

Not long after, and quite inexplicably it seemed to me, Mom began to reveal tantalising titbits of her life before Edenville. The large apartment in the bustling city where she'd lived with her devoted parents and brothers. She'd had a happy childhood, success at school, and holidays. Holidays. Imagine that? To far-flung countries. I listened to her stories, my eyes on stalks, and wondered if she'd regretted giving it all up to follow the light?

And then last night, when we were cooking supper together, she grew suddenly wistful.

'I used to love to dance. Your dad did, too. He was an excellent dancer.'

My ears pricked up, tall and alert. My *dad* was one of those off-limit subjects. Whenever I asked her about him – who he was, where he was, what he did – the shutters came down furious and fast. *There are some things it's best not to know*, she'd say, or, *what you don't know can't hurt you*. And now, here she was, bringing him up, all of her own free will.

So, my dad liked to dance. This was news indeed. Dancing was forbidden in Edenville, which meant she'd met him before she moved here.

'Trouble was,' she continued, 'my family didn't approve.'

Things were starting to make sense. Is that why she'd come here? I did the maths. It was possible he'd moved here with her. 'Do you miss your family?'

'Every day.'

I see. 'It must be tough knowing that you'll never see them again.'

'One day I hope I will. If they're still alive.'

'So, you think *they* can be saved then?'

'Of course they will be.'

'But how? They don't live in Edenville.'

'They're good people. That's how.'

'But I thought—'

'Enough now, Lola. My parents will be saved.'

Did she really believe that? Or was it some vain hope she clung to, because what she said made no sense. Unless there was a loophole I didn't know about, which allowed for the salvation of some Otherworldlies. Whatever, I'd had enough of being fobbed off. Years and years of it. Forgetting my shitting-in-my pants promise to God of two nights earlier, I hung on in. ‘So, if they are that good, why did you leave them?’

‘You know why.’

‘No, I don’t. You never told me.’ I held my breath, expecting her to stomp off in the mother of all rages.

But she didn’t. She just gritted her teeth and said, ‘I saw the light.’

‘And do you still see it?’

But that had been one question too far. She marched out of the room and slammed the door. Two hours later, she was holding me in her arms again, telling me she loved me.

‘What’s keeping you, Lola?’

There she goes again. No matter how many times Noah warns her, she keeps on calling me that. A blatant act of defiance? Or a force of habit? I squeeze my eyes shut and remain where I am. Face down on the bed.

‘Lola. Get a move on. You’re going to be late.’

Stifling a cry, I raise myself on my elbows and grip the quilt until my knuckles turn white. Oh Jesus. It’s actually happening. And with Christmas so close. And Armageddon not far off.

‘Lola! Where are you?’

The door swings open. I try to speak, but no words come out, only a wounded-cat kinda moan.

‘What on earth are you doing? And what’s happened to your scarf? Honestly, Lola, sometimes I despair of you. I really do.’ Her voice is soft and gentle, as though she doesn’t mean what she’s saying.

Slowly, I turn to face her. ‘I don’t understand why I have to wear it.’

‘Yes, you do. It’s the rules.’

‘I hate the rules.’

She flops down next to me. 'Lola.'

'Lois. My name is Lois. And if you're not going to cover your hair then neither am I. This scarf is impossible. It keeps slipping off.'

She puts her arm around me. 'Lois, sweetheart, I'm not covering my hair because I'm not coming with you.'

This is news to me. Although now I come to think of it, she's never once said she was. I give it a go but I can't imagine life without her. We may have had our differences, but she's been the one solid presence in my life. She's picked me up when I've fallen down, wiped away my tears when I've been sad. Fed me, sung to me, taught and scolded me. Told me endlessly that she loves me, even when I'm being downright mean. An awful thought occurs to me then. She doesn't love me anymore. She wants to get rid of me. Is that it? Has she had enough of my shenanigans? Her word, not mine. What if I never see her again?

'How long will I be staying?'

'I don't know.'

'But you will be allowed to visit?' My voice is small, like an itty-bitty mouse's.

She fiddles with my hair, twirling a lock round and round her finger. 'We'll work something out.'

Well, see, I know what that means. It's adult-speak for *haven't the foggiest*. Or maybe something worse, like, *No. This is it. You are never going to see me again*. My heart is thumping so hard against my ribs I'm worried it's about to burst clean out of my chest. I fling my arms around her and grip her tight, afraid to let go. And that's when I hear it. A sob. And I know full well it didn't come from me. Seems I'm not the only one not feeling all that brave.

'Were there parties?' I whisper as I nuzzle her neck.

'Parties?'

'In the Otherworld.'

'What's brought this on?'

'Were there?'

'Oh yes, there were plenty of parties.'

'And were they fun?'

My mother pauses like she always does when I try to start a chit-chat about the Otherworld. I wait for the inevitable. But ... 'Yes, Lola, they were.'

Now I'm having serious second thoughts about my future. I'd been so excited about meeting the Divine Protector I hadn't stopped to think what it actually means. How it will affect my life. What if I can never leave? I'll be trapped in Ascension House forever. As helpless as a fly in a web. 'Let's go find your parents.'

She breaks away. Holding me at arm's length, she studies me intently.

'I don't want to be a prisoner.'

'Darling, you won't be. You're going to live with the Divine Protector. You're not going to jail.'

'But I want to be free.'

'You are free.'

'But that's just it. I'm not, am I? I want choices. I want to make my own decisions. Live my own life. I want to learn to dance. To taste champagne.'

Her eyes widen fleetingly, but then her shoulders slump, and she sighs. A long, exhausted sigh that tells me that she, too, has thought about such things. '"Man is born free, Lola, but is everywhere in chains."'

This is not what I'm expecting her to say. It's like she's agreeing with me and disagreeing at the same time. And I don't like the sound of it, not one little bit. 'I don't understand. Why me? Why now?'

She stares out the window, but I can tell by the far-away look she's not seeing anything. Not outwardly, at least. Eventually, she turns back, her expression, this time, unreadable.

'Lola,' she says, taking both my hands in hers. 'There's something you need to know. Something I should have told you years ago.'

CHAPTER FIVE

It's a crisp December morning, and a weak sun is shining in a china-blue sky. A woman on a mission, Donna walks briskly down the Queen's Road on her way to visit Jos, the sense something is wrong with her son weighing heavily on her mind. She can't relax until she sees, with her own eyes, that he's okay. Propelled by this overarching need, she's distracted, nevertheless, by a young man in a shop doorway curled up in a heap of blankets. Only his head is visible, his cheeks strewn with dirt, his hair matted with dust. She has no idea who he is, but it could just as easily be Jos. Trying to ignore the lump in her throat, she reaches inside her handbag for her purse and empties the coins into the jam jar beside him.

The young man opens his bloodshot, red-rimmed eyes and sits up. 'Thank you, Miss. Very kind.'

She whips off her hat, another woolly gift from Patricia. 'Here, take this. It might help stave off the cold.' As he holds out his grubby hand, she sees the puncture marks on his arms and frowns. 'Promise me you'll buy food.'

Although the young man nods, Donna doubts he will.

Making a mental note to bring coffee and sandwiches next time, she sets off again, her heart even heavier.

It's only the second time Donna has visited the squat and a while since her disastrous first visit. She shivers, recalling the exchange that took place on the doorstep. She heard Jos before she saw him, chatting away behind the partially open front door, his laugh, instantly recognisable, although she hadn't heard it in far too long. He's happy, that's good, she thought and, crossing her fingers, knocked.

The second he saw her, Jos' laughter evaporated. 'What the hell are you doing here?'

She flinched but moved towards him, arms open. 'It's good to see you, Jos.'

Eyes glinting, he backed away. 'You can't just waltz in here. This is my home. It's private.'

'Darling, I'm your mother.'

'You think I don't fucking know?'

She recoiled, shocked by her son's clenched fists, the stony look in his narrowed eyes. He'd been grumpy and moody, but he'd never sworn at her before. 'I should have warned you I was coming.'

'You shouldn't have come at all. Get out.'

'Jos, please.'

'I said, get out.'

She touched him on the arm, but he shook her off and pushed her into the street. 'I wanted to catch up. It's been ages since I've seen you. Darling, please.' She knew what was coming before he slammed the door in her face.

Today will be different, though, because she's prepared. The door is ajar again but, this time, she walks straight in.

The squat is damp and smells of an overpowering mixture of mould, dope, old socks, stewed vegetables – odd, considering the filthy stove clearly hasn't been used in years – stale sweat, and something else. Loneliness and regret, perhaps. The linoleum is blistered and stained, and the buckled door hangs off its hinges. A trio of bluebottles are buzzing around a torn black bin liner full of goodness knows what, slumped against a rusty bike, and are those mouse droppings beside it? Haphazard towers of LPs and books flank a wall with chunks of plaster missing, while the table, a pile of bricks in place of its missing fourth leg, is covered in overloaded ashtrays and packets of Rizla papers. And in pride of place on the windowsill – the only window with a pane of glass, albeit cracked – a line of marijuana plants.

When did you get so middle-class? she wonders, drawing her afghan coat tightly around her.

'Hi. Can I help you?'

Donna turns with a start. A willowy girl, with hennaed hair, dressed in a mauve maxi dress and black Doc Martens is smiling at her, seemingly unfazed to find a stranger in her kitchen. 'I'm looking for Jos. Is he about?'

'Er ... no, I think he's out somewhere with Naomi.'

'Naomi?'

'Love the coat. You must give me the name of the charity shop you picked it up from. I'm Stacy, by the way.'

Charity shop! But seeing the funny side, Donna smiles. 'I didn't buy it from a charity shop. It's just old, Stacy. Like me.'

An aged hippie, she thinks, at once casting her mind back to the afternoon she wafted into Biba with Marty, her film producer boyfriend. Watching her parading around the shop in the coat, he stunned her by whisking out his wallet and buying it. She was happy. In love, a supporting role in a West End play, rave reviews, and an upcoming audition for a Hollywood film directed by a friend of Marty's, she had the world at her feet. But life can play the cruellest jokes. Three months later over dinner in a Soho restaurant, Marty told her he was hopelessly in love and reached inside his pocket. To her surprise, he brought out a handkerchief, not the ring she was expecting, and handed it to her.

'Pancreatic cancer,' he said. 'I'm afraid the men in white coats have given me three weeks.'

Donna barely had time to recover from his earth-shattering revelation before the darling man was dead. Sobbing into Marty's handkerchief as his coffin was lowered into his grave, she vowed never to fall in love again.

And if losing her lover wasn't heartbreak enough, the part she hoped would mark a turning point in her career went to a young American actress who, overnight, became a star. It was back to the grindstone; single mother of three working all hours of the day and night, waiting in restaurants, pulling pints in pubs and teaching English to foreign students to meet the mortgage payments, the endless household bills, while struggling to clothe her children and put food on the table. The only time she could relax was when she landed a role in a television advert, a small part in a serial, or found work as a voiceover artist. Gruelling didn't cover it, and yet she always managed to eke out enough time to focus on her campaigns.

Stacy whistles. 'Wow. Like vintage fashion. No. I've got that wrong. But you know what I mean.'

'Perfectly. I'm Donna. Jos' mum.'

'Oh right. The activist.'

Donna winces. 'I value my children's future. Nuclear war would be the biggest, most hideous catastrophe of all time.'

'That is so true, Mrs P. I love how you Greenham Common women are weaponising femininity. It's just what this country needs. Shame the heartless cow in charge won't listen.'

'Well, quite.' An uncomfortable silence follows. For Donna, at least, because Stacy doesn't look the least bit troubled. Her eyes remain locked on Donna's, her broad smile unwavering. Donna clears her throat. 'Stacy, would you mind if I waited for Jos in his room.'

'Knock yourself out, Mrs P. It's the first on the left.'

Jos' guitar is propped up in an enclave and, on the rickety chest of drawers beside a bag of weed and three packets of Rizla papers, is a sheet of music. Donna glances at the lyrics written in Jos' handwriting. Her heart lifts. He hasn't turned his back on every aspect of his old life. Music still plays a part.

She nudges aside the sleeping bag with her foot and, casting a blind eye to the stains, sits on the lumpy mattress and folds her arms. She tries to focus on the Greenham protest, but her thoughts keep returning to Jos. Why won't he talk to her anymore? Ever since he could speak, words had tumbled out of him. No subject was off limits. All three of her children had been the same. A problem shared, she used to tell them, is a problem halved. Obviously, as the girls grew up and began independent lives of their own, certain topics remained private. But not many. Tess still goes into way too much detail about the guys she sleeps with, but surely it's better that way.

Jos was about three when Chrissie, her eldest, started calling him their angel. Angelic in both looks and behaviour and affectionate, too, he was generous with his hugs and eager to tell them he loved them. When he sang, which was often, his voice was light, bright and beautiful. He skipped over the notes as if it took no effort at all.

But after the crying started, his moods darkened. Going to wake him one morning, half an hour earlier than usual, she found him perched on the ledge outside his window. Trembling all over, she begged him to come inside, which he did. She clasped him tightly as he mumbled something about needing some air to clear his head. But Donna wasn't fooled. Lying awake on his floor that night, too scared to let him out of her sight even for a second, she wondered how she'd have coped if he had jumped?

Somehow, they navigated a way through the trauma, and although she could remember it in all its awful, vivid detail, neither of them ever mentioned it again. Donna moved back into her room, and Jos remained cocooned in his. Constantly on edge, frightened and mentally exhausted, Donna took time off work and the campaign trail, to care for her depressed and damaged son. For eighteen weeks, she devoted all her time and energy into caring for him. Nothing she did made any difference, though, and, as time wore on and her own mood took a downward turn, she wondered if she was heading for a breakdown, too.

And then the Embrace the Base letter arrived. Finally, she could do something positive for her children. Their future was what mattered. Jos and his outpouring of grief about the futility of his existence in a world so intent on destruction had opened her eyes to that. But the first day she visited the base, Jos started smoking weed. It was the inevitability of the progression that worried her. What would he do next?

'You're too young,' she told him. 'It'll mess with your brain.'

'Like you'd know,' he snapped and walked away.

He grew his hair and stopped washing it so it became greasy and lank. He stopped hugging, he stopped chatting. He stopped telling her he loved her. Six months ago, he muttered something about becoming a roadie. Shortly after, he dropped out of school, got a job in HMV, and moved into this squat with seven strangers. Just like that. As a child he dreamed of becoming a marine biologist, as a young teenager he set his heart on becoming a record producer, but now he drifts from one dead-end job to the next, smoking dope to his heart's content.

Tess sees him the most. She tells Donna not to worry, that he's happier now. But she is worried. Tess has no idea about his attempted suicide. How could she when Donna hasn't told a soul? What if he tries again? He'd been a sensitive child who loved his home, adored by his mother and doted on by his older sisters; a close-knit little group, despite the absence of a father. How will he cope in the big wide world out there on his own? And how will she manage without her son? Never mind his moods, home seems emptier for the lack of him.

Still, she reasons, it's not long until Christmas; all the family snuggled together in front of the fire, the tree, the lights, the decorations, the carols, the Turkish Delight. Jos' favourite. She'll get two boxes this year. And some chocolate coins. He loves those. And she'll work more shifts and buy him a new Walkman. She doubts he's replaced the one that was stolen. And she'll organise a family outing to the cinema to see *Ghandi*. Patricia saw it last weekend and said it was brilliant. The cinematography is phenomenal, apparently, and Ben Kingsley is a dead ringer for the guru. And she'll order a takeaway curry for afterwards. She'll make it the best Christmas ever. Jos will kick his depression into touch and move back in. He might even go back to college, take his A levels.

A thought pops into her head. What if Jos won't come home for Christmas? What will you do then?

Of course he will. We're his family. And if he refuses, then I shall insist.

But she can't ignore the little warning voice insisting Jos is no longer a child. He's a young adult, and life isn't that simple anymore.

A wave of exhaustion rushes over her. Forgetting the shoddy mattress, she lies down.

He used to tell me everything, she thinks for the umpteenth time.

It's not healthy, though, is it? her conscience nags. He's sixteen. He's not a child. Cut him some slack. You were no different at his age, running away to London with Paddy O'Neill, the rebel from next door, without a word to your poor doormat of a mother. Living in the flat above a chemist on Tooting High Street for nigh on six months with barely a penny to rub together. She must have been worried sick, but what did you care? Fleeing the nest. It's what kids do. It's healthy. And as for living in a squat. Everybody's doing it nowadays. All these run-down, empty houses. Goodness knows, but the lad dossing on the street would be far better off in one. And why not? It's not as if the Tories are doing anything to help the homeless.

Her attention shifts to a cobweb, dangling from the crumbling cornice, silvery-white like tangled strands of angel hair. She watches it for a while, hypnotised by its Gothic beauty, until she realises she's wasting her time. Jos clearly isn't coming back anytime soon. All the hours spent at the peace camp have seen her list of household chores stack up. If she's to get them done before her evening shift at the pub, she needs to get going.

She rolls onto her hands and knees and is about to clamber to her feet when she spies the crumpled corner of a photograph sticking out of the pillow case. She takes it out and gasps. Rupert. What on earth is Jos doing with a picture of his father?

Hearing voices in the hallway – male and female – she rushes to the door, expecting to see Jos and the mysterious Naomi but comes face to face with Stacy and a man dressed in a grey beanie and navy overalls.

'Hello again, Mrs P,' Stacy says without her previous bonhomie. 'This is Martin, Jos' friend.'

The unease Donna's been feeling these past few weeks returns with a vengeance.

'I hope you don't mind us barging in.' Stacy shifts her weight from foot to foot. 'But Martin has told me something and ...'

'Oh, for heaven's sake, what is it?'

'It's Jos, Mrs P. He's ... er ... well, he's gone.'

'Gone. Gone where?'

The man in the overalls sniffs. 'To America. With Naomi.'

'Oh my God.' Donna reels backwards, clasping her face.

'It's not like he's dead or anyfink,' the man adds charmlessly. 'He's just gone to the bleedin' States.'

CHAPTER SIX

I'm watching my mother, waiting for her to tell me whatever it is she thinks I need to know, but she keeps on staring at her fingernails as if it's the first time she's seen them. And then Isabel appears and gawps at me like I'm a ghost. Hanging jaw, goggle eyes.

Mom frowns. 'Can you leave us for a moment, Isabel.'

'There's a Principality at the door. Says she's here for Lois.' Isabel's baby blues are still glued on me.

'Right, well, tell her we'll be with her in a minute.'

But, other than swaying from foot to foot, Isabel doesn't budge. Not one inch. And now she starts to *click–click–click* her tongue like she's got something real important to ask but is holding back as if it's the hardest thing she's ever had to do.

'Do as I say, please, Isabel.'

Isabel glares, hands on her hips, as though she means business which, being Isabel, she probably does. 'Why is Lois wearing white? She's not allowed to wear white.'

'Isabel!' The raised vein on my mother's neck is a sure sign her temperature is rising.

'But, Mom—'

'Now!'

Isabel springs back, as if she's thrust her hand in a hornet's nest. She glares at Mom, then me and, huffing and puffing, stomps from the room.

'You haven't told her,' I say quietly.

'Not yet.'

For a while neither of us speak. I, for one, am too tied up with thoughts to know what to say. I glance around, committing the contents of the room to memory. My sisters' bunks set against the back wall, my wooden bed under the sloping roof I'm always bumping my head on, the chest of drawers, the wardrobe with the squeaky door, and the quilt I made when I was twelve. Sewing does not come naturally to me – I haven't the patience for one thing, let alone the skill – so, boy, was I proud when I laid that little beauty on my bed. The tantrums I had when I was unpicking all those wonky seams. My throbbing fingers from endlessly pricking myself with my needle. The boredom. I honestly thought I'd never finish it. But against all the odds, I did. My greatest achievement, perhaps.

'White suits you,' Mom says, breaking the silence.

'You think?'

'It suits your father, too.'

Pardon me? Why are we bringing *him* up again? But I don't say anything. I simply continue to stare at my quilt. Just a thought, but maybe I can bring it with me.

'Do you understand what I'm saying, Lola?'

I roll my eyeballs. 'Yup. My father and I measure up in white. Good to know.'

'Michael–is–your–father.'

It comes out in one long, agonised word, like she's

speaking in tongues. I have to unravel it just to make sense of it. 'Michael ... is ... my ... father.'

She grabs my arms. 'Yes.'

Whoa. It's like I've turned a dozen somersaults and have no idea which way up I am. I take a deep breath, steadying myself. 'The Divine Protector? My Father? You mean like he's your Father and everyone else's Father?'

'No, Lola. He's *your* dad. You are his daughter. His only child.'

Is this for real? Or has my mother taken a break from reality? 'You mean you slept with him?' See, I know how babies are made. We all do. It's one thing they make sure of early on. 'But I thought ... he wasn't allowed—'

'We were in love.' She says this quietly, without drama.

I tilt my head and eye her quizzically. 'You and ... the Divine Protector?'

'It was a long time ago, but yes. He couldn't marry me, of course. God wouldn't allow it. And it was tough. Tough for us both.'

It's too much to take in. My mother's pained expression. The mind-blowing detail of her confession. My mother slept with the Divine Protector. I'm his daughter, which if *The Tablet* was covering the story, makes me front-page news. This kind of thing doesn't happen to me. But hang on? Why send the Powers to our house? Why frighten me like that? Unless ... 'Has he just found out, too?'

'Goodness me, no. He was there at your birth.'

'Jesus bloody Christ.'

'Lola! Please.'

My mind is in overdrive, dashing forwards and back, racing round corners. I need to get this straight. 'But the other night. The Powers. He sent them.'

'I imagine he wanted to protect you.'

It makes perfect, twisted sense. 'Sorry, sorry, sorry.' My head is bursting, thousands of questions hammering to get out. 'Did he ... did he hold me?'

'He was the first person to hold you. The first person to kiss you.'

I leap up and jump and clap my hands. And I'm thinking, wow, wow, wow. This is better than Christmas. Better, even, than Michaelmas. The best thing ever. Wait till Abi hears about it. It'll blow her mind.

An idea pops into my head, loud and angry and with such speed, it's as if I've been punched by a mighty fist. *Wham.* I stop jumping. I stop smiling. There is something very wrong about this. If he's my dad, why have I never met him? Why didn't I know? Doesn't he like me? I roll my lip over in my teeth. 'Did I do something wrong?'

'Wrong?'

'Yeah, like upset him. Did I make him mad? Did he want a boy? What did I do? Tell me, Mom. I need to know.'

'Oh, sweetheart, you didn't do anything. Michael couldn't be a father. It wasn't his calling. And anyway, it wouldn't be fair.'

'Fair? On who?'

'On everyone. It would look like favouritism.'

I chew on this answer. It's tough and tastes bitter, so I spit it out. 'But what about me? I'm his daughter. And you. You were in love. How did you feel?'

Mom is gazing at me with such sad eyes she doesn't need to say anything. 'It wasn't easy. But I understood. It wasn't about me and him. It was about the good of all. He wanted to maintain the status quo. And as for you, well, what you don't know can't hurt.'

See, the thing about Mom is there's logic in everything she says. No matter how hard I try and unravel 'em, her explanations are like knots that cannot be untied. But not this time. This time I see a flaw. And it's glaring. 'I know now.'

I feel no triumph, only sadness.

My mother takes my hands and kisses them, and smiles, although I can't help noticing it doesn't reach her eyes. 'Recently, he changed his mind, which is why he wants you to move in with him. But, Lola, I want you to remember I am your mother and I love you very much. No matter where you are, who you're with, or what they might tell you, never forget that.'

And that's when I know for sure, I am not going to see my mother, or my sisters, or Abi, Benjamin, and David ever again. And I want to scream and howl and stamp my feet but I can't. I'm in a daze.

Mom leads me downstairs to the front door where Principality Keziah is waiting. Like me, she is dressed in white. Well, not exactly like me. Her scarf is securely in place, and her dress seems to be a part of her, unlike my more obvious, ill-fitting disguise.

'Are you ready, Lois?' she asks.

No, I'm not. Not at all, but Mom is making those *go on, Lola* eyes of hers at me, so I nod.

Holy shit. This is it.

'You won't forget me, will you, darling?'

What a question? I don't answer it because a) I'm trying to ignore the tear that's rolling down her cheek and b) I've already decided. One of the first things I'm going to ask the Divine ... Michael ... my father, after I've wheedled my way into his good books, is if he'd allow Mom to visit. If he won't agree to it, maybe I'll be able to persuade him to let me visit her. Oh God. It's happening too fast. I'm not ready. Not by any stretch of the imagination. And my imagination is extremely flexible, I've been told.

My arms are around my mother's neck, and I'm sobbing into her hair. Hair that smells of jasmine and frangipani. But Keziah is pulling me away. I claw at my mother's clothing, begging her to let me stay. But Keziah keeps on tugging.

'It's okay, Lois,' Mom whispers through her tears. 'The Divine Protector has big plans for you.'

'I don't care. I don't want to go.'

'Come on now.' Keziah yanks hard. 'You're making a scene.'

And suddenly I'm angry and want to kick Keziah in the shins, tear off her scarf, and rip out her glossy brown hair by the roots until she's begging for mercy. But, of course, I don't. I'm not completely stupid. Leaving my mother, my family, my home, is a done deal. The Divine Protector has summoned me. It doesn't matter what I think. I stop crying and bite my lip until I taste blood. It does the trick. Distracted by pain, I set off down the road towards Ascension House, focusing on the mountains behind it, taking great care not to look back.

I don't like Keziah. There, I've said it. She's a witch. She didn't speak to me the entire walk. Not one word. Not even when Elijah, labouring under the weight of his enormous grudge, hurled a mean mouth-load of insults my way from Dairyman Paul's roof, or when Martha, Peter, and Clem, seeing my dress and scarf, stopped on their way to school to jeer and holler as if it was the funniest thing they'd ever seen. It was only after she'd led me through Ascension House's heavily guarded gates into a vast courtyard, past the gleaming cars – one white, one black – through another smaller gate into a square with the greenest grass I'd ever seen, that she said anything at all. And really, it wasn't worth her breath.

'This is the quadrangle. That's the Almond Tree, and over there is the Olive.'

As if I cared about a couple of stupid trees when there was so much else to take in. A group of Dominions dressed in white. The heavy wooden doors. The arched, covered wooden walkway around the grassy square. All so much bigger than I'd imagined. And grander.

'The Divine Protector's rooms are along there and there.' She pointed to two sides. 'You are not to go into them unless summoned. The same goes for Raphael's quarters in the corner over there.'

Who?

'The Dominions, myself, and the other five Principalities, live in the rest of that wing and along here,' she gestured, completing the square. 'The Powers have rooms off the cloisters in the outer courtyard.'

The Powers that close? Oh my.

'They are not allowed in here at any time, and you are not allowed out there after dark. Speaking to them is forbidden.'

Don't worry, I won't.

'And do not pick the fruit.'

As if.

Then she showed me to my room to the right of the gate we'd walked through. The far-too-close living arrangement of the Powers slipping from my mind, I gawped at the enormous bed and the private bathroom attached.

'Take a shower,' she said.

I parked my hands on my hips. 'I've already had one.'

'Take another. And be sure to use the soap this time.'

And with that she was gone, thank the Good Lord.

Hepzibah is with me now. She's also a Principality but, being lumpy and dumpy, her white dress doesn't look as good on her. I can tell, already, she's kinder but, honestly, what I need right now is space to think. Everything's happened so fast, my mind is playing catch-up. Am I really here because the DP has this sudden urge to see his daughter? Why now, after all these years?

'Don't you scrub up well? And you smell deliciously of almonds.'

I give her the stink eye. I can't help it. I mean, what a thing to say.

'Ooh, now, dearie. Don't go making that face when you meet the Divine Protector.'

Hepzibah has a strange way of talking. Although I want to, I find it impossible to stay angry with her. Everything she says comes coated in candy, and from such a good place in her heart, to be cross with her would be cruel. So, I smile my best smile and say in my sweetest voice, 'I wouldn't dream of it, Hepzibah.'

For some reason this makes her laugh so hard she has to dry her eyes with the hem of her white apron. Does *she* know why I'm here? I wonder, as she pulls herself together. I open my mouth to speak, but she beats me to it.

'It's time,' she says and rings a bell.

The first thing I notice about the Divine Protector is his aureole. See, it's not in its usual place. I glance around the room. Maybe he's hung it on a peg somewhere because it got a bit hot. Do they get hot? My peepers are everywhere. But I can't see it. What has he done with it? I spy the oh-so-familiar, larger-than-life painting of him hanging on one of the white walls. There it is. A glowing, radiant light, perfectly in place around his body. I look back to the actual Divine Protector, expectantly. Nope, nothing, not even a halo. How is that possible? Somebody help me out here.

But nobody can. It's just the halo-less aureole-free DP and me.

'Is everything okay, Lois? You seem a little ... distracted.'

'I ... er ... I was admiring the room.'

He arches an eyebrow. 'And is it to your liking?'

'It's very ... white.' Stupid, dumb thing to say, but the truth is I've been preoccupied. I give it the once-over. White walls and ceiling. Uh-huh. Greyish-white tiled floor. Neat. Silver pots. Marble table with gilded legs and chairs to match. And, wow, the most brilliant thing I've ever seen, a waterfall of glass teardrops hanging from the ceiling.

'Do you like the chandelier?'

'It's magical. What's it for?'

'It's a light. A very splendid light. Come closer, Lois. Let me see your face.'

He opens his arms, but I don't budge. Something else about him isn't right. Not his voice, that's as warm and velvety as ever. Nor his eyes, the darkest chocolate colour. It's his height. The Divine Protector, Michael, my father, is surprisingly small. Man-sized, in fact. And his clothes. They aren't what I'm expecting either. Jeans and a T-shirt. Both white, fair do's, but where are his robes?

His aureole?

His halo?

His ordinariness is unexpected. And funny. So hilarious I can feel a giggle rumbling around in my chest. My hands dart in front of my mouth. I cannot laugh in front of the DP. I lower my head, close my eyes, and try to control it, but it has a mind of its own. And it's strong. My body convulses, once, twice, three times. My eyes are watering and, worse, I'm making strange gurgling noises. This is a disaster. The worst possible thing. Fast running out of options, I bend over and cough.

'Are you all right, Lois?'

Before I can stop it, a belly-load of laughter bursts out of me.

'What on earth is the matter?'

I shake my head. Tears stream down my cheeks. I bite my lip, half-crying now, frightened of what I've done.

'You're distressed. Of course you are. This is all so new.' He claps his hands, which makes me jump, and I stop laughing for a second, but almost immediately the fit kicks off again.

Hepzibah appears. One look at me and her eyes bulge. But the DP doesn't notice. He's one hundred per cent focused on me. And there's concern on his face, like he cares. My laughter dries on my tongue. He walks over, wipes my cheeks, and kisses one and then the other.

Whoa! Touching the Divine Protector is forbidden. But, hang on, this is different. He's touching me. All the same, I turn rigid. I can't help it. He may be my father, but I don't know him and I don't like it. It feels odd.

'Do you have a kiss for your father?'

He smiles, but I'm not so stupid to think it's a question. I lean in and brush my lips against his skin. The teeniest peck.

'Go back to your room,' he says, eyes shining. 'Get some sleep. We'll talk again tomorrow. At first light.'

. . .

The bed is heavenly, all goose down and feathers, the sheets soft and white. Hepzibah told me as much after she wished me goodnight, but not before she'd given me a piece of her mind.

'What were you thinking of, dearie? There'll be big trouble if you carry on like that. Mark my words.'

'I'm sorry. I couldn't help it.'

'Nerves, I shouldn't wonder. It's a good thing he thought you were upset. Now, into bed. You'll get your best ever sleep in that bed, so you will.'

Wrong, Hepzibah. I haven't slept a wink. How could I? For starters there's the issue with the room. I'd been so impressed with the private bathroom I hadn't seen the too-high, tiny window I can't possibly see out of. For the first time in my life I'm on my own. And it happened so quick, as if I fell through a crack I hadn't noticed into a deep dark hole. Will I ever see my mom again? My heart aches with missing her. And I'm scared. The Powers are a hair's breadth away. It's like I've leapt from my life into one less ordinary. I don't want to be here. Maybe if I ask the DP politely he'll let me go home.

My chest tightens, and all of a sudden, I'm gasping for breath. I sit up and gulp air until my breathing calms.

What in God's name is going to happen tomorrow? But no matter how hard my mind tries, it can't come up with anything and, pretty soon, I'm crazy with nerves again, and tomorrow is already today.

I slide out of bed, slip on my white dress, and pace the room in my bare feet, so as not to wake Hepzibah. Or anyone else for that matter. Up and down, up and down, until I can't stand it any longer. I simply have to see him.

Now.

I creep into the quadrangle and glance about. The gate

to the outer courtyard and the Powers is closed, thank goodness. I zip across the grass, past the Almond and the Olive Tree and stop sharp. Guards loom either side of the wooden door. But they're dressed in white, not black. Dominions. Phew.

'Where do you think you're going?' the taller one says.

Dammit. I stand a little straighter. 'My father is expecting me.'

'Haven't you forgotten something?' He points to his head.

Jesus. My scarf. I grit my teeth and look him in the eye. 'No.'

The other guard grins and nudges him in the ribs.

'Right,' the taller one says, opening the door. 'This way, my lady.'

My lady! Jeez. I'm going to have to up my game. I sniff, just loud enough for him to hear, and raise my hand. 'Hey, it's cool. I know the way.'

I pad into the dark corridor. The door clicks closed behind me. I let out a whopping great lungful of air and give my arms and legs a real good shake.

Now what?

My brain draws a blank, so I decide to retrace my steps to the white room. I tiptoe down the corridor, but a figure looms out of the darkness. A man. Oh my God, Jesus Christ. I cross myself and hold my hands in prayer. Neither of us moves. Neither of us breathes. Adjusting to the dark, I take in his colourless features, his colourless robe. Why doesn't he move? I step closer. Nothing, not even a flicker of his eyelids. Slowly, I reach out my hand until my fingertips settle on the skin of his arm. It's smooth and cold as stone. Of course, the statues. Jesus, Mary, and Michael. I noticed them yesterday.

Hearing footsteps, I duck down behind Jesus. Just in time, because a slim woman with blonde, shoulder-length hair approaches. She opens the door opposite and disappears inside. I hang back for a minute and, without thinking of the consequences, follow her.

The room is vast with a low bed on a raised plinth in the centre. Through the open door of the bathroom on the far side, someone moans. I scuttle across the floorboards and press my back against the wall. I count to ten and peer round the frame.

Two bodies, the DP and the young woman, are locked together. Skin on skin. Lip on lip.

And then I see them.

Ethereal. Magnificent.

The wings on Michael's back.

CHAPTER
SEVEN

It's Christmas Eve, and Donna is sitting on Jos' bed, still made up with its Brighton and Hove Albion duvet cover, clasping his Action Man, still dressed in its Red Devil outfit. There are grass stains on the suit, the ping-pong ball helmet is dented, and the parachute is worn and frayed. It doesn't seem all that long ago since he was hurling it through the attic window. Donna sighs and puts it back on the shelf, between the Evel Knievel motorbike and the Pelham Puppet Dragon he used to take everywhere with him – the hours she spent untangling those strings. Strange he should have kept them all, she thinks, her gaze straying to the sticker-splattered skateboard, propped against the wall next to the air rifle she bought in a moment of utter folly, when he turned thirteen. He proved himself to be an excellent shot, hitting the bull's-eye on targets he pinned to the old oak at the bottom of the garden. But then he started killing squirrels from his bedroom window, which upset his sisters. Taking aim one day, he missed his prey and shot the neighbour's cat instead. Fortunately, the animal survived, but Mrs Patterson made her displeasure clear.

'Your children are out of control,' she said, wagging her finger. 'And is it any wonder, the hours you waste on your endless causes. They're neglected, that's what they are. Make no mistake, Donna, you'll live to regret it.'

Did I neglect him? she wonders, clutching the duvet.

Eleven days have passed since Jos' unlikely friend, Martin, delivered the earth-shattering news. He thought she'd overreacted, but how on earth could this no-hoper who lived in somebody else's house, who owned nothing, not even a job, possibly begin to understand how she felt? He'd only known her son five minutes, whereas she'd given birth to him, had cared for him and doted on him for sixteen years, only for him to leave with a young woman she'd never met, at Christmas, without a word to his family. Darling Jos who used to tell her everything.

Tess, God bless her, had done some digging. Jos had gone into town one evening a fortnight ago and had returned to the squat with Naomi, a pretty, blue-eyed, blonde-haired Californian, and they'd been inseparable ever since. She was twenty-four, eight years older than Jos.

'Well, we all know what the attraction is there,' Tess said. 'Stacy showed me a photo of the two of them taken at a party. Jos was happy. His eyes were shining, and so was his hair.'

Donna lies down and draws her knees to her chest. It's at times like these she misses having a man in her life. She may have toughened up her act – a single mother of three young kids she had to – but she's only human. What she needs right now is a shoulder to cry on. If only she knew what is going on in Jos' head. Why the animosity towards her? And why the sudden infatuation with the blue-eyed blonde, Naomi, who'd swept him off his feet and flown him to another country a mere two weeks after meeting him? Surely there are plenty of girls Jos' age as attractive. Pretty little Angie Morris from three doors down, for one. Donna has seen the way she ogles Jos, all doe-eyed and dreamy. She clearly fancies the pants off him. If only he'd plucked up the courage to ask her out.

Or is she making too big a deal of it? Jos has been surrounded by older women all his life. Chances are he finds girls his own age giggly and childish but, even so, eight years is a big gap. Perhaps not for Jos, but if you flip it the other way, what does a pretty woman find so attractive about a grubby teenage boy who lives in a squat?

And what about the photograph of Rupert? Where had Jos got hold of it? Had Rupert resurfaced after all these years and got in touch with his son? Or was it the other way around? Had Jos tracked down his dad? It would explain the change in his behaviour if he had. If only he'd talk to her, tell her what's going on in that beautiful, mixed-up head of his, she might be able to help.

She takes the photo of a beaming Rupert from her pocket and is immediately hit by a raft of memories, not least the memory of his smile. It was one of the things which had first attracted her to him. That and his insanely glamorous name, Rupert Prince. What girl didn't want a prince and a teddy bear in their life? He was fun, too, energetic, and wildly radical. He played the guitar, performed in a band, was into jazz. He could recite the names of all the US presidents and down a pint of beer in five seconds flat. He wrote poetry.

They met on the Aldermaston March in April, 1958. The moment they got chatting, Donna knew he was the man of her dreams. Lying in bed with him in an attic room in a run-down pub that night, she realised it was love at first sight for him, too. They'd found their significant other. Together they would take on the world. She was nineteen, Rupert twenty-seven. Same age difference as Jos and Naomi, except the other way around.

Is it inconceivable they feel the same?

Nine months later, she gave birth to Chrissie. Tess followed two years later after which, and much to her parents' relief, Rupert finally proposed. Five years into married life, Jos arrived. Rupert was delighted. He'd made no secret of the fact he wanted a son. So why, four days after celebrating Jos' first birthday, did he walk out of his life? No, that's not strictly true. He disappeared. Vanished into thin air without a word to anyone. Never to be seen again.

September 1967. One minute they were a happy family of five, the next she was a single mother to three young children. It had been tough trying to rebuild her life. Her heart was broken. Her world shattered. Worse still were the feelings of rejection, the crying in the bathroom, the breaking down in front of her parents, the keeping it together in front of the kids, and the endless hours spent wondering why the husband she loved with all her heart had left. He'd been disillusioned with what was going on in the world, the Vietnam and Biafran Wars, that much she knew. They'd just lived through the 'summer of love', but it had passed them by. In demand as a graphic designer, and with a family to provide for, he'd been working ridiculously long hours with little time or energy for anything else. In her darkest hours, she wondered if the depression she'd failed to put a name to as Rupert moped about the house at weekends, had driven him to kill himself. At night she dreamt of him in the arms of another woman. Was she to blame? Her friends told her not to be so hard on herself. She had her work cut out with three young kids. She was not responsible for his happiness.

Hard to believe I was ever married to him, he's been gone so long, she thinks, staring at the handsome face she'd once known better than her own.

Donna hasn't spoken to Pauline for fourteen years. Her choice, not Pauline's. They got on well enough for the first year after Rupert left, but then the accusations started. Pauline blamed Donna for her brother's abrupt disappearance and, although she tried, there was nothing Donna could say or do to change Pauline's mind.

She pauses by the telephone. Is it likely Rupert has been in touch with his sister and not her? And if he has, will Pauline tell her where he is? And if she does, will Rupert be of any help? He hasn't seen his son for fifteen years. Why would he care where he was or who he was with?

But the photograph. Why, after all this time, does Jos have a picture of his father? It can mean only one thing. Rupert has to have been in touch. Either that or Pauline has sent her nephew the photo out of loyalty to her brother.

Her hand trembling, Donna picks up the handset and dials. The phone rings and rings. Deflated, she's about to put it down when she hears a muffled voice on the other end. 'Pauline? Is that you?'

'Yes, why? Who's speaking, please?'

'It's me. Donna.'

There's a deep inhalation of breath.

'Please, Pauline, don't put the phone down. It's about Jos.'

It's Donna's trump card. In happier times, she and

Rupert had made Pauline Jos' godmother. Pauline had doted on him and, even when she and Donna were no longer speaking, she continued to send Jos cards and presents every birthday and Christmas. Is it so inconceivable Jos has told her where he's living?

'What's happened? Is he okay?'

'I think he might have been in touch with Rupert.'

'So what if he has? He has every right to speak to his father. Honestly, Donna, do you have any idea how crazy you sound? Now, if you don't mind, it's Christmas Eve—'

'Hang on, Pauline, please. He's run away. To America.'

'Ah. Right. I see.'

The chatter of an excited male voice, followed by Tess' instantly recognisable laugh, sends Donna hurtling downstairs into the kitchen. Cringing, she takes in the scattered leaflets, unopened bills, dog-eared magazines, the dirty dishes, and the hastily strung fairy lights draped along the wall. Oblivious to the chaos, Tess is lording it at the hob, singing 'Frosty the Snowman' as she pours a bottle of red wine into a saucepan while her current boyfriend, Marcus, equally unfazed, sits at the cluttered table reading *Private Eye*. Swallowing hard, Donna wishes them a merry Christmas. Marcus drops the magazine and springs to his feet grinning, and she immediately feels guilty. She likes Marcus. He's a good lad and, better still, makes Tess happy.

'Happy Christmas, Donna,' he says and pecks her on the cheek.

Tess bounds over and hugs her. 'For an awful minute I thought you weren't here.'

'It's Christmas Eve. Where on earth would I be?'

'Greenham Common.'

There's no hint of accusation, but all the same, Donna winces.

'What is it? What's wrong? You're awfully pale. Isn't she awfully pale, Marcus?'

But before Marcus can reply, the front door bursts open again and Donna and Tess charge into the hall.

'Hello, Chrissie. Hello, Bob.' Tess kisses them one after the other. 'You're just in time, I'm making mulled wine. Ooh, but you've got champagne. How extravagant. You must be doing well, Bob.'

A look passes between her eldest daughter and her boyfriend. What's that about? Donna wonders. Quashing her disappointment again she embraces first Chrissie and then Bob, and forces a smile. 'We're in the kitchen. Come on through.'

As Bob and Marcus shake hands, Tess finds a chopping board and slices an orange while Chrissie sets about tidying up the mess, loading the dishwasher and washing the pans.

Donna joins her at the sink. 'I'm sorry. I'd meant to do this earlier.'

'Still no word from Jos, then?'

'Nothing. Not even a phone call.'

'Don't worry, Mum. He'll be here.'

'He's leaving it rather late. America's not exactly down the road.'

'Jos loves Christmas. He wouldn't miss it for the world. And you never know, he might even bring the mysterious Naomi.'

'I wish I shared your optimism.'

'She might prove to be the best thing that's ever happened to him.'

'But running away like that.'

'Don't take it personally. He probably needed to stretch his wings.'

'I haven't exactly mollycoddled him,' Donna says, recalling Mrs Patterson's criticism.

'No, you haven't.'

'You think I haven't done enough then. Is that it?'

Chrissie drops the scourer and drapes her arm around Donna. 'Mum, stop. You're putting words in my mouth. I mean, he's sixteen. He's not a child anymore.'

Donna leans into her daughter and smiles. 'When did you become so wise?'

'Mulled wine.' Tess thrusts a mug into her hands. 'And you, Chrissie.'

'Er, no. Not just now, thanks.'

'Hungover, are we?'

'Nope. Just don't fancy it.'

'All the more for me then.' Tess says and bounds back to Marcus who is laughing uproariously at one of Bob's jokes.

'Oh, Chrissie. You're not ill, are you?'

'No, I'm not, but I do have some news which might cheer you up.'

The champagne. Of course. Donna puts the mug down and claps her hands. 'Bob's asked you to marry him.'

'Er ... no.'

'Oh, darling, I'm sorry. I'm sure he will—'

'Mum, shush.' Chrissie presses a finger to Donna's lips. 'It's good news. I'm going to have a baby.'

'A baby?'

'We've got the order wrong, I know, but we will get married. Afterwards.'

'After the baby?'

'Yes. For now, we want to focus on the birth.'

'I'm going to be a granny?'

Chrissie cocks her head. 'Are you pleased?'

'Oh, darling, I'm ecstatic.' Beaming, Donna flings her arms around her daughter. 'That's fantastic news. Where's that champagne? Oh, this is wonderful. I'm so happy for you both. Tess. Tess. Have you heard Chrissie's news? She's—'

But the sound of the doorbell ringing, loud and long, drowns out her words.

'Jos,' says Chrissie. 'Told you he'd come.'

Donna dashes into the hall and opens the door, but it isn't Jos, it's the postman with a parcel.

It's late on Christmas Eve when Donna decides to come clean about her conversation with Pauline. The subject having preyed on her all day, she's been trying to work out a way to drop it into the conversation. The television is on in the sitting room, something funny, judging by the laughter. Sensing now is as good a time as any, Donna takes a deep breath and opens the door.

Cuddled up with Marcus on the sofa, Tess looks up as she enters. 'You okay, Mum?'

'Yes, I'm fine. I ... er ... I spoke to Pauline earlier.'

'Oh,' says Chrissie. 'How did that go?'

'Quite well, as it happens.' It was true, after a frosty start, Pauline had thawed. She'd been sympathetic, eager to help – the mother in her, no doubt. When she'd confessed Rupert had got in touch with her five years ago but hadn't mentioned it for fear of reopening old wounds, Donna had somehow managed to cling on to her temper. Letting rip at her sister-in-law wouldn't help get Jos back. 'She gave me your father's number.'

'Wow!' says Marcus.

Tess inches forward, eyes bright. 'Have you rung him?'

Donna baulks. This conversation is going to be even harder than she thought. All three of them have avoided the subject of Rupert's disappearance for years and yet, clearly, Tess misses her dad. She was old enough when he left to remember him. Is it so odd she's keen to have him back in her life? 'Not yet, no.'

'Oh! That's a shame.' Tess slumps against the cushions, and Marcus puts a protective arm around her.

I've gone about this all wrong, thinks Donna, wearily. 'It's been so long, Tess.'

Tess nods, folds her arms, and concentrates on the screen. *The Goodies Christmas Special,* Donna notices. She's been looking forward to watching that.

'Where's he living?' Chrissie asks.

'America,' says Bob.

Tess whips around and glares at him. 'That's not funny, Bob.'

'Sorry. Sorry.'

'Mum?' Chrissie says, eyeing Donna suspiciously.

Donna steels herself. 'Actually, Bob's right. Rupert is in America. I think Jos has gone to meet his dad.'

CHAPTER
EIGHT

I'm perched on a white chair in the white room, calm and sweet as you like, as if this is just another day in my oh-so-dull existence. Strikes me it's the way to play it, in case someone walks in. My insides, though, tell a completely different story. My nerves are in knots, and my stomach is a piece of elastic, pinging about all over the place. I shouldn't be here. I should be wearing a scarf. And I'm pretty sure I've seen things I'm not supposed to see. First off, the wings. No more doubts. Michael is The Divine Protector. He may be small, he may have mislaid his aureole. But those wings. They're the real deal. I mean, we've all heard the rumours, but I've never met anyone who's actually seen them. Although, now I come to think of it, I guess Mom has. Ew! And the woman he was kissing, she'll have seen them, too.

That's the bit that's bothering me. What's the Divine Protector doing with her if he can't be with Mom?

The wait is killing me. I've been here for what seems like forever, Hepzibah is bound to have discovered I'm missing. She might even sound an alarm. But I'd be crazy to leave because the guards know I'm here. God only knows how the DP's gonna react. He may be my father, something I'm still struggling to take in, but we're strangers. Sure, I *know* a lot about him. I've been learning about him, listening to him, and worshipping him my entire life. But up until yesterday, I was just a dim and distant memory, a fleeting moment he turned his back on. And now, hey presto, here I am, the very bones and flesh of me. I want him to like me. Not only because he's my father, or because he has the ear of God, but because he's my saviour. Without him we'd be damned, like the poor lost souls of the Other-world. I have taken his lessons to heart and abided by his rules all my life – well, generally speaking. It's not easy being perpetually good, unless you're a saint, or an angel, in which case I imagine you're probably born with the knack of resisting temptation. So, sure, I've had my moments, but that's in the past. I'm determined to be a better person. If I'm to make a success of this father/daughter thing, I really need him to like and trust me. It would be awful if he disowned me. So why, I wonder, did I sneak past his guards and waltz into his house without so much as a by-your-leave? And to think I was going to ask him if I could see Mom.

Jeez, as starts go, this is pretty disastrous.

The longer I wait, the worse I feel. My armpits are soggy, and I'm nauseous. I wish I was a million miles away. Anywhere but here. If he doesn't show up soon I'm gonna hurl. And then what? How will I explain away a puddle of vomit amongst all this gleaming whiteness? Ugh. This can't be happening. What am I doing here? Why did Mom agree to let me come?

Okay, okay. I need to calm down. It's possible I'm over-reacting. The DP has no idea I've been spying on him. He's going to be surprised to find me here, but I'll blag a way out. Mom's always saying I've a special talent for that.

'Lois! What on earth are you doing here?'

I whirl around, heart thumping. The DP is staring at me. And boy, is he angry, the crimson face and hands on hips a dead giveaway. 'You told me to meet you at first light. So, here I am.'

'But how did you get in?' He looks up, down, and all around like a man who's lost something he's certain he had with him.

'Front door. Same as yesterday.'

He's blinking now, scratching his temple. 'And your scarf. What happened to your scarf?'

I pat my head, all innocent like. 'Oh no. I'm sorry, I must have forgotten to put it on.' Like you did your aureole, I want to add. *Again*. 'Shall I fetch it?'

'No. There's no need.' He sinks down in the chair next to mine, never for one minute taking his chocolate browns off me, like he's working real hard to figure me out.

I don't speak because I think it's probably for the best. I'm in enough trouble as it is, and the DP, well, he seems plain confused. So, I smile my prettiest smile.

'Lois, my child.' He reaches for my hands.

Awkward but, at the same time, a whopping relief. Seems I'm off the hook.

'I hope you'll be happy here. I have big plans for you.'

'I'm sure I will. It's kind of you to invite me. It's a great honour. There's nowhere else I'd rather be.' Enough, Lois. Stop talking.

'I'm pleased to hear it. I think we're going to rub along very well. Although we've been living separate lives, I feel as if I know you already. But then you are a part of me.' He lets go of me to touch his heart.

Holy moly. This is going better than expected. Far, far better. I want to laugh, shout, dance, and cry all at once. 'I just wish we had more time.'

He cups my cheeks. 'Little angel, we have all the time in the world.'

I chew this over. See, I know he can't have forgotten that the world ends on the twelfth of May next year. The news came straight from his mouth after all. But perhaps his mind, like mine, has been overtaken by events. 'But the Apocalypse,' I whisper.

He smiles. 'You are forgetting something, Lois. Are you not?'

Am I? Nope. I don't think so.

'After the Apocalypse, on the Day of Enlightenment, you and I, and all the other Guardians of God, will ascend to the spiritual realm to enjoy eternal life.'

I'm beaming now, my face fit to split. I've had my doubts about this but, hearing it from the DP's own lips, I know it's true. Okay, so there'll be a battle, the kind of which mankind has never known, blah blah blah, but the DP will lead Heaven's Army to victory over Satan. And if he thinks he can win then so do I. 'And Mom will be with us.'

His right eye twitches. 'Of course.'

I spring up and spin on one leg, arms overhead, something I'm really good at. I can't help myself. I'm that happy.

'Meantime, Lois, even though you're my daughter, there are certain rules you must abide by.'

I stop twirling and pull my most serious face. 'I promise I will wear my scarf at all times.'

He throws back his head and laughs, so hard I can see every polished white tooth in his head. 'Oh goodness me, I couldn't care less about the scarf. In fact, I'd rather you didn't wear one. You have such lovely hair. And anyway, it's not necessary. It's merely ... No, never mind.' He strolls over to the table on the far side of the room, picks up a small silver bell, and rings it. 'There's someone I want you to meet.'

Oh, but we're having so much fun. Can't it wait? There's stuff I need to know. Where's your aureole, for one? I shift from foot to foot, trying to disguise my frustration, as a tall man dressed in a white linen tunic walks in, a wing-topped staff in one hand and an odd-looking cup with a silver straw in the other. His face is pinched, his nose pointed, and what is left of his dark hair is flecked with silver.

'Your tea, my Lord.'

'Thank you, Raphael.'

I examine the man suspiciously, taking in his hollow cheeks, the crinkles around his beady black eyes, and dear Lord, his necklace strung with teeth.

'Raphael, my daughter, Lois.'

The man turns to me and nods. 'Honoured to meet you, Lois.'

I slap my hand over my mouth. I mustn't laugh, but it's so over-the-top I can't help myself.

The DP frowns. 'Lois!'

As tellings-off go, it's short and sweet. But a telling-off it is. I wipe the smile off my face and hold out my hand. 'Pleasure to meet you, too, sir ... Raphael.'

Raphael clasps it in his. They are large and cold and uncomfortably dry, I notice, as he fixes me with an intense stare. I shift my gaze an inch to the snakes wound around his creepy-as-hell staff. What's that all about, I'd like to know?

'Raphael is a great healer,' the DP says. 'And a man with whom I would trust my life. I'm about to appoint him second-in-command.'

At last, Raphael lets go. I drop my head and stare at my feet.

'Look at me, Lois.'

I do as I'm told, grateful not to have to ogle Raphael. There's something about him that makes me uneasy. Something sinister. Something Otherworldly, perhaps.

'As my only child and heir, I have big plans for you.'

'Your heir?'

The DP takes a sip of tea. 'You know what that means?'

I nod, my shoulders drooping under the weight of his words. He can't be serious. Me? His heir? Wow! 'But why? Are you ill—'

He raises a palm. 'You are young and inexperienced, so I have offered your hand to Raphael.'

Wait a minute, what?

'I can think of no man better suited to you. If anything should happen to me, God forbid, he is the man to guide you. You will marry on Ash Wednesday.'

'But he's so—'

'Lois! This is not the wish of your father. It is the will of God.'

CHAPTER NINE

It's Christmas morning. Donna and the remnants of her family are in the sitting room opening presents but, instead of the usual hilarity and mickey-taking, there's a subdued air about the place.

Last night, Donna had dialled Rupert's number over and again, letting it ring and ring in the hope an answer-phone might kick in so she could at least leave a message. But either Rupert didn't have one, or he'd forgotten to turn it on. He couldn't be ignoring it. The sound of the telephone's incessant ringing surely would have driven him to answer it or, at the very least, take it off the hook. Whatever the reason, Donna's frustration has turned to despair.

To lighten the mood, Marcus and Bob have mixed some spicy Bloody Marys, served in long glasses, each with a leafy stick of celery.

'To mop your brow,' explains Marcus as he hands them around. 'If you start to sweat.'

But nobody laughs. Not even Tess.

The smell of turkey roasting reminds Donna she has a meal to prepare. She's not in the mood for cooking. She'd far rather close the curtains, crawl into bed, and cry her eyes out. But what good would that do? She may not want to but she has to plough on. She has to stay strong for the girls. It's what she does and she's good at it. There's bound to be a perfectly simple explanation for Jos' mad dash to the States. A fleeting visit, perhaps – a fortnight's vacation to meet his dad, with Naomi for support. Chances are he won't get on with Rupert anyway. Abandoned by him as a baby, he's grown up fatherless. He's bound to be angry. Bound to have lots of difficult questions. Not the best platform from which to launch a father/son relationship.

She'd prepared the vegetables late last night with Chrissie, while listening to the carols from Kings Chrissie had tape-recorded earlier, a family tradition they'd sleep-walked into. But neither of them had paid much attention to the music, they'd been too lost in their thoughts. Donna had assumed Chrissie, like her, was thinking about Rupert. She hadn't asked because she didn't think it fair. If Chrissie wanted to talk about her father then she would in her own time.

She rises slowly to her feet, and Chrissie moves to join her. 'I've got this.' She takes in her daughter's pallid complexion, the bags under her eyes. What a shame this mess has overshadowed her exciting news. 'Put your feet up for a bit.'

'I'd rather keep busy.'

'Marcus and I thought we'd pop down the pub,' Bob says. 'Unless you need our help.'

Donna waves her hand. 'No, no. Go ahead.'

'Think I'll join you,' mutters Tess. 'I could use the anaesthetic.'

'How bloody predictable,' snaps Chrissie.

'It's not as if I've got anything better to do.'

'You could lay the table,' Donna suggests, keeping her tone light. It's not like Chrissie to make snide remarks.

'Fine! I'll join you boys when I'm finished,' Tess says and stomps off.

The radio is playing in the kitchen. Donna puts the kettle on, the sound of it coming to the boil immediately drowning out the angry rattling of cutlery in the small dining room next door. 'How are you bearing up?'

'Same as you, I should think.'

'Angry, frustrated, and confused?'

'Yup, and sad, too.'

She wraps her arms around Chrissie. 'Oh, honey, I'm sorry.'

'Why? It's not your fault.'

Isn't it? she wonders for the millionth time.

'Listen, Mum. Marilyn Monroe. Remember the Christmas Jos performed this?'

Recognising the song, 'I Wanna Be Loved by You', Donna smiles. 'Oh, yes.'

Age nine, Jos sneaked away from the table and reappeared in an old blonde wig of hers, Chrissie's brand-new makeup, and one of Tess' dresses that reached his ankles. Chrissie wanted to throttle him, but he looked so funny, she couldn't help laughing along with everyone else. He was always so entertaining when he was a kid, dressing up and clowning around.

'I should drain the potatoes,' Chrissie says. 'Before they turn to mush.'

Donna lets go of her daughter, picks up the saucepan of parsnips, and puts it on the hob. She scoops some of the turkey fat into a smaller pan for the gravy, while Chrissie shakes the potatoes and tips them into a tray sizzling with hot oil. She's thinking what a great team they make when the doorbell rings.

'Tess, can you get that?'

Cutlery clatters on the table and, with an audible expletive, Tess thuds down the hall. The door opens with its familiar squeak. I must get around to oiling it, Donna thinks, as Tess shrieks excitedly.

'Jos!' Donna sprints into the hall but pulls up with a start. It isn't Jos standing in the doorway. It's Rupert. Rooted to the spot, she tries to take it in. Her husband. The children's father. Here, on the threshold of the family home. For the first time in fifteen years.

'Hello, Dad. I'm Chrissie, your eldest,' Chrissie says, slipping past her.

Dumbstruck, Donna can only watch as Rupert shake his daughter's hand. 'It's good to see you.'

That voice, deep and gravelly. Instantly recognisable.

'It's been a long time,' Chrissie adds.

His suggestion of a smile flickers. 'Yes, it has.'

Oh my God, really? thinks Donna. Is that all you can say after fifteen years?

'We thought you were in America,' Tess says.

'I am, I mean, I was. I'm staying with Pauline over Christmas. I arrived last night.'

'She might have said,' mutters Donna.

Rupert catches her eye. 'Hello, Donna.'

'Hello, Rupert,' she says, willing herself to sound casual, like she couldn't care less whether he was here or not. But she does care. This is the man she once adored. The lover she thought she couldn't live without. The half of her that made her whole. The father of her three children. But that was another lifetime ago. She studies him, this man she used to know so well. His thick, dark hair is longer than it used to be and flecked with grey, lending him a gravitas he didn't have before. His tanned face is thinner and etched with age; creases on his forehead, crow's feet around his deep-brown eyes, fine lines bracketing his mouth, those lips she loved to kiss. But he is handsome, still, and slim for a man of his age. Fit and healthy, too. Steeling herself, she makes a show of checking her watch. 'What kept you?'

Rupert winces. 'I didn't come around to start a fight.'

'Oh, so I'm supposed to forget the last fifteen years ever happened and forgive you, just like that?'

The girls shrink back.

'No, Donna. I don't expect you to forgive me. Ever. I treated you badly. You didn't deserve it.'

She stalls. There are so many questions she wants to ask him: What did I do to make you run away? Where did you go? Are you in love with someone else? But a deep-rooted fear she won't like what he has to say stops her. 'You could have called. Let me know you were okay. I thought you were dead.'

'I'm sorry. Look, one day I hope we'll be able to sit down and talk about it, but until we do ... It's good to see you, Donna. You haven't changed a bit.'

She sniffs. 'Better get your eyes tested.'

'I mean it. You're just as I remember.'

Something stirs within her. Affection? Or some innate, misplaced lust? Her emotions in freefall, she girds herself and fires the question that's been bothering her all day. 'Have you been in touch with Jos?'

Rupert tugs his ear, a habit once so familiar. Seeing it again, Donna thinks she might cry.

'That's why I'm here. I don't know where he is. I haven't seen Jos, or spoken to him, in fifteen years.'

The room starts to swim. To steady herself, Donna slumps against the hall table.

'Mum!' chorus Tess and Chrissie.

Rupert steps towards her. 'Donna?'

She raises a trembling hand. 'I'm okay. Sorry. I—'

'Tess and I will make some tea,' she hears Chrissie say, as her eldest daughter leads her into the sitting room and deposits her in an armchair. 'We won't be long.'

Donna nods, grateful Marcus and Bob have made themselves scarce, furious Rupert has taken up residence on the sofa opposite. She eyes him askance, sitting on her furniture, in her house, comfortable as you like, what appears to be an expensive watch strapped to his wrist. Aside from the seventeen hundred pounds he left in their joint account – intentionally or not, she didn't know – the bastard hadn't contributed a penny to the upbringing of his children since. How dare he come here, pretending to care. The nerve of the man. She glances at the Christmas tree, festooned with the lights, tinsel, baubles and ornaments she and the children have collected over the years; a lifetime of memories made in his absence, thank you very much. Why doesn't he piss off back under the stone he's crawled out from? She's on the verge of suggesting it when Tess and Chrissie breeze back in with mugs of tea and a plate of beautifully iced tree-shaped biscuits.

Tess offers them to Rupert. 'Chrissie made them. And they're as delicious as they look.'

'We thought Jos had got in touch with you,' Chrissie says. 'He hasn't been himself recently. He dropped out of school. Moved into a squat. And now he's gone to the States. One of his friends told us that's where they were headed.'

Donna takes a sip of the tea Chrissie hands her. She

wishes she was coping as well as the girls. They seem perfectly happy discussing Jos' disappearance, as if talking to a father they barely remember, who walked out on them without explanation, is the most natural thing in the world. She's not sure if she's angry they can, or sad.

'His girlfriend, Naomi, is Californian, you see,' adds Chrissie.

'Naomi?'

Donna glances at Rupert. He is frowning again, tugging his ear.

Tess nods. 'Yes, and she's older than Jos.'

'My age,' adds Chrissie.

'Where is she from? In California, I mean?'

'Haven't the foggiest,' says Tess.

His frown deepens. 'Have you met her?'

Tess shakes her head. 'I've only seen a photo.'

Rupert stares into the distance, still tugging his ear.

'What is it?' Donna asks, finding her voice at last. 'What's wrong?'

'It's a long shot but...' He reaches inside his jacket for his wallet and draws out a small, rectangular picture. The type you'd take in a booth. The type they'd taken together in the early stages of their marriage. Mostly they'd goofed around in front of the camera, but in one or two they'd kissed. He hands it to Tess. 'Is this her?'

'I think so.'

'Yes or no, Tess. It's important.'

Clearly shocked by his tone, Tess bites her lip and studies the photo again. 'Yes. Yes, it's her. I never forget a face.'

A shiver runs down Donna's spine. She clasps the back of her neck. Why does Rupert have a picture of Jos' girlfriend in his wallet? Or is it? Can Tess be absolutely sure it's

Jos' Naomi? There must be hundreds of blonde-haired, blue-eyed Naomis living in California. It might just as easily be her doppelganger.

Chrissie whistles. 'Wow! That's one helluva coincidence.'

And then it hits her. 'Your girlfriend, I assume.'

Wincing, Tess hands the photo back to Rupert.

'Naomi? God, no.' He stuffs it back in his wallet

And yet you carry her photo. Donna clenches her jaw and tries to quash the feelings of jealousy and betrayal rising, like bile, in her throat.

'I ... She ...' His voice peters out.

She folds her arms and glares at him.

'I knew her mother. She ... er ... she died. I helped out with ... er ... Naomi after she died.'

Jesus, Rupert, thinks Donna, as the girls exchange worried looks. Do you honestly expect us to believe that? Mother and daughter. Wow! Have you no scruples?

He shifts awkwardly, eyebrows squished together. 'A year ago, Naomi got involved with a group of happy-clappy Christians. She moved in with them and asked me to join her. She said I'd been carrying so many regrets for so many years, and punishing myself for them, she reckoned I'd be happier there. Told me I deserved to be happy. That everyone did.'

For heaven's sake. If he'd regretted walking out on his family, then all he'd had to do was call. Okay, so she might have slammed down the phone, but—

'Thing is, I didn't think I did. As far as I was concerned, I'd got what I deserved. And anyway, I hated the idea. It wasn't my scene. Never has been. I told her so in no uncertain terms and tried to talk her out of going back. She left in a huff, back to wherever it was she'd been living. I found out where, a few weeks later, from a guy I met at a bar. Turns out he'd had a fling with her. Love-bombing, I think it's called. Part of the Guardian of God's recruitment process.'

Love-bombing? Guardians of God? Donna doesn't like the sound of this. Is Rupert saying that Naomi, by some strange coincidence, has targeted her son? 'Are you telling me it's a cult?'

'God no, it's a commune. There's been no trouble. No funny stuff. No banner-waving. No indoctrination. They're just a harmless bunch of religious do-gooders. All they want is to save people's souls.'

Tess shakes her head. 'Jos isn't the least bit religious. He wouldn't be seen dead in a place like that.'

'Haven't you been listening?' says Chrissie. 'Naomi 'love-bombed' Jos into going.'

No, Chrissie, thinks Donna, recalling the photo of Rupert she'd found in the squat. Jos hadn't just been loved-bombed. He thought he was going to meet his father, too. Naomi, the cruel-hearted bitch, had set Jos a trap.

CHAPTER TEN

Esther hauls up the last sack of the day and unhooks it from the hoist. Breathing heavily, she mops her brow with the hem of her fawn apron and thanks God they don't work the mill in the hundred-degree heat of the summer anymore. Despite his workers fainting, it wasn't until one of the gin ponies collapsed and died that Miller Isaac proposed they store the grain after the harvest for grinding in the cooler months of winter, and spin the cotton, a far less arduous task, in the summer months instead.

I'm getting too old for this, she thinks as she heaves the sack across the wooden boards. She pauses for a minute to catch her breath, tips the grain into the hopper, and watches it flow down the shoe into the eye of the millstones on the floor below.

Her shift over, she hangs up her apron and says goodbye to Leah, her co-worker, who acknowledges her departure with a swift wave of her hand. Pausing at the gin gang to stroke Felix, her favourite mill pony, on the nose, she rolls up her sleeve to check the time, but her wrist is bare. She gasps, at once covering her mouth with her hand.

'Are you looking for this?'

She spins around. Miller Isaac's son, David, slips a watch out of his pocket, the instantly recognisable gold strap glistening in the beam of sunlight streaming in through the window. She stares at him, her cheeks burning.

'It's okay, I can keep a secret.' He holds it out to her.

She glances around, fretfully. Seeing no one, she snatches it back. 'It's a sentimental thing.'

'You don't have to explain.'

'Thank you.' She flashes a weak smile and, clutching her watch to her breast, charges off down the road. She's lost her daughter. She couldn't bear to lose this, too. A twenty-first birthday present from her parents, she'd kept it even though it's forbidden.

'Say hi to Lois,' David calls after her.

'I will.' She closes her eyes for a moment and prays David will be true to his word. Why wouldn't he be? she wonders irritably as she fastens the clasp. He's a sweet boy with a kind heart. And Lola adores him.

The hum of the fortnightly aeroplane delivering the latest band of recruits has her checking the time. Bang on schedule, which means fifteen minutes until her shift at The Bakery. It's a mile's walk but, if she looks sharp, she should make it. She's got away with the watch, but it won't do to be late. She'll get a black mark. Too many and she'll be isolated and, that way, madness lies. Three weeks was all it took to transform Anna from confident milkmaid to gibbering wreck, never to recover.

With that sobering thought in mind, Esther conceals her watch with her sleeve and increases her pace to almost a run so that by the time she arrives at The Bakery, she's panting and drenched in sweat. But at least she isn't late. She tucks a stray hair behind her ear, neatens her dress, and heads inside. Baker Amos nods, and Dorcas raises her eyes, but nobody else in the busy room takes any notice. Why would they? No one here knows her secret.

But what if someone finds out? she wonders, hurrying to her station and slipping on her white apron. What will happen to her then?

Best not to think about it, she thinks, measuring out the flour in a large bowl. She adds the yeast, a dash of salt, a splash of oil, and half a jug of water, and mixes it together. That done, she scatters a light dusting of flour on the wooden counter and kneads the dough, pushing it down and then outwards with the heels of her hands. It's a repetitive and hypnotic task but, even so, her thoughts return to Lola. She loves Michael with all her heart, but nobody should have to give up their daughter, not even if their father is the Prince of Light.

Should they?

When the request came through from Ascension House, she knew this was the greatest expression of her love for the Divine Protector, and therefore, God. To refuse would be to ignore the needs of the group. It would be selfish.

But mulling it over that night, she had second thoughts.

A day later, she received a brief, handwritten note from Michael. Not quite a command but not far off.

If you love Lois, truly love her, you will let her go.

Up until then, Esther had never doubted her love for her daughter. A smiley, gurgling baby who rarely cried, Lola held a special place in her heart. Growing up, she seemed to occupy more space than any other child. She was bright, she was precocious. She captured the attention of everyone she met, however unwittingly. She was a free spirit who found humour in the most banal situations. She could light up any room simply by being there. She was kind.

Home is quieter now, the atmosphere less charged, her life less vibrant. She misses Lola's laughter. Her cute smile. Her dimpled cheeks. The light in her pale-blue eyes. Esther feels her absence keenly, and it hurts, as if a part of her has been surgically removed.

She was the dearest thing in my life and yet I gave her away. I shouldn't have done that. I should have fought for her. That's what mother's do.

You had no choice, her conscience nags. It was God's wish. And who are you to argue with Him? Anyway, it's not as if she's dead. Stop thinking about her in the past tense.

Not yet, thinks Esther with a shudder as she plonks the silky-smooth dough in a bowl to prove. But the Apocalypse isn't far off.

It's eight o'clock on Christmas morning, but Esther is still in bed. Noah is away on business. No surprises there. Since becoming a Virtue he's away more and more. Jemima and Isabel are celebrating with Elijah this year, although they'd begged to stay with her and, for the first time, Lola is with her father. Esther has no idea what Michael does on Christ's birthday, but she hopes, with all her heart, he has something special planned. Lola has always loved Christmas, despite the low-key Edenville approach – a single gift and a special meal – but then, unlike Esther, she has nothing to compare it to.

Esther shuts her eyes and casts her mind back to the

family Christmases of her childhood. The memories still sharp after all these years, she can indulge her senses at will: the earthy smell of the freshly cut fir, the ropes of fairy lights, the silver tinsel and the multicoloured baubles; the staircase, lavishly decorated with branches of spruce and clove-studded oranges; the sumptuous feast prepared by her vivacious mother for her brothers, grandparents, aunts, uncles, and cousins; the carols sung on Christmas Eve at the tops of their voices; the beautifully wrapped gifts left by Father Christmas on the end of her bed.

She releases a long sigh and rolls onto her side. No good ever came from reflecting on the past. Best to bury those memories. It was her choice to leave her family. The dream may have gone a little sour, but she must try and make the most of what she still has.

Taking care not to bang her head on the sloping eaves, she hauls herself up, dresses, and heads downstairs to the kitchen to give it the once-over, but the room is spotlessly clean. The pantry, too, is full, but as she isn't hungry, she can see no sense in cooking. Still, there's always plenty to do in the garden, chickens to feed, vegetables to tend, watering, weeding. But at the back door, she stalls. Her limbs are leaden, her joints stiff, and a dull ache is throbbing at her temple. Trying to make sense of this latest turn of events has drained her.

She slumps into the nearest chair, laces her fingers behind her head, and tries, once again, to grapple with the questions Lola's abduction – because that's how it feels – has raised. Why had God decided to reunite Michael with his daughter? Why leave it this long? Does He have something planned for her? Or with the Apocalypse fast approaching, does He feel she'll be safer with her father? She squeezes her elbows together and groans. No matter how often she tells herself otherwise, she can't quash the feeling something is wrong. Lola needs her mother. She isn't prepared for such a dramatic change to her life, never mind that she's still young and hopelessly naïve.

If only there was someone Esther could talk to. Ironic, really, considering the countless times she's longed for privacy. But no one leads a solitary life in Edenville. They're one big, happy family, hundreds of like-minded people sharing the same beliefs, working towards the same goal, every day chock-full of activity. Early morning Religious Instruction is followed by shifts at The Mill and The Bakery. Evenings are filled with Meetings, Workshops, and the training of any new recruits. Esther never has a moment to herself. But today there are no classes, there is no work and, for the first time in what seems like forever, she's alone. With nothing to occupy her, she has all the time in the world to sit and think. And now she is, she's conscious of how muddled she's become. She needs to marshal her thoughts, work out how she's going to explain Lola's disappearance to Noah, for starters. He has no idea who Lola's father is. Michael made her promise never to tell a soul.

'It would ruin me,' he said.

So, she told Noah the same thing she'd told Zachary and Elijah, that she didn't know, that it was one of two men and she felt uncomfortable naming either of them.

But now Lola is in Michael's care she has to come up with some sort of explanation. Lola isn't the obvious choice of candidate for a position in Ascension House. The idea Michael has plucked her from obscurity won't hold up under scrutiny. She's too mischievous for one thing, she steals books – not that Esther has told Noah about that little incident. He wouldn't think twice about reporting

Lola to the authorities – and far too young. But Noah is no fool. He's bound to be suspicious.

If only Michael had bothered to explain. But then again, why change the habit of a lifetime? He'd kept their relationship a secret, too.

'It's what God wants,' he'd said.

Esther hadn't questioned it. She loved Michael and she believed in him. When he told her God had been speaking to him in dreams for years, she hadn't doubted him for a second. She'd witnessed the trance-like states he fell into without warning, had heard him talking in his sleep. He'd been relieved. He thought he was going mad.

The week after they moved into Edenville, Esther discovered she was pregnant. The same day, Michael informed her he wouldn't be living with her. She was devastated, distraught. Michael was her life. Her reason for being. Why hadn't he mentioned this earlier? Didn't he love her anymore? She was pregnant with his child. Didn't he want to be a father?

'God spoke to me last night. It's not my calling. But I'm happy for you, Esther. You will make an excellent mother.'

'But I love you, Michael.'

He laid his hand on her shoulder like a priest, not a lover. 'Zachary is your husband now.'

She stamped her foot. Hadn't he heard her? How could any man replace him, let alone one she hardly knew? 'You can't mean that. It's crazy.'

'It's God's will,' Michael said, raising his hand as he walked away.

Zachary was the first husband Michael chose for her. An architect in his former life, he planned, designed, and managed the year-long construction of Edenville. Hard-working, thoughtful and kind, he looked after her as a husband should while bringing Lola up as if she were his own. Esther didn't love him, but she enjoyed his company and, in the five years they were together, felt cared for and increasingly happy. But then Michael decreed Zachary move in with Priscilla and David, Miller Isaac's wife and son, and Builder Elijah move in with her.

Elijah brought with him two scared little girls, Jemima and Isabel, whose mother, having hung herself, was found posthumously guilty of committing a mortal sin. But, barely a month into the relationship, Esther reached the conclusion that the driving force behind Tabitha's suicide was Elijah's abusive behaviour. Six long years later, and much to her relief, he moved out, leaving behind his girls, and Noah moved in.

She wasn't in love with Noah either – she could never love a man as she loved Michael – but Noah quickly proved himself to be decent and attentive and, as with Zachary, she learnt to love him like a brother. She supposes that's how it is with all 'marriages' in Edenville. Not that she dares ask anyone how they feel about their chosen spouses. It wouldn't do to question the status quo.

The last time she'd been alone with Michael was when she'd gone into labour. It had thrilled her to see him holding their newborn baby, tenderly kissing her bright-pink cheeks. He'd named her Lois. Then handed her back.

And that had been that. Until now.

She slaps her palms on the table. It's all very well to have done as God wishes, but what if Lola misbehaves? What if she speaks out of turn? She has such a tongue on her, and absolutely no filter between her brain and mouth. She might air some doubts, or talk about parties, or some other nonsense she learned from that book. Where on earth did she find it? *The Great Gatsby*, of all things.

A memory pops into Esther's head, of hiding away in her room, utterly absorbed by the same novel at the same age. Her mother had cooed her approval, adding that it was one of, if not the, greatest American novels of all time. Not so Esther. When she found the book hidden in Lola's drawer, she panicked. She knew what happened when you broke the rules. So, she took it and burnt it.

What else could she have done?

She shivers, recalling the size of the fire the day, five years ago, Michael proclaimed all novels banned.

Where they burn books, they will, too, in the end, burn people.

Esther rolls back her shoulders. She's being ridiculous. Times have changed, but no one in Edenville is going to burn. And Lola will be fine. No matter how tired she's feeling, she must get on. The chickens need feeding, the vegetable plot needs weeding, the plants need watering.

She grits her teeth and marches into the back yard. The sun is shining in a forget-me-not sky. Even the weather, it seems, reminds her of Lola.

'No good ever came from feeling sorry for yourself,' she mutters and, squinting in the bright light, heads off down the path. The chickens, in anticipation of an overdue meal, strut briskly towards her, ruffling their feathers and clucking loudly. 'Not long now, girls.'

She opens the shed but immediately recoils, hit by the stench of something rotten. A dead squirrel, or a rat. Heaven forbid, a skunk, she thinks and, holding her nose, steps inside. Unaccustomed to the darkness, she treads gingerly over to the feed bin. Something moves behind her. She wheels round and screams as a man leaps out of the shadows, knocking over a hoe in his haste to cover her mouth with his filthy hand.

CHAPTER ELEVEN

Scat, Lois. Scat. Get the hell out of Ascension House. This is not what you want. Go home. And quick. You can't marry this man. You don't like the look of him. But the DP has rung the silver bell, and Hepzibah has appeared. Has she been here all along? What on God's earth is happening? Am I the only one with no idea what's going on?

'I'll make the announcement tomorrow night.' The DP rings the bell again, and a Dominion walks in from a door I hadn't noticed on the opposite side of the room. 'Have the Guardians assemble in the Meeting Room at six.'

The Dominion nods, bows, then leaves.

I'm hot and queasy. I tug at my clothes, wishing I was anywhere but here. Next thing, Hepzibah is looping her arm in mine and steering me out of the room, out of the wing cooing, as we cross the courtyard, about what an honour it is and how lucky I am. I want to holler at her that it's nothing of the sort. Is she blind? Didn't she see that man? My betrothed. He's old. Like crazy old. Older than any man I've ever seen. That's odd for a start. *Isn't it?*

I don't know. I'm not sure of anything anymore.

Oh God, I think I'm gonna puke.

Hepzibah is still babbling when we reach my room. I've no idea what she's saying because I stopped listening the moment she mentioned luck. As *if*. And, anyway, I'm too nauseous to take much in. I need to figure out a way to get home. It's going to be tricky. The gates are guarded and so am I. At least I'm pretty sure that's Hepzibah's role.

But a pesky thought is bothering me. On and on, it drones, so's I can't ignore it anymore. What if I manage to escape and Mom brings me straight back?

Wham, bam, thank you, ma'am.

'Missy had rather an early start this morning. I think a lie down is in order, don't you?'

Hepzibah's knowing look tells me she's onto me, and there'll be no more sneaking around. Well, we'll see about that. But not right now. Now I'm happy to be left alone. In fact, I can think of nothing better.

I force a smile. 'Yes, Hepzibah, I think it is.'

'There's a good girl.' And with a swish of her crisp, white skirt, she leaves, closing the door behind her.

The lock clicks. I hear it loud and clear. No mistaking it. I am a prisoner in my father's house. I sprint to the bathroom and throw up.

Man is born free but is everywhere in chains, my mother said. How godawful lousy the Otherworld must be, despite its music, its parties, its champagne, and its green lights, if it truly is a whole lot worse than this.

It's been hours since Hepzibah left, and I'm wrung out. My head is pounding, too, from racking my brains. I fling myself on the bed and stare at the ceiling. After a lifetime of being told *do this* and *do that*, planning my next move is proving harder than I thought.

Voices filter through the tiny window. I prick up my ears. A man and a woman having the mother of all squabbles. Oh my, that's not good. Raised voices, cussing and fighting are a big no-no in Edenville.

'You told me you were taking me to paradise.'

Ah ha! A new recruit. Another soul from the Otherworld Noah and his band of Virtues have saved. Hooray for Noah!

'I did, and here we are.'

'Weird idea you have of paradise.'

'Don't be such a child.'

'You didn't tell me there'd be so many people, or about the *Little House on the Prairie* outfits.'

Little House on the what? What in Michael's divine name is he on about?

'Will you please shush. Someone might hear.'

'So what?

'So, you're being rude and disrespectful, that's what,' she says, in a sugary voice that would sure irritate the pants off me. 'And that kind of behaviour is not tolerated here.'

See. Told ya!

'Christ, you sound like my mother.'

Ha! Mine, too.

'You'll think differently when you meet The Divine Protector.'

'What the f—'

'And just so you know, he wears white, like everybody else in Ascension House. And please, Joseph, stop swearing.'

'Don't call me that.'

'Yeah, well, be sure to introduce yourself as that when you meet him.'

'Why, for God's sake?'

'Because it's relevant.'

'Jesus. You do talk crap. When are we going to meet my father?'

The woman sniffs. 'Not yet. He's away on important business.'

'When will he be back?'

'Soon, Joseph, soon. Now, stop whining and be grateful. This is the most blessed place on Earth.'

'Blessed, my arse. If I—'

But that's all I hear because the click of the lock announces Hepzibah's arrival.

It's Christmas Day. My first away from home. All day I've tried not to think about it because every time I do I feel like blubbing. But, hey, you won't win at life if you don't square up. Aside from Hepzibah's tour of Ascension House, and the lunch in the refectory – when I felt like a freak because the ten remaining Dominions, sitting at the long table, had gawped at me – the day has dragged. There's been no gift, no special meal, and I haven't even seen my father. Imagine? What kind of father doesn't spend Christmas Day with his only kid? Duh, mine, of course. I mean, why break the habit of a lifetime?

Still, I'll be with him soon. It's only thirty minutes until the Big Announcement. Boy, have we had a lot of those over the years. Too many to count, in fact. But not once, as I sat mousy quiet on our bench in the Meeting Room listening to the DP's wise words, did I imagine the subject would ever be me. Abi and Ben will get the shock of their short lives when they see me by his side. Because that's where I'll be. Hepzibah told me, so it must be true. Imagine the looks on their faces?

'There now, that's better.' Hepzibah teases yet another knot from my hair. 'You're so much prettier when you smile. Raphael is a lucky man.'

Jeez, Hepzibah. Hit a girl when she's down, why don't you. My smile evaporates. *Poof*! And I have to fight the urge to run from the room, out of Ascension House, back to my mother. I was happy with her. Well, most of the time, anyways. We had our differences, didn't always see eye to eye, but we rubbed along pretty well.

I clench my fists. No one should do this to their child. It's mean and selfish and horrible. What kind of a mother is she, sending me away?

Never mind. I'll think of a way out of this mess by myself. Mom's always telling me I'm a cunning little putti, disappearing when I shouldn't, roaming around after Curfew, et cetera, et cetera. See if don't prove her right.

'I think we're done here, don't you?' Hepzibah, who's been fiddling around with my face and hair for what seems an eternity, hands me a mirror.

Oh my. The reflection staring back at me – the dark makeup around my eyes, the curls and sparkly gems in my hair – belongs to a stranger. I may not feel it but I sure look the part. 'It isn't me, though.'

'Yes, it is. It's the very best version of you.'

And as Hepzibah beams at me, I find myself wondering if she means it, or whether she's saying it because she must? 'Why can't I just be me? The normal version, I mean.'

'Oh, come now, child. You know why. Now stop pouting and smile. You don't want to upset your father.'

It's not a question, I realise, but a matter of fact. A rule. *Thou shalt not anger the Divine Protector.* I stop pouting, if that's what I'm doing. But I don't smile. I can't. So, I relax my face to its neutral state. It seems to do the trick because Hepzibah loops her arm in mine again. And that's it. We're off to the next sorry chapter of my rinky-dink life.

The room seems whiter than ever. Whiter than the feathers of the swans that swim on the canal by Farmer Samuel's barn. Whiter than Heaven, perhaps.

On the far side of the room, the DP is locked in conversation with a young man, laughing and purring, and clicking his tongue. After the poking and preening I've been subjected to, I'm annoyed he hasn't noticed my *would-you-look-at-me* arrival. My mood darkening, I stand in obedient silence and listen.

'Gabriel, my Gabriel,' he says and shakes him warmly by the hand.

The young man frowns. 'My name is Jos.'

The DP inclines his head. 'Jos?'

'It's short for Joseph. But everyone calls me Jos.'

Right. Now I get it. He may have rediscovered his manners, but this is the antsy, whiny guy I heard talking outside my room. The new recruit. But where's the woman? I glance around, but it's just me, Hepzibah, the DP, and the newcomer, Jos, whom the DP has grasped with both hands, his peepers grown so big I'm worried they might pop clean out of his head.

'Yes, yes, of course. A sign.'

The man clearly doesn't have a clue what the DP's on about, his nose and mouth pulled back in a *what the heck* expression. I say man, but if you delve beneath the honey-coloured hair and the wispy excuse of a beard, he's probably not quite a man. Hmm. But not quite a boy either. A man-boy. Yeah, that's it. And he reminds me of someone. Can't for the life of me think who. But someone familiar.

'You are Gabriel, sent by God.'

Wow! The man-boy's face is a picture.

'No, I'm not, I'm Jos. And I'm from Brighton.'

The DP's right eye twitches. 'I don't think you understand. You've been sent to me from God. You are His strength. The bringer of good news. It is a sign. The time is near.'

A timely knock on the door saves the man-boy from replying. Just as well because, judging by his half mystified, half horrified expression, I'm pretty sure he was about to say something that'd upset the DP. And we don't want that now, do we?

'Come in,' the DP says.

The door opens, and Raphael appears clasping his snake staff. He marches up to the DP, whispers in his ear and slips something into his pocket. The DP, all smiles and twinkles, pats him on the back.

Raphael spies me ogling the two of 'em, and nods, his tooth necklace glinting in the bright light. It sets my nerves on edge, so I concentrate on the man-boy, Gabriel, who's a whole lot easier on the eye. At least he would be if he lost the knitted brow and brooding, black-look thing. Shifting a fraction, he catches sight of me, waiting patiently at the back, trussed up like a Michaelmas turkey in all my finery. His jaw drops.

Ha! This really is a day of surprises for him.

The DP follows the man-boy's gaze. 'Ah, there you are, Lois. I wasn't aware you'd arrived.'

No shit.

He prances over and kisses me on the cheek. I hold my breath – I don't know why, but it helps – and kiss him back.

He studies me, his ginormous eyes scrutinising every single cell of me. 'My goodness, I hardly recognise you. You're beautiful. Beautiful.' He flings his arms wide and spins round to face Gabriel again. 'May I introduce my daughter, Lois.'

All the hard edges have left the man-boy's face, but now his cheeks are glowing red. 'Hi, Lois.'

His accent is a dead ringer for the DP's, and in a blinding flash of panic, I wonder if the DP is the father he's searching for? He fathered one kid, who's to say there aren't more of us about?

'Pleased to meet you, Gabriel.' See, I want to say Jos, but I figure it won't help. And now the man-boy smiles. Like properly: goofy teeth and dimples, all that stuff. I remember what I look like and giggle. But just a little. Hepzibah has her beady eye on me.

'And this is Raphael,' the DP adds.

At the mention of my future husband, my smile slips. Fortunately, the DP doesn't go into details. Less said about that the better, in my opinion.

The man-boy checks him over with an *are you for real* expression on his cute face, which makes me feel a whole lot better. He stops with the narky questions, too, and listens to whatever it is Raphael is telling him in that hoarse whisper of his, his eyes occasionally darting my way. Goodness me, but Jos is so familiar. Who does he remind me of? Think, Lola, think.

And then it hits me.

Jesus Christ.

Whoa!

I take a step back. No, it's not possible. It's too soon.

And anyway, the DP wouldn't have called him Gabriel if he was. Would he? Or have I missed something? My mind does have a habit of drifting. Mom's always saying so.

'Lois!' The sharpness in the DP's voice brings me hurtling back to the here and now. 'It's time.'

CHAPTER TWELVE

'Please. Don't scream. I mean you no harm,' the man says. 'Nod if you can promise you won't call out.'

A coldness hits at Esther's core. She stands stock-still, breathing in the sour odour of his filthy skin. What will happen if I don't? she wonders, hesitating. But thinking better of it, nods.

True to his word, the man removes his hand. 'Bless you, kind lady. I'm sorry, I didn't mean to frighten you.'

Swaying slightly, she examines him. His shirt and trousers, once Dominion-white, are grubby and torn. He has stubble on his chin, dirt under his fingernails, and bags under his hazel eyes. Daniel, she's sure of it. She shuffles backwards but, with the fugitive now blocking the door, there's no hope of escape.

He raises his palms. 'Please, don't be scared.'

'The Divine Protector has issued a warrant for your arrest.'

'I swear on my life, Thomas and I have done nothing wrong.'

So, it is Daniel, latterly Yahriel. Michael's trusted

English friend. A good man, he's been with them from the start. But where is his partner in crime, Thomas, previously Zophiel? Is he hiding in here, too? Fearing a two-pronged attack, she scans the shed.

'It's okay. I'm alone.'

'What happened to Thomas?'

'With all my heart, I hope he's escaped. He's young, an innocent caught up in events not of his making.'

He can't mean that, can he? Esther eyes him suspiciously, but apart from his ragged appearance, there doesn't seem to be anything dangerous about him. In fact, he seems harmless and completely sane. 'How long have you been here?'

'Not long. I was in the shed next door but I hopped over the fence after the Powers searched your house. I thought they were unlikely to come back. At least for a while.'

Cobbler Absalom and Bernice's place. He should be counting his lucky stars. Bernice, a seamstress, has an eagle's eye. 'Two days then.'

'Is it? I'm afraid I've lost track of time.'

'So, what did you do? You created panic. The Powers were armed.'

'Victims of circumstance, unfortunately.'

She tilts her head. 'How so?'

'Kind lady, please believe me when I tell you I've been devoted to Michael for years.' He smiles. 'Yes, I call him by his name. We were friends, you see. Close friends, like brothers, in fact. But three years ago, Raphael swept into town, or John as he was known back then.'

'Raphael?'

'His appointment has yet to be announced, but he's to be Michael's second-in-command.'

'Really?' This news makes about as much sense as Michael's sudden reacquaintance with his daughter.

'Michael *claims* it was God's instruction.'

'You doubt him?'

'Michael is my leader. I love and respect him, but Raphael has inveigled his way into his affection and confidence. He is a very clever man, but he has a dark heart. Alas, Michael is blind to it.'

'That's a terrible thing to say.'

'It pains me, but it's the truth. Raphael is ... well ... a shaman.'

'A shaman? In Edenville. You can't be serious?' Don't shamans commune with the spirit world? Surely that's against God's wishes. Daniel must be mistaken. Either that or he's lying.

'I am completely serious.' He shivers and shakes his head. 'He is an arch manipulator, too, and has cleverly blackened my name.'

'Blackened? In what way?'

'Amongst other things, he claimed I was a threat, that I wanted to overthrow Michael by any means possible which is, no doubt, what he intends to do.'

'That's quite an accusation.' If Daniel is telling the truth, and if Raphael succeeds, what will happen to Lola?

'Trust me, I don't make it lightly.'

'Word has it you were tried and found guilty. Thomas, too.'

'Indeed, we were, and my punishment was to be publicly flogged, by Raphael, of course. I wasn't sure I'd be allowed to survive so I fled, along with Thomas.'

She doesn't want to believe him, but there's an openness and honesty about him she finds compelling. But Michael forming a close bond with a shaman? Flogging a person to death. It's ridiculous. Isolation is the punishment dealt out in Edenville. Even the mentally tough can crack after a month spent locked away in a cold, dark mountain cell. It has to be a ploy. Daniel has to convince her, otherwise she'll report him to the Powers. 'What was Thomas' crime?'

He lowers his gaze. 'That, I cannot say.'

Can't or won't? 'What will you do? You can't hide in my shed forever.'

'I shall try to escape.'

'But the Apocalypse. What about your Salvation?'

'I'm prepared to take my chances. Meantime, could I bother you for some food, kind lady? I can't remember ever being this hungry.'

She takes in his hollow cheeks and pallid complexion. It wouldn't hurt to help him. He hasn't recognised her, and it will give her time to question him more about Raphael and Michael. 'I'll see what I can do but now I have to feed the chickens.'

She picks up a bucket and loads it with corn. As she turns to go, Daniel grabs her arm. Her breathing quickens. She's been wrong to trust him.

'One more thing, kind lady. I beg you not to tell anyone you've seen me. Or repeat anything I've said. For your sake, as much as mine.'

She forces her wavering lips into a smile. 'You have my word.'

'From the bottom of my heart, I thank you. Happy Christmas, kind lady.' Letting go, he retreats into the shadows.

'I'll bring food when I can,' she says, backing out of the shed and swiftly closing the door.

Seeing her, the chickens' squawks grow louder and

more frantic. Relieved to have escaped unscathed, she opens the pen, fills the feeder, and hurries back to the house. Thinking it best to provide Daniel with food while the girls are still with their father, she takes a slab of cheese from the fridge and sets about making some sandwiches.

What are you doing? her conscience nags as she smears butter on the bread. What if Daniel isn't innocent? Once he's eaten, there's every chance he'll turn on you. Never mind if Bernice sees what you're up to. Or Julia or Herdsman Jethro for that matter. Julia's always sticking her nose in where it's not wanted. What if she reports you? What will happen to Lola?

She's halfway through the fourth sandwich when she hears the front door open.

Noah. Oh God. Her heart, which has barely settled into its natural rhythm, starts to pound.

'Hi, Esther. I'm home.'

She glances at the sandwiches, but it's too late to hide them. Noah is striding towards her, a beautifully wrapped present in his hand. She puts down the butter knife and flings her arms around him so he can't see the falseness in her smile, the fear in her eyes.

'It's good to see you. I've missed you.' He prises her off, kisses her on the mouth, and hands her the gift. 'Some of that face cream you like,' he says, at once ruining the surprise.

She peels off the paper, grateful to have something to concentrate on other than him. 'Oh, how lovely. Thank you.'

'Lois not about?'

'No, she's not. She's ... er ... she's out. She'll be upset to miss you, though.'

Noah's chest visibly swells. Her inability to bear him a

child has always been a bone of contention. Promoting the idea his stepchildren adore him is her way of applying balm to the wound.

'I heard she'd been summoned.'

'Hmm.'

'Bit odd, over Christmas.'

'Right.'

'Any idea why?'

'Yeah. Er ... er ... Virtue training.'

'At her age?' He purses his lips, his cheeks flushing red.

'Well, Naomi's pretty young. And ... and you were surprised at how quickly she was promoted? You thought it terribly unfair. Remember?'

'Yeah, well, I was wrong. Naomi is brilliant at what she does. And she's twenty-four. Hardly young. Wow, that's a lot of sandwiches. Expecting guests?'

Unable to meet his eye, she turns away and places the face cream on the table. 'Force of habit, I expect.'

'Never mind, I'll help you eat them, although it's not much of a Christmas lunch.' He grabs a couple of plates, a flagon of homemade cider, and pulls out a chair. 'And afterwards, what say we make the most of Lois' absence? Come on, tuck in.'

Esther hasn't the stomach for food, but she takes a bite hoping, if she chews long enough, she'll manage to swallow it. She shouldn't have lied to Noah. She should come clean about Lola before he finds out. And she must figure out what to do about Daniel. Then she needs to find out what Michael has planned for Lola. She is her mother after all.

'Earth to Esther. Hello!'

'Sorry, what?'

'You haven't heard a word I've said, have you.'

'I ... er—'

'What's up? Did something happen while I was away? There are a lot of journalists at the gate. Is the Divine Protector talking to the media again?'

Thomas. He must have escaped. 'No, I don't think so.'

'So, you haven't heard about the runaway Dominions?'

She bats the air. 'Oh, that? It was a few days ago now.'

'You don't seem terribly concerned. I heard they're armed. What about the girls? They could get hurt.'

Her heart is going like the clappers. This is the perfect opportunity to tell him the truth about Lola. But something is holding her back. Fear, perhaps, or guilt? 'Yes, I know, and I was worried, but things have calmed down.'

'Really? I heard the Powers were on patrol.'

'Er, yes, they searched the house.'

Noah stiffens, his lips pressed into a fine line. 'And did they find anything?'

Her chest constricts so fast and so hard she can barely breathe. Noah's stare is intense. Has he guessed she's lying? Is he testing her? She puts the sandwich down and looks him square in the eye. 'No, Noah. Of course they didn't.'

Esther is sitting in her designated place on the bench in the Meeting Room, flanked by Isabel and Jemima – who neither fidget nor chat, as Lola used to do – and behind Zachary and Priscilla (who, despite convention, have somehow remained together), their nine-year-old twins Peter and Jacob, and Priscilla and Miller Isaac's son, David. For the third time since they arrived, Lola's best friend, Abigail, seated two rows in front, peers over her shoulder and tries to catch her eye.

Hands clasped in her lap, her face a mask of composure,

Esther avoids Abigail's gaze, and everyone else's in the room, and stares at the blank screen, grateful at least that David has kept quiet about her watch. Every now and again, Noah leans across, touches her on the shoulder, and beams at her. And why not? His mind, unlike hers, is clear. He has no idea his wife is harbouring a fugitive in their shed; a fugitive she finally managed to feed under the pretence of locking up the chickens when Noah was taking a shower. Or that the daughter he has brought up as his own is now living with her true father, the man Noah has devoted his life to and whom he loves with all his heart. She has lied to him as no wife should lie to her husband. And now the fear the lie is about to be exposed is squeezing the breath from her lungs. How will Noah and the girls react if Michael has called them all to Meeting to introduce his daughter? Will they understand her need for secrecy? Or will they hold it against her? And how will they feel about Michael, when he made it clear that, as the Father of the group, he could neither take a wife nor father a child? How will anyone feel? To admit it would surely shatter his followers' illusions. Or perhaps Daniel was telling the truth about Raphael, and Michael is going to announce his appointment as second-in-command. Despite her reservations about the wisdom of this decision, she clings to this hope.

The lights dim, and almost immediately, Michael's image, glowing with the Divine Light, appears on the screen. As he opens his arms in greeting, Esther crosses her fingers and holds her breath.

'My people, the time of the Apocalypse draws ever nearer. And on that day, the atmosphere will shift. There will be earthquakes, terrible storms, tidal waves, the like of which has never been seen. But you must not be afraid, for I will deliver you all from evil by leading God's Army to victory over Satan and his forces. And afterwards, when I have locked Satan in the Abyss for one thousand years, the earth will shift into the fifth dimension, and I will lead you towards the light. You, the privileged few, have nothing to fear.

'That time draws ever closer, but we are gathered here today because I have news. Great news. God has spoken. I will not be alone in this monstrous battle. I will have the support of another.'

The rasp of rapid inhalations is followed by the hum of whispers.

'I have called you here today to introduce you to my brother, Raphael, the Guardian of the Tree of Life. In the days leading up to the Great Battle, he will nourish and heal your souls. And after the second coming of Christ, he will watch over you all to ensure your safe, smooth passage into God's Kingdom.'

Unable to fully grasp what Michael is saying, Esther watches numbly, as a tall, erect man in his late forties she vaguely recognises, surrounded by a glowing aureole and carrying a winged-top staff of entwined snakes, enters the frame to cries and grumblings from the crowd.

Immediately, Michael claps his hands, and the room falls silent again. 'My people, there is a second person I would like you to meet.'

Esther's hand flies to her mouth, but nobody notices. All eyes are glued to the screen.

'My daughter, Sophia.'

Farmer Samuel leaps to his feet. 'A daughter. How is that possible?'

'I would have thought that was obvious,' mutters Brewer Cyrus from the row behind.

Lola, barely recognisable from the tangle-haired teenager of three days earlier, walks into shot; a beautiful vision in a long white dress, shimmering with the same holy light.

'Wait a minute, isn't that Esther's girl?' Cobbler Absalom calls out from the back.

'Yes, it's Lois,' Elijah says, wheeling around to face the room from his seat at the front. 'So that's why he summoned her. I did wonder.'

Esther's cheeks are smarting. And now Isabel and Jemima are bombarding her with questions, pawing at her and pleading to be told what's going on. Esther stares ahead. She's not prepared for this. Not one bit. If only she could disappear.

But Noah has grabbed her arm and is hissing in her ear, 'Is this true?'

She lowers her head, hands clasped.

'Answer me!'

Esther winces.

'You said she'd been selected to train as a Virtue. Tell me the truth, goddamn it. I demand you.'

Her world is spinning violently on its axis. She's no idea what to say or do.

But Michael hasn't finished. He's clapping his hands again, calling for quiet, as though he's here in the room. She looks up and gapes at the unexpected tableau, at Michael, whose eyes seem larger than normal, at her daughter with the fake smile plastered on her lips, and the stern-faced man with the caduceus staff.

'This is a day not only for rejoicing in the gifts God has sent us, but also a day of celebration. God has spoken again. My only daughter is to be betrothed to Raphael.'

. . .

Esther is slumped in a heap on the kitchen floor. Her lungs are burning. She hasn't run so fast in years. The second Michael announced Lola's engagement, she fled the Meeting Room without looking back. God decreeing Lola be married was shock enough, but to betroth her to a man more than three times her age is beyond comprehension. It's all her fault. She shouldn't have entrusted Lola to Michael. She doesn't know him anymore. How could he allow God to do this to his only child? And what about her? Her reputation? She is Lois' mother, ergo she has slept with Michael. It's hardly rocket science.

The furious Guardians fired questions at her and yelled abuse as she sprinted from the room, but what could she possibly say to appease them? Would they believe her if she told them that it wasn't until after she was pregnant God told Michael he couldn't father children. Life was completely different back then. They were in a relationship. Edenville was merely a dream. She wasn't called Esther, and Michael wasn't the leader of God's Army. She knows that. Michael knows that. But nobody else does. So, unless Michael explains, there is no telling what will happen to her. Consigned to oblivion most likely. And what about Lola? Dear God, what will become of her now? How could Michael marry off his daughter without telling her? To a man she knows nothing about. It must be a mistake. The Apocalypse, less than six months away, he must be anxious. He can't have heard God correctly.

But then a doubt enters her brain. She tries to dispel it but, like a moth intent on a flame, it persists in worrying her. What if God didn't tell him Lola should marry Raphael? What if he made it up? What if he made everything up?

Esther clasps her aching head. No. No. No. It's not possible. Michael wouldn't do that. He wouldn't lie. The ideology upon which the Guardians of God is built derives from Michael's unique relationship with God. The world and everybody in it depends on him, even those who haven't realised it yet.

The front door slamming has her leaping to her feet. Her mouth is dry, her palms are sweating, but she knows she must not show her fear. To do so would be to admit she's guilty. And she isn't. Not by any stretch of the imagination. Tucking a stray wisp of hair behind her ear, she smooths the creases in her skirt and braces herself.

'Isabel, Jemima, go to your rooms.'

The girls say something Esther cannot hear.

'Later. Now scoot.'

She listens to their footsteps on the stairs and Noah's heavier tread as he marches into the kitchen. His usually soft face is hard, and there's an ugly glint in his bright blue eyes. She lowers her head and breathes deeply; in through the nose, out through the mouth. Having made a spectacle of herself fleeing the Meeting Room, it's important she stays calm.

'There you are,' Noah says gently.

Her spirits lifting, she raises her head. 'I'm sorry. I shouldn't have run away. I was shocked, that's all. Raphael is ... well ... old ... and I know nothing about him.'

'Hmm.' Noah turns away, cracking his knuckles, a habit she loathes, and paces the room. *Crack-crack-crick. Crack-crack-crick.* Just when she thinks she might scream, he stops. 'All hell broke loose after you'd gone.'

'Oh!'

'You seem surprised? Funny, I thought that's why you left.'

'No, I told you. I was thinking of Lol ... Lois.'

But Noah, his back to her, isn't listening. 'The people

are up in arms. They're accusing the Divine Protector of falling. There's even talk of a rebellion.'

'Falling? I ... I don't understand.'

'Because, let me see now, sixteen years ago he slept with you. That's what happened, isn't it, Esther? You slept with the Divine Protector. Even though it's forbidden.'

Her shoulders slump. 'No, you've got it wrong.'

'I don't think so.'

'I mean it wasn't forbidden then.' Esther tugs on Noah's arm, willing him to look at her, but he sloughs her off and continues pacing. 'Please, if you'll let me—'

'They say Lois is a Nephilim.'

She staggers backwards. 'What? But that's—'

'They think it's a sign the Apocalypse is already upon us.'

'I ... I don't understand.'

'People are angry. Furious, in fact.'

'Michael will explain.'

'Michael, is it? My, that's quite some plot you hatched.'

'Plot? What do you mean? Noah, please, let me explain.'

'A bit late, don't you think?' He spins around, eyes flashing, slaps her hard across the cheek, and storms out of the room, out of the house, leaving Esther alone to ponder her fate.

CHAPTER THIRTEEN

I'm in the inner courtyard, sitting on the greener-than-green lawn in the shade of the Almond Tree, planted by my father. Not that I feel comfortable calling him that. It's just fact, pure and simple. I'm staring at The Book and twirling a succulent blade of grass between my fingers. I'm meant to be reading it. It's what I told Hepzibah I wanted to do to, so I hope I look convincing. I couldn't think of any other reason why I should be in the courtyard at this time. It sounds highfalutin, but it's not. I can't just hang around. I must be seen to be doing something. An idle mind breeds idle thoughts, they say. Don't waste a second. Kinda makes sense, as time is running out for us all. In this life, at least. Not that it matters because the next one is going to be awesome. Anyway, it worked because Hepzibah beamed and told me it was an excellent idea and I should take as long as I liked.

So far so good. It's dusk, I'm in the same spot, and nobody gives a damn, not even Principality Judith who actually smiled at me when she passed by. Now I'm hoping and praying the man-boy finds his way here, too. It's what we planned. Well, not exactly. It was more a suggestion he hurriedly whispered in my ear after the Big Announcement, when everyone else was caught up in conversation and we'd got chatting. How he'll manage it, though, I've no idea. Hopefully his life is freer than mine. Still, it won't be easy for him. And I'm pretty sure, if we're discovered, one or other or both of us will be in a whole heap of trouble. Thing is, I don't care. No punishment could be as bad as having to marry Raphael. Come *on*. That's a life sentence in itself.

'*Psst*. Lois.'

I turn, oh so nonchalantly. The man-boy is skulking in the shadows of the cloisters, beckoning me to come over. Slowly and deliberately, I close The Book and sidle over.

'It's safer here. Darker,' he says.

I purse my lips. 'You embarrassed to be seen with me?'

'God, no.'

The speed at which he says this makes me giggle.

'Lois, don't.' He presses a finger to my lips. 'Someone will hear.'

'Oh-oh-oh.'

He backs off, as if I've struck him.

'I'm sorry.' It's true. I am. I hadn't meant to gasp, but his touch made my belly flitter-flutter.

'Are you okay?' He edges closer, hand out as if wanting, but not daring, to touch me again.

I nod quickly, to put him out of his misery.

'Good, because I was worried, you know.'

'About me? Why?'

'You mean you want to marry that old geezer?'

Geezer? Oh, Raphael. 'No, I do not. He's so old.'

'And creepy. Seriously, what's Michael thinking?'

My eyes widen. 'The Divine Protector.'

'His own daughter. How could he?'

'Ah! See, we've only just met.'

His face is blank. Not a thing going on.

'He wasn't allowed to be a father. It was God's wish.'

The man-boy rubs furiously at his brow like he's got the mother of all headaches. 'You mean Michael?'

I frown. 'The Divine Protector, but yeah.'

'And you know this because?'

'Because God told him. Duh.'

'But that's bonkers.'

'Bonkers?'

'Totally insane.'

'No, it's not. The Divine Protector is the Prince of the Seventh Heaven. His work is God's bidding.'

He gawks at me like I'm out and out crazy. 'Christ! And you believe that?'

'Sure I do.'

'Because?'

'Because it's true.'

'You mean, it's what you've been told. Just as you were told your name is now Sophia?'

Hmm.

He knits his brow. 'So, what does that make you? An angel?'

'Er ... no. I don't think so.'

'You don't think so. Wow! What about Naomi?'

'Who?'

'The idiot who brought me here and then buggered off.'

I giggle. 'Oh right. She's a Virtue. So ...' I screw up my eyes. '... yeah. Probably.'

'What the hell is a Virtue?'

'Miracle workers who provide peace and hope. She's not here because Virtues don't live in Ascension House.'

'Why not?'

'No room at the inn.' Noah was always telling us, but having seen things for myself, there really isn't.

He does that boggle-eyed stare again, like I've lost my mind. 'Has it ever occurred to you Michael is lying?'

'No. No. No. You can't say that. It's blasphemous.'

'But you must realise it's total bullshit. I mean, where's the proof?'

I jut out my chin. 'I've seen his wings, so there.' The words tumble out of me, all in a rush. Immediately, I want to take them back. Too late. They're said.

'Wings?' His shoulders slump. 'I see.'

I want to tell him they weren't white like I'd expected, but from his grim expression, I know he wouldn't believe me. 'He named you Gabriel. Which makes you special, too.'

He shakes his head and sighs, long and hard. 'No, Lois. I'm a man, a regular guy.'

I narrow my eyes. 'You're not, though, are you?'

'Yes. Lois, I am. I'm Jos Prince from Brighton, a seaside town in the South of England.'

'Oh! Oh! Oh!' Imagine. A real-life prince like in the fairy tales Mom used to tell me – one temptation she couldn't resist.

'And I've no idea what I'm doing in this crazy place. Goodnight, Lois.' He turns and slopes away.

No, wait. You can't leave. Shivering, I reach out, but he already has his arms around me and is holding me close and whispering in my ear, 'Lois, you can't marry that man. Let me help you.'

My feet feel like they're hovering above the ground. And it feels good. Oh, so good. The best thing ever. And the peppery smell of him, I can't get enough. My fingers are tingling. My whole body, fit to burst. So, I reach up, plant my lips on his, and kiss him as if my life depends on it.

Today, I'm with the DP. Just the two of us, walking around his secret garden – which he has explained is a gift from God – getting to know one another. Ring-a-ding-ding. I've never seen a garden before. I've read about Gethsemane, and we all know about Eden, but this truly is a paradise. I can't speak for taking it all in. Gravel paths weave their way through giant boulders and mossy carpets, past azalea bushes, and trees with red feathery leaves called maples. There are stone lanterns, and a meandering stream runs prettily over a rocky waterfall into a pond, which the DP tells me is full of fish called koi carp. The trees and bushes mirrored in the water look like an exquisite painting, and a curved bamboo bridge leads to a wooden building on a small island that fair steals my breath away.

The DP explains that it's a teahouse which, like the garden, is Japanese in style. 'Japan is a country in Asia, Lois. I spent a year there when I was young and developed a fondness for their stroll gardens.'

My eyes widen. 'God is Japanese?'

'Don't be ridiculous, Lois. Of course not. Peaceful, decorative and serene, it's the perfect place for quiet reflection and, with parts of it shaded by the mountains, not too hot.'

We sit on patterned cushions on a wooden platform, outside the open teahouse, sipping strange bittersweet tea in wooden cups through silver straws, and talking. Well, the DP talks and I listen.

'It's important we explore our father/daughter relationship. We've missed out on so many years.'

I nod but I'm thinking, well, maybe you should've thought about that before you left my mom. But I'm also thinking of course he had to leave us because he couldn't go against God's wishes, which is also why he's marrying me to Raphael. And far be it from me to go against our Lord.

Anyway, now I'm getting to know the DP, he seems okay. Kinda cool, in fact. I don't remember Zac, I was too young, although whenever I see him he's always real friendly. He doesn't criticise me or bother me like Elijah did (less said about that the better), or lecture me, like Noah. He seems to actually like me. Why else would he cancel his appointments for an entire morning? So, that's a first, as father's go.

My thoughts being kinda knotted, I'm also wondering why Jos accused him of lying; that he's not really the Divine Protector. He's literally carrying the weight of the world on his shoulders, what with the Great Battle looming and all. Nobody would wish that on themselves. Nor lie about it neither. Not in a gazillion years. Jos has only been here five minutes. It's all new to him, so he's bound to have his doubts. It's only natural. But Jesus had his doubters, too. Doesn't mean he wasn't the son of God.

And that's another thing bothering me. Jos seems certain he's a man, which is hardly to his advantage. Us mortals are way down the pecking order. Perhaps it's cos he doesn't like to brag. I mean, if I'm right and he is who I think he is and not Gabriel, then he far outranks the DP. Of course, he'd be humble and modest and wait until the right moment to break such momentous news. Unless he doesn't know. It's possible the light hasn't awoken within him yet.

Talking of light, I'm still confused about the DP's aureole. See, I saw it the night of the Big Announcement back in its usual place. Things happened so fast. One minute I was in the white room, being introduced to 'Gabriel', next, the Dominion, Zadkiel, was pushing me in front of a camera – if it's stolen my soul, God alone knows how I'll ascend – in a small, brightly lit room. The DP and Raphael were already there, encircled by the Divine Light. Thing is, they returned to the white room without it. How is that possible? Is it like a lamp you can switch on and off?

'You seem distracted, again, Lois. Is everything all right?'

And that's another thing bothering me. Why does he call me Lois when, the other night, he introduced me as Sophia? Lola-Lois-Sophia. A Holy Trinity of names. I'm on the point of asking when Principality Ruth rushes towards us, panic-stricken.

'My Lord, a word.'

He frowns. 'What is it, Ruth? I asked not to be disturbed.'

'Well, actually, it concerns ...' She jerks her head at me, almost imperceptibly. But I see it. And I listen good.

'Go on.'

'There's trouble in the town. Rumours are flying about. Talk of Nephilim. Watchers.'

He puts down the cup. 'Ah. I see.'

And I'm thinking: What, Michael, what do you see?

Principality Ruth leans in and whispers in his ear. But all I hear are the words *is in danger.*

His face drains of colour. 'Call a Meeting.'

The DP has told me I'm to be by his side when he speaks to his people. He hasn't told me what he plans to say, only that it's important I'm there. With him. He hasn't explained what's wrong or what the rumours flying about town are. And having not listened as hard as I probably should during Religious Instruction – my mind having a habit of wandering when I'm bored – I have no idea what Nephilims or Watchers are, but I sense there might be something sinister about them. Why else would he call a Meeting? I've asked him what's happened, but he's just told me not to worry, that once he's spoken, harmony will be restored.

I really hope he's right because more than anything I want to see Jos. I've so many questions I want to ask him, never mind that I'm dying to kiss him again. Meantime, Hepzibah has been and gone, but not until she's got me camera-ready. So, I'm all dolled up and waiting to find out, yet again, what on earth is going on.

CHAPTER FOURTEEN

Esther wakes from a fitful sleep fully clothed. The room is uncomfortably hot and stuffy with the window closed and the door jammed shut with a broom in case Noah returned while she was asleep. Not that she thinks he'll do her any harm. It's just that he might. He surprised her, lashing out like that. It wasn't like him.

Or was it?

If the last twenty-four hours have taught Esther anything, it's that she can't be certain about anything anymore. How well does she actually know Noah? In the five years they've been together he's never once struck her, let alone walked out on an argument. Not that they've ever fought. She's been the dutiful wife, so he's never had cause. On the odd occasion Lola said or did something stupid, Esther rallied to her defence – if she didn't, nobody else would – otherwise she's been wholly submissive. Marriage to Elijah taught her it was counterproductive to challenge one's husband. Wilful wives, he'd gleefully point out, were isolated unless, or until, they repented. Stupidly old-fashioned and a slap in the face for all the feminists who burned their bras. Do they still do that? Or have they moved on to better things? Tucked away in this desert oasis for sixteen years, Esther has no idea of women's roles in the real world anymore. Maybe they are on an equal footing with men these days. If so, then Edenville has taken giant retrograde steps. And she's been happy to go along with it. Anything to maintain the status quo.

She clasps her head and groans. How has it come to this? During their brief but intense relationship, Michael treated her as his equal, even consulting her about God's commands. Between them they'd come up with the idea of Edenville. It would be a peaceful town. A better place. An earthly paradise where people could live in perfect harmony, shielded from the world's evil. She didn't, for one second, suspect Michael would leave her the moment they moved in. Broken-hearted, and left to fend for herself with the temporary husbands he selected, she knuckled down, working hard while raising three girls, including *his* daughter.

Six years in, and with a population swelled to four times its original number, God appeared to Michael in a vision. Instead of everybody being equal and mucking in with whatever needed doing, they would be assigned jobs. But that wasn't all. A chosen few would be promoted to positions of authority, and live in a walled compound alongside him. The group accepted it unanimously. If this was God's bidding, then so be it.

The remodelled Edenville was nothing like the transcendental sanctuary she and Michael had imagined. Jealousy and dissension were rife. Again, God spoke to Michael. Members were expected to toe the line. If you didn't you'd be isolated. This, Michael explained, was the only way forward. The town had simply grown too big to carry on as before. It was a difficult time, and she didn't envy him.

Despite this seismic shift, she hadn't noticed how powerful Michael had become. Still desperately in love with him, she nurtured the hope that, one day, they'd be together as the happy family she'd always expected them to be. And if not here on Earth then in the spiritual realm that Michael, under God's instruction, was guiding them towards.

But with Lola gone and the members in uproar over Esther's relationship with Michael, her utopian dream has shattered. Denied life's choices, her every waking moment controlled by him, she's utterly dependent on his whims. Somewhere along the line she's lost sight of her authentic self. What happened to the cheerful twenty-two-year-old with the bright future? Who has she become?

She heaves a sigh, leans on her elbow, and looks out the window. The red-tinged glow of morning is gathering over Zachary's assiduously planned rows of identical wooden A-frame houses, the immaculate yards, and clean, car-less streets of Edenville. The sky will be blue, the day hot. People will get up and go about their business as they always do, happy and content.

But not Esther. Not today. She is trapped. A sitting duck.

She must find a way to talk to Michael. If Noah is telling the truth and the people are accusing Michael of falling, then his behaviour will be under the microscope, too. What a mess he's created, coming clean about Lois when he's made it perfectly clear on countless occasions he couldn't be a father. Surely he realises that by introducing his daughter – a child of whom he now seems inordinately proud – he is admitting to having lived a monstrous lie. He should have told them sixteen years ago, should have explained the order of events: that God only issued his command after Esther fell pregnant; that he'd sacrificed being a father to his child to be Father to them all. The ideology has always been clear. His purpose, and those of his inner circle, is to praise and glorify God, to mediate between God and mankind, to watch over mankind, and to oversee the running of the universe. To sleep with a daughter of man is immoral and a sin. Those who do will be barred from Heaven. Worse still, even though she is Lola's mother, he didn't bother to consult her. When did he become so selfish?

Esther buries her head in her hands and casts her mind back to the day she first saw him, preaching from a platform in a shopping mall, a small figure with big brown eyes and big ideas. Did he wink at her? She can't remember. But after he finished speaking about self-knowledge, contrition, soldiers of good, and precisely what else, she can't recall, he asked her out for a drink. The drink morphed into dinner, after which she invited him back to her flat. She'd been embarrassed by its opulence, but he told her not to worry. Material possessions, wealth and greed, were things of the past. The future was what mattered now. They were blissfully in love. The life they were planning, exciting and exhilarating. They made a great team.

'You hardly know him,' her mother said as they sat on Esther's bed the night before she left. 'And you're still young. Why not give it another year, finish your law degree. You may feel differently then.'

She'd been happy at home, enjoyed an idyllic childhood, her parents there for her no matter what. But her love for Michael was too strong. Equipped with the same missionary zeal, she left home to immerse herself in what, in the end, turned out to be Michael's world, never to set eyes on her parents again.

She fingers her watch, trying to ignore the ache in her chest. How must they feel, their only daughter lost to them, who'd since given birth to a child of her own? A grandchild they don't even know they have. It was cruel and short-sighted of her. If only she could seek their advice. But telephones, like televisions, newspapers, radios, cinemas, books, and holidays are forbidden in Edenville. It is, Michael assures them, the only way to protect them from all evil. She knows nothing about the outside world, has no idea what's happened these past sixteen years. Why, her parents might even be dead.

She slaps the mattress. Crying over spilt milk won't help. It's vital she stays positive. She mustn't give up. Her parents are, most probably, fit and well. What she needs to do is formulate a plan, otherwise she'll have no option but to go into hiding. Like Daniel.

Daniel. Oh God.

She leaps out of bed and tiptoes across the landing. Jemima and Isabel are fast asleep, their covers kicked off. They're peaceful now but how will they feel when they wake? Will they scream at her? Will they cry? Or will they rally to her defence as Lola used to do when family life hit a wrong note? And if they do, what will that mean for them? How will her marred reputation impact their lives? They may not be her biological daughters, but she loves them both as if they are. Perhaps they'll be sent to live with Elijah. He may be a brute but he is their father. Either way, she'd hate them to suffer on her account.

Trying to ignore the ache in her chest, she takes a long look at them and hurries down the stairs. She slips her bare feet inside her clogs, grabs a cotton bag, and throws into it a loaf of bread, some cheese, and all the oranges she can find. She fills a pitcher with water, steps outside, and pauses to check for prying eyes. Confident the coast is clear, she rushes through the yard to the shed, opens the door, and peers inside, but the sudden change from bright to dark makes it impossible to see.

'Daniel,' she whispers. 'Are you there?'

The foul smell hits her, knocking her off balance. Something tickles her hand. Seeing it's a spider, she flicks it away and turns to leave, but a shape rising from the shadows halts her in her tracks. She holds her breath.

'Hello. Yes, I'm still here.'

Although hoarser and weaker, Daniel's voice is instantly recognisable. His face is thinner, too, she notices, as he steps into the shaft of light. Gaunt, in fact, and filthy. How long has he been here? Three, maybe four days? Too long, in any case. 'Here, I have food.'

'Thank you, kind lady.' He takes the pitcher, tips back his head, and gulps down every drop. Wiping the trickles of water from his chin with the grubby sleeve of his shirt, he picks up the bread and tears off chunks, which he wolfs down without chewing.

'You ought to take it steady. You'll make yourself sick.'

He licks his lips. 'My God, I needed this.'

'I'm sorry it's taken so long.'

'Please don't apologise. I am eternally grateful you're here now.'

She watches him make a start on the cheese, slower this time. A once proud member of Michael's inner circle turned outcast in the blink of an eye. A shadow of the man he used to be. Is this what fate has in store for her? 'I want to request a meeting with Michael. But I don't know how.'

Daniel stops eating and eyes her warily.

'I'm in trouble. Big trouble, and only he can help.' She stalls, eager to find the right words. 'You were right about Raphael ... about Michael appointing him second-in-command.'

Daniel nods and takes another bite out of the loaf.

'My daughter is to marry him.'

He stops chewing. 'Ah. I see.'

'No, I don't think you do.' She takes a deep breath and prays Daniel won't react the same way as Noah. 'She's Michael's daughter, too.'

His eyes widen.

'Now you see,' she says tonelessly.

'Yes. Yes, I do. Esther, that's your name, isn't it? I thought you seemed familiar. I remember you from the early days. You were also close to Michael.'

She nods hesitantly, unsure of his feelings on the matter. 'The town is up in arms, as you can imagine.'

'You told them?'

'Michael announced it at a Meeting.'

'Ah!'

'I'm scared for my daughter. Scared for Michael, to be honest. But I don't know what to do.'

Daniel studies her as if weighing up her words. Clearly, she's shocked him, but is he angry? Disappointed? His expression inscrutable, there's no way of telling.

He lowers himself gingerly onto an upturned crate. 'Things are not always as they seem in Edenville. Tell me everything, and we'll try and work out what to do.'

'We don't have time. You're not safe here anymore, Daniel. You'll have to leave.'

'Come with me then. I'll take care of you. It's the least I can do.'

She touches her chest, grateful at least one person is on

her side. 'I can't. Not without my daughter. I can't let her marry that man. She's only fifteen.'

'Ah. I see. Yes, yes. Quite right. You must go to Michael.'

'But how? The guards won't let me pass.'

Daniel scratches his neck, eyes glued on hers as if he's considering his options. After a while, he leans in close until his lips almost touch her ear. 'There's a door hidden behind a bushy curtain of cat's claw creeper in the back wall. An emergency exit, if you like. It leads to his private garden. Only the privileged few are allowed in there. If you go after dark, you should be able to gain entry to his wing undetected.'

Her spirits lift but almost immediately plummet, and she has to lean against the wall to steady herself. 'But surely it's locked.'

'Well, yes, but I have a key.'

'You have?' So that's explains his miraculous escape. 'Does Michael know?'

'Nobody does, apart from Thomas, of course. Go tonight, if you can. I'll wait in Farmer Samuel's barn. If you don't come, I'll leave alone.'

Esther flings her arms around him. 'How can I ever thank you?'

'Kind lady, there is no need for thanks. If it weren't for you, I would not be alive.'

CHAPTER
FIFTEEN

My head is about to explode, I'm struggling that hard to make sense of it all. The DP is talking to his people. About me, of all things. And I don't like what I hear. Or maybe I do. Who knows? I mean this is huge. This changes everything. Doesn't it? See, one minute, the DP and I are on a teeny-weeny bonding walk in his garden, sipping weird tea while I buzz with happiness about being his daughter. Next, he's telling the Guardians I'm an Aeon sent from God's Kingdom to bring wisdom to our town. At least Sophia is, if Lois and Sophia are the same. Are they? I'm so muddled right now I can't be sure.

'To challenge her, or to steal her light, will plunge us into chaos,' he says. 'Without her wisdom we will not ascend.'

It's one helluva responsibility. Am I capable of that? My knees are quaking, like the mule fawn's we found trapped in our back yard last year. I've goosebumps, too, and my stomach is flipping over. Meantime, I'm trying not to let my face in on the secret. My instructions were to smile. Kinda hard when all you want to do is yelp.

'Esther was the vessel God chose to transport Sophia here,' the DP continues. 'Like Mary was for Jesus.'

I pinch myself. Did I hear that right? Vessel? That's pretty mean. Last time I looked, Mom definitely was a woman. And me an Aeon. How come I didn't know about any of this? And what, in heaven's name, is an Aeon? Surely God should have mentioned it to me, cos, frankly, in forgetting to appear to me in one lousy vision to tell me how the land lies, he's set himself up for the mother of all shit-shows.

I will fail.

I mean, I'm bound to. I'm not up to any of this. For starters, I'm not wise. Not in the least. Mom will vouch for that. She's spent a lifetime telling me how dumb I am, that I never listen, that I ask way too many stupid questions, not to mention my habit of landing myself in trouble. There is no way I will succeed. Unless ...

What if this is how stuff works? What if I'm about to experience a lightning-bolt moment of empowerment? One minute I'm an idiot, the next – *poof* – I'm the smartest kid in town.

Oh boy. I'm struggling to get my dopey head around it all. Am I, or am I not, a *somebody* of epic proportions? I swear if I was, if I'd been hit by a thunderbolt, I should feel wise. Powerful. Divine. I should be blinding everyone with a most brilliant light. But I don't and I'm not. I'm just the same old Lola-Lois, pig-ignorant and klutzy, trying my hardest to understand what the DP is saying.

Reading between the lines – something I've learned is more important than the actual written word here in Edenville – I've figured people are unhappy. Seems they've been questioning my birthright, hence this mind-blowing explanation. And who can blame them? But why would they think my arrival is a sign of the impending Apocalypse? That the Divine Protector has fallen? That I am a Nephilim (must ask him what that is later)? All of which he is going to great lengths to deny.

'And let us consider Esther for a moment,' he says sharply. 'No harm must befall this most holy of women. Under any circumstance.'

Now that's a massive kick to the belly. Even I can work out he wouldn't have to say such a thing if the intention to hurt my mother wasn't out there. Is that why he called the Meeting? Has something happened to her?

Dear God, please may I have got this whole thing very badly wrong.

Fighting the urge to cross myself, I concentrate instead on the DP, now talking about Thomas and Daniel, previously the Dominions, Zophiel and Yahriel. Only turns out they weren't Dominions at all but agents of Satan in disguise. Apostates, I believe the DP called them. Fallen angels intent on stirring up a whole heap of trouble out there in the Otherworld.

'They will come after us,' he says.

Who? I wonder. Thomas and Daniel? Satan and his army? The Otherworldlies? I can't make head nor tail of it. And I'm far too worked up about what has happened to Mom to be capable of figuring it out. Not that any of the other stuff matters anyway, because we all know the Divine Protector and his army will defend us when Satan and his cronies hit town.

'But we need not fear,' the DP says. 'God has given us the means to protect ourselves.'

See!

'He has given us a sign.' Opening his arms wide, he stares down the lens. 'Sophia.'

Jeez. Why throw my hat into the ring again? How am I a sign? This is too much for me. Way too much. I haven't a clue what's going on. My head is spinning. I feel nauseous. I want Mom. I need her. There are specks in front of my eyes. Oh, sweet Jesus, no. This mustn't happen. No ... no ...

Somebody shouts *Cut.*

And the room goes dark.

I wake up covered in a crisp, white sheet. Instinctively, I know it's not my room. It doesn't smell the same. It's muskier. Not unpleasant, just different. I prop myself on my elbows and glance nervously around. I'm on a large, low bed in the centre of a white room.

Whoa. This must be it. My thunderbolt moment. The point when all is revealed and I am transformed.

I hold my breath and try to ignore my booming heart. It won't be a picnic. Coming face to face with God requires courage. I must not screw it up. I must not ...

But hang on a minute. I've been here before.

The DP's bedroom. The DP's bed? That's not right. Unless this is the place God has chosen ...

Dear Lord, but I feel groggy. And my mouth is bone dry? Did something happen already?

'Welcome back, missy.'

Hepzibah appears like a celestial vision, and I come crashing down to earth. Holy Mary, Mother of God, I fainted.

'You gave the Divine Protector quite the fright. Here, drink this.' She hands me a glass of orange juice.

I take a sip. It's cool and citrusy sweet.

'All of it, mind. There's a good girl.' She wags her finger as she turns to leave. 'Now, stay right where you are while I go fetch him. He wanted to see you the moment you woke up.'

But I'm too busy running over the details of his announcement to pay much attention. I'm an Aeon sent by God to bring wisdom so the righteous can ascend. An Aeon who happened to faint. Is that even possible? Do Aeons faint? Although now I come to think of it, my fainting fits are usually over pretty quick. How long have I been out? Maybe it's got something to do with the air down here. It's not rarefied enough for an Aeon. Not what I'm used to.

Nervous as hell as to what's going to happen next, but too weak to face it head-on, I lie back on the soft, white pillows while the sugary liquid takes effect. Almost immediately, there's a knock at the door.

'Come in,' I manage to say, when no one does.

Jos' face appears. I've never been so relieved to see anybody in my sad excuse for a life. I sit up and grin idiotically.

His scared-little-mouse eyes brighten. 'You're okay.'

'Fit as a butcher's dog,' I say, parroting another of my mother's expressions.

He rushes over, flings his arms around me, squashing the air from my lungs, which makes me giddy all over again.

'You had me worried there for a moment,' he whispers in my ear.

I cling to him, smiling.

'Michael sent me to see you,' he says, gently prising me off.

'The Divine Pro—'

'He'll be along in a minute.'

'Is he mad?'

He whistles. 'One hundred per cent certifiable.'

He ponders my *hell, this is worse than I thought* expression for a moment, then clicks his fingers.

'Oh, you mean angry? No, he's as worried about you as the rest of us.'

'But the cameras.'

'The broadcast was over. Lights off. I mean, who falls for this stuff anyway?'

I haven't a clue what he's talking about, so I shrug.

'Well, thank goodness for that. Although, why you would when you've seen how he does it. That would be too weird. Even for this place.'

Does what? I wonder. And why weird? But Jos doesn't elaborate, so I dive into his big brown eyes and imagine kissing him again.

'So, Lois.' He reaches out and touches my hair.

Shockwaves prickle my skin. I feel for his hand and curl my fingers through his.

'Why didn't you tell me you were an Aeon, sent by God to save the world? I should be bowing and scraping, oh divine one.' He smiles, but when I don't reply, he says, 'What's your plan? The Big Idea? How are you going to save humanity?'

'Haven't a clue. None whatsoever.'

'No kidding.'

'You're making fun of me.' I let go of his hand, but he reaches up and strokes my cheek, and my entire body floods with warmth.

'I'm sorry. That was mean.'

And I'm thinking, yes, it was, but I'm also wondering whether he's fooling around. 'Why did the D ...' Oh, what the heck. '... why did Michael send you?'

His face falls. 'Do you want me to go?'

'No. No.' My cheeks burning, I lower my head.

'Michael's taken a shine to me, for some reason. Wants me to move in with him. What do you think of that, Sophia?'

'Please, don't call me that.'

'I'm sorry, Lois.'

I tilt my chin. 'Actually, my name is Lola.'

He eyes me quizzically.

'It's what my mother calls me when we're alone.'

'I like that. It suits you. I shall call you Lola, too.'

'Only in private. No one must find out, or she'll get into trouble. You will, too.'

'I promise to only call you Lola when we're alone.'

I smile again, coyly this time, liking the way he says it. 'Is she okay? I ... I'm worried about her.'

'She's pissed people off, apparently. It's nuts. All she did was have a baby. A very pretty one, mind you.' Leaning across, he presses his lips on mine. The lightest of kisses.

I close my eyes and inhale his sweet breath. When I open them again, he's staring at me intensely. My emotions lurching this way and that, I lower my head again.

'Do you know why they're angry, Lola?'

'I told you, God wouldn't allow the ... Michael to be a father.'

'Oh, I get it. Ha. Dirty devil couldn't resist getting his leg over anyway.'

I shrink back. 'Why would you say that? The Devil is Michael's enemy.' A hot tear trickles down my cheek. Quick as a flash, I flick it away.

Jos wraps his arms around me and, although I'm mad at him, I'm glad he's holding me again. 'Oh, Lola, I can't get my head around this crazy life of yours.'

'I don't understand your crazy life either.' *Like all of it.* 'But at least you're safe now, here with us. I just hope Mom is safe, too.' I snuggle into his shoulder, and we stay like that, locked together, and it feels real good.

Eventually, Jos breaks away. 'You love your mother.'

I realise it's not a question, but all the same it sets me thinking. The other day I thought I hated her. She sent me here, away from my old life, away from her, from my friends, my sisters, as if I meant diddly-squat. But now she's in trouble, it frightens me. Why would I feel like that if I didn't love her? 'Yeah, I do.'

'In that case, we won't leave without her.'

'Leave?'

'Don't tell me you want to stay in this nuthouse.'

And I'm thinking, sure I do? I mean, where would I go? All my family are here. And even if they weren't, I know nothing of the Otherworld. Not one little thing. 'But we can't leave. Only Virtues can.'

'Now you're being ridiculous. I can leave whenever I want.'

The ghost of Gideon flits across my vision, and I shiver. 'No, Jos. You can't. Not anymore.'

'I'm a guest. I can leave any time.'

I want to tell him he's wrong, that since that business with Daniel and Thomas it's not allowed because it's not safe. 'Those are the rules and, anyway, the Apocalypse ...'

He places his finger on my lips. 'Trust me, Lola.'

The door handle squeaks, and Jos leaps off the bed. In the nick of time, because the DP walks into the room. He'd be mad as hell to see us touching when he hasn't given us permission. His face an odd mix of happiness and concern, he clasps Jos by the shoulders and kisses him on both cheeks. 'You have restored her, Gabriel. I knew you would.' Smiling, he perches awkwardly on the bed, picks up my hand, and squeezes it. 'Dear Lois.'

I'm on the point of correcting him, but over his shoulder I see Jos shake his head. For once, I hold my tongue.

'Raphael is a very lucky man.'

My heart plummets. It's all I can do not to cry out in protest. What with the worry of my mother, I'd clean forgot about that reptile.

'But now, you need rest.' He pats my leg, stands, and walks away. 'Come, Gabriel. There is much to talk about. Much I need to show you.'

Jos follows, hot on his heels, without so much as a *see you later, alligator*, and all the shiny new hope drains out of me.

But at the door, he turns and winks. *Trust me, Lola*, he seems to say.

The next day I'm as right as rain. Another of my mother's sayings. This one, though, is on the nose because rain is so rare in Edenville. First thing I notice is that things have changed. The DP's door, when I try it, gingerly so as not to attract attention, isn't locked, and there's no sign of Hepzibah either. Well now, seems I've won some trust at last.

I stick my head out. Not a soul about. I saunter down the corridor, past the statues, towards the oh-so-familiar smell of freshly baked bread. My heart flips. What say the DP, out of some over-the-top concern for my health, has found it in his heart to bring Mom here?

I up my speed to not quite a run, but the sound of male voices stops me in my tracks.

'Your tea, my Lord.'

I squirm. I'd recognise Raphael's husk of a voice at a

hundred paces.

'I asked for a cup for Gabriel. I believe you two have already met.'

'You can't be serious.'

'Indeed, I am, and he'll be working alongside us in the weeks to come.'

'Have you lost your mind?'

My hand flies to my mouth. Nobody answers the Divine Protector back.

'Are you questioning God's wishes, Raphael?' Jos asks.

'What do you think you're playing at, you jumped-up little upstart?' barks Raphael. 'You've barely been here five minutes.'

A chair scrapes across the floor.

'Whoa! Get your hands off me.'

'Raphael, enough! Explain yourself or leave.'

'Forgive me,' Raphael says, through obviously clenched teeth. 'I don't know what got into me.'

'I should hope not. Blasphemy! Insults! There's no place for talk of that kind in my house.'

'My mistake.'

'Anyone would think you're harbouring doubts.'

'Never.'

'So, you accept God has sent Gabriel to us in our hour of need.'

'I do.'

'And as such is a cause for celebration.'

'Of course.'

'Then I look forward to working with you, Raphael. I'm sure we will prove a force to be reckoned with,' Jos pipes up in a jaunty voice sure to irritate the pants off Raphael.

'My Lord, I have a lot of pressing work to be getting on with.'

'Very good, Raphael.'

Thinking it would be a bad idea to be caught eavesdropping, I make my entrance.

'There you are, Lois.' The DP opens his arms extravagantly as Raphael struts past me with a barely disguised sneer.

We sit down to a bizarre breakfast – prepared and served by a stern-faced man with jet-black hair – of rice and fish, the bread I smelled baking, and Raphael's bittersweet tea which we'd drunk in the teahouse.

'You'll be living with me from now on, Lois. Gabriel, too. A happy little family,' the DP says. 'And because we are family, from now on you will call me Michael.'

My first thought, *why?* is nudged aside by a silent *whoop, whoop*, and I pump my fist under the table. Free at last.

Well, sort of, because under no circumstances am I to leave Ascension House.

But that little fact I already knew.

Other than me and Jos, no one lives with the DP ... sorry, Michael. Not even the pretty young woman I sneaked a peek at in his room that first morning (what's become of her, I wonder?). His wing is private. No unauthorised personnel allowed. At least, at night. During the day, the Dominions buzz about their daily tasks, whatever they may be, toing and froing, busy as bees. You can't go anywhere without running into one. Seems they have an awful lot to do, because they pass me in the dark corridor without so much as a howdy-do. And on the rare occasion one of them chooses to make eye contact, it's in a peer-down-the nose kinda way, as if I'm not Sophia the Aeon sent to save them but plain old Lois, daughter of disgraced Guardian, Esther. Thankfully, I haven't had the misfortune to cross paths with the witch, Keziah, again. Lord knows how she reacted to the news of my nobility. But I don't give a damn what she or anyone else thinks. I am privileged, as is Jos. I have my own room, and so does he. Michael has explained we may roam his wing as we please, although he has asked us not to disturb him at night. Fair enough. We all need some privacy. And we must have permission to enter the chapel. But there is one room we're forbidden to enter. His study. That room is oh so out of bounds. It's also locked, so we couldn't go in even if we wanted to. Weird, but knowing I can't brings out the nosy parker in me. What does he have in there he doesn't want anyone to see? The garden most likely. You can only reach it through his study. Still, I could kick myself for not taking more notice when we walked through it the other day.

Dismissed this morning after breakfast, because Michael had some work he wanted to run by Jos – wonders will never cease – I've been checking things out and can report there are nine rooms in total, all with the same tiny high windows. There's a chapel and the studio attached to it, the kitchen, the gleaming white room, three bedrooms, and a box-like room so small there's hardly space for the two chairs and table squeezed inside. On the table is a television. I know what it is even though I've never actually seen one. Why would I when its contents corrupt? Though looking at it now, a metal box with a glass screen, Lord alone knows how. And on the shelves lining one wall are books. I'm not talking floppy manuals, like we're given at school, or The Book we're presented with at birth, but solid storybooks. Loads and loads of *Great Gatsby*-like tales. Thirty-two of 'em, I counted. That's thirty-one more than

I've ever seen. It's fair blown my mind. I've been standing here for ages, desperate to open one and yet not daring to. But staring at them has got me thinking. If they're forbidden, what in God's Eden are they doing here?

'Boo!'

'Shit!'

'Language, Lola, please.'

Jos! I spin around and give him a playful whack. 'You scared me half to death.'

'Sorry. Couldn't resist.' He lifts me up and spins me around, and I laugh.

'You're in a good mood,' I say when he puts me down.

'Yes, I am. C'mon.' He takes my hand and leads me down the corridor to Michael's study. 'Ready?'

I pull a face. 'For what?'

He grins and knocks on the door. My body tenses. Why, I don't know. It's not as if I'm scared of Michael anymore. Not really. But I needn't have worried. There's no answer.

'Bet you're wondering what's inside,' he says.

'No.'

'Liar.'

Just as I'm thinking that will be that, Jos slips a hairpin from his pocket, unwinds it, and starts fiddling with the lock.

'What are you doing?'

'A trick I learnt in the squat.'

Squat? But he's already opened the door, and I'm too freaked out to ask. 'Are you crazy? We're not allowed in there.'

He sticks out his tongue, rolls his eyes, and twirls his finger around his temple.

'That's not funny, Jos.'

Next thing, he's in the room, and I'm left standing there,

mouth open, catching flies. I scour the corridor, but no Dominions are about.

'Close the door behind you.'

What the hell? But you know what, I do as he says.

Jos whistles. 'Aladdin's cave or what? Look! State-of-the-art stereo, TV, camera. Bit of a hypocrite, our Michael.'

See, I've heard about Aladdin, thanks to Mom's bedtime stories. Nerves jangling, I peer at the treasures Jos has listed, and which I couldn't have put a name to even if I had noticed them the other day. But I've barely time to register them because he is reaching for a wooden box on Michael's desk and is taking out a key, like he knew it was there.

'The spare.' He locks the door and replaces it.

I have to pinch myself. But heck, it ain't a dream.

He nods to shelves stacked with what appears to be more books. 'All Zadkiel's recordings of Michael's smoke-and-mirror shows are on those tapes. He used to be a TV producer, you know.'

Smoke-and-mirror shows? Tapes? TV producer?

'He's a regular Paul Daniels, your dad. C'mon.' Sliding open the glass door on the other side of the room, he saunters into the garden, confident as you like.

I hesitate, hopping from foot to foot.

'Oh, c'mon, Lola. Don't be a spoilsport. This whole setup is nuts, but the garden is completely bonkers. Why should Michael have all the fun?'

'We can't.'

He flings open his arms and laughs. 'I think you'll find I just did.'

We are sitting inside the teahouse, holding hands. I'm happier than I have ever been. The trees and the lake are so pretty, and the garden so peaceful, it's as if I'm in Heaven already. The soft mat-like floor, Jos tells me, is stuffed with straw, and the sliding doors are made of parchment. According to him, it's Chinese in origin. He knows this because he watched a programme on television called the *Water Margin* when he was a kid. If you say so, Jos, but I'm pretty sure Michael told me it was Japanese. Maybe they're the same. Who knows? It doesn't matter anyway because, best of all, we're alone. Jos has asked me oodles of questions about what it was like growing up, why we wear the clothes we do, our living arrangements, whether we go to school, and why we're not allowed televisions or radios. Fair do's. He's curious. I get that. But he keeps on saying things like *You can't be serious*, or *I can't get my head round that*, so my answers get shorter and shorter. He already thinks I'm pretty dumb. I'd hate him to think even less of me.

'Jesus, you must have been bored. No wonder you like books.'

I roll my lip over in my teeth. If I tell him they're banned, I might let slip about the one I stole. Less people who know about that the better.

'And what about when you leave school? What happens then?'

'You're given a job.'

'Are you paid?'

I shake my head.

'Wow! I can't get my head round that. Did you have a dog?'

I scrunch up my face. 'No dogs.'

'Another rule?'

'Uh-huh.'

'But you know what they are?'

'Sure I do.' It's true. Mom told me about Tipper the terrier who followed her everywhere when she was young. I wish she hadn't; the way she talked about the happiness he'd brought her and the love she'd felt for him, I couldn't help but be jealous. 'Do you have a dog?'

He lets out a pained sigh. 'I did. Rufus meant the world to me. He died a couple of years ago. Worst day of my life.'

I rest my head on his shoulder. 'I'm sorry.'

'Yeah, well. Shit happens, I s'pose.'

I glance at the mirrored reflection of the trees in the still-as-glass water and wonder which is worse, not being allowed a dog or loving one so much that when it died you were torn apart with grief.

'So, where's the church?' he asks suddenly.

I shrug like I always do when I don't understand the question but don't want to let on.

'No church, huh? Bit weird. What about Communion? Do you eat flesh? You know, like the Catholics?'

I stare at him like he's got two heads.

'They believe it's Christ's body, but it's just a wafer some priest has consecrated. Stupid, eh?'

'Insane.'

'What about the Powers? They've got guns, but would they use them on you? They're not actually soldiers. It would be against the law if they did. Mind you, you're so cut off from the rest of the world, I don't suppose anyone would know. Or care.'

I shiver. I don't like the direction our chat has taken. Does he think I haven't thought about this, too? So, I lean across and kiss him on the lips, bold as you like. Jos kisses me back, real hard. My belly flip-flopping, I close my eyes and wind my fingers through his silky locks.

He strokes my cheek with the back of his hand. 'You're going to get me in a whole heap of trouble.'

'Speak for yourself. You broke in here.'

'I mean it. You're so beautiful, I can't resist you.'

We sit there in silence for a while, face to face, hands clasped. Looking at Jos is like looking at the best ever painting, the bluest sky, or the brightest star. How different my life would be if Michael had betrothed me to him and not that creep, Raphael. It's obvious Michael likes him. At breakfast he kept ruffling his hair. Jos hated it, I could tell, because he ran his hand through it afterwards and once even ducked out of the way. The conversation was different, too. More relaxed. More normal. Michael laughed a lot at the things Jos said, as if he was a regular guy, not the Divine Protector sent by God to save the world. Seems he knows this Brighton place where Jos grew up as well. He talked about visits to the seaside when he was a teenager, playing the slot machines on the West Pier – was it like Daisy's pier? I wanted to ask – and dancing the night away in seedy clubs. Of games called football and cricket, pop concerts and theatre, art galleries and boat trips and tons of Otherworldly stuff I'd never heard of. And as they chattered away, I tried to conjure up an image of all these things that were terribly evil but which sounded such incredible fun.

'Michael really likes you,' I say.

'Yeah. Good, isn't it, and all part of the plan.'

'Plan?'

'Christ, for a bright girl you can be incredibly dumb at times.'

I'm about to challenge him but, hearing voices, leap to my feet. Whimpering, I glance around for somewhere to hide.

'Quick, in here.' Jos slides open a door I haven't noticed,

at the back of the teahouse. 'Lie flat, behind that, and they won't see us.' He points to a low table and quickly closes the door.

'What if they come in?'

He shushes me and gesticulates to the mat. The voices draw nearer. Without uttering another word, I lie down beside him. Just as well because, through the parchment panel, I can see the outline of my father and my *betrothed* a few inches from where we were kissing seconds earlier. I clamp my lips and pray they can't hear my booming heart. Caught snooping in the Divine Protector's private garden, having broken into his study, would take a helluva lot of explaining.

'You're making a grave mistake,' Raphael says.

'It's God's wish, not mine.'

'The people grow increasingly angry.'

'Exactly. Gabriel is the tonic they need. They'll adore him. Now, if you haven't already, see that Naomi is rewarded for her exceptional work.'

'And what, might I ask,' continues Raphael in the same brusque tone, 'did God suggest you do about Esther?'

My breathing grows more ragged.

'I'll speak to her. Reassure her.'

I gasp. Jos prods me. I hold my breath. Neither men speak for what seems an eternity. Have they heard me? Dear God, no.

'And the wedding preparations,' Michael says eventually. 'How are they coming along?'

I shudder and squeeze my eyes shut, wishing I could close my ears as well.

'You can rest assured, it will be a day to remember.'

'Hmm. Quite so. Quite so.'

'Are you having doubts?'

I cross my fingers. Oh Lord, say yes.

'What? No, no. It's God's wish. But she's only fifteen, and I worry—'

'No need to worry,' Raphael says hurriedly. 'I can assure you of that.'

'Good. Right, about Matthew. He nearly gave the game away last week. I think it's time I had a word, don't you?'

The veranda creaks as the men step off it, but it's not until the footsteps fade into the distance that I open my eyes.

'You should've told me.' Jos is lying on his back, staring at the ceiling, his face drained of colour.

'Told you what?'

'It's disgusting.' He rises slowly to his feet. 'Michael should be ashamed of himself.' He clasps his head. 'Jesus, I could've been arrested.'

I spring to my feet and reach for his hand, but he backs away. 'What are you talking about?'

'Your father, the pimp.'

'Pimp?'

Jos curls his lip. 'Don't play the innocent. Not now. I've had it up to here with liars.'

The way he's glaring at me, like I'm shit on his shoe, the things I've just heard. Suddenly, it's all too much. A tear springs from my eye. Angry, I swipe it away. 'I'm not. Please, Jos, I don't know what you mean.'

'You're fifteen, for Christ's sake. Under*age*. You're not *legal*. You should have told me.' He jumps up, slides open the door without once looking at me, and marches through the heavenly garden, leaving me no option but to follow silently behind.

CHAPTER SIXTEEN

Apart from the faint light from the sickle moon, it's almost as black as the night Lola went walkabout. Was that really only ten days ago? So much has happened since their far-too-close encounter with the Powers. So much heartache, so much change. And now, thanks to Michael's outlandish announcement, the Guardians' critical finger is firmly pointed at her. Confined to the house and with Noah still absent, Esther has nevertheless heard the rumours from her daughters who, terrified by the anger Lola's new-found status as an Aeon has whipped up, continue to confide in her. Many worrying conclusions have been drawn. Some are saying Lola is not an Aeon at all but a Nephilim. Others point out that Nephilims are giants and she is simply too small.

Last night, during supper, Jemima asked her how the Divine Protector could be both a saviour sent by God to save us and a fallen angel. 'Because if he isn't who he claims to be, surely everything he's told us is a lie.'

'He's not a fallen angel,' Esther said.

'Abi's Mom reckons God actually wants Raphael to lead

his army,' chimed in Isabel, unknowingly backing up Daniel's claim about the mystery man's ambitions. 'But I don't understand why Raphael's allowed to take a wife if the Divine Protector isn't?'

The list of contradictions was generating concern about the group's future. And all because of some misguided whim. But therein lay the rub. Michael had always been a stickler for detail. It was uncharacteristic of him to go out on a limb. Was he receiving mixed messages from God?

Esther forces her mind back to the present. She needs to stop trying to second-guess Michael and focus on tonight's goal. No doubt top of the Guardians' list of things to do is to push Public Enemy Number One, the Nephilim's mother, into doing something she shouldn't. And yet, here she is, sneaking through Edenville's back yards well after Curfew. Lord alone knows what will happen if she's caught.

She shivers and draws her cloak tight. She has to stay positive. That there is only a sickle moon is a good thing. Less chance she'll be seen. With Edenville in disarray, the Powers' presence has intensified. More men, it seems, are needed to keep the peace. And more guns.

When Michael first mooted the idea of a private army, three years ago, his reasoning seemed justified. There'd been a spate of protests about the Dominion selection process, cries of inconsistency, inequality and favouritism, words that were anathema to the ethos of the town. He reasoned that a visible presence of an armed authority would scotch any further dissension. And with the terrors of the outside world and the threat of annihilation bearing down on them, 'Prevention,' he said, 'was better than cure.'

How could she have been so naïve? Weapons bring out the evil in man. Back in the days when it had seemed universal love could conquer all, she and Michael agreed wholeheartedly on this. They'd discussed the future battle against Satan, too. It terrified her to think of Michael in combat with the Devil. Did she honestly think it would be a war fought without arms? That Michael could defeat him with his bare hands? Was she so blinded by love she'd lost her mind?

But using force against his own people is an entirely different matter. According to Daniel, Raphael is manipulating Michael. He arrived around the same time the Powers were selected – a group of boisterous young men who'd be whipped into shape. Were they his idea? If only she could have talked to Daniel longer.

Esther heaves her tired body over Baker Amos' fence, the last in the row. Her senses on high alert, she scrutinises the area. She needs to get to the rear wall of Ascension House without the midnight patrol spotting her. The door being a well-kept secret, she should be relatively safe once she gets there. All she has to do is find it.

If, in fact, it exists.

Scurrying around like a rat avoiding a trap, she's having doubts. Why does Michael need a secret door? Does he like to sneak about at night, like Lola? What if Daniel has lied? What if Michael is using him to lure her into a trap?

She groans. She's becoming paranoid. The key must open something. Why not a hidden door? At the very least, it explains how Daniel escaped without detection.

But a secret garden, in a desert. Really?

The howl of a coyote has her jumping in alarm. But after that, all is quiet. She takes a deep breath. Only the alfalfa field and the citrus orchard to negotiate. Her eyes adjusted to the darkness, she makes swift progress and is quickly swallowed up by sweet-scented orange and lemon trees laden with ripening fruit. At the edge of the grove, she lingers in the shadows and surveys the wall, covered top to bottom in cat's claw creeper.

A twig snaps.

She peers fretfully over her shoulder and scans the orchard.

Nothing.

Trembling, she leans against a gnarled trunk and wonders whether it would be better to give up on this foolish plan and go home. But what would be the point? Home isn't the place it used to be. Lola has gone, Noah has walked out, and the everyday lives of her stepdaughters are fraught with uncertainty and fear. No, better to brazen this out and at least try to find the door. And if she does and she's arrested, then so be it.

She rolls up her sleeve and looks at her watch. Twelve-thirty. Now's her chance.

Esther's hands are scratched and bleeding from groping through the creeper, she notices, when she checks the time again. One fifteen. Forty-five minutes until the next patrol. With only a small stretch still to search, she ignores the stinging pain and carries on. But the wall yields nothing. Certain that Daniel has played her for a fool, she's about to give up when she hears a loud clunk.

She drops to the ground. Not a moment too soon because, about twelve feet from where she's crouched, the cat's claw curtain parts to reveal a figure swathed in a hooded cloak. Throwing a cursory glance left and right, it scuttles off into the darkness. The door. It must be. But who was it? Michael heading off on a nocturnal wander? A Power on a covert mission? Raphael?

Esther scurries to the spot where the figure materialised

and rummages beneath the creeper. Within seconds, her fingers settle on wood and a cool, round metal handle. She yanks back the cat's claw to expose a solid door. Pulling the key from her pocket, she thrusts it in the lock and twists. But try as she might, it won't budge. She has another go, pushing and twisting until her fingers ache. Tears of frustration pricking her eyes, she grabs it with both hands and wrenches. Just as she's thinking she might burst with the effort, there's a satisfying clunk. She turns the handle and shoves. The hinges creak and the door opens slowly inwards. She steps inside, but instead of the garden she's expecting, she comes up against another wall.

Her heart sinks. Michael must have discovered the Dominion's escape route and sealed it off. In which case, the hooded figure must have been trying to get in, too. It was a miracle they didn't bump into each other.

She sags against the wall, flicks the sweat off her brow, and rotates her stiff neck side to side. A circle of light to her left catches her attention. A passageway? She sidesteps tentatively to the end, counts to ten, and pokes her head out. She gasps, unable to believe her eyes. A garden bathed in soft light emanating from a line of stone lanterns either side of a meandering gravel path. Gathering herself, she takes note of the ferns, succulents, sedums, and mosses growing on the wall from which she's emerged, and follows the sound of flowing water.

The stream she reaches wends its way through mossy carpets, cloud-shaped azaleas, sculpted pines, cherry trees, and Japanese maples, to a gentle waterfall trickling over rocks. An arched bamboo bridge leads to an oriental pavilion on a small island, overlooking the rest of the large pond. A teahouse. In a Japanese garden. In the Colorado desert. Incredible.

A curl of pungent, floral smoke wafts towards her on the cool night air. Girding herself, she tiptoes over the bridge and peers around the back of the building. A man with shoulder-length hair is sitting cross-legged on a patterned cushion on the wooden veranda, puffing on a spliff. All of a sudden, he dips his head and makes a strange mewling noise.

'Michael?' she says without thinking.

The man jerks backwards. 'Lois?'

Her heart jolts. Out of love, or fear, she couldn't say. She steps into the light. 'No, it's me, Esther.'

He leaps to his feet. 'Good God!'

'I'm sorry, I didn't mean to startle you.'

He flicks the joint away, eyeing the area, frantically, as if sensing an ambush. Seeing she's alone, his gaze settles on her. 'How on earth did you get in?'

'The door. I have a key.'

He blinks rapidly. 'A key? How did you come by a key?'

'I need to talk to you,' she says hurriedly. 'I'm worried about Lois.'

Michael sinks onto the cushion, rounding his back as if the giant load he's been carrying all these years has suddenly grown too heavy.

'How did it come to this?' she asks.

'I don't know what you mean.'

'I think you do,' she says, hardly recognising herself. When did she become so bold? 'You're upset. It might help to talk.'

He shakes his head, picks up a worn wooden cup, and takes a sip through a silver straw.

'Is it so ridiculous? We loved each other once.'

Staring straight ahead, he pats the cushion next to his. 'Sit down, Esther.'

She pauses, but Michael reaches for her hand. Her breath hitching, she does as she is bid, and for a while they sit in silence, staring out across the smooth, black water of the lake.

'Somewhere along the line I lost sight of things,' he says eventually.

She studies his face, taking in the crow's feet around his eyes, the marionette lines.

'Do you like the garden?' he asks when she doesn't respond.

'It's exquisite. Even more so for being unexpected.' She glances at the tatami mat inside the open shoji. 'But it must have cost a fortune.'

'A man must enjoy some pleasure.'

A woman, too, she thinks bitterly. But no one else in Edenville has access to such luxury. *Possessions are the devil,* Michael preached. *We must put self aside for the greater good. What's yours is mine*, and so on. Had Raphael persuaded Michael to raid the group's coffers for this? 'Did Raphael design it?' she asks, although he clearly hadn't. The garden is far too mature.

'Good heavens, no. He's a doctor. The garden is a gift from God. A miracle.'

She stares at him open-mouthed. Does he honestly expect her to believe that? 'You must hold Raphael in high esteem,' she says, finding her voice and steering the subject back to Lola's fiancé.

'He is my brother from another realm. A great healer, highly intelligent and forward-thinking. We make a good team.'

'And you think a suitable husband for Lois?' Although angry he refers to Raphael as his brother, she keeps her tone light. That would make him Lola's uncle. Truly, it is too preposterous for words. And, anyway, what's wrong with Doctor Luke and Doctor Seth?

'As my successor, she needs a guide in life. Someone wise and strong. I thought Raphael fitted that bill.'

'You're speaking as if you expect life to go on? And what do you mean you *thought* Raphael fitted that bill? What's changed?'

Michael puts down the cup. 'I don't like the guns. I never wanted them.'

So, the Powers are Raphael's doing. But why would a doctor insist on an army?

'I wanted to make a better life for you, for me, for all my followers.' He sighs wearily. 'Dear Esther. Is your life so very bad?'

'The people are angry. They've branded you a Watcher. A Grigori, Michael. They think you've deceived them. They think I have, too. Noah has left me, and my girls are scared.'

'I have tried, very hard, to put things right.'

He sounds and looks so sad, Esther can't help but believe him. 'How is our daughter?'

Michael beams. 'Funny. Beautiful. The light of my life.'

'And yet so many years gone to waste.'

The smile evaporates, and he lets go of her hand. 'Be careful, Esther.'

She steels herself. 'Does Lola miss me?'

His expression darkens. 'Lola?'

'Is she happy about her marriage?' she asks, silently cursing herself.

Michael turns away.

'I take it that's a no.'

'Of course, *Lois* misses you.'

'Why, Michael? How can you do this to your daughter? Raphael is so old. What's so special about this doctor that you'd not only let him marry our beautiful, innocent child, but elevate him to such a powerful position, too?'

Michael clenches his jaw.

'The press are congregating at the gates,' she goads.

His cheek muscle twitches.

'Sophia! I mean, really. Dominions fleeing the town at risk of their lives. It's not good, Michael. And Armageddon only months away. The Apocalypse is still coming, isn't it?'

'Enough!' Michael leaps to his feet. 'It's time you went.'

She clenches her fists. 'I want to see my daughter.'

'Impossible.'

'Why?'

'Do not question me.'

'What is to become of me then?' she asks, her voice rising. 'Did you consider my future when you made those wild claims about Lois? You know perfectly well I wasn't God's chosen vessel. I was there, remember?'

Eyes glinting, he strikes out and smacks Esther with the back of his hand.

She gasps and stares at him as if seeing him for the first time.

'Sorry. I'm sorry. Now go, please.' He backs away, palms raised.

'Do I mean nothing to you?'

'You shouldn't be here. Go now, or I'll call the guards.' He veers away, over the bridge, down the path towards the house, dry-washing his hands.

'I don't know how you live with yourself, Michael. I really don't.'

But Michael ignores her and continues walking. She thinks about pursuing him, but her cheek is stinging, his threat ringing in her ears. Letting out a frustrated groan, she kicks the wooden cup into the lake and sets off in the opposite direction, her heart sinking deeper with every step she takes. At the living wall, she takes one last look at the exquisite oasis, slips into the narrow channel, and inches along it. She's about to slot the key in the lock when someone grabs her from behind. A short, sharp scream escapes her.

This is it, she thinks, her knees buckling. I'm done for.

CHAPTER SEVENTEEN

Esther squeals as she's turned roughly around but, instead of the Power she's expecting, comes face to face with Michael. She smiles and throws open her arms.

Michael backs away and holds up his hand. 'Give it to me.'

The bubble of optimism bursts. She stares at him blankly.

'The key, Esther. Give it to me.' He lays his palm flat.

Head hanging, she hands it over.

Immediately, Michael barges past her, unlocks the door, and hauls her outside. 'Be sure to give my regards to Daniel and Thomas.' The door slams shut, and the cat's claw curtain closes.

Esther stamps her feet until, puffing and fighting back tears, she slumps to the ground. How could he be so heartless? She's the mother of his only child, and yet he's thrown her out like a piece of garbage. Has he forgotten the promises they made to one another, lying in bed in her San Francisco apartment? The life of spiritual *and* physical harmony they'd share, the family they'd talked about? He *had* loved her. He'd told her often enough. It wasn't as if she'd asked for much, just the chance to speak to her daughter. Hardly a crime. Couldn't he have found it in his heart to allow them a little time together?

The timid rays of the early morning sun creep over the horizon. Esther staggers to her feet and sets off, stumbling through the fragrant orchard and the green alfalfa field until she reaches the first house in her street. But instead of continuing home, she heads to the winter wheat fields, only coming to a standstill when she reaches Farmer Samuel's barn. With no idea why she's here, she's about to throw back her head and howl when she notices a man with scarecrow hair, beckoning to her from the opening.

Heedless, she walks towards him, her gaze flitting over his dirty face, sunken cheeks, and red-rimmed eyes. 'Daniel?'

'Oh dear, I must look quite a fright if you have to ask. Quick, in here. I'm afraid the opening to my hideaway is quite small.' He ushers her inside, kneels down, and slithers on his stomach through a crack between two bales.

Esther follows, wriggling on her elbows.

'It's not much, I'm afraid,' he says as the tunnel disgorges her. 'But it's home for now.'

Her eyes adjusting to the near darkness, she makes out a cramped, dusty cavity and a breathless Daniel, sitting cross-legged, opposite.

'We can't stand but at least we can sit. I must say, I find that easier these days.'

Esther stretches out her legs. They are scratched and bruised, she notices. Not that she cares. Her life is in pieces, her heart shattered.

'Did you see your daughter?'

She shakes her head.

'But you found the door?'

She nods and doubles over.

Daniel crawls towards her and drapes his arm around her. 'Dear Esther.'

The tears she's been fighting stream down her face. Defeated, she rests her head on his bony shoulder and closes her eyes until her breathing calms.

'Michael's not the man I used to know. That's why I'm upset. And I can only assume it's Raphael's doing.' She sniffs and wipes her nose with the back of her hand. 'But I think he has misgivings about him.'

'What makes you say that?'

'The sense of regret I felt when he spoke of him.'

'Well, that's something, I suppose. Raphael's up to no good, I'm sure of it. I've seen him at work. The concoctions he mixes for Michael with the devilish names. Vine of the Soul, Flesh of the Gods, Semen of the Sun, the Divine Leaf of Immortality. And Michael accepts them all as if he's under his spell.'

A shiver runs down Esther's spine. Michael must have been drinking one from the strange wooden cup. But why, if God has promised him life in the Eternal Realm, would he go seeking immortality? He said Raphael was a doctor. But what kind of a doctor gives their patients such strange-sounding potions? A New-Age doctor, perhaps? A shaman? But such nefarious practices are against God's will.

There must be another explanation. Daniel is angry with Raphael. He'd sentenced him to a public flogging after all. It makes sense he'd want to blacken his name. And yet, try as she might, she can't dismiss the idea he is telling the truth. In God's name, what does that mean for Lola?

'Would you consider going back for Lois?'

She hugs her knees to her chest. 'More than anything, but I can't. I no longer have the key. I'm sorry.'

'Don't be. I have no need of it.'

'There's another key, though.'

'I'm sure there is.'

She raises her head. 'No, you don't understand. I mean someone else has a key. I saw them leave. I was lucky I didn't bump into them.'

Daniel's eyes widen. 'Who was it?'

'They were cloaked in a hood, and it was dark. I couldn't see.' She frowns, mulling it over. Who had she seen? Raphael, perhaps? But where was he going, sneaking around in the dark? Nefarious practices, covert undertakings, Michael's blind faith in Raphael, the weird drinks, Lola's marriage. Trying to decipher it is making her head throb.

'I'll climb the wall tomorrow after the second patrol.'

'But it's so dangerous. You could be killed.'

Daniel shifts his body into a more comfortable position, the large tear in his shirt exposing his protruding ribcage. A chill runs through her.

'I'm afraid I will starve to death if I don't at least try. Come with me.'

Why not? she wonders. After all, what does she have to look forward to? A furious husband, two terrified stepdaughters, and endless days spent peering over her shoulder; hardly a future, more a struggle for survival. She closes her eyes and imagines the alternative. An emotional reunion with her family who'd doubtless forgive her, even if it takes a while, and the chance to live a normal life for the few months she has left.

Without Lola.

She opens her eyes and shakes her head.

'You wouldn't be alone. I'd take care of you, as you have me. You'd be happier in the real world. I'm sure of it.'

'Maybe I would but I can't, Daniel. Not without my daughter. I can't leave her behind to marry that man.'

He nods and, with his thumbs, gently wipes away the tears pooled in the wells beneath her eyes.

It's still early when Esther emerges from Farmer Samuel's Barn. Blinking in the early morning sunlight, she makes out the distant figure of Dairyman Paul herding the cows to the milking parlour, but the wheat and cotton fields, closest to the barn, are deserted. Eyes peeled, she heads to the canal. As she passes The Mill, Felix pops his head out of the stable and, seeing her, brays excitedly. She pauses to stroke his muzzle, cooing in his ear to stay quiet. Spying a sack of carrots, she feeds a handful to Felix and the other three ponies, at the same time picking straw from her hair. The animals appeased, she carries on to the canal. About four hundred yards away, Fisherman Cain and his apprentice, David, heave their early morning catch from the boat onto the wooden jetty. Absorbed in his work, Fisherman Cain takes no notice of her, but David, ever observant, throws her a sympathetic smile. Unable to meet his gaze, Esther hurriedly scoops up handfuls of water, washing her face, the dried blood from her arms and legs, the dirt beneath her nails.

Cleaner, and feeling less like a fugitive, she sets out on the walk home without a backward glance. With every step she takes, her feet drag. She has no plan. No idea what to do. Maybe it would be better to run away with Daniel and go back to her family. Her father could use his influence to get Lola out and, when they're together again, they could build a new life for themselves.

Ah, but times have changed. Chances are her father would fail. Armed Powers at the gate prevent visitors entering and members leaving. Is that even legal? She isn't sure. She abandoned her law studies so many years ago, she can't remember.

She creeps past the forge but is surprised to see it's empty. Perhaps Smithy Simeon, a notoriously early riser, is unwell. She pauses at the standpipe and looks around. The bakery is deserted, too, which is odd, and the school, although lessons don't start for an hour or so. Unless it's Sunday. No. No, it's definitely Friday.

Isn't it?

She scrubs her face with her hand. I'm losing my mind, she thinks and sets off again at a brisk trot. The A-frames on the outskirts of town now clearly visible, Esther slows to a snail's pace. Any minute now, she's bound to run into a fellow Guardian. Stay strong, she tells herself and, holding her head high, turns into Main Street.

The sound of a motor has her hopping into the shadow cast by a large Palo Verde tree but, instead of the black limousine she's expecting, Michael's Silver Shadow purrs into view. The sun's glare reflected in the sparkling white paintwork, she shields her eyes, thinking how ludicrous that a man who preaches utilitarian values should parade around in such an ostentatious car.

Next thing she knows she's charging it down, shouting and waving her arms. The driver swerves to avoid her, but she spots Michael in the back, sprints after it and raps on the window. Michael stares stonily ahead, but the passenger beside him cranes his neck in her direction. She runs beside it for a few yards, yelling, but Michael, without once looking at her, taps his chauffeur on the shoulder, and the car speeds away.

Spitting expletives, she throws her hands in the air, at the same time noticing the small crowd which has gathered to watch. 'What are you staring at?' she bawls as the last of her self-respect deserts her.

Nobody answers. Nobody moves.

'What, no one? Not you, Potter Ishmael?' She jabs him in the chest with her index finger. 'Or you, Eve?' she asks, moving down the line. 'What's the matter, cat got your tongue? And what about you, Builder Aaron? I've never known you short of an opinion.'

Somebody links arms and tries to yank her away, but she digs in her heels. 'Get off me.'

'Esther, please,' the woman mutters. 'You're not doing yourself any favours. Stop this now, before it gets out of hand.'

She's about to give her a good hard shove, but seeing it's Leah, one of her co-workers from The Mill, allows her to lead her away.

'Jezebel,' someone screams.

'Satan's whore,' yells another.

'Nephilim hatcher!'

Esther hangs her head.

'What on earth has happened to you?' Leah asks once they're out of earshot.

But Esther doesn't reply. She can't. There are no words for what she's been through.

'Listen, I couldn't give a monkey's what you and the Divine Protector got up to once upon a time, but you're my friend. Let me help you.'

Friend? No one has friends in Edenville.

'I'll never forget what you did, saving me from that ape,

Levi, four summers ago,' Leah adds. 'It was the bravest thing I've ever seen.'

A memory stirs; Levi, a big bull of a man, screaming as Esther thrusts a pitchfork into his thigh. His blood spurting like a fountain when he yanks it out.

Esther winces. It had been uncharacteristic, as if some primal instinct had been driving her. 'I didn't mean to hurt him. I only meant to frighten him.'

'I know, but if you hadn't fought him off, God only knows what he'd have done to me. So, please, let me help?'

Esther sighs. What can Leah possibly do? The only person who can help is Michael. And he's made it perfectly clear he won't. Work might be a distraction, though. 'Are you headed to The Mill?'

'No. Michael's called us all to Meeting.'

'Another one? At this hour?'

'Yes, but this one he's doing in person.'

Esther rubs her forehead. Michael hasn't stood in front of his people in years. 'Must be serious. Better get a move on then.'

'You're coming? Do you think that's wise?'

'Wouldn't miss it for the world.'

The streets have emptied by the time they reach the Meeting Room, Leah having suggested they hang back to avoid further aggravation. Even so, she is biting her lip and glancing about fretfully. Despite her own precarious situation, Esther can't help but feel sorry for her. She'd been brave to help. Siding with an outcast is a dangerous business at the best of times.

'You go ahead,' Esther says. 'I'll stand at the back.'

'If you're sure?'

'Perfectly.'

A ghost of a smile settles on Leah's lips. 'Be careful,' she says and dashes inside, leaving Esther alone once more.

The rumblings of murmured conversations drifting towards her, Esther slips inside, closes the door, and presses her back against the wall. But with every eye trained on the stage, eagerly awaiting the Divine Protector, no one notices.

The lights dim. There's a blinding flash, and Michael appears in a floor-length white robe, trimmed with gold.

Esther's eyes widen. He looks nothing like the shell of a man she'd chatted to less than six hours earlier.

Standing beneath the glare of a spotlight, Michael spreads his arms in benediction. 'I was sent by God to defend you from the evil in this world.' His voice hushed, the audience has to strain to hear him. 'As I have told you many times, your lives have a higher purpose than those earthly beings who have embraced the wiles of Satan. For years you have listened to the prophecies and proclamations I have delivered directly from God. In doing so, you have dispelled the darkness of ignorance. The time for me to face Satan's army draws ever closer. If I am to win the Great Battle, if I am to slay the beast, it is vital we do not allow ourselves to become distracted by forces outside our control. For only in victory will I be able to fulfil my promise to you. Only then can I lead you towards the light. So! I ASK THE ENEMY WITHIN, THOSE OF YOU WHO DOUBT AND QUESTION ME, TO STAND UP, NOW.'

Esther takes in the stunned expressions, the shared glances, the bowed heads. A handful can be heard muttering, but not a single person rises.

Michael narrows his eyes. 'What? No one?'

Nobody moves. Nobody speaks.

Michael raises his finger. 'THERE IS NO ROOM FOR COWARDS AND LIARS IN THE KINGDOM OF GOD.'

This proclamation is greeted with a deafening silence.

'After the great battle, once God's Army has defeated Satan, every single one of you here will stand before God's judgment. So, I ask you again. STAND UP ALL THOSE WHO DOUBT AND QUESTION ME.'

The tension emanating from the audience is palpable.

Michael raises his palms. 'I implore you then to stop bickering. Embrace the truth entrusted to me by God. Do not continue to incite his anger. Focus your minds. We have no time to waste.'

The Guardians nod, their expressions grave.

'Rejoice, for God has sent us another sign.' He spreads his arms again and raises his eyes heavenwards. 'God's voice. The bringer of good news. The Angel of Revelation. Gabriel.'

There's another blinding flash, a roll of thunder, and a handsome young man, with dark-blond, shoulder-length hair appears beside him.

The audience gasp. The bright light explodes again, and the room falls dark.

Nobody takes any notice of Esther as they pile out of the Meeting Room, they're too busy discussing what they've seen. The majority seem inspired, some appear shell-shocked, while a handful simply look terrified – the guilty few, no doubt, who've been whipping up resentment. Serves them right, she thinks, scanning the crowd for Noah and her girls. Unable to spot them, she weaves her way through the hordes. For all her anger towards Michael, she's impressed by his display of strength. He certainly knows how to put on a show because that's surely what it was. He hadn't apparated onto the stage. He'd arrived by car with the young man, Gabriel. She'd seen them. Surely other Guardians had seen them, too. Nevertheless, her overriding feeling is of relief. Although he hadn't said *don't take your anger out on Esther*, it's what he'd implied. He'd grabbed their attention, reeled them in, and had them hanging off his every word. It had been a massive gamble. It had been brave, but he'd pulled it off with aplomb. Now, perhaps, she can pick up where she'd left off; be a proper mother to her stepdaughters again, a wife to Noah.

'If it's any consolation, Esther, I know how you feel.'

The angry voice breaks through her musings. Naomi is standing over her, arms folded, glowering.

'You do?'

'Gabriel. I mean, honestly.' Naomi throws up her hands. 'The guy's a loser. Lives in a squat.'

'I'm sorry, I don't under—'

But Naomi is stomping off and someone else is touching her on the arm. Zachary, and his face is etched with concern. 'Are you okay, Esther? I've been worried.'

I am not alone, she thinks, and smiles. 'I'm fine, but thank you.'

'Promise me you'll take care.'

'I promise.'

I must find a way to tell Daniel what's happened, she thinks, as Zachary dashes back to Priscilla's side. A spring in her step, Esther heads into her street, nodding at Cobbler Absalom and Bernice. Feeling a good ten years younger than she had first thing this morning, she opens the wooden gate and skips down the path. The front door open, she rushes in and collides headlong into Elijah.

'Oh!' she says, eyeing the sack he's carrying. 'Hello.'

Elijah frowns and barges past. 'Get a move on, girls.'

Isabel and Jemima, who is clutching her moth-eaten teddy to her chest, traipse down the stairs.

'Come on,' Elijah calls from the path. 'Hurry up.'

Jemima looks so lost and forlorn, Esther moves to hug her. 'It's okay. I'm home now.'

Quick as a flash, Elijah darts back, grabs his daughter's arm, and drags her away. 'They're *my* daughters and they're going to live with *me*.'

'But why?'

'You're a disgrace, Esther. And, by God, do you deserve what's coming.'

'But Michael said—'

Esther hears the thud of boots approaching. She spirals around and quails. The men in black surround her menacingly.

Jemima screams, a horrible piercing sound that cuts right through her. Scowling, Elijah picks up his daughter and forces Isabel, whose face has drained of colour, behind him.

Esther reaches out her hand. 'Don't do this, Elijah. Think of the girls.'

'That is precisely what I'm doing.'

The Powers pounce. Esther bucks and kicks and tries to wriggle free, but a blow to the back of her head leaves her dazed.

And all she is aware of, as they haul her away, are her legs dragging awkwardly along the ground.

CHAPTER EIGHTEEN

Donna closes her eyes to the craggy mountains and dusty, desert landscape, leans out of the car window, and soaks up the warmth of the Californian sun. She is tired and stiff from the flight but, after the heartache and madness of the Christmas holidays, she's relieved to be here.

Boxing Day had been particularly tough because Pauline invited her girls over for supper with Rupert. She'd no idea how it had gone. She hadn't asked, and they hadn't spoken about it, out of respect for her feelings, she presumed. She'd heard them chatting late into the night, though. She doubted he'd been a disappointment. A charismatic man and a brilliant raconteur if the mood took him, Rupert had the capability of charming the pants off everyone he met. If her daughters wanted him back in their lives, she could hardly stand in their way. He was their father, after all, even if it was in name only.

She needn't have worried. As quickly as he reappeared, he disappeared back to the States. With Tess at uni and Chrissie back teaching, Donna was alone. The evenings dragged. All she could think about was Jos, where he was, what he was doing. Was he happy? Did he think of her at all? Did he wonder how his absence was affecting her, the pain she was in? Because no one, not Naomi, nor any other person on this godforsaken planet, could love another being as she loved Jos. She tried her hardest to come to terms with his sudden departure, tried to accept her daughters' assurances that, despite not receiving a single phone call, postcard, telex, or telegram from Jos in all this time, there was nothing to worry about. He was, they told her repeatedly, a young man simply spreading his wings.

But she couldn't stop worrying. Something was wrong. She may not have proof but she could feel it in her bones.

And then last night, Rupert rang with news. He'd read a disturbing article in the *San Francisco Chronicle*, and the commune had been referenced.

'I'm flying out tomorrow,' she said.

Instantly, he offered to stump up the cash. A generous gesture, she'd been wrong-footed. Her funds at an all-time low, there was no way she could afford the fare.

'It's the least I can do,' he added.

'Yes,' she replied as she fought to restrain herself from giving him the full two barrels. 'It is.'

And if that wasn't enough, in some desperate attempt to set things right, he insisted on joining her on her quest to retrieve her son. The stupid, selfish, irresponsible fuckwit. Because Jos was *her* son. Rupert may have contributed fifty per cent of his DNA, but that's where his fatherly role began and ended. Where was he when Jos was growing up, when he scraped his knee, fell ill with the measles, broke his arm, got in trouble at school? Where was he during all those parents' evenings, the school plays and concerts, the interminable football and cricket matches, the birthday parties?

Where was he when she was struggling to make ends meet? Lazing by a pool in the Californian sunshine with some blonde-haired bimbo, half his age, that's where.

Donna hadn't bought into the *looking out for an old friend's daughter* line. Sure, he was angry with Naomi and concerned about the place she'd taken Jos. But Rupert had lied about their relationship and, consequently, was furious that his spurned and bitter ex had had the nerve to hit on Jos. How dare he presume to care? Walking out on his son fifteen years ago, Rupert wouldn't know him if he passed him in the street. And while he'd frittered away his time on Naomi and, no doubt, a whole raft of other younger women, Donna had gone it alone.

Somehow, the anger she'd held back for so long hadn't spilled over when he'd scooped her up from the airport. She couldn't disguise her irritation, though. And yet, despite the put-downs and the long periods she'd turned her back and ignored him during the journey, Rupert had been so damn reasonable, making sure she was okay, had enough to eat and drink, endlessly asking how she was feeling. The situation was as maddening as it was nonsensical. Why was he so keen to help?

It occurs to her then that this cock-and-bull story about a newspaper article might simply be a ruse to entice her to the States. But does she honestly think that, after fifteen years without contact, Rupert would use his son's disappearance to re-engage?

No. The idea is ridiculous. She's losing her mind.

Donna opens her eyes and stares at the lush green fields of the Palo Verde Valley, a startling contrast to the arid landscape of moments earlier. A Dolly Parton song she doesn't recognise is playing on the radio. She tries but fails to concentrate on it. Never mind that she'd brought up three children alone, Jos would never have taken off like this if Rupert hadn't gone AWOL in the first place. At least, not to a religious commune in the Colorado desert with an old squeeze of his father's called Naomi.

She clenches her jaw to stop herself screaming. She knows she doesn't have to forgive him, but Chrissie was right to encourage her to try to get along with him. At least until Jos is safe. If he sees his mother at loggerheads with the father he most likely left home in search of, it's bound to make the job of persuading him to come home far harder. All the same, having nursed her anger all the way from Brighton, she's reluctant to let it go.

'Here we are,' Rupert says, drawing the car to a halt.

Donna releases a pent-up sigh. Not long now until I'm reunited with my son, she thinks, peering through the mucky windscreen at the word **EDENVILLE** spelled out in bold black letters on a vast white sign. She takes in the mountains, the breezeblock wall, the iron gate, and the six or seven men gathered in front of it, half of whom are carrying cameras.

'Seems we're not the only ones visiting,' Rupert says. 'I wonder what's going on?'

Without waiting for a response, he heads over to the group and immediately engages with an eager young man in a green-and-white baseball cap. After a short chat, the man beckons to another bloke, who breaks off his conversation to join them. Blond and dressed almost identically to Rupert in un unbuttoned denim shirt over a T-shirt and jeans, he's neither as tall nor as handsome, and the look doesn't suit him so well. More animated than the first, he gesticulates while he talks, and clearly has a lot to say because Rupert listens intently, nodding and only occasionally chipping in. Back when they first met, this effortless ability to join in, no matter how diverse the surroundings, or how odd the situation, was one of the things Donna found so attractive about him.

She bounces her palm off her forehead. God sakes, what am I doing? I can't stand the man. Kicking open the door, she eases herself out and, ignoring her cramped muscles, strides towards them.

'Ah, good. This is Todd.' Rupert places a hand in the small of her back and gestures to the younger of the two men. 'And this is Steve. They're journalists from the *Palo Verde Valley Times* and the *San Francisco Chronicle*. Gentlemen, my wife, Donna.'

She bristles. Why touch me? And why introduce me as his wife? 'Pleased to meet you.' She forces a smile and shakes their hands. 'Okay. So, what's the story?'

Todd clicks his tongue. 'Well, see, we're not exactly sure.'

'Fine, now if you don't mind, I need to find my son.'

The elder of the two takes hold of her wrist. 'I wouldn't do that if I were you.'

'Excuse me!' She wrests herself free and glares at Rupert. 'Are you coming with me or not?'

'It's not safe, Donna,' he says gently.

'What do you mean, it's not safe? You told me it was a commune full of religious nuts.' She digs her hands in the pockets of her dungarees and marches to the gate, taking in the guards' sinister black headdresses, the assault rifles slung over their shoulders. Never one to be intimidated by a soldier, Donna grabs hold of the gate's gleaming black bars. 'I'd like a word with my son, please. He's currently a guest of yours.'

'Can't you read.' The taller guard points the barrel of his gun at the smaller sign.

PRIVATE. KEEP OUT.

'I'm his mother, for heaven's sake. Now, be a good fellow and let me in.'

The men raise their guns.

Donna steps back, arms wide. 'Oh, c'mon. Thou shalt not kill and all that.'

The men take aim.

She tilts her chin, her heart pumping furiously. 'You wouldn't dare.'

'Come away, Donna,' Rupert says, appearing at her side.

'I'm not moving until I've spoken to Jos.'

But Rupert takes her arm and half leads, half drags her away. 'I think you should listen to what Todd has to say.'

'Get your hands off me.'

'Donna, please. The vibe has changed.'

Vibe! Since when did Rupert use words like vibe? 'Fine.' She shakes Rupert off and trudges with him, back to the group.

Engaged in conversation with two other men, Steve doesn't register their return, but the younger man, Todd, greets her with a rueful smile.

Glowering, Donna folds her arms. 'So, are you going to tell me what the hell is happening here?' Out of the corner of her eye she sees Rupert wince. He always was a stickler for good manners. Well, tough, she thinks, pursing her lips.

'Er ... right. The details are a little sketchy, but a week or so ago a guy turned up in Blythe, the nearest town that-away,' Todd jerks his thumb westwards, 'having escaped.'

Donna laughs. 'Escaped? What is this place, Alcatraz?'

Rupert tugs his earlobe. 'You've seen the guns.'

Todd throws a nervous look at Steve, but he's still chatting away and doesn't register. 'Up until recently, the locals thought the Guardians of God were a bunch of hippies with alternative views who'd distanced themselves from what they saw as the failing narrative of society. In the sixteen years since they persuaded the powers-that-be to sell them these one thousand acres, along with access to sufficient irrigation water from the Colorado River and, of course, electricity, they've caused no trouble, building this town and farming the land as promised.'

'They built it?' Donna asks. 'By themselves?'

'Yeah, irrigation ditches and all, and paid for it, too.'

Rupert whistles. 'Must have taken a whole lot of dosh.'

'The Guardians have incredibly deep pockets. The group boasts architects, engineers, builders, lawyers, nurses, doctors, accountants, and teachers among its members – you name it, they got it covered.'

'And the locals sounded them out?'

'Sure, and so did the press. Communes that disengage from reality are profoundly fascinating for those of us leading normal lives. They attract the very thing they're trying to avoid. Scrutiny. The leader was more than happy to answer the press and public's questions. The journalists dug but were unable to find any dirt, so they moved on.'

Donna waves her arms in exasperation. 'So, they're harmless.'

Todd frowns. 'But when the rumours started a few weeks ago, the media's interest was piqued again. Only this time, the leader clammed up.'

'Rumours? What rumours?'

'That all was not well in Edenville,' Steve says in a horror-film voice, finally breaking off his conversation and turning to face them.

'The clue is in the tight security,' says Todd. 'The guards, of course, the guns, and the razor wire on the wall.'

Donna follows the line of his finger, wondering how she hadn't noticed it before.

'That's why we're still here.'

Donna wraps her arms around herself. Everything Todd says makes perfect sense. But, then again, the press have a habit of pissing people off. They'd certainly managed to in their coverage of the Greenham protests. Perhaps the group felt they'd been demonised for being different and upped their security. It wouldn't be the first time.

'One evening before Christmas, before the razor wire appeared, I managed to climb in,' continues Todd. 'I wanted to see the place for myself. A storm was brewing, so it was an unusually dark night, which was ideal. I'd taken a camera but, unfortunately, the flash attracted the attention of a patrol of those black-clothed guards. They were searching for someone, I'm sure of it. But seeing my flash came after me. I got away, thank God.'

'Maybe they just value their privacy,' says Donna.

Todd shakes his head. 'You've seen them. They're armed.'

'Isn't everyone in America?'

Steve rolls his eyes. 'Oh yeah, sure they are.'

'It freaked me out,' Todd says. 'I honestly thought they were going to shoot me.'

Donna flinches. However you dress it up, it isn't good.

'What did the guy who escaped have to say about it all?' Rupert asks.

Steve runs a hand through his mop of blond hair. 'We haven't had the opportunity to ask him yet. He's in hospital guarded by a local cop.'

Donna blinks rapidly 'Why? What happened to him?'

'We don't know,' says Todd.

'I'm sorry about your son.' Steve looks her directly in

the eye. 'And I don't want to worry you, but I think you're going to struggle to get him out.'

'But that's absurd.'

'Only a select few ever leave, and we think that's to harvest new recruits. Thing is, if people can't leave, this ain't no commune, it's a cult.'

Donna's hand flies to her mouth. If Steve's right and if Jos is in there, then he's essentially a prisoner. Unless ... unless he wants to be there. But why would he want to hang out with a crowd of people with guns? Darling Jos who wouldn't harm a fly.

But then she remembers the squirrels. Mrs Patterson's cat.

'Why do you think that a group of apparently harmless people have armed themselves?' Rupert asks, breaking the silence. 'What do they see as the threat?'

Steve shrugs. 'That's the six-million-dollar question.'

'Okay, so what about their leader?' Rupert asks. 'What's his message?'

'His name is Michael but, other than that, we know zip. It's like he breezed in under the radar. Which is why I've got my feelers out. Got a man back in San Francisco doing some digging.'

Donna throws up her hands again. 'This is ridiculous. What do you think they're going to do? Start a war?'

'I don't know, but I intend to find out before it's too late.'

CHAPTER NINETEEN

There is only one store in Blythe, and Rupert is in it, shopping for provisions. He thinks Donna is having a lie down in the cheap motel they booked into. The first place they spotted on the main thoroughfare running through the town, only a double was available but, thankfully, the room offered two single beds. Donna would never have agreed to it otherwise. Her nerves on edge, she's far too anxious to rest. If she can't get past Edenville's gates she at least needs to find out if her son is actually in there. Rupert is convinced he is, but Donna needs proof, which is why, despite her jet lag, she's on her way to the hospital – the only one in town, according to the man at the gas station. She hasn't left a note telling Rupert where she's going. Why should she? When it comes to detailing his whereabouts, the stupid scumbag has form.

Palms and other indigenous trees Donna can't put a name to stand in occasional lines in front of the low buildings bordering the road and, looming in the murky distance, the jagged outline of the Big Maria Mountain Range. Gas stations, Mexican restaurants, and fast-food outlets make up the rest of Blythe, giving the town the feel of a two-mile drive-through. She's not sure what to make of it all. The desert, the unrelenting sunshine, the overpowering smell of insecticide, a total contrast to the cosmopolitan bohemia of Brighton. She's never been to California, never been to America, never been in such close proximity to a cult.

She shudders. Nobody has any proof The Guardians of God is a cult and not a harmless religious sect as previously thought.

But the guns, her conscience nags. What about the guns?

Seated on a plastic chair in the waiting area opposite the runaway's room, Donna flicks through a long since out-of-date copy of *Time* magazine, plotting her next move. She's been keeping an eye on the police officer guarding the door for almost an hour, knows every detail of his young, acne-strewn face, but the only idea she's come up with is to sneak into the room when he leaves his post for a bathroom break. Wishful thinking, but what else can she reasonably do? She can hardly walk in pretending to be a concerned relative. If the Guardians of God is a cult then the man probably hasn't seen his family for years. But speak to him she must, because if she's to succeed in getting Jos out of Edenville, she needs to know what she's up against.

A blond-haired doctor wearing a pair of horn-rimmed spectacles and a white coat approaches the officer, brandishing a clipboard. A dead-ringer for the journalist from the *San Francisco Chronicle*, she thinks, as he opens the door and strides into the room. In fact, I'd bet my life it's him.

She tosses the magazine onto the table and crosses her arms and legs. Damn. Why didn't I think of that?

By the time the journalist re-emerges, Donna has bitten her nails to the quick. Bold as you like, he thanks the officer and sets off down the corridor. She follows at a discreet distance, but when he turns a corner into a far more crowded area, she loses sight of him. Making her way against the tide of hospital staff and visitors, it's not until she's in the lobby that she spots him again but, by then, he's way ahead of her.

'Oi,' she says as he walks outside. 'I need to talk to you.'

But the man either doesn't hear her or assumes she must be talking to someone else because he saunters into the car park. Donna breaks into a run but, by the time she reaches him, he has shed the white-coat-and-glasses disguise and is sitting in the driver's seat of a baby-blue Buick.

She grabs hold of the door. 'Please. Wait.'

Scowling, he yanks it closed and fires the ignition.

'Please.' Donna hammers on the glass, desperately trying to catch her breath. 'It's me. Donna. We met earlier. Outside Edenville.'

A flicker of recognition crosses his face. Smiling, he winds down the window. 'Well, hi there. I'm sorry, I thought you were a loony hotfooting it from the psychiatric wing.'

She frowns. 'I need to talk to you.'

'Great. How 'bout we grab ourselves a drink?'

'Oh. Yes. I'd like that, thank you. Er ...'

'Steve.'

Yes, of course, Steve.

Grinning, he reaches across, opens the passenger door, and she folds herself into the seat beside him. 'Coffee? Or something stronger?'

'Something stronger sounds good.'

'Husband not with you?'

'Er ... no. He's taking a nap.'

'Right.'

'It's been a long day.' Why explain, she wonders, cringing. It's not as if I'll ever see this guy again.

'Bit of a coincidence bumping into you like this.'

'What are the chances?'

He clicks his tongue. 'Pretty damn slim, I should say.'

A ponytailed man in a plaid shirt is playing pool with a bald, bull-necked guy, their bottles of beer balanced on the side rail, but other than that, the dimly lit bar is empty. Steve leads her to a booth that's seen better days and flings his keys on the table. A pretty young waitress in a short, tight dress, zipped up the front, rushes over and takes their order. A bourbon for him, a white wine for her.

'Oh, and some peanuts, please,' Steve says, winking at the girl.

Donna frowns.

'My daughter.'

'Oh, I see.'

'Jeez. I'm kidding. Kid's seen a lot of me these last few days. This bar's become like a second home.'

Donna takes in the sticky tabletop, the cracked linoleum floor, and the nicotine-stained ceiling. Some home.

'So, are you going to tell me what you were doing at the hospital?' he asks. 'Or do I have to guess?'

'I'd have thought that was obvious.'

'Hey, Donna. Loosen up a little.'

'I'm perfectly fine.'

'No, you're not. You're coiled up ready to explode.'

The waitress returns with the drinks and nuts. Donna watches, appalled, as Steve's eyes settle on the soft swell of the girl's breasts. He flirts with her for a bit while she sets down the glasses. To her credit, she doesn't seem the least bit bothered and even throws him a pretend kiss when she leaves.

'Bright girl, that one. Knows how to work a good tip.'

Donna slaps her palms on the table, slightly louder than intended. 'Look, Steve. I'd really appreciate it if you could tell me what he said.'

'He raises his eyebrows. 'What who said?'

'The runaway.'

'You been spying on me, Donna?'

She shifts uncomfortably. 'No. Yes. I mean, you had the same idea as me. Well, almost. I didn't dress up as a doctor.'

'Psychiatrist, actually. Neat, huh?'

The weight of her jet lag bearing down on her, she strains to keep a lid on her temper. 'Frankly, I'm amazed he believed you. Now, if you'll excuse me.'

She rises, but Steve grabs her arm. 'Sit down, Donna.'

What is it with this guy, always manhandling me? She tries to wrest herself free, but Steve clings on, so she glares at him through gimlet eyes.

'I'm sorry, okay?' He lets go. 'Now, please, sit down.'

Donna's not sure why, but she does as he says.

'Right. I only had half an hour with Thomas, and he thought I was a psychiatrist, so he was a bit guarded.'

'Did he ... did Thomas tell you how he got out?'

'Over the wall a way back from the gates. He made a

dash for it in the dark, climbing over with a ladder he'd found in a barn. Somehow, he managed to evade the guards, who incidentally, only appeared since he went into hiding.'

'Really?'

'Apparently so. He had no money on him, no idea where he was going. He was severely dehydrated, too, skinnier than a rake, his arms and legs ripped to shreds by the razor wire, and could barely walk. Lucky for him, a car happened to be passing. The driver stopped and offered to take him to hospital.'

Donna shudders. 'Why did he leave?'

'He wouldn't say.'

'If the guards had seen him, do you think they'd have shot him?'

'Thomas is certain they would. And you heard how scared Todd was.'

For a split second, Donna's breathing is suspended. When she manages to speak, her voice is little more than a whisper. 'But why?'

'To stop him talking, I guess. When I asked him why he'd been so intent on leaving, he simply said the dynamic of the group had changed.'

'In what way?'

'I don't know. He clammed up. Refused to say another word. Poor guy is clearly terrified of speaking out.'

Donna shoulders slump. She'd been hoping for more. 'I wish I could speak to him.'

Steve's grin returns, broader than ever. 'Swell idea.'

'No, I'm serious.'

'So am I.' He downs his bourbon and grabs his keys. 'Drink up and we'll go.'

. . .

Donna is not remotely convinced Steve's plan will work. It's so foolhardy as to be laughable. Yet, despite voicing her reservations, he's managed to persuade her to tag along.

'I can't see what the problem is. The cop outside his room is barely out of diapers. The worst that can happen is he won't believe you. It's not as if he's going to sling you into jail.'

A witness to his earlier success, Donna assumes that Steve's unwavering confidence is the key. That and his refusal to take no for an answer. Fortified by the wine as much as Steve's cavalier assurances, Donna hovers in the background, curling and uncurling her fingers as Steve approaches the young officer. The youth listens intently to the preposterous story Steve concocted in the car, nodding sagely while he explains that this unexpected, but most welcome, visit from Thomas' long-lost and deeply concerned aunt, will speed up the laborious deprogramming process.

'Go ahead,' the officer says, opening the door. 'Poor kid needs all the help he can get.'

Donna bites her lip to stop herself smiling and walks into the room, followed by Steve who swiftly closes the door behind him.

'Hello again, Thomas,' Steve says to the prone figure with bandaged arms, hooked up to a saline drip in the bed. 'Meet Donna.'

Startled awake, the young man heaves himself into a seated position. His gaunt, pale face and the dark hollows beneath his eyes make it difficult for Donna to put an age to him, but she'd guess he's probably younger than he looks. The same age as Jos, perhaps.

'I hope you don't mind, but she has a few questions she'd like to ask you.'

Thomas sweeps his lank shoulder-length hair off his face. 'Who is she?'

'A learned colleague. You, pal, are a most interesting case.'

'I am?'

'Indeed you are, which is why it's important we find the underlying cause of your dilemma before the press get hold of you.'

Thomas' wan face turns even paler. 'The press?'

'Yup. So, we need to get your story straight. The press can be merciless if they smell a rat.'

'A rat?' Thomas pulls the sheet to his chin with quivering hands.

'You're hiding something, Thomas. Why? Because you're frightened. But there's no need. We're your friends.'

One by one, the lies trip off Steve's tongue. There's something sinister about his oh-so-friendly manner that makes Donna uncomfortable. The lad is clearly terrified, his blue eyes darting about as his fingers worry the crisp, white bedsheet. And is it any wonder? Steve clearly intends scaring him into submission. She knows what they're doing is unethical, but the fear she feels for the safety of her son is walking roughshod over her morals. Any attempt to reassure the poor chap would mean blowing their cover.

'Donna has a few questions. I'd like you to answer them. There's a good fella. Let's start with the group's dynamic? You mentioned it changed? Why do you think that is?'

Thomas rests his head against the bank of pillows, as white as his face, and closes his eyes. He looks exhausted. Haunted, too, and vulnerable, Donna thinks, pricked by another stab of guilt.

'An extremely dangerous man has wheedled his way

into Michael's good books. Michael doesn't realise it, but he's poisoning him.'

Donna's hand flies to her throat. 'What, literally?'

'Michael is going to appoint him second-in-command,' Thomas continues in the same monotone.

'You make it sound like an army,' says Donna.

Thomas eyes snap open. 'It is an army. A celestial army. Michael is the leader. He is God's warrior, the Prince of the Seventh Heaven.'

'Oh great. Another lunatic with a Christ complex,' mutters Steve.

Thomas jerks upright, his cheeks flushed crimson. 'Michael is the Divine Protector. He is the only person who can save us.' Eyes narrowed, he points a trembling figure at Steve. 'Save you.'

Steve laughs. 'So he says.'

'So God says. But you don't need to take my word for it. You'll find out for yourself soon enough.' Thomas folds his arms and, pressing his lips together, reclines against the pillows.

Steve taps his leg. 'You're talking about the Apocalypse, right?'

Donna throws him a questioning look, but Steve's eyes remain locked on Thomas who tilts his chin and turns to stare at the wall.

'Do you have a date?' Steve asks.

'The twelfth of May 1983.'

'But that's only a few months away,' says Donna. 'Surely you don't actually believe that?'

'It's not a question of belief. Michael knows.' Thomas' head whips around. White spittle has collected in the corners of his mouth, and his flushed skin has taken on a mottled appearance. 'And on the day of enlightenment, he will lead his heavenly army into battle against the forces of Satan. They will win the war and lock Satan in the abyss for a thousand years. But only the members of The Guardians of God will be saved.'

Donna clasps her cheeks. 'But that's crazy. Completely nuts.'

'Ah, but is it?' Steve raises a finger. 'It's all there in the Book of Revelations. The opening of the Seven Seals. The Four Horsemen of the Apocalypse. Yada, yada, yada.' He sits on the bed, places his hand on Thomas' knee, and says in a far gentler voice, 'But I sense there's more to it, Thomas. If we're to help you recover, it's important we understand everything.'

Thomas shrinks back, flattening himself against the pillows.

Steve pats the trembling youth's leg. 'I sense you were close to Michael. What was your role within the group?'

Thomas glances from Steve to Donna and back. 'I am ... I mean I *was* a Dominion.'

'And what, for the uninitiated, are Dominions, Thomas?'

'The select few who govern the duties of those beneath us.'

'I see.' Steve slips off the bed and, stroking the stubble on his chin, paces the room.

'What?' asks Donna. 'What do you see?'

Steve spins around, his expression smug. 'I'd have thought that was obvious.'

'Not to me, no.'

'Within the Guardians of God, Michael has established ranks his people can aspire to.'

'It isn't like that,' Thomas snaps. 'Michael is led by God. The hierarchy was of God's making.'

Steve nods. 'Right. Right. A hierarchy. So, the guys with the guns. You told me they're a recent addition.'

'The Powers act as guides for lost souls,' Thomas mumbles, 'by maintaining order.'

'The law-enforcers. Okay. And what about the other tiers?'

'I don't see why I should tell you. You'll just twist it around to suit yourself.'

Steve strides back to the bed and rests a hand on Thomas' shoulder. 'I give you my word I'll do no such thing.'

Is this how spies extract information? Donna wonders as Thomas scours Steve's face, up and down, side to side, searching for something. Though what that might be, she hasn't a clue.

'The Virtues,' Thomas murmurs, 'work God's miracles by recruiting lost souls, and the Principalities are the educators. They encourage people to strengthen their faith.'

Steve springs back, grinning. 'Ah, now I get it. The angelic hierarchy first put forward by ... shit, what was his name. Syrian guy. Masqueraded as the Athenian convert of Paul the Apostle. Hang on ...' Steve clicks his fingers. Once, twice, three times. 'Dionysius. Or to give him his full name, Pseudo-Dionysius the Areopagite. Yeah, that's the one.'

'Who?' Donna asks.

'A Christian theologian and Neoplatonic philosopher from the fourth or fifth century. He studied what the Bible said about angels and developed a scheme of three hierarchies, emanating from the most spiritual origins – in other words, God – down to man. A bit like the rungs on a ladder. Only by ascending all the rungs can you achieve divine ascension, or something. I can't remember exactly but I touched on it briefly at Harvard,' Steve says blithely, while at the same time batting the reference away with a swish of his hand. 'According to Dionysius, each hierarchy has three orders ... no, choirs ... but what those are, I can't remember. It doesn't matter because I'm pretty sure they include Virtues and Powers above Archangels and Angels, with Thrones, Seraphim, and Cherubim at the top, and Principalities and presumably Dominions somewhere in between. And actually, if you think about it, it's quite brilliant.' He slaps his thigh. 'Such attention to detail. Groups with structure tend to be more focused, more successful. But to gift a person a celestial title. How attractive is that?'

'Attractive but ridiculous,' Donna says. 'Surely, no one believes it?'

Steve turns to Thomas. 'So, that means you, Thomas, and every member of his inner circle, are angels.'

Thomas smiles a self-satisfied smile. 'Not here on Earth but in the next realm.'

'Oh my God, they do,' mutters Donna.

'The only thing Michael got wrong was the name,' Steve says, slapping his thigh again. 'He should have called it—'

The door swings open, halting Steve in mid-sentence. Donna swivels around and sees a red-faced man storm into the room, followed by the now fraught-looking police officer.

The man marches up to Steve, forefinger outstretched. 'Who the fuck are you?'

'The psychiatrist,' says Thomas helpfully. 'And his learned friend.'

'Psychiatrist, my ass! I'm the psychiatrist. What the hell are you playing at?'

'Studying my patient.' Steve stuffs his hands in the pockets of his white coat. 'A most interesting case.'

'He is my patient, and you have no right to be in here.'

His face puce, he turns to the deputy, now cowering on the other side of the bed. 'You were under strict instructions not to let anyone in.'

As Steve gently steers her towards the door, Donna throws a concerned glance at the bewildered patient.

They haven't got far when the doctor flies over in two giant strides and slams it shut. 'Oh no you don't. I know exactly who you are. You're a fucking journalist.'

Thomas gasps.

Shit, Donna thinks. We're busted.

'This is not the time for a game of who's fucking who,' says Steve. 'This is a very serious situation. My patient requires urgent medical attention.'

But the doctor isn't listening. He's picked up the handset of the phone by the bed and is yelling into it. 'SECURITY. ROOM THREE-SIX-TWO. NOW!'

CHAPTER TWENTY

I'm getting used to Michael's breakfasts . Or rather Chef Kishi's breakfasts. Grilled fish, steamed rice, fried egg, and fermented soya beans, washed down with the bitter-sweet tea. It's a kooky combination, and I don't much like it, even if it is good for me. But we have toast with it, or bread, which reminds me of Mom, so I save that for last. It also means the icky fishy taste doesn't hang around all day.

Jos, however, eats everything Kishi puts in front of him – especially sashimi, Jos' all-time favourite. Yuk. Why would anyone want to eat raw fish? – and I'm talking platefuls. Far more than Ben and Gideon. It's pretty disgusting, actually, although Michael doesn't think so. He's always saying how impressed he is by Jos' appetite. Why? It's not like it's a talent.

But then again, everything Jos does impresses Michael.

I'm getting used to the breakfast meetings with Raphael, too. Michael summons him, and he stands there while we eat our strange food, his nostrils flared, top lip curled. He seems irritated by whatever Michael has to say, which is a lot. I wonder how long it will be until he explodes? If Jos continues to chip in, as he's been doing today, anytime soon, I would guess.

Meanwhile, I try and avoid eye contact with Jos. Difficult. And I try my hardest not to look at Raphael either. When I do, I find myself studying that cruel face of his, which has me worrying what our marriage will be like. So, I stare at the ceiling, or the floor, or at Kishi and whatever it is he's cooking. It makes for an uncomfortable twenty minutes, that's for sure.

This morning's briefing over, Michael dismisses Raphael. The muscles in his cheeks working overtime, my future husband leaves the room. Now it's time for our *happy* (Michael's word, not mine) little family to troop through his study for a stroll around his garden. See, I'm really not that chipper. Jos hardly talks to me anymore, barely even registers me. Spends his free time hanging out with the Dominions, exercising and lifting weights, and playing dominoes – things I'm not allowed to do. And when they pray, go to lectures, or study The Book, he sits on his own on the grassy square, strumming Michael's guitar. Boy, does he love that guitar. Strange, cos I had it in my head Gabriel was a trumpeter.

Anyway, I'm set on asking him if he's found his father, but since he hasn't told me he's searching for him, I daren't. I've tried asking him what the problem with my age is, though. But he rolls his eyes and says, *Jesus Christ, Lois. Don't be so stupid.*

And that's another thing that makes me sad. He doesn't call me Lola anymore. It's like his feelings for me were a running tap he's turned off. Just like that. It hurts me more than I can find the words to explain.

Michael isn't just impressed by Jos. When he's not

laughing at some lame joke, or being sucked into one of his stories, he's ruffling his hair, patting him on the back, or putting his arm around him. He hugs me and he kisses me. Well, he would. I'm his real daughter. But he's not impressed by me or interested in anything I have to say. My life hasn't been a patch on Jos' but, all the same, it's kinda frustrating.

Jos never mentions leaving Edenville anymore either. I assume he's still looking for his father. His proper dad, not his pretend dad. Because, although they have the same big brown eyes, I am one hundred per cent certain Jos, with all his concerns about legal stuff, would never have kissed me if he was Michael's son. Seeing how he'll be supporting Michael and Raphael in the battle to come, I suppose it's a good thing he's hanging around. That said, it's odd how quickly he changes his mind. One minute he's all over me, the next he can't come within touching distance. One minute he's talking about running away, the next he's basking in Michael's attention. Maybe he just needed time to become Gabriel. Perhaps that's how it works when God bestows his glory on you, or whatever it is he does. I hope it works for me pretty soon because, sure as Hell is hot, I don't feel anything like Sophia. But then I don't feel like Raphael's future wife either. Oh God, how I'm dreading that day. I've no idea what'll happen, no idea how I'll deal with what's expected of me. I'd give anything for a few hours back home to talk things through with Mom.

'Are you okay, Lois?' Michael asks when we stop to feed the fish. 'You're awfully quiet these days.'

'I'm fine.' I glance away so he can't see I'm lying.

In the distance, Gardener Takae is spraying the plant-covered wall with a fine mist of water. He does this every morning and evening so it'll keep on living, even though, like the garden, it has its own irrigation system. I like Takae. He's a peaceful man with twinkly eyes. Michael insists on calling him Timothy. Crazy, because although his English is better than Kishi's, it isn't great, so he never replies, and Michael ends up calling him Takae anyway. He goes about his business calmly and methodically as if nothing else matters. Quite an achievement with the Big Battle looming and all.

'Are you missing your family, Lois?' Michael asks.

It's quite a knack, his ability to read my mind. I nod and toe the gravel. If I talk about my mother now I'm gonna cry and, once I start, I might never stop.

'There's no need, you know. We're your family now.'

He says it warmly, like it's a good thing but, for the first time since coming here, I think how easy it would be to hate this man who took me away from the person I love most in the world. So I look at the pond and focus on the brightly coloured carps' gaping mouths and strange barbed whiskers as they writhe around in the water. All of a sudden, a dark shadow looms up from the depths. It snatches some food and, with a flourish of its trailing black fins, disappears back down. An outsider, just like me.

'There he is,' Jos says. 'The Lucky Fish.'

Michael grins. 'Bang on time, as usual. Best get on.'

Out of the corner of my eye, I see Michael put his hand on Jos' shoulder. I shake my head and walk back down the path.

'What's the plan for today?' Jos asks.

'I want to run through the filming of Lois' wedding with Zadkiel. Only a few days to go, so it's important we get it right.'

My skin crawls like it's got legs and wants out. Am I never allowed a minute to forget my fate?

'Oh, right. Cool,' Jos says, although his tone seems to imply the opposite.

I steal a peek and see he's frowning. No surprises there. He's bound to disapprove. Raphael is a hundred times older than him.

'It'll be a momentous day,' Michael says. 'One that Edenville will never forget.'

They won't have long enough, I think, kicking angrily at the gravel. Which is something, I suppose.

Back inside Michael's study, I mumble goodbye, but they're too wrapped up in each other to hear, so I make a beeline for the storybooks in the box-like room. I've searched the shelves and rummaged through the boxes but I haven't found *The Great Gatsby*. I have, however, discovered a couple I like by a woman called Dolores Scott. I prise *The Crimson Sunrise* from its place on the top shelf and open the cover to the bit about the author I've read a hundred times already.

Dolores Scott, affectionately known as Lola.

It's quite something, sharing the pet name of a real-life writer, makes me all warm and fuzzy. I smile and flick the page.

To Zosia.

Such a pretty name and one I've never heard before. Who is Zosia, and what does she mean to Lola? I wonder, as I sit down and pick up where I left off.

Within seconds I'm lost in the story of Hannah, a young woman who can't outgrow her childhood or her family, but who is tearing them apart as she tries. It doesn't matter that there's so much I don't understand about the world she lives in, or the life she leads, because the words this Lola uses to describe Hannah's life paint a powerful and emotional picture. It's almost as if I'm there, with her, struggling to lighten the weight of her past.

I reach the end of the chapter and sigh. Did God actually mean Lola and Zosia to be damned for all eternity? If only I felt more Sophia-ish, I'd likely not only know the answer but be able to save them, too.

The familiar whirr of the aeroplane overhead distracts me. Until I moved to Ascension House, I assumed it was delivering recruits. Now I know it delivers fresh food for Kishi – tuna, salmon, octopus, and abalone – and various other unusual ingredients like sushi rice, seaweed, wasabi, and miso, when his stores run low. I imagine climbing inside and flying high in the sky, soaring and diving, carefree as a bird. No chance of that, but a girl can dream.

I have so much time on my hands – too much really – now I don't go to school. I'd give anything to jump on Fisherman Cain's boat and fish for catfish with David, or go searching for racoons with Abi and Ben. I suppose this is how it feels to be lonely. I've tried talking to the Dominions. I recognise a few from when they were plain old Guardians. Reuben and Barnabas, for example, now Hashmal and Naneel, and Moses and Shem, now Gadreel and Kushiel. They're friendly enough but they're too busy running errands for Michael, training and studying, to hang around with me.

Sometimes, I head to the kitchen to watch Kishi. He's a man of few words, like Gardener Takae, and those he does speak, I don't understand. He bows often and smiles when he sees me, which makes for an easy life. But, boy, does he have some mighty skills. His fingers are so quick and nimble, and he's a real whiz with the knife, slicing and chopping vegetables, meat, and fish at breakneck speed. I'd like him to teach me. It would be real handy come the Great Battle. Cos that's another thing that's troubling me. Michael hasn't told me what my role will be. Not knowing makes me sick with fear. What if it's something I can't do? Highly likely, seeing how short I am in the talent department.

The door flies open, and I jump so high the book falls from my hands.

'Hi, Lois,' Jos says. 'What's that you're reading?'

I pick up the book with trembling hands and show him the cover.

'Nope, never heard of it. Any good?'

Seems Mister Know-it-All still doesn't know 'bout this particular rule. 'It's brilliant. Best I've ever read.'

'Cool.' He takes it and reads the back. 'Whatever rocks your socks.'

'Do you like books?'

He tosses it away. 'Yeah. S'pose.'

My spirits lift. 'Have you heard of *The Great Gatsby*?'

'Sure. My A level text.'

'Did you like it?'

'Didn't read it. Left school and moved into a squat.'

'Oh yeah, right.' Did he tell me that already? I can't remember. But seeing how I've snagged his attention, I've other questions I want to ask: what was it like at his school? How many books has he read? What are A levels? Squats? But it's been ages since we've been alone. Last thing I want to do is scare him off again.

'I saw the film so I know what happens. Daisy kills Tom's lover, and Gatsby gets shot by her husband.'

'Oh!' My hands fly to my mouth.

'You haven't read it?'

'I read some but then I lost it.' It's near enough the truth, so I don't feel bad for leaving bits out.

'And now I've ruined it for you.'

I attempt a smile. 'That's okay. Was Daisy very upset?'

'Nah. Stupid cow moved away with Tom.'

My oh my, but that's a blow to my heart. 'But she and Gatsby were so in love.'

'Yeah, well, that's life. Probably a good thing you didn't finish it. Anyway, I came to tell you that creep, Raphael, wants to see you.'

I shiver as I always do at the mention of his name.

'You don't have to marry him, you know. America is a free, democratic society. You have a choice.'

I roll back my shoulders and quote the line I've heard so often, 'It's different here in Edenville.'

He groans. 'Why?'

'You know why.'

'No, I don't.'

I lower my head. Yes, you do. Please don't make me say it.

'Go on, Lois. Tell me why it's different here?'

I guess it's not my lucky day. Either that or he's testing my loyalty. I take a deep breath. 'God makes the rules.'

'You've got to stop believing this crap. Michael makes it up as he goes along.'

No, he doesn't, I think, angrily. 'I thought you liked Michael.'

'I do, but he's not an angel. Neither is Raphael and neither am I. There are no angels. They don't exist.'

I bunch my hands into fists to stop myself shaking. I hate it when he talks like this. And I don't understand why he does. Gabriel shouldn't say such things. It's not right. 'Michael is. I've seen his wings.'

Jos laughs, but it's a joyless sound. 'Wings? He hasn't got wings.'

I stamp my foot. 'Yes, he has. I told you already. I've seen them. But they're not white, they're black.' I close my eyes and picture the wings on Michael's back. The colour had surprised me. I'd assumed angel wings were white and feathery. But there could be no denying them. I'd seen them with my own eyes. I tilt my chin, hands on hips. 'And I've had sex, too. Plenty of times and with men far older than you. So there!'

He raises his hands and backs away. 'Whoa. That's not right. In fact, it's repulsive. Worse still, it's illegal.'

Illegal. Illegal. Illegal. Ugh. Why is he so hung up on this? 'It is right. Sex between a man and a woman is an expression of your love for God, and therefore your love for Michael. So long as you don't become too attached, you can express this love with as many people as you like.'

'Bullshit, and anyway, you're too young.'

'No, I'm not. Women are supposed to provide for the sexual needs of men.'

'Says who?'

'It's what God wants.'

He shakes his head. 'Jesus, you really believe all this shit.'

'Yes, because it's true.'

'But you're not a woman, are you, *Sophia*. You're an Aeon, whatever the fuck that is. Still, I suppose that's why *you* get to marry an angel, no matter how old or how repulsive he happens to be, and your mother can't. It would be hypocritical otherwise, don't you think?'

My mind scrambling to understand, I blink rapidly.

'What, don't have an answer?'

I rub my forehead vigorously. Images of myself having sex with Raphael flash through my mind. His dry, wrinkled skin on mine, his sour breath on my face.

But then another more vivid image appears, of Elijah, stealing into my bed to have silent sex with me while my sisters slept. *Sharing God's love,* he said, when I asked him what he was doing the first time. *It's a special thing, but it's our secret. Not a word to anybody, you understand.* He'd clamped his hand over my mouth, and I remember wanting to feel special but could only think how much it hurt and how much I wanted it to end.

I want this to end, too. I want to see my mom. But nobody talks about her anymore. 'I don't want to marry Raphael. I don't want to be an Aeon. I never asked for any of this.'

The room suddenly feels too small for the two of us. I'm stiflingly hot, can barely breathe. I have to get out of here. I need to be alone. I take a deep breath and run.

I'm on my bed curled up in a tight little ball, too numb to cry. My mind is a mess. I want to believe Jos is lying. It's what Otherworldlies do because they're evil. But I can't quite believe it of him. Satan, yes, but not Jos.

I don't know. What if he isn't? What if he's telling the truth? And anyway, he's living in Edenville now so he's not an Otherworldly and, therefore, isn't evil. And Michael likes him. A lot.

I spend an hour hidden away, my thoughts zig-zagging this way and that until, exhausted, I lie there staring blindly at the ceiling. I must have dozed off at some point, because

I'm woken by voices in the corridor. I sit bolt upright and listen.

'And what about the yagé. Was it on the plane, too?'

Michael.

'It was, but I think you should hold off for a bit. It's started to mess with your mind.'

And Raphael.

'It helps, just as you said.'

'Yes, but—'

'Any news on Thomas and Daniel?'

'The Powers continue to search, but I'm afraid they've left us.'

'Think they'll talk?'

Raphael clicks his tongue. 'We can but hope they won't.'

Michael says something I can't make out.

'I'm not comfortable with that at all,' says Raphael.

But that's the last thing I hear before they move out of earshot.

I cross my legs and mull it over. I thought the Powers were looking for Thomas and Daniel because they'd done something wrong. Now I'm not so sure. Michael sounded anxious. But why?

That's what happens when you pick up fag ends, I think, recalling another of Mom's expressions. No sense ever comes of it.

I miss supper. I'm not hungry, but worse, I can't face Jos. I send my apologies via a passing Dominion – Muriel, I think, although I can't be sure. When everyone dresses in white, wears their hair the same length, it's hard to tell people apart in the gloom.

Later, Michael drops by my room to check on me. He sees me lying on the bed, and his face falls. 'Are you ill, Lois?'

'Nope.'

'What then?'

'Nothing.'

'I think we both know that's not true.'

I purse my lips and stare at the ceiling.

'Has someone upset you? Tell me, Lois. I might be able to help.'

I sit up, suddenly hopeful. 'Could you? Would you?'

'Of course. You're my daughter. My little angel. I'd protect you to the ends of the earth. You know that.'

Judging by his pained expression, I realise that if my father doesn't yet love me, he cares about me. 'I don't want to marry Raphael. He's too old for me. And he scares me.' The words tumble out of me, all in a rush.

Michael flinches, as if I've hit him, and paces the room, shaking his head and making *tsk-tsk* sounds. I hold my breath. After what seems forever, he sits down next to me. But he isn't smiling.

I've gone too far this time, I think, as I reach for my pillow and clutch it to my chest. Michael fixes his god-like eyes on mine. They are dull, I notice, the light gone out of them. He's judging me. He knows what I am.

Exhaling loudly, he pats my leg. 'I understand.'

He does? 'You do?' I fling my arms around him. 'Oh, oh, oh! Thank you, Father,' I say, trying the word for size. It's a good fit, so I try it again. 'Oh, Father, thank you.'

A small smile settles on Michael's lips. 'Well then. What say we forget about this for now and take a stroll around the garden.'

. . .

The notes of a song I don't recognise float over the bridge towards us. I stop and look questioningly at Michael, but he puts a finger to his lips. His eyes have a heavenly glow to them again, as if it's the Holy Spirit himself he's listening to. My heart sinks. Yet again, we won't be alone.

Sure enough, Jos is sitting cross-legged on the veranda, eyes closed and singing. I should have guessed when I heard the guitar. He has a pretty voice, there's no denying it, sweet and clear. But the words about a world without countries and religion, where everyone lives in peace. It's a bit shocking. Isn't it?

'Beautiful,' says Michael. 'I've always loved that song.'

Seems not.

Jos opens his eyes as if we've startled him. I'd like to think he isn't expecting us, really, I would, but an itty-bitty part of me suspects that almost everything Jos does is planned.

Michael ruffles his hair. 'Clever of you to play it on the guitar.'

'Why is it?' I ask, irritated that, yet again, I haven't a clue what they're talking about.

'John Lennon wrote it for the piano,' Jos says. 'Do you like it?'

And I'm thinking, are you for real? Have you forgotten how you spoke to me earlier? But Michael is there, so I shrug. 'Sure.'

'I've another song you might like.' He smiles sheepishly as if I give a monkey's about any of this. 'Also written for the piano.'

Michael lets out a bark of a laugh and claps his hands. 'Ingenious boy. Then we must hear it, mustn't we, Lois?' Without waiting for a response, he settles himself on a cushion.

But I don't budge. I have no idea what's going on but I will not play along. I will *not*.

'It's from the same album,' Jos says. 'Although a couple of years ago it was a hit for Bryan Ferry.'

He's talking about people and stuff from the Otherworld, and that's forbidden. I throw Michael a nervous glance, but he's smiling indulgently.

'It's called "Jealous Guy".' Catching my eye, Jos winks.

I clench my jaw and stare at my fingernails, determined he won't make a fool of me a second time today. I won't listen, I think, as he starts to sing.

But I can't help myself. The song. Its name. The words. About being jealous and losing control. About not meaning to hurt someone and making them cry. It's like Jos is speaking to me. If he is then it's probably some kind of sick joke. He thinks I'm too young. And anyway, I'm promised to Raphael.

Only now he's staring right at me, and the way he's singing the words, I know he means me to listen. He was insecure, he trills, because I no longer loved him.

But who said anything about love? Love is for Michael and God, not boys like him. And I want to scream at him to stop. I can't cope with any more. Friends one minute. Enemies the next. But I don't want to make Michael angry. He might change his mind and force me to marry Raphael.

'Dear boy, you have the voice of an angel. Truly,' Michael says when the song ends, as if either he hasn't listened to the words or else he's forgotten what he's taught me and all the other Guardians in Edenville, that songs like this are Satan's weapons. And it makes me think the world has gone mad.

Jos peers up at me from beneath his curls, and I realise

that, while my thoughts have been running riot, I've been unable to take my eyes off him.

He winks at me again and mouths *I'm no angel.*

My cheeks burning, I turn away.

It's the middle of the night, but I can't sleep for tossing and turning. Could it be that Jos isn't angry with me now? And if he isn't, why am I still angry with him? If it is anger I'm feeling and not something else – hurt, perhaps, or shame? Should I be ashamed of what I've done? The way Jos looked at me when I told him I'd had sex with other men like I was filthy and worthless. Has Michael said something to change his mind? Has he changed his mind? What if I've got the wrong end of the stick?

By morning I'm exhausted. Too tired for breakfast, I lie in and sleep until lunchtime. In a rush to dress, I don't notice the piece of paper peeking out from under the door until I step on it. I pick it up and unfold it with fumbling fingers.

> *Please forgive me, Lola.*
>
> *I was wrong to judge you. It was mean of me, and I'm no bully. Honest.*
>
> *Everything is going to be okay.*
>
> *Trust me.*
>
> *J xx*

I press it against my heart. My chest swells, and the dark thoughts of the night scatter. I slip the note under the mattress and hurry to the kitchen with a spring in my step.

Raphael is there, drumming his fingers on the table. He fixes his beady black eyes on me. 'Good morning, Lois.'

I smile stiffly, fighting the urge to cut and run. Where are the others? I glance around. But it's no use. We're alone.

Raphael reaches for his serpent staff and stands. 'Come with me, please.'

'Why? Where are we going?'

But Raphael just flings his cloak over his shoulder and strides from the room.

I stay right where I am. There ain't no way I'm going anywhere with this snake. Especially since Michael said I don't have to marry him.

He bangs his staff. 'Lois! Come!'

Great, so he has beady eyes in the back of his head, too. Well, I'll show him. I jut out my jaw and fold my arms. But he turns and gives me the evil eye. Shivering, I lower my arms. Something isn't right.

'Where's Michael?'

His nostrils flare. 'In the chapel, praying for forgiveness.'

'Why? What has he done?'

'Come with me, please, Lois.' His voice is softer now, gentle. 'We'll speak somewhere more private.'

I clench my fists. 'No one's around. We can talk here.'

'I see you're as obstinate as your father.' He sighs and shakes his head, and his tooth necklace rattles. 'I warned him, but he wouldn't listen. If he had, it might have turned out differently for your mother.' A beat. 'I'm sorry.'

Mom? 'What's happened? Tell me.'

My knees buckle. Next thing I know, Raphael has drawn me inside his cloak, and all I'm aware of is the steady beat of his heart.

CHAPTER TWENTY-ONE

It's not the first time Donna has been arrested. Her life as an activist has landed her on the wrong side of the law more times than she cares to remember. This is her first stay in an overseas jail, however, and the first time Rupert has had to bail her out. Steve, too, although how her 'husband' suddenly has all this money to burn is beyond her. When she asked why he wanted to help out a total stranger, he smiled and said it would be churlish to let the poor man rot in jail. Since when did he use words like churlish?

Aware that this, and all the other questions she longs to ask, would kick-start an all-out interrogation and most likely a row, she keeps her mouth shut.

Minding her manners – always the best policy when stuck in deep water – she apologises to the sheriff and thanks him for his hospitality.

'Still can't fathom why you were questioning the poor fella. He probably ran away because he did something wrong. I imagine he's mighty embarrassed about it, too. Last thing he needs is more grief from the likes of you.'

'My son is in Edenville. I'm extremely worried and want to see him but I can't because the guards are armed and won't let me in.'

The sheriff sniffs. 'They have permits. No crime in that. With people snooping around day and night, is it any wonder they're protecting their privacy? Why not write your boy a note? Save us all a heap of bother.'

Donna rubs the back of her neck. Why hadn't she thought of that? 'So, you're absolutely convinced they're not dangerous?'

'One hundred per cent. They're harmless. In fact, the G.O.G have given us less trouble in fifteen years than you have in the twenty-four hours you've been here. Now, if you'll excuse me, Mrs Prince, I'll go and tell Mr Anderson the good news.' And with that, the Sheriff of Riverside County opens the door and bids her good day.

Thanking her lucky stars she's free once more, Donna steps outside and follows Rupert to the car.

Rupert. No matter how hard she tries, Donna cannot comprehend how her long-lost husband is, once again, a feature of her life. And yet here he is, all dashing, six-feet-two of him. Is it, as he claims, out of concern for Jos? Or does he have some other agenda? And why is she so damn angry he's back when she's spent far too many years wishing he was? When he showed up unannounced at Christmas, she'd automatically assumed the moral high ground. She was the injured party, after all. But as to why he left, she still has no idea. He hasn't told her anything. Or blamed her for his leaving either. Instead, he's behaved like a perfect gentleman, even rescuing her in her hour of need. Her pride dented, the last thing she wants to do is thank him. But thank him she must. As to the matter of his surprising wealth, she'll deal with that after she's had a shower and caught up with some much-needed sleep. With the overweight and inebriated man in the adjoining cell breaking wind and snoring loud enough to rattle the bars all night, she didn't snatch a single wink.

She takes a deep breath and mumbles a few words of gratitude, a gesture made easier by the thought that without his benevolence she'd be spending another twenty-four hours alone in the tiny cell.

'It's the least I could do,' he says, turning into the motel and pulling up in their allotted parking space.

'Well, that's true.'

His grip on the steering wheel tightens. 'You know what, Donna? You haven't changed a bit.' Shaking his head, he gets out of the car and heads off towards the motel without a backward glance.

Donna wakes to a ringing telephone. She picks up the receiver, glancing at Rupert's travel clock on the table between the two beds, and sees that she's been asleep for two hours.

'Hi, it's Steve. I'm outside.'

'Oh, right.'

'Your husband's gone out.'

What? Was he stalking her now?

'But I'm guessing you'd rather not entertain a stranger in your motel bedroom. So, shift your ass and get outta there. I've got news.'

A Guns N' Roses record is playing on the neon-lit jukebox and, on the table next to them, a man with wiry hair is working his way through a soggy pizza, but otherwise the dimly lit bar is as empty as before. The same waitress, wearing the same too-tight dress, hurries over to take their order. Steve engages in his customary banter, and she answers him back with a cheeky smile, clearly pleased to see him. And why not? Although not exactly blessed with Robert Redford looks, he has a rugged charm about him: strong jaw, full head of hair, manly scar above his right eye.

'Great guy,' he says once the drinks have been served and the waitress has left. 'Your man,' he adds, grinning. 'Bailing me out like that.'

'He's not my man.'

'I'm sorry, your husband then. Real good of him.'

'Yes,' she says through gritted teeth. 'It was.'

Steve eyes her curiously but instead of probing into her private life, launches straight in. 'Right, so Nate's been in touch. He's the guy I've had digging around.' He whips a telex out of his back pocket and unfolds it. 'He's unearthed some fascinating background info about the cult's leader.'

Donna's scalp prickles. The word itself unnerves her, let alone its awful connotations. 'The sheriff is convinced it's a harmless commune, that the guards are there to protect their privacy. He suggested I write Jos a letter.'

'Swell idea. If you don't get an answer, then we'll know for sure things aren't good.'

Oh God, she thinks, holding back a cry. I hadn't thought of that.

'Now, do you want to hear my news or not?'

She nods, steeling herself for the awful information she both does and doesn't want to hear.

'Right, well, as we know, the leader goes by the name of Michael. Means *who is as God*, apparently. His real name, however, is Terry Leech.' Steve slaps the paper with the back of his hand. 'Ha. So, you can see why he changed it. Oh, and he's British.'

'Really?'

'Yeah,' says Steve with an exaggerated nod. 'As a young man he trained and worked for Leonard Lewis, the hairdresser who went on to make Twiggy famous.'

'Wow!'

'He was a talented stylist, apparently, in demand, but was had up for embezzlement. He claimed to be innocent, but Lewis, who Leech later told the court resented his success, had incontrovertible proof, and Leech was prosecuted. Twenty-four years old and disillusioned with England, Leech packed up and set off to explore the big wide world, changing his name to Michael and cutting hair as he went to fund his travels. He spent time in South America and lived in Kyoto for a year, before moving to the States. Despite his criminal record, he blagged his way in and ended up in Los Angeles. Somewhere along the line, he must have experienced a moment of enlightenment, because he gave up styling hair, moved to San Francisco, and began preaching. His message: that the world was an evil place, and everyone in it was destined to rot in Hell. He also claimed God had requisitioned his body for humanity's survival, and promised salvation and eternal life to everyone who followed him. You know the type of thing?

'Anyway, while he was in San Francisco, he met and fell in love with trainee lawyer, Zosia Scott. As luck would have it, Zosia happened to be the daughter of Cameron Scott, an extremely wealthy Californian businessman, and the critically acclaimed author, Dolores 'Lola' Scott.' Steve peers at her over the top of the telex. 'You may have heard of her.'

'Nope.' Maybe she should have? It's hard to tell from

Steve's expression, part quizzical, part amused as he leans back in his chair.

'Right, well, seems Zosia fell for Leech hook, line, and sinker. She believed every warped little lie he told her. They got engaged, although it's unclear whether they actually married. It doesn't matter, the point being that the unmitigated support of such an intelligent, likeable and, apparently, sane woman lent credence to Leech's incredible theories. According to reports, he is the type of man whom men admire and women want to fuck.'

Donna winces. Why must he be so direct all the time?

'But perhaps the most interesting fact Nate uncovered is that throughout the group's sixteen-year history, not one member has left. Until now.'

Donna rests her elbows on the table and clasps her head. 'But he escaped. He didn't leave. And you saw him, he was terrified.'

'Right, because some man who he thinks is dangerous and who may, or may not, be poisoning Michael, has been appointed second-in-command.'

Donna lowers her hands. 'What are you saying?'

'The cult has a hierarchy. Perhaps Thomas thought he was destined for higher things and this new guy kiboshed that.'

'That's what you think?'

'Actually, no, I don't. Typically, success for any cult leader is dependent on his followers' complete compliance. By brainwashing and isolating them, he induces not only dependency but also dread. If you don't agree, we'll convince you. If we can't convince you, you're the enemy. In other words, he rules by fear. Pretty standard cult stuff. The question we should be asking is, have others tried to leave? Or are they being held against their will? The guns suggest they are. Choice, you see, is a casualty in any cult. We need to find out what it is that Mr Leech and his sidekick are trying to hide.'

Donna listens with an increasing sense of foreboding. It's incredible how seemingly sane, clever people are so taken in by the nonsense spouted by a superficially charming person, they are prepared to give up everything – their family, wealth, possessions – to blindly follow.

Is that what's happened to Jos? Does he buy into what Naomi is selling him? Does he believe he is damned? Is he hoping for salvation despite never having shown any interest in God, Jesus, or any religion? Or has he been flattered by beautiful Naomi's attention and blinded by fantastic sex? Not that the whys and wherefores matter. If Steve is right, he's essentially a prisoner in a potentially dangerous cult.

'As a self-proclaimed leader of a religious cult, Leech undoubtedly has a grandiose idea of who he is and what he can achieve,' continues Steve. 'In this case, Archangel Michael, God's right-hand man and leader of his army, the only being who can save our souls.'

Donna slaps the table. 'Exactly. It's complete and utter nonsense. Why would anyone fall for it?'

'I know, it's mind-boggling, but not if you consider that Michael not only has a handle on the world's problems but the solutions as well. That's kinda attractive, isn't it?'

'For someone with low self-esteem, perhaps, but his followers, the accountants and lawyers, surely they're too intelligent to fall for it. And what about Zosia Scott? She comes from a stable background and sounds pretty grounded, too.'

'Sure, but love can do strange things to a person. Maybe she felt her life had been mapped out for her and by joining ranks with Terry she was seizing control of her destiny. You don't have to be depressed to find the world an intimidating place. And if a handsome man is telling you the world will end on the twelfth of May 1983 but can offer you eternal life in a spiritual realm, then he's a superhero – or in this case an angel – and that's not only exciting but incredibly sexy, too.'

It's late by the time Donna returns to the motel. She opens the door as quietly as possible so as not to wake Rupert, but seeing him sitting in bed, reading, her heart sinks. She braces herself but is surprised when, instead of demanding to know what she's been doing, he simply asks her if she's okay and whether she needs anything. When she tells him she's tired and desperate for sleep, he closes his book and, after she's changed into her nightdress in the privacy of the bathroom, turns out the light.

'Goodnight, Donna,' he says. 'Sleep well.'

Exhausted though she is, sleep eludes her. Not so Rupert. She listens, enviously, to his steady, almost silent breathing, studying the curve of his lips, the strong line of his jaw, his straight-as-an-arrow nose. The handsome man she used to love. He told her earlier she hadn't changed. Irrespective of whether he meant it as a compliment or a criticism, how, in the little time they've spent together, can he possibly tell? So much has happened to her in the years since he walked out, she can't possibly be the same. He certainly isn't. He doesn't snore anymore, for starters. And what has happened to his famous temper that flared up like a firework every time she overstepped the line? He'd rant and rave, accuse her of this and that, then quickly offer his heartfelt apologies, smothering her in kisses as they tumbled into bed for mind-blowing make-up sex. And what about his machismo, his can-do attitude, his refusal to shy away from a problem, no matter how difficult?

It isn't like him to take a back seat. Perhaps he's taken up yoga. Isn't that the latest Californian fad? Or has he simply realised this sorry mess is all his fault? If it wasn't for him, Jos would never have met Naomi. He wouldn't have been captured by a cult. And she wouldn't be here, in California, trying to rescue him.

Donna groans, rolls onto her side, and closes her eyes, but the image of a blonde-haired, blue-eyed bimbo has her snapping them open again. Ridiculous really. She has no idea what Naomi looks like. She still hasn't seen the photo. Her imagination has her down as a floozy, though, which helps her feel superior. What kind of relationship did they have? Rupert's stuttered explanation that he'd helped out with her because she was the daughter of an old friend seems ludicrous. He said Naomi suggested he join the commune because it was what he needed. Surely there was more to it than that. To have taken the trouble to entrap his son, Naomi must have been pretty keen on Rupert. Hell hath no fury like a woman scorned. Perhaps she'd fallen in love with him and, heartbroken when he called it off, sought solace in a cult from where she plotted her revenge. And what better way to reap it than to take out all her pain, anger, and jealousy on the son of the man she loved.

And yet, somehow, it doesn't add up. If that was the case, Naomi must have known he was married, that he'd left his wife and hadn't spoken to her, or his children, for years. What could she hope to gain from coercing Rupert's son? A son he doesn't know. She'd ruffle some feathers but she can't have expected Rupert to go running back to his wife, the woman from whom he'd fled, with his tail between his legs. What would be the point?

The beginnings of a headache gnawing at her temple, Donna reaches for the bottle of Tylenol by her bed, swallows a couple of tablets, and flops onto her back. Best to forget about Naomi and all the other girlfriends Rupert may have had, and focus instead on the plan of attack Steve laid out in the bar.

'Given the sheriff's unshakable belief the cult is a harmless sanctuary for the disenfranchised, it's time,' he said, 'to harness the full force of the press. I'm gonna reach out on a global scale. Tomorrow's headline in the *San Francisco Chronicle* will make for very interesting reading indeed.'

Donna has adopted the same strategy dozens of times. An insider with contacts at his disposal and all manner of media tricks up his sleeve, Steve will get their message across and lend weight to their campaign. He let slip he went to Harvard. Clearly he's intelligent but he is zealous, too, prepared to leave no stone unturned in his pursuit of the truth. He knows what he's doing, knows the lay of the land. She's more than happy to ride on his coattails. Meantime, she'll do as the sheriff suggested and write a note to her son.

And with those optimistic thoughts buzzing around her brain, she drifts off to sleep.

The first thing Donna notices when she and Rupert arrive at the compound the following afternoon is the increased media presence. The half a dozen journalists camped outside have swelled to at least three times that number and, judging by the white van with ABC7 emblazoned on the side, they include a television correspondent. Great. The more people who know about the strange goings-on in the Palo Verde Valley the better.

She scans the group, but there's no sign of Steve. Perhaps he's working on another story, or telexing his team, or his contacts, or whatever journalists do. With nothing else to occupy her, she's wondering whether now would be a good time to instigate a conversation with Rupert about his vanishing act all those years ago, something she'll have to endure sooner or later, when Todd rushes over brandishing a newspaper.

He hands it to her, grinning broadly. 'Steve got the front page.'

Donna glances at the attention-grabbing headline, ANGEL TOWN: ONE MAN'S VISION TO SAVE THE WORLD.

'If that doesn't get the authorities sitting up and thinking, then I don't know what will,' Todd says.

Smiling, Donna scans the article about Terry Leech, the British hairdresser who claims to be the reincarnation of Archangel Michael sent by God to save the souls of his dedicated followers, and the hierarchical cult he's created in the desert, policed by ninja-hooded 'angels', armed with guns.

Leech's earthly mission is to lead his troops into battle at Armageddon. But what will really happen on the twelfth of May 1983? A great war between God's Celestial Army and Satan and his demons, or another Jonestown-style mass suicide?

The hairs on the nape of Donna's neck stand on end. Was Steve being melodramatic for effect? The communist cult led by Reverend Jim Jones made international headlines four years ago, when over nine hundred people died in Guyana's jungle after drinking Flavor Aid, laced with a deadly cocktail of drugs. Initially, it was thought to be a mass suicide but, given the number of children involved, was later deemed to be a ritualistic mass murder. She remembers the quip *don't drink the punch* they bandied around at parties. But that was entirely different, wasn't it? Jim Jones was a lunatic.

She thrusts the article at Rupert.

'Talk about pouring fuel on a fire,' he mutters. 'Our son's in there. What the hell is he playing at?'

My son, Donna thinks, but she's too shaken to correct him.

Despite the flurry of activity Steve's article has created, with nothing newsworthy to report, the media bandwagon moves on, leaving behind only Todd and the original handful of journalists. Bored of mooching around and waiting – for what, she has no idea – Donna roots through her handbag for the pad of paper she snaffled from the motel and pens a note to Jos, filling it with warnings about Michael, the potential danger of the commune, and how much she misses him.

She passes it to Rupert. 'The sheriff suggested I write to Jos.'

He examines it and shakes his head. 'He might not be the only one who reads it.'

Irritated by the stream of good advice that continues to flow from him, she rips out the page and scrunches it into a ball. 'So, what do you suggest?'

'Why not say you're here visiting his father and invite him to meet us tomorrow at the motel. Should grab his attention.'

He's right, she thinks, resignedly. She scribbles another note, signs it with two kisses, then walks over to the guard – a different one from her previous visit – who nods when she asks if he can deliver it to her son. Just to be sure he knows whom she means, she shows him Jos' photo.

Relieved to have finally done something constructive, she returns to the car and settles down to wait. No doubt the guard will also report back to Michael, if they haven't already, about the day's goings-on. Would it fan the flames as Rupert predicted? And what exactly were the flames? From the titbits Thomas has told them, there isn't much to go on.

She rubs her eyes and sighs. Why had she been so quick to throw her lot in with Steve? As Rupert so wisely pointed out, Steve is out to make a name for himself. The more sensational a story he concocts about the cult, the more people will buy his paper, the better it'll be for him. He isn't interested in saving Jos. What's needed is patience. If she wants to see her son, she has to be prepared to play the long game. Tomorrow, they'll have a better idea of when that will be. It makes perfect sense and, for the first time since Rupert waltzed back into her life, Donna is grateful he's here.

It's dark by the time Steve returns to the compound.

Rupert nudges her. 'Brace yourself.'

But instead of heading her way, Steve wanders over to Todd who, like them, is sitting on the bonnet of his car munching on a sandwich.

Her breath hitches, catching her off guard. God sakes, Donna, get a grip, she berates herself as she watches the journalists chat animatedly to one another. He's an outrageous flirt and probably has a woman in every town. Either that, or he's married. And anyway, now is most definitely not the time.

She glances at her watch. Jos should have received the note by now. The night air chilly, she hops off the bonnet and is reaching for the door handle when the unmistakable crack of a gunshot rents the silence. She starts and twists round. A cylindrical beam of a searchlight arcing through the night sky settles on an emaciated man perched on the wall, bright enough to illuminate the expression of sheer terror on his face. There's a loud blast, and a volley of bullets peppers his torso. His bloodied body jerks, buckles, and falls backwards, landing, in the ensuing silence, with a thud on the far side of the wall.

CHAPTER TWENTY-TWO

I wake up and groan. My brain is a cotton wool ball, and my tongue is sandpaper dry. It's dark, so I'm pretty sure it's night. Odd, though, because I can't remember going to bed.

I reach for the tumbler of water on the bedside table but, apart from the lamp, there's nothing there. I flick the switch, prop myself up on my elbow and, squinting, glance around the room expecting to see Hepzibah, but there's no one here 'cept lil' ole me. And now my head is throbbing.

I flop onto the pillows. How did I get here? Think, Lola, think.

I shut my eyes and rummage for a memory, but there's nothing, not one little nugget. And my thirst has grown so bad I can't ignore it anymore.

I slip out of bed, slowly, trying not to fall over I'm that woozy, and stagger on unsteady tippy toes into the corridor. A figure is loitering outside Michael's door. I spring back, but the floorboard I step on creaks. The nightwalker turns and, blow me, if it isn't the woman I saw in Michael's room that first night. Seems I'm not the only one who can sneak past guards. She sees me and freezes. Course she does. She shouldn't be here. Not that I care. And just to prove it, I smile and edge closer. Only now I realise I'm wrong. It's not a woman at all, but a man. A beautiful young man. I stare at him, bamboozled, because I see now, plain as day, it's David. His hair grown to Dominion length and dressed in white, I didn't recognise him.

I grin and clap my hands. I've never been so pleased to see anyone in my life. 'David. It's me, Lois. Gee, this is a turn-up. You're a Dominion, so we'll get to hang out. Bet you miss your fishing, though,' I add, cos he looks real sad.

He puts a finger to his lips. 'You haven't seen me, Lois. Okay?'

I screw up my nose. 'Sure.'

'Promise me, Lois. You mustn't tell a soul.'

I'm about to ask why, but the ear-splitting blare of an alarm stops me in my tracks. My heart, too, with a whopping great jolt. I peer over my shoulder. Raphael is striding purposefully down the corridor, a small blue jar in one hand, snake-staff in the other, his cloak billowing behind him, he's walking so fast.

'Go back to your room, Lois.'

I stick out my tongue at his departing back. Boy, does that feel good. But the rap of his staff on Michael's door has me hopping into the shadows. Just as well, because he flicks his head left, then right.

Mercy me, David. I glance around desperately but, here's the thing, there's no sign of him. The coast clear, Raphael marches in, although I swear Michael hasn't answered.

Jos' door flings open, and out he struts, his hair a tangled mess. 'What the hell is going on?'

I shrug, one eye on Jos, the other still scouring the area for David. But he's vanished into thin air.

'Only one way to find out. C'mon.' Jos grabs my arm and sets off at such a brisk pace I have to hitch up my nightdress to stop myself tripping over.

Out the front door we run, past the Almond and the Olive Trees, to the entrance to the outer courtyard where we pull up sharp. The gates are open, and the Powers are storming out of Ascension House. I shiver. First David and now this. Something is very wrong.

'You coming?' Jos asks once the last pair have left.

I stare at him like he's lost his mind, which of course he has, because there's no way on earth I'm stepping one foot outta Ascension House.

'Well?'

'We can't. We're not allowed.'

Too late. He's off. And just as I'm thinking nothing in this world frightens Jos, and he must surely be Gabriel, Trumpeter of the Last Judgment, after all, I realise my legs have acquired a mind of their own and are sprinting after him.

Quite a crowd has gathered beneath the wall at the front gate. I've been here once or twice as a dare, but it's Out of Bounds, so I didn't hang around for a full-on recce. It's too dark to see much now, but I can make out the outlines of other Guardians. Seems we're not the only ones flouting the rules. Every now and again a bright beam of light sweeps across us. I spot Miller Isaac and Tamar, Blacksmith Simeon, and Lydia from two doors down, Fisherman Cain, Abi's parents, Carpenter Ezra and Susanna, and Herdsman Jethro. Dressed in white nightgowns, they resemble a panic-stricken Heavenly Choir. I lower my gaze, but no one takes the blindest bit of notice of me. They're all hypnotised by whatever it is the Powers, locked shoulder to shoulder together, are shielding. Nobody tries to get a closer look. Nobody dares. Not even Jos, thank the Good Lord. They aren't aiming their guns at us, but every single Power has his finger on the trigger. It scares me to my bones to think they might shoot. And as I wonder what it would take, I remember how brave I used to be doing dares and breaking rules in the years before I became an Aeon.

The captain barks an order, making me, and everyone else, jump. The Powers part, and four of them march out, carrying something on a wooden plank. The crowd slopes forward, dragging me with it, close enough to see it's a body covered in a bloodstained sheet.

Up go the guns.

With a loud gasp, the crowd scurries back, a startled animal with many legs.

The Powers bundle the body into the trunk of the black car like it's a sack of flour and not a person, which I guess it isn't anymore. Because I'm certain that whoever it once was is dead.

And now the murmuring begins, a mosquito hum that swells to a clamouring hullabaloo.

'What's happening?'

'Are we under attack?'

A woman, Deborah, I think, throws up her hands, stares at the sky, and moans. 'It's a sign from God. The End of the World is nigh.'

'Satan is among us,' says Fisherman Cain.

Shivering, I scan the Guardians' heads for horns, their feet for hooves. But if the Devil is here, he's in disguise.

A shot rings out above my head. I gasp and reel backwards.

The captain steps forward, black-eyed and menacing. 'Go back to your houses.'

Bam. We bow our heads, meek as lambs, and turn back down the road towards Edenville. We haven't gone far when the car carrying the body overtakes us at a lick. Perhaps the victim is still alive. I glance questioningly at Jos, but he's staring at the ground. What does he see there, I wonder?

We pass the forge, the school, and the bakery. When we reach the standpipe at the top of Main Street, the Guardians peel off towards their houses, the crowd thins, and soon it's just me, Jos, and the Powers. Seems we're the only ones crazy enough to have left Ascension House.

We lag behind so as not to be noticed, no mean feat when you're dressed in white and everyone else is wearing black. Holy shit, we're in big, big trouble. I'm trembling all over, can hardly breathe, I'm that scared. I know what happens when you break the rules. There's not much street left, just a few houses, including mine. Maybe we should go home like everybody else. The Powers won't be any the wiser. And it would be good to see Mom.

A memory sneaks up, almost tripping me over. Last thing I remember before I woke was Raphael telling me Michael had arrested her. I must have passed out from shock. My insides turn to water. It's all I can do to stay upright but, somehow, I stagger on. Michael must have known how dangerous he'd make life for Mom when he introduced me as his daughter. That's why he told the Guardians not to harm her. But they hadn't listened, so somebody had to take the rap. Mom. What a cruel, cowardly thing to do. I only came to Ascension House because after a lifetime of being a nobody, turned out I was Michael's only child. If I'd refused, Mom would still be free.

Dear Sweet Jesus. I'm as much to blame.

I stop dead. No way am I taking another step until I've sorted out this mess. Jos is too busy muttering expletives to notice, but the captain does.

He fixes me with his raven eyes. 'What are you playing at?'

'Nothing.' It's true. I'm not playing. I'm not doing anything, I'm that mad.

'Then go home.'

'No.'

The eyes glint. 'Go home.'

'Fine.' I make for the gate, vaguely aware Jos is gawping at me as if I've lost my mind. But I don't care. I'm damned if I do and damned if I don't.

The captain clenches his jaw. 'I said, go home.'

'I heard you.'

'Like hell you did.' The captain clicks his fingers and, immediately, I'm surrounded.

I ball my hands into fists and press them into my thighs. A Power reaches out to grab me, but the gates have swung open and Raphael appears. He throws back his cloak and bangs his staff on the ground. One, twice, three times.

The Powers fall back and stand to attention.

With a jerk of his thumb and a nod of his head, Raphael motions us towards the courtyard.

Breathing hard, I hold my ground.

The muscle in his cheek working overtime, he strides over and thrusts his face to within inches of mine. 'Go to your room, Lois. Or it'll be your mother who pays.'

. . .

I press my back against the cool, white wall of the corridor and glance at Jos, slumped on the floor opposite. His silence frightens me. I need his strength. Need him to tell me that everything will be all right.

'I've got to get out of here,' he says, more to himself than to me.

I shake my head. Surely he knows it's impossible. And anyway, what about the body? What about Mom? I take a deep breath. 'Michael had my mother arrested.' I look at my hands and see they're shaking.

'You're kidding?'

'No, I'm not. Raphael told me.'

Jos clicks his tongue and scowls. 'And you believe him?'

I nod dumbly. I mean, why would he lie? What could he hope to gain? 'It's all my fault.'

'That's ridiculous. Why would you think that?'

I want to tell him I've been nothing but trouble my whole life. I want to tell him about the book I stole. But I can't. Not now he thinks better of me.

'Something's not right. Your father ...' He leaps to his feet. 'Stay here. I'll be back in a tick.'

'Jos, no.'

But Jos is already sprinting down the corridor.

I sink to the floor. I have no idea what to do or what to think. Raphael told me Michael had arrested my mother. Why would he say it if it wasn't true? I stuff my fist in my mouth to stop myself crying and think back to the words Mom pressed upon me before she said goodbye.

I want you to remember I am your mother and I love you very much. No matter where you are, who you're with, or what they might tell you, never forget that.

A tear rolls down my cheek. Michael shouldn't have had her arrested. She should be safe at home with Jemima,

Isabel, and Noah. If only I could see her. Maybe if I shout loud enough at Michael, for long enough, he'll set her free. No, I can do better than that. I'll demand he does, or else!

Or else what, Lola?

My shoulders droop. I don't know what to think anymore. I've devoted my whole life to Michael. Our Father, who also happened to be the man my mother loved, who couldn't be *my* father because God had bigger plans for him.

There must be another way around this, unless ... unless God instructed him to arrest my mother. Is God angry with her? Angry with Michael? Angry with me? Because He would know what they've done, whether Michael told his people or not. He'd know who I was.

He knows everything.

Jos is back, nudging me with his foot. 'Quick, get up. We need to talk.'

'You heard Raphael. We're supposed to go to our rooms.'

But Jos has heaved me to my feet and is dragging me down the corridor to Michael's study.

Could this day get any worse? I wonder. Too tired to protest, I hang back as he picks the lock. Always playing with fire, it's like he has a death wish. Or is it more complicated? He appeared out of nowhere. *Poof.* A genie from a lamp. Perhaps Brighton is one of the Seven Realms of Heaven and God has sent him here to test me. I'm pretty sure Gabriel is Ruler of the Sixth, so it's possible, isn't it?

Jeez, I don't know.

It's quiet in the garden. Kinda eerie, too. But, at least, we're alone. I trudge after him to the pond, over the bridge to the teahouse. Dog-tired, I flop onto a cushion while Jos, furiously chewing the inside of his cheek, paces the wooden platform. After the hell of the last few hours, I'm glad I'm with him, glad we're friends again. But I'm scared, too, of what he might do.

'I think Raphael is drugging Michael,' he says eventually. 'Or rather, I know he is. I just tried talking to him, but he hadn't a clue who I was.'

'You went into his room?'

'A bit odd, don't you think, given someone's been killed?'

I shrink into the cushion, not wanting to remember.

'I knew Raphael was supplying him weed. Funny that, given it's a sin. And I know there's something odd about the tea he gives us at breakfast.'

'The tea?'

'Haven't you noticed how wide awake and invincible you feel after drinking it? And Michael knocks it back it by the bucket-load, so no wonder he's away with the fairies. But I'd no idea Raphael was dishing out amphetamines, too. Still, it explains why Michael hasn't slept in over a week and is now spark out.'

I've long since stopped wondering how Jos knows stuff I don't and, although he's speaking in a language I don't understand, I get the drift. Because now he comes to mention it, I do feel more positive and energetic after breakfast. And what about the jar I saw Raphael take into Michael's room? And whatever it was he'd slipped into Michael's pocket that day in the white room. All of which has me thinking, I was out so long after Raphael told me about Mom, did he drug me as well?

'I doubt he was in his right mind when he had your mum arrested if, in fact, Raphael was telling the truth.'

'But why would he lie?'

'I don't know, but there's something shady about

Raphael. We should search his rooms. See if we can find out what he's up to. And then we should find your mum. We can't leave without her.'

I sit bolt upright. I don't like the sound of any of this. What if we're caught? What then? 'Jos, we can't.'

'I can't stay in this loony bin, and I'm not leaving you here at the mercy of that evil bastard.'

My heart's beating like a tom-tom. 'But the gates are guarded, and the Powers have guns.'

He looks at me then, out of one eye, scrunching up his cheeks like the truth has finally caught up with him. 'I'll ... I'll find a way. They can't make me stay. I'm not one of you. They wouldn't dare shoot me. I'm English. All hell would break loose if they did.'

I shudder. 'You think the Powers shot ...? But that's—'

He wraps his arms around me and gathers me to his chest. 'It'll be okay, Lola. My father lives here. That's why I came. I haven't seen him yet. I haven't seen him for fifteen years ... he walked out on me ... on all of us ...when I was one. But I have some photos. Naomi gave them to me. I met her in Brighton and, well ... anyway, I showed one to Michael, but he didn't recognise him. No surprises there. He's so spaced out he probably has no idea who lives here. But if we can find him he'll help us. I know he will.'

I take it in, every word. From the way he's speaking, I get that the sharing of his secret is a big deal. And I'm real glad he has because it means he trusts me. But I don't have the heart to tell him he's wrong. His father, whoever he might be, follows Michael and will not help us leave. So, I keep that thought to myself, shut my eyes, and soak up his warmth, and let him believe it for as long as he can.

The cocks are crowing, which means the night, at last, is over. I haven't slept a wink. I couldn't. I was too worried about Mom. Too worried about Jos. And terrified about whatever it is Raphael is up to. Perhaps he's convinced Michael I should marry him as planned. And if he has, in four weeks I'll be his wife. Breathing the same air as that reptile has the flesh creeping from my bones, but the thought of sleeping with him makes me sick with fear. After a night spent worrying about him drugging me into submission, death seems the better option. Maybe I should throw my lot in with Jos and leave. And if we're shot? Well, that'll be that.

I drum the mattress with my legs. No. I can't leave. Not without my mother.

I drag my weary body out of bed, throw on my dress, and head to the kitchen. I'm not the least bit hungry but I'm in desperate need of human company.

Kishi is preparing fish. He greets me with a brisk nod and a *konichi wa*. I nod back and watch as he slides his knife through the fish's belly, imagining the razor-sharp blade slicing through flesh. Would that be worse than being shot?

Recalling the corpse covered in a bloodied sheet, I gag, but my stomach is empty. Fortunately, Kishi has his back to me and doesn't notice. Sighing, I slump into a chair.

Jos wanders in, still wearing last night's haunted expression. Michael follows, dry-washing his hands, his cheeks pale, his hair unkempt.

'Oh good, there you both are.' His gaze flits around the room as if he's not sure where he is. 'Are you quite well, Gabriel? Lois?'

Is he for real? What about last night? I leap to my feet. 'Where's my mother? What have you done to her?'

A shadow darts across his face. 'Esther is at home.' His

right eye flickers. 'Or work. What day is it? Tuesday? Wednesday? So, yes, she is at work. At The Mill. That's where she works, isn't it? Yes, yes.'

But I'm not having it. 'Don't lie to me. You said no one should harm her because she was holy, and yet you had her arrested. Raphael told me so himself.'

His right eye twitches, like it's taken on a life of its own. 'You're mistaken. Why would I do such a thing?'

But I don't hear him for the angry roar erupting out of me. 'And that's not all. Someone was killed last night. Why weren't you there? We were scared. We needed you.'

'Dear child, you need to calm down,' Michael says without attempting to comfort me. 'The apostate, Daniel, died last night, shot by the Devil's spawn. Stop these histrionics. You need to get ready. I have called a Meeting.'

One of the runaway Dominions. I'd forgotten about them. I thump my fist on the table. 'What's the matter with you? Haven't you been listening to me? I'm not going anywhere until I've seen Mom. And neither is Jos.'

'Lois,' Jos says gently. 'Michael's right. Now is not the time.'

I stare at him goggle-eyed. Why isn't he backing me up?

'Quite right, Gabriel,' says Michael dully. 'Now is most definitely not the time.'

The cream seats in Michael's car are shiny and smooth, and the silver angel, perched on the hood, leans forward, wings spread, an expression of sheer excitement on her exquisite face. Children cheer and run alongside us as we purr down Main Street. They see Sophia the Aeon, sent by God to protect them, not Esther's daughter, plain old Lois. But instead of pride I feel numb with shame. God has put his trust in me, but I've no idea what I'm supposed to do. I will fail. And, come the glorious day of judgment, He will pass me over.

The driver, Ophaniel, turns off the road and stops outside the rear doors of the Meeting Room, guarded by two Powers, their eyes covered by mirrored shades. Like me, they were sent from God but, unlike me, they look like the inhabitants of a distant star.

I touch the angel, make a wish for courage, and follow Michael into the area behind the stage. My jaw drops. If Michael's study is an Aladdin's cave, then Lord alone knows what this is.

'Smoke and mirrors,' Jos says. 'See?'

I take in the lights, the speakers, the screen, the ropes and pulleys, a long board with knobs and buttons, and a large black box, but I can't spot a single mirror, or any smoke.

Michael claps his hands. 'Remember, whatever happens, neither of you will speak. Once I have landed, Gabriel, you will enter from the right, Sophia, you will enter from my left.' And with that, he is gone.

Landed? All Michael has told us is that he's acting under God's command. We are not to ask questions but must do as instructed or else incur God's wrath. I'm that jittery about getting things wrong, I've broken out in a cold sweat.

A Guardian I recognise as Matthew guides me into position on the far side of the stage. 'You might be blinded temporarily, so eyes down and take care not to fall over when you walk on.'

I follow his gaze to a metal beam high above us, that runs across the full length of the stage.

He gives a thumbs-up. There's a blinding flash. A thunderous crash. Darkness. Hissing. A gust of air and, suddenly, we're clouded in smoke.

'Ready?' Matthew asks.

I gulp and somehow manage to nod.

'Good. Now go.'

I stumble into position. My throat is dry, and I want to cough but I mustn't. The spotlights flare into bright, white life, and the music starts. Remembering Matthew's instruction, I look at my feet but I can't see them in the swirling mist.

The audience gasps and stares at a point above my head.

Sweet Jesus. Michael is hovering in the air, his wings outstretched. Beautiful and white, the feathers, fluttering in the slight breeze. I blink long and slow but I'm not dreaming. As sure as night becomes day, Michael's wings are real.

'Those who come from their father, the Devil, desire to do his bidding,' a loud, echoing voice booms from the rafters, deep and powerful enough to rattle my bones. 'The Devil was a murderer from the beginning. He has never been truthful. He does not know what the truth is. Whenever he tells a lie, he is doing what comes naturally to him. He is the father of lies. Last night, your brother, Daniel, was slain, shot by those who came from their father, the Devil. A fugitive, he was drawn to them. But he paid for his mistake with the ultimate sacrifice. His life.'

In the awestruck silence that follows, Michael, arms and wings spread, slowly descends. 'God has spoken. You have all heard what He has to say. His word is the truth.'

I nod furiously, terrified out of my wits. Never in my wildest dreams did I imagine God would speak to me. To us.

'Point made,' Jos mouths, catching my eye.

I frown, not understanding.

'It is a sign,' continues Michael. 'The salvation, the power, the Kingdom of our God, and the authority of his Messiah have come. For the one who accuses our brothers day and night in the presence of our God, has been thrown out.'

Lights flash, thunder claps, and with a loud hiss, smoke rolls around our ankles until we're up to our waist in it. It's cold and dry and tickles the back of my throat, and I have to hold my breath to stop myself coughing.

Michael rises into the air, arms outstretched. 'PUT ON THE ARMOUR OF GOD. RESIST THE TACTICS OF THE DEVIL. THE WAR IS BEGUN.'

CHAPTER
TWENTY-THREE

Fifteen hours have passed since the shooting, but the memory of the man's body, buckling as the bullets eviscerated his body, remains scorched on Donna's retinas. War, weapons, and all their grisly connotations, are atrocities she's spent her life campaigning against. Never in her worst nightmares did she imagine she'd witness a murder. And to be close enough to see the expression of terror on the poor man's face. Even after all the cups of tea Rupert has made her since, the rug he produced from the back of the car and draped around her, she can't stop shivering. Jos is in there. What if he tries to leave? Will they kill him, too?

Rupert has tried his hardest to reassure her. 'From what you've told me about Jos, he's unlikely to rock the boat. And even if he does, they're hardly likely to murder a teenager recently arrived from England. Imagine the diplomatic row it would spark.'

She wants to believe him. Rupert may have a greater understanding of American Law than her, but he doesn't know his son, has no idea what he's capable of. Truth is,

Jos' character has changed so much these past couple of years, neither does she. At least the authorities will have to get involved now. Americans might have the right to keep and bear arms, but they did not have the right to kill a person in cold blood. If only they could get hold of the sheriff. The journalists spent the night trying, but Hank Rivera continued to elude them. Out of sheer frustration, they'd contacted the Blythe Police, but Edenville, they explained, fell under the jurisdiction of the Riverside County Sheriff's Department.

'Here he is.' Rupert points to the police car speeding down the track.

Donna closes her eyes. 'At last.'

'It sounds a bit far-fetched,' the sheriff says after Steve's relayed the details of the shooting.

'Why on earth would we make it up?' Donna asks.

'I can think of plenty of reasons.'

Her temperature rising, Donna tears the rug off her shoulders. 'Thomas was certain if they'd seen him they'd have shot him, too.'

The sheriff arches an eyebrow. 'But they didn't, did they?'

'For heaven's sake. A man was killed in the full glare of a searchlight. We all saw it. It's murder in the first degree. Pull your finger out and go and find out what the hell is going on.'

'Watch yourself, lady, or I'll be forced to arrest you again.'

'For what? Telling the truth?' asks Donna, heat flaring her cheeks.

'Come on, Donna.' Rupert picks up the rug, puts his arm around her, and steers her away.

'Don't you think you should at least take a look, Hank?' she hears Steve say. 'If there is a body and the death isn't reported, it'll be your reputation on the line, not ours.'

It's well over an hour since the sheriff drove into Edenville to meet with Michael, taking with him another letter for Jos which, to Donna's surprise and relief, he'd been happy to deliver. The remaining journalists, having promised to remain silent on the matter until the sheriff is in full possession of the facts, are taking the opportunity to nap in their cars. Donna wishes she could do the same but she's still jittery with shock and sleep is out of the question. So, she sits on Rupert's bonnet in the full glare of the sun, biting what's left of her nails, eyes locked on the gate. The wait is driving her nuts. She desperately needs to know her son is okay and not being held against his will.

Rupert eases himself from the passenger seat, where he's been snoozing, to perch beside her. 'You should try and get some rest. Or, at least, sit in the shade.'

Donna shakes her head.

He pats her on the back. 'It'll be okay.'

'And you know this because?'

'Because the sheriff will find the body, and it will be full of bullet holes. Michael will be arrested, and Jos will come home.'

She nods. He's right, of course. She just needs to be patient.

'Now what say you try and grab forty winks?'

'I can't sleep until I know he's okay.' She laces her hands

behind her head and peers at the sky, bright blue with not a cloud in sight. If she believed in God she'd probably be praying for the safe return of her son. As if a supernatural power, who lords it over all humanity, could possibly single out a lone voice from the cacophony of a billion others clamouring for favours. It's ironic. Here she is, trying to retrieve her son from a group of people, blindly following a man who claims to be a saviour sent from the same God she doesn't believe in. The sheriff maintains Edenville is a peaceful commune. And maybe it used to be but, whether Hank Rivera accepts it or not, last night they witnessed a murder. Thomas told them the group's dynamics had changed, that someone was poisoning Michael. He'd felt threatened, that's why he'd run away. Presumably, the man they'd seen shot was trying to escape, too.

Did Michael order his execution? Or is the cult being undone from within? And if it is, does that explain the sudden presence of guns? According to Michael, the world ends on the twelfth of May. That's less than four months away. Are the Guardians of God arming themselves for a battle? Or are they gearing up for a mass suicide?

Her blood running cold, Donna hugs herself and inclines her head towards Edenville. To her relief, the sheriff's black-and-white patrol car is heading back down the track towards the gate, which swings open long enough to allow him through. Desperate for news, Donna slides off the bonnet and rushes over.

The sheriff, beating the dust off his cowboy hat, looks up as she approaches. 'I s'pose it was too much to hope you'd gone back to your motel.'

Donna clenches her jaw. Either this man has no children of his own or he's a lousy dad. 'So, have you arrested him?'

He plonks his hat on his head. 'Whoa. Don't you think

you're jumping the gun here, missy?'

Ignoring his sick attempt at humour, Donna peers through the dirt-strewn window of his car, fully expecting to see a handcuffed Terry Leech, but the back seat is unoccupied.

'Hello again, Sheriff,' Rupert says, hurrying over with the journalists.

The sheriff touches his hat and rolls back his shoulders.

Trying her damnedest to keep her anger at bay, Donna nevertheless senses an uneasiness about him, totally at odds with the brusqueness of his remarks.

Steve nods. 'Hank.'

The sheriff clears his throat. 'Right, well, as you are already aware, a man died last night.'

'Ten out of ten so far,' mutters Steve.

The sheriff narrows his eyes. 'Like I said, he died.'

'Right,' says Steve.

'He wasn't murdered.'

'Like hell he wasn't,' says Todd.

The sheriff thrusts out his chest. 'Those are the facts.'

'A man was shot. In cold blood. In front of witnesses,' Donna says through clenched teeth. 'In my book, that's murder.'

'I take it you saw the body,' says Steve.

The sheriff removes his hat and runs his hand through his sweat-matted hair. 'I did not, no.'

Donna throws up her arms. 'Oh, for heaven's sake.'

'Why not, Sheriff?' Rupert asks reasonably.

'The body had been cremated.'

Steve arches an eyebrow. 'How incredibly convenient.'

'It's the Guardian's custom to cremate a body within twenty-four hours of death,' the sheriff says as he replaces his hat. 'They believe it aids the passage of the deceased into the afterlife.'

Donna gapes at him. Was it really that easy to pull the wool over someone's eyes. 'So, it's our word against Terry's, is that it?'

Sheriff Rivera frowns. 'Terry?'

'If he wasn't murdered, how did he die?' asks Steve.

'He shot himself.'

A wry smile settles on Steve's lips. 'And how did you reach that verdict, Hank?'

'The poor man was terribly depressed, apparently. Couldn't cope with the idea of the world ending.'

Steve clicks his fingers. 'Let me get this straight. He didn't want to die and yet he killed himself anyway. Hmm. Makes perfect sense.'

'This is crazy,' snaps Donna. 'The murderer burns the body and, with it, all the evidence, and walks free.'

The sheriff straightens up to his full height. 'Now look here. I've known Michael fifteen years, and in all that time he has never once refused to cooperate. He's always been completely open about what he's doing. He's an intelligent, thoughtful man—'

'A narcissist and possibly a psychopath,' mutters Steve.

'—who cares deeply about the health, safety, and well-being of his followers.'

Steve raises a finger. 'And yet who terrifies them into believing the world is about to end. You've got to admit, Sheriff, there are some glaring contradictions here.'

'Thank you, Mr Anderson. Now if you don't mind, I've a busy day. Blythe ain't the only town in Riverside County, as well you know. Why don't you let me get on with my job just as I intend to let you get on with yours.' And with a loud harrumph, Hank Rivera turns and marches off towards his car.

Fists clenched, Donna chases after him. 'No! You cannot walk away. What about Jos? You can't leave him in there. He's only sixteen.'

The sheriff stops. 'Oh yeah, I almost forgot.' He thrusts a hand in his back pocket, whips out a folded envelope, and hands it to Donna. 'Michael asked me to give you this. A letter from your son. Now, if you have any sense, you'll take my advice and go home.'

Donna is lying on her bed in the motel room. Her rage has dissipated, but her nerves are still jangling. Like Rupert, who once again is fast asleep, she's trying to get some rest, but since reading the note, she wonders if she'll ever be able to sleep again.

She'd waited until she was in the privacy of her car before she'd unsealed the envelope. She'd been excited and terrified in equal measure – happy Jos had replied, scared as to what he had to say. The last thing she'd expected to feel was anger.

Letting out an exhausted sigh, she reaches for the note and reads it again.

Dear Mummy and Daddy,

Thank you for your kind letter. I was very interested to hear that you are holidaying in California and sincerely hope you are having a lovely time. Unfortunately, I won't be able to accept your invitation. It coincides with a workshop I am leading and it would be terribly disappointing for everyone if I cancelled it.

I am really enjoying life in Edenville. I am extremely glad I made the decision to leave home because this wonderful town is everything I dreamed it would be. Michael is an inspiration. If only there were more men like him, the world would be a far happier place. He is kind and generous with his time. We have forged a strong bond and I cannot imagine life without him.

I hope you both enjoy your stay.

Your loving son,

Joseph

It doesn't take an Einstein to work out Jos didn't write the note. It's typed, for starters, with no mistakes and, as far as she knows, Jos has never used a typewriter. It isn't signed, and the tone isn't that of a sixteen-year-old, let alone anything remotely like Jos' – where are the colloquialisms, the slang, and the modish references? The author clearly doesn't know a great deal about him either, because it begins, Dear Mummy and Daddy. In all his sixteen years, Jos has only ever called Donna Mum, and as to calling Rupert, a man he doesn't know, Daddy, well it's ludicrous. And since when did he refer to himself as Joseph? He'd flip out if anyone called him that. There is also no clue as to the shock, anger, happiness, or whatever emotion Jos is bound to have felt that the father he doesn't know has appeared, as if by magic, inviting him to meet up. In fact, it's so obviously not Jos' work, Donna can only assume the author never intended them to think it was. This raises the question of whether *her* letter reached Jos in the first place. Did Michael read it and refuse to pass it on? Or did Jos, on reading it, instruct someone to reply on his behalf. Naomi, perhaps. Or Michael himself. It seems unlikely. He didn't reply to a single one of the letters she sent to the squat. It upset her, but she carried on regardless. She reasoned that, if he read them, he remained connected to his family in some small way. Why would he change his behaviour now? Unless ... unless he's been brainwashed.

Shivering, she draws the blanket tight around her. If the sheriff hadn't been halfway back to Riverside County Station by the time she'd read it, she'd have thrust the note in his hand and banged on and on at him until he admitted it was fake. In my dreams, she thinks miserably. Sheriff Hank Rivera is clearly a man who takes everything at face value; not the best attribute for a man tasked with the responsibility of upholding the law. Michael has proved himself to be a law-abiding citizen, thereby earning the sheriff's unwavering trust. Nothing anyone says or does can change his mind. It's as farcical a situation as it is infuriating.

What now? she wonders, miserably. Wait for another man to die? Or take the law into my own hands as I would if I was in England. But if that bloody man arrests me again, chances are he'll have me deported.

Rupert stirs in the bed opposite. Yawning, he sits up and glances over. 'Get any sleep?'

'Not a second.'

'How about I take you out for something to eat?' He stretches his arms over his head. 'If we're going to get Jos out, you need to keep up your strength.'

She raises her eyebrows. So, Rupert hasn't handed in the towel just yet. She may have her misgivings about him, she may not like him, but it's the best news she's had all day. The thought of battling through this alone is only adding to her anxiety. Back in their joint activist days, Rupert had matched her move for move. Their life together a fast fading memory, she can't help wondering if it was all a dream.

'Okay,' she says, although she doubts she has the stomach for food. 'Let's go.'

Donna takes a tiny sip of her margarita. It's both salty and overly sweet and not to her liking. She puts it down and pushes it away. Other than some odd subliminal hankering for the cocktail – a drink she and Rupert had a thing about in the mid-sixties, when it was *all the rage* – she can't think why she ordered it. The last thing she needs is a fuzzy head. Her stomach grumbling, she glances at the flabby enchilada with its lattice of overcooked cheese, and the dollop of darkening guacamole on the white plate in front of her. Rupert is tucking into his with gusto. Perhaps it tastes better than it looks. She forks up a mouthful and chews, but the swallowing reflex has deserted her, and she gags. Fortunately, Rupert is busy scraping his plate clean and doesn't notice.

She shoves hers towards him. 'Here, have mine.'

He peers at the untouched meal. 'Shall I order you something else. Some bread? A dessert? How about some ice cream?'

'No,' she snaps.

'You should try and eat something.'

His frown is almost imperceptible, but it's there. She folds her arms and turns away, wondering why she agreed to come. What she'd really like is a cigarette but she gave up smoking in 1958 when she was pregnant with Chrissie; a decision she's never regretted until now. Perhaps she should excuse herself and dash out to buy a packet. No one need ever know. Chances are, though, she'll get hooked, which won't be the best timing with Chrissie due to give birth next month. Poor Chrissie. If only she'd rung her last night as she'd intended.

I'll do it now, she decides, shifting. But Rupert is clearing his throat. She winces, recalling from old that it signalled an announcement. I'm not up for this, she thinks.

'I want to give you and the kids some money. I've made a fair bit since setting up my Real Estate business.'

Her mouth drops open. Real Estate? Rupert? Had he cast aside his leftist principles, along with his family, in pursuit of wealth? She's not sure which disgusts her more.

He tugs on his ear. 'I'd have done it sooner but—'

'Dad? It is you, isn't it? I knew you'd come.'

Chrissie? Tess? Donna whirls around, confused by the American accent, but the young woman standing beside them, although roughly the same age as Chrissie, is a tall, fair-haired stranger. 'I don't think so, love.'

'So, who's this then?' The woman nudges Rupert and grins. 'Well, are you going to introduce us?' But something seems to twig and her expression darkens. 'Oh my God, it's her.'

The colour drains from Rupert's face. 'Not here. Not now.' He pushes his chair away.

'You know her?' Donna asks.

But if Rupert hears he doesn't respond, he's too busy ushering the, now furious, young woman from their table. The way he manhandles her, it's obvious he knows her. She called him Dad, so perhaps Rupert is living with her mother. Donna has no idea. She hasn't asked about Rupert's life. All she knows is what he's just told her and she's struggling to get her head around that. So, she sits in stunned silence, helplessly watching the angry exchange playing out at the door, while the diners on the neighbouring tables trade glances and nudge one another.

The woman jabs a finger in Rupert's chest. He opens his arms and remonstrates. Whatever he says does the trick because she tosses her head and storms out of the restaurant, and Rupert trudges back to the table.

Donna buries her head in her hands. She's spent years wondering about the life Rupert lived after he left. Any minute now, he'll start filling in the gaps. And yet, right now, she can't think of anything she'd like less.

Rupert flops onto his chair and clears his throat. 'There's something I need to tell you. Something I should have told you a long time ago.'

She raises her head and sighs. That's got to hurt, she thinks, as Rupert yanks on his ear. 'You honestly think this is the right time?'

'Yes, Donna. I'm sorry, but I do.'

She glares at him. How dare he ambush her like this? As if she doesn't have enough on her plate. Rupert frowns, properly this time, as though she's injured him in some way. Her emotions flitting all over the place, she takes another sip of her margarita and immediately regrets it. It tastes just as awful as before.

'I was married.'

The full force of the weight she's been lugging around for fifteen years bears down on her. Her body tenses. She'd been expecting him to tell her he was in a relationship. But this confession has caught her off guard.

But, hang on. How is that even possible? They're still married. Aren't they?

'I should have told you and I'm sorry. I'm very, very sorry.'

'Actually, you should've got divorced. I'm pretty sure bigamy is illegal.'

'I did get divorced.'

'Can you get divorced without telling your wife?' Donna's not sure why this should bother her so much.

'No, of course you can't.'

'Then we're not divorced, and your marriage isn't—'

'Which is why I waited until after the girls were born.'

Donna gasps and clasps her cheeks.

'I should have told you the moment we met but I thought I'd lose you so I kept quiet.'

The restaurant and all the other diners seem to fade away as, for the first time since they sat down, Rupert comes into sharp focus. She stares at the top of his head, at the dark hair flecked with grey. 'Are you telling me you were married when you met me?'

'Yes,' he says, finally looking her in the eye.

She recoils as if he's hit her which, in a sense, he has. A massive verbal blow to the chest that's left her reeling. Everything they'd ever had was born of a lie. And she'd never, for a single moment, suspected anything. They'd fallen in love the day they met, and it had seemed the most natural thing in the world. But it wasn't. Rupert was already married and, worse still, had kept the truth from her. A whopping great secret.

Who does that? Who doesn't tell their lover they already have a wife? Liars and cheats, that's who. She thumps the table with her fist. 'I had your children. Don't you think I had a right to know?'

The diners on the adjacent table stop talking and stare at them, open-mouthed.

'Yes, you did, and I'm sorry. It was idiotic of me. But I was desperately in love and scared of losing you.'

'You should have given me the option. What you did was ... was ... entrapment. And what about your wife? How on earth must she have felt when you left? Did she know about me? About our kids?' Donna pauses to catch her breath as the awful truth sinks in.

'Trust me, not a day has passed when I haven't regretted my decision.'

'Is that why you're telling me now? To clear your conscience?'

'No.'

She trawls her racing mind for answers. 'But why else would you tell me?' Her eyes fixed on his, she wonders, if she stares hard enough, whether she'll be able to see inside his soul, find out what other dark secrets lie hidden there. And then she sees it, clear as day. 'Shit! That young woman ... just now ... the blonde. She's ...'

He bites his lip.

Sweat prickling her armpits, Donna leans on her elbows to steady herself. No. It can't be.

'... Ingrid and I ... It wasn't only us. There was a child, too. A little girl. Ellie.'

CHAPTER TWENTY-FOUR

I stare blindly at the pages of *To Kill a Mockingbird*. A new addition to the collection in the box-like room, I found it nestled between Dolores Scott's *The Crimson Sunrise* and *In Days Gone By*, as if I was meant to see it. You know, like a sign. My fingers were itching to get hold of it. But it didn't seem right. A new book always set me thinking. If it was here then it had been found, and whoever had hidden it was probably being punished. Who had loved it enough to chance their luck? Had it been worth it? Or were they suffering some place and wishing they'd thrown it on the bonfire with all the others? There for the grace of God, my girl, Mom would've said if she was here and not Lord knows where. So, I paced the room, weighing up the dos and don'ts. Michael had made it clear I could go anywhere apart from his study. There'd been no mention of what I could or couldn't do with these books. They hadn't been burned so they must be here for a reason.

And anyway, I wondered, what is a book if it isn't being read?

I couldn't think of an answer to that particular question

but I knew, if I didn't read it, I'd never find out what a mockingbird was. And, boy, was I curious. Next thing I knew, kazam, the book was in my hands, and I was reading the bit on the back where the author tells you a little bit about the story.

Truth is, I'm grateful for the distraction and can't wait to learn more about Atticus Finch, and his children, Scout and Jem. We don't have attorneys in Edenville because, with Michael issuing instructions straight from God, we have no need of them. I know what they are, though, because Abi's father, Carpenter Ezra, used to be one in his previous life. The interesting thing about this story is that Atticus is defending a black man accused of raping a white woman. I know what rape is. It's not a crime in Edenville, though the reason why is kinda blurred. The more beautiful a woman is, the more depraved she's likely to be, apparently, so if a man rapes her, she only has herself to blame. I'm not entirely sure what depraved means, but it must be something wicked, because to be raped for being beautiful has never made much sense to me. It doesn't seem to be the case in the Otherworld, and I'm longing to find out why, but with my mind fretting about the Great Battle, my eyes can't seem to settle on the words.

I slump forward, I'm that exhausted by it all. Immediately, the image of Michael flying above the stage, his mighty white wings unfurled, pops into my head. What a wonder they'd been. Nothing like the smaller, black wings I'd seen on his back. I've done some thinking and have decided what I'd seen were his wings neatly folded and packed away. They'd be far too bulky and awkward to lug around otherwise. Imagine trying to sit on a chair? Or walk through a narrow door? They'd trip him up, or whack into people and injure them rotten. Seeing them in all their breathtaking, feathery glory, my heart had soared and all my doubts melted away.

Not Jos.

'The wings were strapped to his back, Lola,' he said. 'They might have been made from feathers, but they weren't real. I'll bet there's a flock of swans somewhere in this crazy town. And he wasn't flying. He was in a harness. The guys on the rig were working the pulleys. You must have seen them. The dry ice was a neat touch, the pyrotechnics and the voice of God. Solves the problem of the dead body. Zadkiel is a complete whiz with special effects, but all the same, I'm amazed anyone falls for this crap.'

His words hit me. *Thwack. Thwack. Thwack.*

I'd seen the ropes but I hadn't seen a harness. I'd seen the wings, though, the lightning flash, and I'd heard God's voice. I have to trust my eyes and ears. I have to trust Michael. Liars are the spawn of Satan. If Michael is a liar then my and all the other Guardians' lives, and everything we've been taught, are meaningless. Jos is wrong. He has to be.

The door flings open. Sweet Jesus. Caught red-handed. I yelp and let go of the book. But it's Jos, and his cheeks are crimson.

'What's happened?'

Jos covers his face with his hands. I hear a strangled sob and, without thinking, I fling my arms around him. It does the trick because he stops crying.

'You cannot marry that man. He's evil. Pure evil.' Jos peels me off him and looks at me with his big brown eyes. 'I'm going to show you what I found. You have to see it for yourself.'

I don't like the sound of this. 'You could tell me. I'll believe you. I promise.'

'Please, Lola. You have to see it with your own eyes. Raphael's in Edenville. We won't get caught.'

No. No. No. I will not go sneaking around again. It's too dangerous. Has he lost his mind?

Ah, but hang on a second. Maybe it's not such a bad idea. I want to help Mom. If I go with Jos, then I'll have proof of whatever it is Raphael is up to. And if I have proof I'll be able to persuade Michael to get rid of him and have Mom set free.

Oh God, why does everything have to be so darn difficult?

I groan, long and hard. It doesn't help much, but at least Jos knows how I feel. 'Okay. I'll come with you.'

Jos fiddles with the hairpin, beads of sweat breaking out on his forehead, while I hop from foot to foot. What if Hashmal and Naneel see us picking Raphael's lock? We told them Raphael sent for us, Lord knows, but that's a bare-faced lie.

'Thought he was in Edenville,' Naneel, the taller of the two said. 'But okay.' And with that, he launched back into the conversation he'd been having with Hashmal.

I glance in their direction. Hidden by the Olive Tree, we're not in their line of sight, but if they move a foot either way, they'll see what we were doing. This is a bad idea. The very worst Jos has had. Damn. Damn. Damn. I chew on my thumbnail and pray.

Dear God, please understand, we're not doing this for ourselves, we're doing it for the good of all.

And lo, there's a click.

Quick as a flash, Jos opens the door, pulls me into a small lobby, and leads me to a room at the end. Stone the actual crows. It's like nothing I've ever seen. For starters, it's glowing with a golden light. My eyes on stalks, I take in the turtle shell and deer skull hanging on the wall. The black mask with the yellow and white stripes, wooden nose, and leering, toothless mouth, which surely belongs to the Prince of Darkness himself. Long pipes, and knives with large blades, spears, and brightly coloured feathered head-dresses. Shelves crammed with books by writers with strange names: Virgil, Plato, and Catullus. A padlocked wooden closet, a glass-fronted cabinet stuffed with clear, blue, brown, and green bottles in all shapes and sizes filled with fruits, flowers, and plants with unpronounceable labels: Datura, Brugmansia, Lophophora williamsii, Cinchona, Erythroxylum, and Psilocybe Mexicana. An orange scarf thrown over a table lamp, the reason for the mellow light. If Michael's study is an Aladdin's cave of wonders, then God only knows what this is. There's the whiff of the Devil about it, thrilling but terrifying. What's it all for? And how did Raphael come by it? The hairs on the back of my neck standing to attention, I turn to ask Jos. But despite all the weird and wonderful treasure, he's delving inside one of the cardboard boxes piled in the corner.

He takes out an envelope and waves it. 'See this? It's a letter from my mum.'

A letter? This sure takes me by surprise. Overcome by an ache of longing for mine, it's all I can do not to cry out in pain.

'Hidden away amongst hundreds of letters from concerned relatives, some dating back sixteen years.' He plunges into the box and pulls out a handful. 'Not a single one delivered. How dare he?' He glares at me as if expecting an explanation. 'It's wrong. No, it's worse than wrong, it's pure fucking evil.'

Mother Mary, I've never seen Jos this mad. Must have

hit him real hard cos it's like he's discovered the worst crime ever. Here, in this room with all these evil-looking objects lying about. Thing is, Jos is still new here. There's a whole heap of stuff he's yet to learn. The way I see it, though, it all makes perfect sense. 'Otherworldlies are ignorant obstacles to salvation,' I say, parroting one of Michael's lines. 'By holding on to the letters, Raphael is protecting the Guardians. But have you seen this jar with—?'

'What did you say?'

I bite my tongue, not wanting to repeat it, certain he'll pick holes in it if I do.

Jos sinks into a chair. 'You don't get it. You just don't get it.' He frowns and unfolds the letter.

I watch sullenly as he reads it. I'd give anything to hear from my mom. But there's no point telling him. I don't want to fight. Last time we fell out, I'd never felt as lonely. And I'm far more interested in finding out what all these weird things are. So, I do as Mom used to do when Elijah kicked off, and head off down the long and lonely road of least resistance. I clear my throat. 'How is she?'

It's a while until he answers. 'She's here, in Blythe.'

'Blythe?'

'The town down the road. With Dad.'

Oh! See, I know how desperate Jos is to meet his dad. It's the reason he's here. But how did his dad manage to get out of Edenville? And how come his mom is with him? From what I'd gleaned when Michael and Jos used to chew the fat, Brighton is as far away as the Heaven's Realm I'd believed it to be.

And then it hits me. Wham, bam, thank you, ma'am. I click my fingers. 'He must be a Virtue. You know like ... whatshername.'

'Naomi,' he says quietly, tilting his head. 'You think?'

'Sure. That's why you haven't seen him yet. He'll have been away, recruiting.'

'I have photos.' He stands and, reaching inside his back pocket, hands me a crumpled picture. 'Do you recognise him?'

I study the face, crisscrossed by lines from being folded and unfolded time and again. He has Jos' eyes, the same determined set of his jaw. More than anything I want to tell him what he wants to hear, he's that hopeful. But I can't. I've never seen this man. I shake my head.

'Would you be able to identify all the Guardians?'

I mull the question over. I'm pretty sure I could put a name to most of them – not the newest intake, apart from Jos, of course – but I don't want to crush his spirits. 'I guess not.'

'You didn't recognise Naomi, did you?' he continues breathlessly. 'And she's a Virtue. So it makes sense.'

I clap my hands. 'Well, there you are then. Problem solved.'

Jos nods, his eyes sparkling.

'Sounds like he's recruited your mom.'

'I dunno. It's odd they're together. He left without telling Mum where he was going. Literally vanished into thin air. They haven't spoken since, and now here they are, asking me to meet them at a motel.'

'Hmm. Maybe Naomi told him you were here and he decided to recruit your mom but needs your help.' Total garbage, but I'm hoping it'll soothe him.

'I dunno.' He leans against the wall and slides to the floor. 'Maybe.' He stares at the letter for a moment, but I'm pretty sure he's not reading it. I guess he's just busy figuring things out.

I plonk myself next to him. 'You do want her to join, don't you?'

He presses his lips together.

'It's The Time of The End, Jos. Michael will lead us to the light. She must come or else—'

'Look, I know that's what you believe. And I don't blame you. You've been brainwashed since birth. Edenville, this crazy mixed-up world, is all you've ever known. But it's not true. Not one word of it.'

I keep quiet, as I've been taught to do when doubts are raised. Doubts are the Devil's attempts to deceive. To doubt is to lose your faith. And if you lose your faith, you go to Hell. Jos is conflicted. But I'm sure if he thinks real hard he'll work it out, however difficult it might be.

'Do you miss her?'

Jos shrugs. 'Not really.'

As answers go, it's not very convincing, but he's angry so ... 'I bet she misses you.'

'I doubt it. She's too busy strutting her stuff with the Greenham Common women. But it could just as easily be gay rights, rape victims, or Miss World. You name it, she's either marched for it, or against it.'

Apart from rape, I've no idea what he's talking about. But I'm interested to hear his mother might share Atticus Finch's views and want to ask if all the Otherworldlies do, but I figure now is not the time. So I stare at the shrunken human skull perched on the table, wondering who it belongs to, horrified it's here, curious as to why Jos isn't frightened by it, and wait for him to tell me that he's going to ask Michael if he can go meet his parents. He hasn't admitted it, but I know he wants to. But one sideways glance at his long face, and his foot, tap-tap-tapping against the floor, I see the truth has finally come home to roost. If his father *is* a Virtue, he'll never in a million years allow Jos to leave Edenville.

'What is all this stuff?' I ask.

'That's an opium pipe.' He points to a wooden tube with a tiny bowl at one end. 'The thing by the machete, that large knife, is a blowgun used to shoot poisoned darts, and the stuffed fish with the teeth is a piranha. And in those bottles, amongst other things, are mushrooms, cannabis, and a whole load of other plants Raphael prepares for Michael to eat, smoke, and drink.'

'You think?' I ask, struggling to keep up.

'It's voodoo. Raphael's a witch doctor. He probably drinks blood and sacrifices children. But I'll bet he doesn't believe in God.'

None of it sounds good, but to not believe in God is unimaginable. I let out a long, low whistle. 'Do you think Michael knows what he's up to?'

'Hiya, Raphael,' a woman calls from inside the hallway. 'I did knock, but the front door was open. You gotta minute?'

Keziah, I think, holding back a cry. I'd recognise her witch voice anywhere.

Jos leaps up, hauls me to my feet, and drags me behind the partially closed door. Trembling, I press my back against the wall. As hiding places go, it's a bit shit, but really, what's the alternative?

The door flings open, almost hitting us but not quite. I hold my breath and pray she doesn't think to look behind it.

'Raphael? You in here?'

I close my eyes and will her to leave.

'Curious,' she mutters, pulling the door to. 'I could have sworn I heard voices.'

Neither of us move a muscle until we hear the front door click shut. Exhaling loudly, I double over.

'That was close,' Jos says.

'Too close.'

'Best get out of here. C'mon.'

I follow Jos into the lobby, drumming my fist against my thigh while he peeks outside. He gives me the thumbs-up, and I scamper after him, my tom-tom heart propelling me across the grass, never once looking back.

'Go okay?' Hashmal asks.

'Er ... yeah. Great.'

He eyes me curiously, like I've got two heads or something. 'You sure about that?'

Frowning, I bite my lip.

He laughs. 'If you could see your face.'

'Leave the poor kid alone,' Naneel says, opening the door.

I turn to thank him but over his shoulder I notice Keziah marching towards us. Did she see us leaving Raphael's quarters? I wonder, as I dash inside, Jos hard on my heels.

I'm woken in the middle of the night by shouting. It only takes a second for me to realise it's coming from Jos' room. I throw off the sheet and rush outside before I've even had time to think but hop straight back because Jos' door has flown open, and Michael, naked to the waist, his wings neatly folded on his back, staggers into the corridor.

They *are* real, I think, and lean against my bedroom wall to catch my breath.

'Get lost,' hollers Jos. 'Or else.'

Oh my. This ain't good. No one threatens Michael. No one.

'I said go! Or I'll call the guards.'

I squeeze my eyes shut, wishing it to be over, just as Jos shuts up. And now Michael speaks, in a tone so low I can't hear what he's saying, but I guess he's doing his best to calm Jos down. Jos was real cut up about the letters. Perhaps that's what this is about.

Curiosity gets the better of me. I steal another peep. Michael is standing in front of stone Jesus, his hands clasped in prayer. His hair is wild, his face milky-white, and his eyes overly bright. He looks diminished, forlorn, nothing like the Divine Protector.

All of a sudden, Jos springs into view and jabs his fist into Michael's chest. 'Get the hell away from me.'

Letting out a puff of air, Michael holds his ground. 'Gabriel, I'm sorry.'

'Stop calling me that!'

'It was a misunderstanding. I thought—'

'And you have the nerve to call yourself The Protector. You should be ashamed of yourself, you ... you piece of shit.'

I yelp but quickly cover my mouth.

Michael raises his hands. 'Gabriel, please. Lower your voice.'

'Or what, someone might hear about your dirty little secret?'

'No, that's not what I mean. You're tired. Overwrought. You need to calm down.' Michael steps towards him, arms outstretched. But Jos shoves him roughly away. Eyes glistening, Michael stumbles backwards. 'But I've given you everything.'

'Stay away from me, you filthy pervert.' With an almighty crash, Jos slams the door in his face.

Michael lingers, pacing back and forth, clearly stuck for ideas. All the while, stone Jesus stares right through him, looking as though he might, at any moment, come to life and strike him dead.

The sound of hurried footsteps has me slinking back into my room. The last thing I see before I close the door is Raphael, haring down the corridor followed by two goggle-eyed Dominion guards.

CHAPTER TWENTY-FIVE

Donna squeezes her eyes shut. If she wasn't so dizzy, she'd run away. Away from this diner, away from California, away from him. He's a pathological liar. And she ... she is a dim-witted simpleton. She hadn't had a clue. For the nine years she'd lived with Rupert, she'd loved him unconditionally. And yet he had deceived her, absolutely. How could he have lived with himself, with her, knowing he'd left a wife and child to fend for themselves?

Or had he lived a double life?

A sudden coldness hits her core. Shivering, she wraps her arms around her body.

'I shouldn't have abandoned Ingrid the way I did. And maybe I wouldn't have if she'd told me she was pregnant. But she didn't, so how could I possibly have known?'

Donna opens her eyes and stares at him incredulously. Did he honestly expect her to answer that?

'I didn't find out until Jos was six months. Ingrid and I had been divorced six years by then, but not once during the proceedings did she mention a child. I probably wouldn't have found out at all if Ingrid hadn't died. She was only thirty-two. Cervical cancer, apparently. I'd no idea she was ill. Her friend, Vonnie, got in touch and filled me in. She was furious. Insisted I step up to the mark now Ellie was an orphan. Threatened to tell you if I didn't.'

Ingrid. Vonnie. Ellie. Donna clasps her head. All these people, all these names.

'She was eight years old and alone. No family other than me.'

She thinks she might scream, or slap him, or both. She would if they were on their own. 'So, you left us. You left your family ... your other family... to go and look after *her*. A child you didn't know you had.'

'She needed me.'

'*We* needed you.'

'No, you didn't, Donna. You hadn't needed me for a long, long time.'

A flush of pure hatred runs through her. 'Don't you dare turn this back on me. None of this is my fault.'

'I didn't say it was. I'm just telling you how I felt.'

She slams the table with both hands. 'No, Rupert. You don't get to do that.' The diners gape at them, but Donna is way past caring. 'You told us nothing. Not one word. I was frantic with worry, terrified you were dead. And now here you are, spilling your guts like you expect me to understand. To feel sorry for you. Because I don't. And to come out with it now, while Jos is being held captive by a religious maniac. Jesus, Rupert, what the hell is wrong with you?'

'I'm telling you now because it was Ellie who brought Jos here.'

This is too much, she thinks, clutching fistfuls of her

hair. 'Oh, for Christ's sake. It was Naomi who brought Jos here.'

Frowning, Rupert takes a deep breath. 'Ellie is Naomi.'

Donna sprints into the road in front of a car she hasn't seen. The driver swerves, missing her by inches, blares his horn, and shakes his fist. Donna barely registers. She is dislocated from reality, as if some invisible force is propelling her. Away from the restaurant. Away from Rupert. Away from his confession. But try as she might to outrun it, his confession keeps pace. It's a part of her now, like a facial scar or a crooked limb. And all the time she runs, his words bond together into the grotesque and twisted truth.

Naomi is Ellie.

Ellie is Jos' half-sister.

Naomi is Jos' girlfriend.

Therefore, Jos is sleeping with his sister.

A jolt runs through her, knocking her off balance. She zig-zags forward, stumbling as she fights to remain upright. What cruel trick is this woman, her husband's daughter, his actual, biological daughter, playing on her son? Does she have no morals whatsoever? She must know Jos is her half-brother. She'd hit on him and recruited him into the cult to get back at her father. Hadn't she? The same father who walked out on his son when he was one, to devote his life to looking after her, the daughter he didn't know he had. But oh no, that wasn't enough.

Unless ... unless Rupert hasn't told her about Jos. About us. God, it's so messed up. How will Jos react when he finds out? He's been suffering so much with depression, struggling to find his place in the world. Will this be the final straw that pushes him over the edge?

Hit by a wave of nausea, Donna stops running and dry-heaves into the gutter.

A car draws up beside her, and the driver winds down the window. 'Hi there. You okay?'

Donna shakes her head, wipes her mouth, and lurches onwards. She hasn't the time for this. She needs to speak to Jos. She has to explain what's happened, gently, before he finds out. He won't be able to deal with this alone.

'You take care now,' the woman calls out as she drives away.

Finding out he has a half-sister will be tough enough for him to handle, but to discover he's been sleeping with her will crush him. She has to get inside Edenville. She must speak to her son. Before–it's–too–late.

The pavement she's pounding blurs in front of her eyes. She stops running and bends over. She thinks she's about to collapse. That won't do. That won't do at all. She hauls herself upright, gulping air. Seeing a sign for Bert's Bar, she staggers inside and flops into a booth.

A waitress wanders over. 'Hello again. What can I get you today?'

'Whisky.'

'On the rocks?'

'Yeah, and make it a double.'

She rests her elbows on the table, laces her hands behind her head, and shuts her eyes. The pain she'd endured when Rupert had left her had almost destroyed her, but this – finding out he had another family, the implications – this is brutal.

'Wow, if it isn't my favourite militant! Or do I mean activist? I've never been totally sure of the difference.'

Bloody hell. Of all the bars she could have chosen in this godforsaken town, she had to walk into Steve's.

'Mind if I join you? Looks like you could use a friend.' The plastic squeaks as he sits down opposite. He reaches out and touches her arm. She bristles, and immediately he retracts his hand. 'Hey, I'm only trying to help. We'll get him out, don't you worry about that. Thought I might hire a plane and parachute in. Failing that, I could climb over the wall dressed as the Easter Bunny. I mean, what's the worst that could happen?'

She groans and covers her face with her hands.

'Gee. You didn't strike me as the type of person to give up. Thought you were made of sterner stuff. No, scratch that. I know you are. Want to tell me what's going on? I can be a pretty good listener, given half a chance.'

'You wouldn't believe it if I did,' she mumbles.

He leans across and gently prises her hands from her face. 'Try me.'

A sob rises in her throat. She tries to stifle it. Next thing she knows, tears are streaming down her cheeks.

'That bad, huh?'

'My husband had another wife. Her name was Ingrid. I didn't know about her. I ... I don't think she knew about me either. And then she died. They had a daughter, and this same daughter convinced my son to join the cult.'

'This is some tale,' says Steve, wiping away her tears. 'Honey, I think you're gonna have to start at the beginning.'

Stronger for having finally managed to get some food inside her – a ham sandwich Steve ordered and which she'd eaten in tiny mouthfuls – and lighter for having opened up, Donna nevertheless feels awkward. She's spilled her heart out to a virtual stranger: everything about her marriage to Rupert, from their passion for nuclear disarmament, their shared love of jazz, to the nine years they'd lived happily together, three years in sin, and six as husband and wife. The fifteen years of single motherhood that followed, her struggle to put food on the table, and the devastating revelation Rupert had lived a double life, which he'd thrust upon her moments earlier. The daughter she didn't know he had and who, for some incomprehensible reason, had seduced her son and lured him here. Even Jos' attempted suicide, something she hasn't told a soul. What must Steve think of her now, this sad little Englishwoman, who'd lived in ignorance for years? A flush creeping across her cheeks, she slides down in her seat.

'I'll bet Naomi is a Virtue,' Steve says suddenly.

Donna peers at him through one half-opened eye.

'A recruiter. Thomas called them Virtues. It would explain how she happened to be out and about in Blythe, and why she went after your son and brought him here. It may also be she's our way in.'

The last thing Donna wants to do is talk to Naomi. But Steve's suggestion makes perfect sense. With Sheriff Rivera's sympathies lying with the cult, she may be their only option.

'What say I drop you at the gates then go find her?'

She thinks about this for a minute. 'But where will you look?'

Steve raises his eyebrows.

'Oh right.' Her heart sinks. 'Rupert.'

It's mid-afternoon by the time Donna and Steve pull up outside Edenville's gates.

'Well, I'll be damned,' Steve says, kicking open the door. 'Seems we got company.'

Donna leans forward and peers through the windscreen. Sure enough, a dozen or so people she hasn't seen before have congregated around Todd and the other journalists.

'And not just any ol' body. If I'm not mistaken, the lady in the big straw hat is Dolores Scott. My, my, things are lookin' up.'

'Dolores Scott?'

'Yeah. The one and only.'

'I'm sorry, I—'

'Leech's squeeze Zosia's mother. The famous author. C'mon. Let's go introduce ourselves.'

Donna hangs back as Steve bounds over. Clearly a little starstruck, he greets Dolores Scott with a reverential bow and shakes her warmly by the hand. She may be a famous author, but Donna has no desire to meet her. She's in no mood for small talk. Instead of twiddling her thumbs outside a potentially dangerous cult, chatting to prize-winning novelists, she wants to march inside, find her son, and take him home. She shouldn't be here. She should be in Brighton helping Chrissie prepare for the birth of her first child and looking forward to becoming a grandmother. But she can't leave until she's talked to Jos. He was so angry with her when they last spoke, had left England without saying goodbye. Chances are she's the last person he'll want to see. All she can do is hope he'll understand her reasons for coming. If he does, she'll tell him about the murder, the danger he's in, and try to persuade him to leave. She can tackle the problem of his relationship with Naomi another time.

Ah, but what if he wants to remain in Edenville? Aren't people like Jos, who are damaged in some way, more likely to seek refuge in a cult? His two best friends let him down, so throwing in his lot with a total stranger sort of makes sense. She may think he isn't the type to succumb to brain-washing, but it's not impossible. These charismatic leaders wield extraordinary power over their followers. Leech may have already indoctrinated Jos, and if Jos is staying here of his own free will, if he's happier now, then she's just wasting her time.

She shakes her head. What a ridiculous notion. Of course she isn't wasting her time. Jos is her son. She needs to know he's all right, needs to warn him about the shooting. If he still refuses to leave, maybe the news he's about to be an uncle will sway him. And if all that fails, then she'll have no option but to deal with it. It'll be tough, but she'll find a way. If only Rupert hadn't lobbed his damn grenade into the mix. Losing Jos to a cult is bad enough. She can't deal with the other stuff. She feels as if she's deconstructing, piece by piece.

A lump catches in her throat. Do not break down, Donna. You are not that person. Forget about Ingrid and Naomi, forget about Rupert. Trust your intuition. This cult is dangerous. You witnessed a murder, for heaven's sake. If Jos is a prisoner, chances are he'll be delighted to see you. Do not give up because the going got a bit tough. That's not who you are.

She glances over at Dolores Scott, engrossed in conversation with Steve and Todd. She hasn't seen her daughter for sixteen years. How do you deal with something like that? Judging by her well-put-together appearance – neat bob, white shirt, smart beige trousers – it seems like she's coping pretty well. Perhaps it gets easier with time. Her life eventually had after Rupert walked out.

Oh God. Why do all my thoughts keep returning to

him? The creep isn't worth it. I should talk to Dolores. It may help. Steeling herself, she wanders over.

'You okay?' Steve asks.

She shrugs.

Dolores Scott holds out her hand. 'Lola Scott, pleased to meet you.'

Donna shakes it, noticing how cool and pale the woman's skin is. Some feat in the searing heat. 'Donna Prince.'

'I'm sorry about your son.'

'It's hardly your fault.'

She adjusts her large straw hat. 'Logically, no, it isn't, but I can't help feeling responsible in some way,'

Donna rolls her eyes. Is now really the time to pick over the bones?

'I didn't like Terry – oh yes, Cam found out his real name,' Lola says, when Steve raises an eyebrow, 'from the off. I didn't trust him. And as for the nonsense he spouted, I didn't think Zosia would fall for it. She's an intelligent girl, a law graduate with a bright future, or so I thought. You see, she gave it all up when she met him.'

'So I heard,' says Donna.

'She was thinking with her heart, of course,' Lola continues, in the manner of someone who's had many years to gain a perspective on the subject. 'And as I thought the relationship wouldn't last more than a couple of years, I didn't put my foot down as I should have when she told me about this utopia they were planning to build.' She sniffs and tucks a loose strand of steel-grey hair behind her ear. 'It's a contradiction, of course. Where there are people, there will always be conflict.'

Steve nods. 'And hierarchies.'

'Well, quite. Anyway, to live is to learn from your

mistakes. I assumed Zosia would figure it out for herself within a few months. But she didn't. And I blame myself for not doing more to dissuade her because he would never have succeeded without her support. And I'm talking financial, not emotional. The man's a—'

'Leech!' interjects Steve.

Lola smiles wryly. 'The perfect patronym.'

Donna folds her arms. She hadn't had the chance to talk Jos out of leaving with Naomi, but if she had, she would have at least tried. Dolores Scott is a writer. She doesn't live in the real world. Even so, there is no way Donna can lay the blame for what is happening in Edenville at her door. It would be like saying she's to blame for Rupert's lying to her because she fell in love with him. But she is intrigued how Lola has managed to carry on with her life. 'Did you try and get in touch with Zosia when she didn't come back?'

'Sure, we did. By then the group had left so Cam hired a private investigator. He tracked the group down, and we flew straight here. But we couldn't get past the gate. It was guarded, although they weren't armed back then or clad head to foot in black. The sheriff wasn't interested either. Kept insisting it was a peaceful community where people came to escape the rigours of everyday life. In fact, he became rather wistful when he talked about it, as though he fancied joining them. He pointed out Zosia knew where we were if she needed us, and the best way to get in touch with her was to write. We sent hundreds of letters but didn't receive a single reply. I doubt they ever got to Zosia. Cult leaders are sustained by the absolute devotion of their followers. Relations can be a right pain in the ass, so isolating their followers is key to their survival. In the end, we backed off and tried to get on with our lives. But Steve's piece in the *Chronicle* put a whole different slant on things.'

Steve clicks his fingers. 'I'll bet Michael has something on the sheriff.'

Lola nods. 'It would explain his intransigence.'

'My guess is he's bunging him cash.'

The rumble of traffic on the deserted highway diverts their attention. Two cars are hurtling towards them, one of which is the sheriff's. The first car screeches to a halt and a tall, robust man in his late sixties gets out and strides towards them.

'Cam,' Lola says. 'Looks like he's hopping mad.'

Steve rubs his hands together. 'Excellent. Here's hoping he's knocked some sense into Hank's thick skull.'

'Here's hoping he doesn't give himself a stroke,' Lola mutters as a third car wends its way down the track.

Rupert. What's he doing here? Donna wonders angrily. But then she notices the blonde in the seat beside him. Oh God, Naomi.

Steve, Lola, and Cameron are locked in a heated discussion with the sheriff by the time Rupert gets out of the car. Donna glances around in sheer panic, but there is nowhere to hide. It's bad enough that she's had to confront a past she knew nothing about, but to have her private life dissected in public with relative strangers in the middle of nowhere doesn't bear thinking about. Mumbling an apology, she reluctantly slips away from the group.

Rupert hurries towards her. 'I'm sorry, Donna. I'm sure I'm the last person you want to see, but I thought Ellie ... I mean, Naomi ... might be useful. And ... well, basically, I couldn't think what else to do.'

She frowns, irritated that her unravelling mind has

rendered her incapable of delivering a suitably acerbic riposte.

'My thinking was that she could get us past the guards.' He tugs on his earlobe until it's stretched to twice its original length.

Great minds, thinks Donna ruefully. Except Rupert's mind isn't great. It is dark, duplicitous, and depraved. She grits her teeth and glares at the attractive young woman leaning nonchalantly against his car. Catching Donna's eye, she smirks as if delighted by the chaos she's caused. Is this all just a twisted game to her? A way of getting back at her dad? At Donna? But for what exactly? She wishes she could march over, grab the smug bitch by the hair, and shake the living daylights out of her. Instead, she turns to Rupert. 'Great idea. Let's go.'

'Ah, well, turns out it's not that simple.'

She narrows her eyes. 'Of course it is. She asks the guards and—'

'She's left.'

'I'm sorry?'

'She had enough. Things were getting weird, apparently. So, she left, ostensibly on a mission, before they sealed the gates. I only found this out on the way over, otherwise I wouldn't have brought her here.'

The last of Donna's patience deserts her. She flies at Rupert, pummelling his chest with her fists. 'This is all your fault. None of this would have happened if you'd been honest with me from the start.'

'I know and I'm sorry. I should have told you I was married. I should have told you why I left but I'd never have guessed Ellie was capable of something like this.'

'But that's your trouble, isn't it? You don't think.'

'Everything okay?' Steve asks, hurrying over.

'Stay out of this, mate.'

'Ugh!' Donna stamps her foot. 'Steve is not your mate. And your scheming cow of a daughter is not going to get away with this.' Arms flailing, she addresses Steve. 'Naomi has washed her hands of the cult and can't get us in.'

'Really? Well, we'll see about that.' Without waiting for a response, Steve strides over to Naomi. Whatever he says wipes the smile clean off her face.

That's more like it, thinks Donna and, turning her back on Rupert, makes her way over to them.

'I think you'll want to hear this,' Dolores Scott says, catching up with her.

Something about her manner halts Donna in her tracks. 'Go on.'

'Cam persuaded the sheriff to let him speak to Thomas. Seems Thomas was in a relationship with Michael. But Michael switched his affections to another, younger man. Homosexuality in the cult is considered a crime, apparently, so when some guy called Raphael got wind of it, Thomas was petrified. He ran away because he feared for his life.'

'Jesus. Thomas told him all this?'

'Trust me, when it comes to extracting information, Cam is top of the class. Anyway, he asked him how young his replacement is, because turns out Thomas is only seventeen. He reckoned he's at least a year younger. The sheriff will have to arrest Michael now.' She shakes her head. 'God only knows how my daughter fits into all this.'

Or my son, thinks Donna. Alarm bells ringing, she hurries over to Steve.

CHAPTER
TWENTY-SIX

I'm hugging my knees, trying not to panic. It won't help. If I'm gonna work out what to do I need to stay calm. Jos is crying. I can hear him through the wall. But that's all. No Raphael, hollering orders. No stomping guards. No Michael. Just the sound of Jos weeping.

I slip off the bed, rush to the door, and dither. I'm scared to go out there. But if I don't, what then? Lord, it's one helluva choice.

I cross myself and pop my head out. I look left. I look right, straining my eyes in the darkness until I'm certain the coast is clear. Weird, considering the shenanigans, but it is. I creep up to Jos' door and knock, real quiet in case someone is lurking. Trouble is, Jos doesn't hear. Or if he does, he's decided he's not gonna answer. I try the handle. But the door doesn't budge. I try again and shove. Nothing. Our rooms don't have keys, so it can't be locked.

'Jos,' I whisper. 'It's me, Lola.' I hear a sniff and raise my voice, ever such a little. 'It's no good ignoring me. I know you're there. So, are you gonna let me in or what?'

'Go away. Leave me alone.'

I'm sweating buckets but I won't give up. 'I'm not going anywhere. Least not until you tell me what's happened?'

Another sniff.

I shoulder the door, hard. It shifts an inch. Something must be wedged against it. 'Please, Jos. You're scaring me.'

'I said, go away.'

Oh heavens. He can't mean that. 'No, Jos. I won't.' I hop from foot to foot and peer into the darkness, expecting to see Raphael and his guards charging towards me but, apart from the cold stares of the statues, there's not a soul watching me. It's deathly quiet, too. Why isn't Raphael here? He should be reading Jos the riot act. And Michael. Where is he? I think about checking his room, but a big, red warning sign is flashing in my mind. Doubt, too, is bothering me with some pretty challenging questions. Why would the great warrior, the Leader of Heaven's armies, beg and snivel and allow Jos to scream at him like that?

I shudder. This town, this pint-sized world of Edenville, is supposed to be God's earthly paradise but, the way things are going, it's becoming less like the Eden it's supposed to be and more like a hellish purgatory. There's no suffering in Heaven. Nobody fights. Nobody is arrested. Peace and harmony are king and queen. Evil is taboo. At least that's what I've been taught. Since I moved to Ascension House, though, and started reading the storybooks, I've got to thinking more and more about the Otherworldies and what sets them apart from us. The Principalities teach that we are blessed and the Otherworldlies are damned. But it seems there are good people out there, as well as bad. Some of these good people are bad sometimes, just as the bad people are sometimes good. Wouldn't it be better, say, to be like Atticus Finch, and try to figure out what's causing the badness? Be sympathetic to their ideas and behaviour, not merciless. If you cut to the nitty-gritty, what we're doing here, setting ourselves apart from the Otherworldlies and peering down our noses, makes us no better than them anyway.

But if that's true, where does that leave Michael, God's angel, put on this earth to save all of us from evil?

Jeez, I can't figure the answer to anything anymore.

I fall to my knees and wrap my arms around Jesus' ankles, wishing he was real and not a cold lump of stone. I badly need someone to talk to. If not Jos, then David, perhaps. He'd know what to do. Quite the mystery, but I haven't seen him since the night Daniel was shot and there's no way I can go searching for him now.

'Please, Jos,' I say, my voice cracking. 'Please talk to me. I'm real scared.'

The sound of something heavy scraping over wood is followed by a squeak. I raise my head and, through the tiny slit, see a red-rimmed, puffy eye.

I spring to my feet. 'Can I come in?'

The eye blinks and disappears, and the door opens a fraction more. I slip through the gap, lickety-split. Just as well, because Jos slams it shut, rams the chest of drawers against it, limps to his bed, and sits there, staring blindly at his knees.

Chilly with sweat, I sidle up to him and slip a hand in his. I expect him to push me away, but he doesn't, so we stay like that, hand in hand, not speaking, for quite some time.

'I have to go into Edenville and find my dad,' he says eventually.

And I see him then for what he is, a little kid lost, like me. I nod. If I remind him we're not allowed out of Ascension House, it'll only add to his woes.

He sniffs. 'Did you know?'

'Know what?'

He releases a long sigh, as though the effort of having to explain physically hurts. 'That your father is a pervert.'

I wince and shake my head.

'You don't know what a pervert is, though, do you, Lola?'

'No,' I whisper. 'I don't.'

'It means he's immoral. Ironic, don't you think? This is no lie, Lola. He tried to force me to have sex with him.'

Holy Mary. That's the worst, most evil thing I've heard. It can't be true. Why would Michael do that?

A tear rolls down Jos' cheek. It clings to his chin for a moment before dropping on his leg. 'He's gay, your father. Nothing wrong with that. Plenty of my Brighton mates prefer men. Only, Michael likes them young.' He swipes his nose with the back of his hand. 'Which makes him a paedo, too. He tried to force himself on me, and that's not right. I ... I thought he was going to rape me. I was shit-scared. What if I couldn't fend him off? He might have AIDS.'

My heart pummels my ribs, winding me. I don't understand everything Jos is saying but I get the gist.

'Oh God, it was awful. Just thinking about it makes me want to throw up.' Shuddering, he clasps his head. 'Why me? Jesus, I am so sick of bullies.'

I put my arm around him and make shushing noises, although my eyes are watering. The man Jos is describing sounds real bad.

'I'm pretty much a prisoner in his house,' he says through sobs. 'There was no way I could get away from him. Not unless I made a dash for it. But if I did he'd probably have me shot. That's why I yelled at him. He backed off and told me he loved me. No, that he was *in* love with me.

That he could make me the happiest boy on earth. He could have anyone, he said, and yet he chose me. Didn't I know how lucky I was? Oh God.'

I crinkle my nose and tug at my nightdress. My father, a lover of men. It can't be true.

Jos lowers his hands. 'He tried to hug me then, so I punched him as hard as I could and called him all the names under the sun.' His voice steady now, he leaps to his feet and paces the room. 'But still he tried to convince me it was what I wanted, too. Thing is, I don't know why I was surprised. I mean, all the signs were there. The endless ruffling of my hair, the hugs, the way he was always touching me, the fact he hung on my every word, that he cared. I kept thinking this is how it must feel to have a dad. And it felt so good, and we got on so well, I began to wonder why I was bothering to try and find my real dad, who knew where I lived but who hadn't bothered to get in touch. How stupid could I be? No wonder Michael told everyone God wouldn't allow him to marry. If he did, he'd have to have sex with a woman. And that'd be torture for him.'

I draw my knees to my chest and wrap my arms around them. If what Jos is saying is true, where does that leave me?

He stops pacing and looks at me. 'Who do you think knows?'

I shake my head.

'Apart from the poor sods he's buggered, I mean. Because I'm certain I'm not his only victim.' He flops down next to me. 'Maybe they're not all victims. Jeez, I hadn't thought of that.'

I don't want to believe Jos, but it's got me thinking about the two times I bumped into David, prowling the corridor. Was it him I'd seen in Michael's room, naked, having sex, and not a blonde woman after all? No. The Principalities preach it's wrong to love someone of the same sex, that God will punish us if we do. David is a good boy. He wouldn't do a thing like that. Would he? Hell. Does Michael honestly think God won't find out? Or does he think he's above God's law? Maybe he is. Maybe the same doesn't apply to angels. Maybe it's okay for them to be – what did Jos call him? – gay? But it doesn't alter the fact Michael has been lying.

'And those angel wings you thought you saw. They're a tattoo.'

I tilt my head.

'Body art made by injecting ink into the skin. With a needle.'

'Body art?' My head is spinning. I can't keep up. Needles into the skin. Is Jos saying Michael's wings are just a painting? Why would anybody put themselves through something like that? Wouldn't it hurt? Surely, Jos has got it wrong. Michael is an Archangel. Archangels have wings. Okay, so his aren't white all the time, but that's only when he folds them away. Isn't it?

'I'm sorry, Lola.' Jos draws me to him and leans his head against mine. 'This must be a massive shock. There's so much you don't know about the real world. But that's the whole point of this place, isn't it? No one knows the truth about anything here. How could they? Edenville is a fictional world sprung from Michael's warped imagination.'

We must have drifted off to sleep, because I wake up with Jos' warm body pressed against mine. It's dark and quiet, but I'm pretty sure it's morning. I lie as still as possible, comforted by the steady beat of his heart. If only it could be like this always. Not hidden away here but in our own little house in Edenville. Just Jos and me. We'd wake with the sun on our faces. We'd be happier. We'd be free. But Michael would never allow it.

Michael. My father.

The Divine Protector. Prince of God.

Lover of men.

Lover of Jos.

Or has Jos got the wrong end of the stick? Michael must have had sex with at least one woman. I am living proof.

I close my eyes and cast my mind back to the moment Michael first encountered Jos. The way he'd looked at him, talked to him like he was a gift from God. He'd called us a happy little family. I'd been jealous of Jos. Michael seemed far more interested in him. He *was* more interested, but for entirely different reasons. Michael had wanted to have sex with Jos right from the start, so he'd taken Jos under his wing. His angel wings, which weren't real wings at all, but an ink drawing.

But what about David? Where does he fit in? And the strange tea? The drugs? Raphael?

Only one way to find out.

Careful not to wake Jos, I eel out from under his arm and tiptoe across the floor. I shift the chest, moving it real quiet, slip through the crack, and make a beeline for Michael's room. The door unlocked, I march right in. Truth is, I'm not scared anymore. The way I see it, I hold all the cards. I'm not the one who's broken the rules.

The bedroom empty, I march into the bathroom, but he's not there either. It's spotlessly clean and tidy, like everywhere else in Michael's wing, apart from a small blue jar on the sink, its top unscrewed. I glance at the grey-brown powder and read the label – *Semen of the Sun* – and cross myself. Catching sight of my reflection in the mirror, I pick up Michael's hairbrush and run it through my mussed-up hair. 'You can do this, Lola,' I say. Nodding, I fling down the brush, race out of the room, and head off to the kitchen. Kishi is there chopping fish.

'*Konichiwa*, Kishi-*san*.'

He jumps, spins round, and places his hand on his heart. 'Oh-oh-oh!'

'I'm sorry, Kishi. I didn't mean to startle you.'

Muttering, he turns his back and continues chopping. I watch him for a moment and try to imagine how tough it must be for him, not being able to communicate, especially since things started going so wrong.

'Bye, Kishi.'

He shakes his head. '*Ki wo tsukete*.'

I grit my teeth and set off down the corridor to Michael's study. I try the handle but, of course, it's locked. I pound the door with my fist. When no one answers, I call out his name, my voice not far off a shout.

Nothing.

I rush down the corridor and out the front door.

'Morning, Miss Sophia,' chorus Hashmal and Naneel.

'It's Lois,' I snap, squinting in the early morning sun. The quadrangle is deserted. I set off past the Almond and Olive Trees, through the gate into the outer courtyard where I almost collide with Hepzibah, hurrying in the opposite direction. Somehow, she doesn't drop the huge pile of towels she's carrying.

'Have you seen Michael?' I ask before she has time to scold me.

'No, dearie. Not this morning.'

A group of Powers, idling beside the far wall, glance over in our direction. I clench my fists. 'Have you?'

'Lois! You know you mustn't talk to them.'

One of the Powers raises an eyebrow. 'Have we what?'

'Seen Michael.'

Hepzibah's hand flies to her forehead.

'Not yet, Sophia.' He smirks, and the other Powers laugh.

A commotion outside catches my attention. The gates are closed as usual and, with them being colossal and made of the thickest wood, I can't see what's going on. I have a sudden urge to *be* Sophia and command the Powers to open them. If I could get into Edenville and find Naomi, she might be able to help us find Jos' father.

'The Guardians are gathering,' Hepzibah says. 'Best get back to your quarters, dearie.'

'The Great Battle?'

Hepzibah shakes her head.

The chatty Power saunters over. 'They're not happy, Sophia.'

I can't see his face but I recognise his voice. Abraham, Potter Ishmael's son. Nineteen years old, a brute and a bully. Weird, but knowing who he once was spurs me on. 'Lois. My name is Lois.'

'I give up,' says Hepzibah and, lowering her eyes, walks away.

Abraham grins. 'Right. The Divine Protector's bastard.'

The other Powers laugh, one of them whistles, a couple jeer.

I feel my cheeks redden but I don't budge. 'Why aren't the Guardians happy?'

Abraham's peepers creep and crawl their way over my body, and I squirm. I can't help myself.

'Because of the rumours.'

'What rumours?'

'That Satan is among us.' He leans forward, his flinty eyes inches from my face. Unblinking, menacing. 'But you'd know all about that, wouldn't you?'

Sweat pricks my armpits. 'No, why would I?'

But he just clicks his tongue and strolls back to the group.

Trembling, I stumble towards the inner courtyard, aware of every single one of those Powers' eyes on my back.

Beyond the walls, someone shouts. Quickly, several others join in. Drums, too. One of the Powers barks an order. I glance over my shoulder. The gates swing open, and the Powers storm out, their boots hammering the paving stones. I see the mob gathered outside, their fiery faces and the boards they're brandishing with red slogans scrawled across them. I catch a glimpse of Elijah's mean mug. Herdsman Jethro and Dairyman Paul. Baker Amos. Cobbler Absalom.

Run, I tell myself. Now's your chance.

Too late.

The gates close with a loud clang. The shouting builds to an angry pitch. A gun blasts. I jump and stagger backwards. Someone screams. Another shot is fired, and another and another. My muscles twitch. My mouth goes dry.

And then the shrieking starts.

I clasp myself tight. The Battle *has* begun.

But then the shrieking stops, the guns fall silent, and all I can hear is my flipped-out heart. Whimpering, I dash across the courtyard.

Naneel, standing to attention now, opens Michael's door. 'You all right, Lois?'

But I dart inside without answering. Slap bang into Raphael. I try to sidestep past him, but he has hold of my wrists. I wriggle, but I can't break free.

'What have you been up to, Lois?'

'The Great Battle ... it's ... it's happening.'

'No, it isn't. The people are upset. Go to your room. You'll be safe there.'

'But Michael told us ... And I heard the guns. The Powers ... Screaming.'

'It's nothing to worry about. Michael will talk to them. Explain—'

'*I* need to talk to him.' I yank my arm, trying to wrest myself free, but Raphael's grip is too strong. 'I need to know what's going on. Jos is distraught. I don't understand why Michael ... last night ... when it's forbidden.'

His expression darkens. 'You shouldn't have seen that.'

'He shouldn't have *done* that. Let go of me or I'm gonna scream.'

Although I'm not expecting him to, Raphael lets go. 'Your father is under a great deal of stress. The Apocalypse weighs heavy on his shoulders, and because of this, his behaviour grows increasingly erratic.'

'Is that why the people are angry? Because he's ...' I rack my brains for the word Jos had used. '...gay.'

Raphael winces almost imperceptibly. 'Your father is flawed like every man.'

'But he's not a man, is he? He's an angel.'

'Yes. Yes. But while he's on this earth amongst mankind, temptation is all around.'

I stamp my foot and flail my arms. 'But he should be above temptation. Like Jesus. And the people are saying Satan is ... Oh!' My hands fly to my mouth. Now I get it. Raphael's staff. His room. Those odd-looking bottles. The shrunken human skull. The evil weapons. I back away, my blood running cold.

'The people are saying things because they are scared. My dear child, without Michael we are doomed. You must trust me on this. Now, do as I say and go to your room. You'll be safe there.'

Trust you? No way. Too scared to move, I stand there, rigid.

Raphael sighs. 'Enough is enough. Come with me.'

'No, I won't. I'm not going anywhere with you.'

'You most certainly are.'

Next thing I know, he's hoisted me over his shoulder and is marching me out the door.

This is it, I think, as I thump his back and holler. I'm toast.

CHAPTER

TWENTY-SEVEN

Esther is woken by a sharp rap. Disorientated, she thinks it's her mother come to wake her, but as the lock slides open, the truth comes tumbling back. She's not a child at home. She's a prisoner. Michael's prisoner; locked in a clean, white room with an unexpectedly comfortable bed. She's thinking how strange her gaoler should knock, when the door swings opens and Hepzibah marches in, swiftly followed by Michael. Her breath catches. Silently cursing herself for letting herself go, she sits up and fiddles with her tangled hair.

'Thank you, Hepzibah. You can leave us now,' Michael says.

Esther has lain around for days and has barely touched her food; she knows that if she tries to stand she'll probably fall. So she swings her legs over the side of the bed and perches on the edge, staring at the floor.

The silence growing increasingly oppressive, she peeks at Michael and is surprised to see him slumped over the dressing table. She rises cautiously, shuffles over, and lays a tentative hand on his shoulder. He flinches but neither moves nor speaks. He is thinner, she notices, his bones more pronounced. Something familiar stirs within her. Something like love. Without thinking, she kisses the top of his head.

The crack of a gunshot and a piercing scream sends Esther jerking backwards. Blast after blast is followed by the rumble of drums. She looks helplessly up at the small window. What's happening? It's months until The Battle.

'What is ... did God ...?' She glances at Michael, but he hasn't moved. Instinctively, she wraps her arms around him from behind. He shudders, so she squeezes tighter and is relieved when he covers her hands with his. They are warm but trembling.

'I really believed He was talking to me,' he whispers.

For a split second she wonders who he's referring to before she realises that, of course, it's God. 'He was,' she says quietly, her mind suddenly clear of all the doubts she's been harbouring. 'He is.'

Michael shakes his head. 'I don't know.'

'Well, I do.'

'I ... I'm not hearing him anymore.'

She reflects on this for a moment. God appointed Michael the Divine Protector sixteen years ago. Since then he's acted on His every command, no matter at what cost to himself. He can't have abandoned Michael. 'It's only natural you're having doubts. It's not long until you go into battle. You must be terrified. But God will be there to guide you. And when you've triumphed, and after He has judged us all, you, Lois, and I will be together again. Hold on to that. It's what I do.'

He rises slowly and, facing her, lays his hands on her shoulders. 'Zosia. Dear Zosia.'

'Oh!' She clutches her hand to her chest. It's a name she hasn't heard in the longest time.

'You haven't a bad bone in your body. I have treated you shoddily. Will you ... can you ever forgive me?'

She peers into his yellowed, bloodshot eyes. 'I forgave you a long time ago. It was God's will you couldn't be a father. I didn't like it but I understood. But I am angry with you for taking Lois away. I miss her terribly. How is she?'

'It's an illness,' he says as if she hasn't spoken. 'It's ... it's out of my control. And you cured me of it for a while. I was deeply in love with you, Zosia. You know that, don't you?'

'Love is not an illness.'

'Raphael has tried his best.' His voice wavering, he wrings his hands. 'He ... he came to me when I sent for him, has listened to me endlessly, and tried his hardest to protect me. He would do anything and everything for me. But I have let him down as well. Temptation was all around, every which way I turned. And I ... I'm as weak as the next man.'

'Are you telling me you left me for another woman?'

He bats the air with his hand. 'No. No, that's not what I'm saying.'

'What then? I don't understand.'

Frowning, he turns to look her directly in the eye. 'I'm gay, Zosia.'

She reels back. 'What? No, it's not possible. You can't be. Me ... you ... us ... all those times ... Lois.'

'I've tried to fight it all my life, and I did for a while, thanks to you.'

Esther wipes her clammy palms on her dress and stares at Michael, open-mouthed. She's always believed that if a man loved another man it's something to be celebrated not punished. But for years Michael declared it a sin. It was forbidden, he said. By God. 'Who? Who did you leave me for?'

He sits on the bed and throws back his head. 'Yahriel.'

'Daniel?' One by one, the pieces of the past slot together. Michael leaving her, suddenly, on God's command when she was pregnant with Lola. Moving in with Daniel, his trusted friend. Her conversations with Daniel who maintained his devotion to Michael despite being passed over for another by heaping the blame on Raphael.

He slumps forward. 'And after Yahriel, Zophiel.'

'Thomas, too.' She crosses herself. Raphael must have found out. No wonder he insisted they were punished. It is the law, after all, whether she agrees with it or not. And Michael, out of guilt, must have gone along with it.

'Then Ariel,' he adds in a quiet voice.

'Ariel?' Three men, and yet she had no idea. Had there been signs? 'But why didn't you tell me?'

'How could I? It would have broken your heart.'

'So why are you telling me now?'

'Because I've fallen in love with someone else.'

She clasps her head, appalled by the ease with which he can transfer his affections. The hypocrisy of his confession. 'But I thought it wasn't allowed ... God forbade it, you said. He must be angry with—'

'Your hair,' he says suddenly. 'How long since it was cut?'

'I ...' She touches it absently. '... don't know.'

He leaps to his feet. 'Let me. Please. Like I used to.'

Her gaze clouding, she allows Michael to lead her into the bathroom. She waits, staring blindly at her reflection while he places the stool beneath the basin. He guides her onto it, lifts her hair, and she tilts back her head as if in a trance. The water is warm, and he caresses her scalp so tenderly, she is transported back to the time they were lovers, and this was one of the many small acts of kindness he used to perform. And as he squeezes the moisture from her hair and wraps it in a towel, she finds herself longing for those days again. Life was simple. They were getting to know one another. They were happy. They were in love. He'd told her often enough. She had no reason to doubt it.

So, why didn't he confide in her? She loved him with all her heart, he could have told her anything. She'd have been devastated, but she would have been free to choose the life she wanted. Would she have stayed? Or would she have taken Lola and gone back to her family, finished her degree, become a lawyer, the career she'd been working towards? She'd have got over Michael in time, perhaps fallen in love again. But he'd denied her the choice. She'd believed in him. Had stayed, obeyed and worshipped him. Suffered the stream of husbands he'd lined up for her, the separation from her daughter.

She is vaguely aware of the tug of the comb's teeth working their way through the knots in her hair. But her mind is elsewhere. She is thinking about the hours spent toiling in The Mill; the heat of The Bakery kitchen; the abuse she suffered at Elijah's hands. The loneliness. Despair. The isolation. And not once had she complained. Michael had broken her heart, and yet she'd gone along with everything he'd asked of her, believing it was God's will. Only, now he's admitting he has sinned but, instead of owning up and taking the rap, he's created a diversion. He must have known how the Guardians would react when he revealed his daughter. And if he had, and if God isn't talking to him anymore, then it must have been his decision to sanction her arrest, and nothing to do with Elijah.

Her body tensing, she listens to the *click-click-click* of the scissors and the whisper of the feathery wisps as they settle on the floor.

Michael runs his fingers through her hair. 'Your beauty restored.'

She leaps to her feet, hands balled by her sides. 'Why, Michael?'

He stares at her blankly.

'Why did you order my arrest?'

'I had to. You were in great danger. The Guardians were angry. With you. With me. With Lois. With God. I had to get them back onside. But when I found out where the Powers had taken you, I had you brought here.'

She shivers and wraps her arms around herself. The Powers had dragged her to a cave in the mountains; a cold, dark cell with weeping walls where they'd taken her watch and left her to rot. She is nothing more than Michael's dupe. His scapegoat. Has been right from the start. He's used her. He's lied to her. He's lied to his people, and more importantly, he has lied to God. Everything he's ever said, everything he has ever done is a lie.

But the important thing about lying, as any lawyer worth their salt knows, is never to offer any surplus information that might catch you out. It has taken years but, finally, Michael has slipped up. And now he is paying the price. No wonder God isn't speaking to him anymore. If, in fact, he ever has.

'I'm sorry, Zosia.'

Her bitten nails digging into her palms, she strides towards him. 'How easily that word trips off your tongue. Sorry for this, sorry for that. It's not good enough, Michael. It's time you started thinking about Lois and me. If you cared about us as much as you claim, it shouldn't be difficult.'

He recoils as if she's struck him, opens the door, and dodges behind it, shielding himself from her anger. 'What do you want? Tell me and I will fix it.'

'I want to see my daughter.'

'Fine, fine. I'll bring her to you.'

'Promise me, Michael.'

'I promise.'

'And after that I'd like to be set free.'

'Yes. Yes.' Michael shuts the door and, instantly, the lock snaps shut.

'No! Esther rushes over and hammers it with her fists. 'LET ME OUT OF HERE. LET ME OUT. LET ME OUT.'

But, of course, there's no answer. Burying her face in her hands, she slumps to the floor.

Barely five minutes have passed when the lock slides open again. Esther leaps to her feet. 'Michael?'

But it isn't Michael. It's a rangy man in his late forties, dressed in a white tunic, a string of teeth looped around his neck. 'I've brought someone to see you. I urge you to talk some sense into her. She needs to tread carefully.' With another brief nod, he backs out of the room.

Esther hardly has time to take in his words before Lola is in her arms, hugging her as if determined never to let go. Fighting back tears, her nose in her daughter's hair, Esther breathes in her familiar scent.

'I ... I ... thought Raphael was going to throw me on the fire,' Lola says in a muffled voice.

'Sweetheart, no.'

'I've missed you so much. Please don't leave me again. I promise to be good.'

'Darling Lola. God knows, given the choice, I never would have.'

'I can't believe you've been so close all this time. This was my prison once. Why didn't Michael tell me you were here?' Lola lets go and looks at her pleadingly. 'I can't go back to him. I won't. I'll stay here with you.'

A tear courses down Esther's cheek. She swipes it away. 'Oh, Lola. I'm sorry. I should've taken you away from Edenville the moment you were born.'

'Mom, please. You have to do something *now*. The Powers told me Satan is among us. I think he's disguised as Raphael. He had Daniel shot. I saw the body.'

'Daniel's dead?'

'Yes. And Michael ... he tried to rape Jos ... but Jos fought back. I was there. I have the room next door. Jos is my friend, but he's hurting, and I want to help him but I can't find Michael. I'm angry with him but I'm scared. I don't know what to do.'

It takes all of Esther's remaining strength to stay on her feet. Michael had fallen, and yet she hadn't realised how far. He'd been playing with fire for so long he probably thought he was immune to the flames. Now, for the first time since Edenville's inception, Guardians are standing up to him and saying no. And he doesn't like it. But instead of trying to placate them, or negotiate another path, he'd killed a man and tried to force himself on another. Homicide and attempted rape. If word gets out he'll be sent down for life. No wonder he's in such a state. No wonder he came to see her. Who better to turn to than the person who loves him most in the world. Loyal old Esther who, no matter how many times he stamps on her, sits up and begs for more. The same blind faith which led her to fail her only child. The child she loves above all others but whom she handed to Michael on a plate.

She clasps her daughter's shoulders with shaking hands. 'Listen to me. Raphael is not the Devil.'

'But he's got a shrunken human skull in his room. And … and strange plants in bottles. A blowpipe which shoots poison darts. He gave Michael a jar with some powder in it. Sun Semen or something. Jos says he's a witch doctor and that he's drugging Michael. I think he may have drugged me, too.'

Esther stiffens. Michael referred to Raphael as his brother, said he was a doctor and that he'd sent for him. But Daniel insisted he was a shaman and was controlling Michael. Are the two of them in this together? Their backs against the wall, there's no telling what they're capable of. She composes herself, determined to keep the fear out of her voice. 'You must be careful. Don't drink anything Raphael gives you. And keep your distance from Michael. He's not himself and he's angry.'

'How can I? I live with him.'

'Try to go along with everything he says. Promise me you will.'

Lola sighs. 'Okay.'

'Good girl.' The idea of Lola challenging her father doesn't bear thinking about. 'There's something else you need to know. There's a locked door hidden behind a living wall in a Japanese garden.'

'Michael's secret garden.'

'You know it. Good. Try and find the key. He'll have hidden it somewhere, so be careful. And then leave Ascension House, with Jos if you can. Hide in Farmer Samuel's barn and wait for me.'

Lola's eyes widen. 'But you're a prisoner. The Powers have guns. And, anyway, how will you know when I've gone?'

'Trust me, I'll know.'

There's a knock, the lock clicks, and Raphael appears.

Lola flings her arms around Esther's neck and clings to her. 'Go away. Leave us alone.'

'Could she stay a little longer?' Esther asks.

'I'm sorry. Michael is trying to find her. It won't be long until he realises what I've done.'

'He doesn't know she's with me?'

'Er ... no.' Raphael clears his throat. 'I urge you to hasten your goodbyes. I'll bring her again, if I can.'

'No.' Lola stamps her foot. 'I'm not coming. Not without Mom.'

'Please, Lola,' Esther whispers. 'It will only mean more trouble for me.'

Lola lets go and juts out her jaw. 'Fine.'

Esther cups her daughter's face in her hands 'I love you. Never forget that.' She steers her to Raphael, who nods and leads her away, locking the door behind him.

Esther staggers to the bed. Will she ever see her dear, sweet child again? If only she could rewind the clock, she'd take her away and suffer the consequences. She's spent so much time worrying about the next world, instead of living in this one, she's ignored the seeds of doubt Michael's erratic behaviour planted in her mind.

And now she is paying the price.

'May God forgive me,' she mutters as she curls into a tight little ball, 'and deliver us from evil.'

CHAPTER TWENTY-EIGHT

I strut past Hepzibah with my nose in the air. I'm mad as hell with her. I thought we were friends, but the malicious harpy has been lying to me along with everyone else. She should have told me Mom was here. But no, it's the same old story. Edenville is a town all tangled up in secrets. Why would Ascension House be any different? Still, at least the fighting has stopped. Guns, drums, and screaming people. Sweet Jesus. It's not what you expect in an earthly paradise.

I linger at the Almond Tree planted by Michael at the beginning of all creation. I can't even begin to imagine how important that makes him. Or how old. Maybe he got bored, wanted to try something new. But sex with a man? I glance at the Olive Tree. An apple tempted Eve; did an olive lead Michael into temptation?

I stare long and hard at the reptile, Raphael. His poker face is more pinched than usual, and his back is bowed. It was good of him to take me to see my mom behind Michael's back, but, then again, Satan would do a sneaky thing like that. Dear Lord, I can't help thinking I'm missing something here.

Talking of God, I wonder if He's keeping up with all the goings-on. Things are moving so fast in the wrong direction perhaps He is struggling, too. Or has Michael lied to Him as well? Is that even possible? Isn't God supposed to be all-knowing? I look up, half expecting to see fire and brimstone raining down from the heavens. But the night is calm, the sky clear, and the scattering of stars twinkling in the night sky seem to wink at me, as if it's all a great big joke.

'Are you okay?' Raphael asks.

'What do you care?'

He frowns. 'You really need to sharpen up you act.'

'What's that supposed to mean?'

'You know perfectly well.'

My shoulders slump as the fight drains out of me. 'Will Michael be forgiven for what he's done?'

'He has spent most of the day repenting so, yes, God will forgive him.'

He pats me on the shoulder in an awkward way, like he's trying to be kind but doesn't know how. Lord, but it freaks me out.

'I must take you to him. He was expecting you an hour ago. Are you ready?'

'As I'll ever be.'

'Good girl.'

I cringe. If it wasn't for Mom's advice, I'd let my feelings be known. But this is no ordinary day in Edenville. Clinging to the hope that I'll find the key to the hidden door, I follow Raphael down the corridor.

'Be careful,' Raphael says when we reach the chapel.

With those words, every single hair on my body stands to attention. I'm that scared I think about asking him to stay. But my conscience butts in with a big, bold *Don't Be Fooled* sign. Satan or not, Raphael is as slippery as a snake.

I brace myself and walk in. Michael is kneeling in front of the altar. There are dark rings around his bloodshot eyes, his face is grey, and his usually glossy hair is in desperate need of a wash. He seems smaller, too, and thinner, as if all his repenting has eaten great chunks out of him. He doesn't smell too pretty either, I notice, as he clambers to his feet and moves towards me, although not so close he can touch me. Thank you, God. Last thing I feel like doing is playing the dutiful daughter. Not after what he tried to do to Jos.

'Where have you been?' he growls.

I shift back a step. Jesus, what am I doing in here? My heart is screaming scoot, but my mind is yelling no. With no alternative, I thrust my hands in my dress' pockets and front it out. 'Looking for you.'

'Where? Raphael has taken quite some time finding you?'

'The outer courtyard. I heard shots. Drums. Screaming. I wanted to see what was happening.'

'The people are upset.'

'Why?'

He bats the air. 'Silly rumours.'

'How silly?'

'ENOUGH!'

I spring away, arms in front of my chest.

'Gabriel is upset, so I've had Kishi prepare a special meal. I meant him no harm as I'm sure you are aware.' His sickly-sweet voice is totally at odds with his ferocious scowl. 'Now, go. I shall see you both in the kitchen at seven.'

I dash out of the chapel and down the corridor with only one thing on my mind. I have to find the key. Now, before it's too late. I don't want to spend another day in this hellhole. Panting, I stop outside Michael's study and try the handle, just in case. Dammit. The key must be in there. Somehow, I'm gonna have to persuade Jos to break in.

With no time to waste, I sprint to Jos' room. Slipping past the chest, I find him huddled in the corner, still in his nightshirt, hugging his knees. 'Good news, Jos. There's a secret door in the Japanese Garden. If we find the key we can escape.'

He raises his head and eyes me doubtfully.

I kneel beside him. 'Mom told me. So it must be true.'

'You've seen her?'

'Yeah. Raphael took me. Weird, huh?'

But Jos just shakes his head and rests his chin on his knees.

'I'll bet it's hidden in Michael's study,' I say, trying to ignore my churning belly. 'Will you help me find it? I can't do it on my own. I don't know how to pick a lock. And we don't have long, because he's organised a special "sorry I messed up" dinner. I know you won't want to go, but, see, we've got to play along. Otherwise he'll lock us up like he has Mom.'

'Did you ask her about Naomi?'

I force my lips into the broadest smile I can muster. 'No, but once we've found the key, we'll look for her. See, Jos? It's the only way we can get out of Ascension House. Mom says we must hide in Farmer Samuel's barn. She'll meet us there, and then we'll escape and find Naomi and your parents. But we can't do any of it until we have the key. Please, Jos. I need you.'

Jos is rummaging through the drawers in Michael's desk while I listen at the door. It's locked, the spare key in the box on the desk so Michael won't suspect anything but, even so, my pulse is flat-out racing. Michael's having the shittiest day. It's likely he'll fancy a calming stroll around his garden, so it feels like we're waiting to be caught. And if we are, we might be isolated, like Gideon, and end up dying of starvation. Or slung out into the desert and eaten by wolves. Or beheaded, or hung from a tree by the hair. Or ... or crucified. Lord, but The Book is full of gruesome deaths. Makes me wonder if God is as good and as all-powerful as they say. Surely he'd put an end to brutal punishments if he was. And wars, too. Fighting and killing must be against his religion. And rape. Heck, I'm pretty certain he'd put his foot down about that, too. But I guess he got so mad with us humans he created, he likes to teach us a lesson from time to time.

I jump at the sound of splintering wood. 'Had to force it,' he says as he tugs open a thin drawer in the centre of the desk.

I slap my forehead. 'Jesus! That's gonna give the game away.'

'I thought you wanted me to find it.'

There's no answer to that, so I keep my mouth shut. Only now I hear footsteps. Worse still, they've stopped outside. Jos must have heard them, too, because he's slid open the door to the garden and is gesticulating wildly. The key rattles in the lock. Trembling all over, I creep across the room.

Jos shoves me outside. 'Run.'

I sprint down the path at such a pace, I trip and almost fall. I stop and steady myself and peer over my shoulder, expecting to see the Devil himself in hot pursuit. But there's no sign of him, nor Michael neither.

'Where did your mum say the door was hidden?' Jos asks, stopping at the pond to catch his breath.

'Behind the living wall,' I say between pants.

'Ta da!' Jos whips the big iron key out of his pocket and grins for the first time in forever.

'You found it.'

'Yeah, beside a gun, would you believe?'

I close my eyes and take a breath. 'But we can't leave now, not in broad daylight.'

'We might have to.'

I follow Jos around the pond, past the bridge to the bottom of the garden. I glance around in confusion. No door, just a wall. Isolation must have made Mom delusional. I scrunch up my eyes and try not to cry.

But Jos has grabbed my arm and is dragging me over. 'It's ingenious. Look! The thinnest of gaps, just wide enough to slip through.'

I clasp his hand and, together, we sidestep down the dark, narrow alley, and there, right in front of my nose, is the door. Jos rams the key in the hole. He tries, but the lock won't budge. He has another go, and another, beads of sweat breaking out on his forehead. At last, it gives. I punch the air with my fist.

'If he's followed us, we go now,' Jos says. 'If not, we wait until tonight. Okay?'

I nod and tell myself to relax, but my muscles aren't having any of it, and I'm certain I'll pass out from the strain. We wait and wait, and just as I'm beginning to think Michael can't have noticed the drawer, I'm aware of someone standing next to me. I whip around and stare straight into the whites of two eyes. I spring backwards with a yelp and step on Jos' toes.

'Lola!'

Struck dumb, I jerk my head.

'Shit!'

The eyes blink, narrow, then widen again. Smiling eyes.

'Takae?' I whisper.

The gardener nods. '*Konichiwa*, Lois-san.'

Dots dance across my vision. It's a wonder I manage to stay on my feet.

'We're playing a game, Takae,' Jos mutters. 'Hide and seek.' He puts a finger to his lips.

Takae grins. 'Secret. *Hai*!' He bows, and copying Jos' gesture, inches back down the passageway.

I throw him a brief smile and, thanking God that, unlike Kishi, Takae understands some English, shut my eyes and pray.

It's dusk when we decide to head back. My legs are lead weights, and my feet drag. Knowing we could now be free of this place, it's the last thing I want to do. I feel bad, too, for persuading Jos to stay.

After Takae left, he changed his mind. 'Michael's a pervert and a nutter, and he's got a gun. Fuck knows what he's capable of. We should go now.'

'No. We have to get through the meal. All hell will break loose if we don't and, anyway, it'll be safer to leave at night.' It's nonsense, really. We'll still have to get past the Powers. Jos is convinced one of them shot Daniel. If they see us, chances are they'll shoot us, too.

This brooding, black cloud hanging over us, we lock the gate, head back down the garden and creep into Michael's study. Without uttering a word, Jos slips the key in the broken drawer.

'I think we should hold on to it,' I say. 'If he sees the

drawer is broken he'll hide it somewhere else, and then what? Here, give it to me.'

Jos hands it over, and I drop it into my pocket. Making sure the coast is clear, we scuttle back to our rooms.

When Jos and I arrive, all spick and span for supper, it's Michael who's hovering over the hob. Kishi is nowhere to be seen. Raphael is there, too, and seems as relieved to see me as I am to see him because a brief smile flickers on his stern face as we take our usual places.

'Thank you for coming,' Michael says, picking up a tray with four small bowls on it.

It's so nuts, I want to laugh. As if we could refuse. But one look at Raphael's frown, and I know that tonight I need to mind my p's and q's. Seems we're not the only ones playing along. But why Raphael feels he must, I've no idea. Of all the inmates of Ascension House, he's the person Michael leans on most. Maybe that's why. Maybe the craziness has got too much for him as well.

Michael places the steaming liquid in front of me without speaking. Fine by me. We have Miso soup almost every day, so no need for any introductions. I don't much like it, but smelling food for the first time today, I realise I'm hungry and wolf it down in seconds flat. Michael hasn't touched his, but then he rarely eats these days. I pick up my chopsticks, wondering whether Kishi has made his delicious gyoza dumplings, or my favourite Yaki udon dish, with pork. My spirits plummet when Michael produces a plate of sashimi instead. Skilfully prepared by Kishi, the transparent paper-thin strips have been cut into individual petals to form a flower. Still, I doubt even a beautiful plate of Jos' favourite raw fish will make things good between him and Michael again.

Jos scowls, but he must be as hungry as me, because he shovels some slices onto his plate. It barely touches the surface before it's in his mouth.

'The ultimate aesthetic experience,' Michael says.

'Oh my God.' Raphael springs upright, sending his chair crashing to the floor. 'STOP!'

I stiffen and glance at Michael who is grinning like a freak.

'Spit it out. Don't eat it.' Raphael rushes over and thumps Jos on the back.

'Ow! Stop that, Raphael. I already did.'

I grab Michael's arm. 'What's wrong? What have you done?'

But Michael shakes me off. 'Lay him out in the chapel when it's over,' he says, and sneering, walks out the door.

CHAPTER
TWENTY-NINE

In the six hours since supper, I have learned that puffer fish contain a poison called tetrodotoxin. It's a neurotoxin one thousand, two hundred times deadlier than cyanide (the preferred drug of wars, according to Raphael). The poison is synthesised by bacteria that live in the fish's liver, intestines, skin, and reproductive organs. A lethal dose is smaller than the head of a pin, and a single fish has enough poison to kill thirty people. Despite the risk, the Japanese consider eating it a delicacy.

'The Russian Roulette of luxury dining,' Raphael explained as he carried Jos to his room.

'The what?'

'Let's just say the people who eat it have a taste for danger.'

It takes a skilled chef years of training to prepare the fish for safe consumption. Raphael was adamant Kishi was more than capable, which means Michael must have forced him to prepare a deadly version.

'Did Michael mean to kill us, too?' I asked.

'I think perhaps he did.'

I cast my eyes over Jos, lying on Raphael's bed, his body twitching, his face flushed. Saliva pools at the corners of his mouth. He touches his lips and grabs his head. Sweat pours from his forehead. He opens his lips to speak but makes a strange guttural noise and clutches his throat, writhing and twisting in agony.

I tug desperately on Raphael's tunic. 'What's happening?'

'He's struggling to breathe.'

'Can't you give him something?'

'There's no known antidote.' Raphael pumps yet more liquid through the tube he's threaded down Jos' throat. Bam. Jos is sick again.

'But you have to do something other than make him sick.'

'There's not a lot I can do, other than pray his body metabolises the poison and excretes it.' He kneels beside Jos. 'Can you sit?'

But Jos just stares at the ceiling with vacant eyes.

Raphael may as well be talking in a foreign language for all I understand. But he clearly wants to save Jos. And as I'm thinking how odd this is, there's a squeak, and the tannoy stirs into life. Oh God. Now what?

'Blasphemy against the Spirit is The Unforgiveable Sin. The arch-seducer who would undo us all is dead, but not before he admitted his heinous crimes. Lay down your banners, your weapons, and put away your anger so that we may live in harmony once more and focus on the great event.'

Is Michael talking about Jos? I glance at Raphael, who rolls his eyes.

Outside the compound, the people who've gathered

start up their hollering again. Seems like they're mad as hell.

'I WILL SHOW YOU THE BODY,' Michael booms, loud and echoing as if God, himself, is speaking from the heavens.

I look at Jos. He isn't twitching anymore. He lies there, a corpse with saucer eyes and lips which are turning blue. My heart skips a beat. 'What's happening?'

'His body has fallen asleep. The tetrodotoxin has blocked the sodium channels in his nerve cells. He's paralysed but conscious. I'm going to help him to breathe.'

'Michael is going to show the people his body.'

'We'll move him to the chapel. I'll do it there.'

I squeal like an injured animal and tug at my hair.

'Lois! I'm going to need your help. You must stay calm.'

With surprising tenderness, Raphael lays Jos on the altar and hooks him up to the machine I lugged over from his room.

'A mobile ventilator,' he explains, sensing my ignorance. 'An old army model. I brought it with me because Edenville is so damn isolated.'

'What's happening to him now?' I ask, certain there isn't a question he can't answer.

'Locked-in syndrome. He's awake, he can hear us, he can see us, and he can feel pain, but he can't move or speak.' Gently, he wipes the spittle from Jos' lips.

'That's horrible.' I clasp my cheeks, thinking how terrified I would be if it was happening to me, but remember Raphael's instruction to stay calm, and pick up Jos' hand and give it a reassuring squeeze. Michael is expecting to see Jos' corpse. How will he react when he walks in and sees

Raphael doing his damnedest to keep him alive? This doctor with his miraculous powers, who cast aside his life in the Otherworld to follow a man he believed was going to lead us all into Heaven. Does Raphael still believe in him? Jos kept telling me it was all an act. Smoke and mirrors, he said. At last I get what he meant. Michael is faking it. It's all just a whopping piece of fiction, like *The Great Gatsby*. Michael is a man, no different from any other. No, that's wrong. How many ordinary men tried to poison people? Or raped boys? And what about Daniel? Did Michael order his death, too?

Raphael turns to me. 'Go and get Michael. The sooner he films Jos the better.'

'But he'll see what you're doing.'

'No, he won't. Not if you warn me first.'

My lower lip trembles. 'How will I do that?'

'I'm sure you'll think of something. Now go.'

CHAPTER THIRTY

'You don't know that,' Steve says, after Donna has confided her fears, 'so don't waste time worrying. Jos may not even have met Leech.'

He's right, she thinks. No good ever came from leaping to conclusions. 'I could ask Naomi.'

'You think she'd give you an honest answer?'

She shrugs and surveys the crowd that has gathered over the course of the afternoon. Steve's latest article, it seems, has attracted a great deal of attention. Concerned relatives, curious locals, and a television crew, now queuing for burgers from an opportunist vendor who's set up shop. The smell of sizzling onions wafting through the dry desert air reminds Donna of the burger bar outside the shopping centre back home in Brighton. Hit by a wave of homesickness, she glances at the ninja guards, listening to the heated debate the Scotts are having with the sheriff. But their impenetrable expressions make it impossible to tell what they're thinking.

'Anyway, from what Thomas told us, Raphael is the

dangerous one, not "Michael",' Steve continues, drawing speech marks in the air.

'Yeah. I only hope the sheriff will agree to pay Leech another visit.'

'Oh, he will. Cameron Scott will not take no for an answer.'

The wait is killing Donna. She wants to get going, but despite Steve's assurances, Cameron Scott is taking an age to convince the sheriff. Not for the first time today, she wishes she'd rung Chrissie and Tess last night. The cult is making global headlines. They must be going out of their head with worry, and if Chrissie is anxious, it won't be good for the baby.

Steve wanders over with a couple of burgers wrapped in greaseproof paper. 'Can I tempt you to one of these? They're actually not too bad.'

She shakes her head. Steve isn't emotionally invested in the situation but, still, she's astonished he can eat at a time like this.

He licks the spills of ketchup off his fingers. 'All the more for me then.'

She turns away, tapping her foot in her eagerness to get going.

'Don't worry, Donna. You'll be in Angel Town any minute now.'

For heaven's sake. Why does he insist on calling it that? Is it one giant joke to him? 'You must be very pleased with yourself.'

'Ouch! Believe it or not, I care what happens to these people.'

Donna frowns and continues to stare at the canal, the

water turning black in the fading light. Beyond it, the ghostly alfalfa fields and, looming in the distance, the murky mountains. Such a remote place, three weeks ago she didn't even know it existed.

'You're not the only one hurting, you know. Your old man is in pieces. Why not try talking to him? It might help.'

She kicks at the dust with the scuffed toe of her trainer. 'I don't think so.'

'Dolores Scott then. She's been there and back and bought the T-shirt and is still capable of a smile.'

'Okay. Okay. You've made your point. Now piss off and leave me alone.'

Steve grins. 'I like you, Donna. When this is all over, I'm going to—'

'Right, we're off.' Cameron Scott, striding towards them, cuts through whatever it was Steve had been about to say. 'You ready, Donna?'

She takes a minute to compose herself. 'I am.'

Steve throws her a reassuring smile. 'Good luck.'

'Thanks. See you later, then.' She touches him briefly on the arm and, without acknowledging Naomi, settles in the back beside her – Cameron Scott being too big for anywhere other than the passenger seat – shuts the door, and closes her eyes. If only she shared Steve's optimism that, with Cameron Scott on board, the situation would be quickly resolved. Steve shows extraordinary and, frankly, irrational faith in the man's abilities. It isn't as if he'll be heading up a business meeting with some hotshot corporation head, something she's no doubt he excels in. He'll be negotiating with a narcissistic psychopath, backed up by a small army, according to Naomi (thus reinforcing Thomas' account) whose face, when Steve told her she'd be accompanying them (for leverage, apparently), had drained of all colour. Having initially refused to cooperate, it was the threat of a prison sentence that finally convinced her. Donna isn't sure you can send someone to jail for refusing to place themselves in a potentially dangerous situation, but it seems Naomi is as ignorant as she is on this point, and anyway, what does she care what happens to her? The stupid cow hasn't exactly played by the rules.

And, come to think of it, psychopaths probably do run the corporate world. Or at the very least, people with psychopathic traits. If you're happy to ride roughshod over everyone for the sake of making millions, it goes without saying you lack empathy. The only difference is that CEO's aren't armed with semi-automatic rifles. How is that even legal?

'Okay, let's get this over with.' The sheriff slips behind the wheel and fires up the engine.

Donna opens her eyes and looks out the window. His feet resting on the dashboard of his car, Rupert appears to be catching up on sleep, but she doubts it. He'd brought his daughter up single-handed and obviously loves her; he must be worried sick about the danger she's in. Donna overheard him tell Steve she'd been the sweetest little girl. The change in her character must have hit him hard. Perhaps, like Jos, something happened in her life to alter her. Something outside of Rupert's influence, which had nothing to do with her upbringing.

Dolores Scott said she felt indirectly accountable for Edenville's existence but, if you follow that logic, surely the blame should be laid at the door of Terry Leech's mum and dad. At some point, parents have to hold up their hands and accept their offspring are sentient beings capable of independent thought, and therefore accountable for their actions. Perhaps the faults in society are to blame, and the idea of living in a utopia under the auspices of a charismatic guru is simply more appealing than the alternative. Self-proclaimed Messiahs are attractive because, unlike politicians, they've correctly identified that capitalism and social inequality, the two mainstays of society, are the sources of evil that will eventually lead to mankind's destruction. You can hardly blame someone for following a rainbow.

The sheriff winds down his window and speaks to the taller guard who, after a cursory glance at the occupants, immediately opens the gate. Craning her neck as they drive away, Donna sees him pick up a walkie-talkie, no doubt to notify Leech. Beside her, Naomi shivers. She knows she should offer the poor girl some sympathy – after all, she is the older half-sister of her three children – but she's too angry to engage with her. So she clenches her jaw and stares straight ahead.

The dusty track now lined with identical A-frame houses, she realises they've reached the town. She spots a standpipe at the corner of the street, rudimentary electricity cables, and several wooden poles with tannoys attached. A man driving a horse and cart loaded with melons frowns at them when they pass and, in a small front garden, a woman in a drab, ankle-length dress, working away at the soil despite the fading light, downs her hoe to stare at them.

Donna taps the sheriff on the shoulder. 'Stop the car! I want to speak to her.'

'I don't think that's a good—'

But Donna has already opened the door, leaving the sheriff no alternative. 'Hi there. Can I have a word?'

The woman glances around, but the street is deserted. Hesitantly, she raises her hand.

'I'm looking for Jos Prince.' Donna rushes into the garden and thrusts his picture under her nose. 'My son. He's sixteen. Do you know him?'

The woman recoils and shakes her head.

'What about Zosia Scott?' Cameron shouts through the window. 'She was engaged to Lee ... er ... Michael.'

The woman scratches her temple. 'The Divine Protector is not allowed to marry.'

'Thank heavens for small mercies,' Cameron says. 'But do you know her?'

'I know no one by that name.'

'You're sure about that? She was one of the founding members.'

The woman shies away and continues hoeing.

'Get back in the car, Donna,' barks Cameron. 'It'd be easier squeezing blood out of a stone.'

'She knows her, I'm sure of it,' Donna says as she clambers in.

'Yes, yes, but unless we torture her, the poor woman isn't going to tell us anything. Drive on, Hank.'

The sheriff snorts. 'This is not a taxi. Please, Mr Scott, show some respect.'

'I told you already. Jos is with Michael,' mutters Naomi.

Donna turns to her, cheeks blazing. 'You honestly expect me to believe a single word that comes out of your lying gob? Hmm?'

Cameron reaches over and places a hand on her shoulder. 'Steady on, Donna.'

'Why? It's the truth.'

Glowering, Naomi folds her arms. 'A bit rich coming from you.'

Donna throws up her hands. 'Oh, really? Wow! Wow!'

The sheriff slaps the steering wheel. 'Mrs Prince, please.'

'So, you think running off with another woman's husband is okay?' Naomi's face is puce.

'What? No.'

'And yet that's exactly what you did.'

Donna leans in close. 'Better get your facts straight, honey. Your darling father forgot to tell me he was married.'

'But I thought—'

'And as for you being his daughter. Well, he didn't mention that little fact until this morning. Capice?'

The sheriff slams on the breaks. 'Okay Ladies, enough. This isn't helping. One more word from either of you and we go back.'

Sucking air through her teeth, Donna settles back and turns to stare out of the window.

'Thank you,' the sheriff says and drives off again.

Pretty soon the houses give way to alfalfa and wheat fields, which in turn give way to a large orchard of orange and lemon trees. It reminds Donna of the kibbutz she and Rupert worked on in the summer of 1958. She'd been pregnant with Chrissie, but that hadn't stopped her picking fruit and cleaning out the chicken coops with the fervent enthusiasm of someone whose eyes had been well and truly opened. *From each according to his ability, to each according to his needs,* was the mantra they'd lived by. Four hundred and fifty-odd people working hard, not for wages but for the collective, producing food, not for market but for need.

The similarities with Edenville are striking. But so are the differences. Terry Leech has created a hierarchy and lords it over his followers, brainwashing them with the ludicrous religious prophesies he preaches. You are either all in or you are out. Utterly dependent on their leader, his people are scared to leave and, just as equally, scared to stay. Naomi, trembling with terror beside her, is living proof that life in Edenville is underpinned by fear. A terrifying cult, not the peaceful commune it professes to be.

An angry mob brandishing pitchforks, hoes, bows and arrows, homemade drums and banners, forces them to a standstill. Donna grips the edge of the seat until her knuckles turn white. The sheriff blares his horn. The startled men jump out the way, and the car stutters slowly forward. Curious faces peer through the windows. One of them recognises Naomi and bangs on the roof. Whimpering, she slides down and covers her face with her hands.

Serves you right, Donna thinks. Inching forward, she catches sight of a tall palisade wall. With its rudimentary lookout turret in the centre, it brings to mind the Wild West fort Jos used to play with as a child. She reads the name painted in large, gold letters above the sturdy wooden gate. Ascension House. Even to a confirmed atheist, the biblical connotations are glaring.

The sheriff kills the engine. 'Probably best if I do the talking.'

'Over my dead body.' Cameron Scott hefts his substantial frame from the car and turns to the man nearest him. 'Is Terry Leech in there?' He jerks his thumb at the building.

'Who?'

Grunting, the sheriff clambers out and jostles into position in front of Cameron. 'We're here to see Michael.'

The man slams his sign into the ground. 'Join the club.'

Donna reads the slogan written in red letters – Sodomite – and winces.

The sheriff puffs out his chest. 'Follow me. I know the form.'

'Chrissakes!' snaps Cameron, who nevertheless does as he's told.

'I wouldn't stay here if I were you,' Donna says to Naomi who, arms folded in silent protest, remains glued to the back seat. 'You'll probably be lynched.'

Naomi scowls, but sensing the truth in Donna's words, reluctantly joins them.

The sheriff forces a path through the jeering horde and waves his arms at a man in the turret, who barks an order to someone below. The gates swing open to expose a small army of black-clothed ninja guards, armed with semi-automatic rifles, standing to attention.

'I thought this place was all about peace,' mutters Cameron.

Donna's stomach churns. So did she.

The guards part to reveal a man with shoulder-length hair, dressed in a white linen kurta and trousers, his hands pressed together in a namaste-style greeting. The crowd backs off, grumbling, but as the man slowly raises his head, an eerie hush settles over them.

He smiles and spreads his arms. 'Welcome to Edenville.'

So, this is Michael, the self-styled Messiah. In his wayfarer sunglasses he has the air of a pop star about him and would tick every box, if it wasn't for his insubstantial height. That he is shorter than Donna makes him seem less threatening.

Don't be fooled, she thinks. He may look like Jesus, but the man is a monster.

'It's good to see you again, Cameron.' If Michael is surprised to see Zosia's father among them, he's doing a great job of covering it up.

Cameron thrusts out his chest. 'You've got nerve, I'll give you that. Now, take me to my daughter.'

'A bit hasty, don't you think?'

'Tardy more like. Should've forced my way in years ago.'

'I mean she doesn't want to see you.'

'Fine, then she can tell me that to my face.' Cameron strides over to Michael. Towering over him, he jabs a finger in his chest. 'Where are you hiding her?'

Michael doesn't flinch.

Donna shuffles forward but glimpses the white Rolls-Royce parked behind him and is temporarily thrown off balance.

'Yes?' Michael asks, smiling beatifically at her.

'Er ... perhaps my son would like to see me.'

'And who might he be?'

'Jos. Jos Prince.'

A shadow flits across his face. 'I'm sorry. I know no one by that name.'

He's lying, Donna thinks. Naomi was telling the truth.

'What's the sheriff doing here? That's what I'd like to know,' a man clasping a pitchfork asks Michael. 'Come to arrest you, has he?'

The crowd stamp their feet. 'SODOMITE. SODOMITE. DEVIL'S FILTH. SODOMITE. SODOMITE. DEVIL'S FILTH.'

It's a deafening wall of sound but, apart from a slight twitch in his right eye, Michael's serene expression doesn't falter. He leans into the sheriff. 'Might I suggest we have this conversation inside?'

The gates securely closed, the sheriff clears his throat. 'Now look, Michael. I have it on good authority you've been breaking the law. If a man has sex with a minor, even if it's consensual, the law states he must be placed on the sex offender list.'

Michael arches an eyebrow. 'I'm not sure I get your meaning.'

'He means buggering a teenager is a crime,' Cameron says gruffly. 'And no one, not even you, is above the law.'

A couple of the guards exchange glances.

Michael smiles. 'Well, quite, but how is it relevant?'

The sheriff, clearly uncomfortable, steeples his hands. 'A young man called Thomas has come forward and accused you of having sex with him.' He shifts his weight and clears his throat. 'He's seventeen.'

'Ah, yes, Thomas.'

'Ha! You admit it,' barks Cameron.

'Far from it. Thomas was in love with me. His desire drove him quite mad, I gather. It could never be requited, you see? That's why he ran away. How is he? Is he well?'

'He's on the mend,' says the sheriff.

'Chrissakes, man,' splutters Cameron. 'Are you deaf as well as blind. His people are protesting. They know what he is. He's dangerous. Do your job and arrest him.'

The sheriff holds up his hand. 'Hang on, Mr Scott.' He clears his throat again. 'Michael, are you saying you deny the allegation?'

A commotion behind the Powers distracts them. All heads turn as a strikingly beautiful young man with blond unkempt hair and overbright eyes bursts through the semi-circle. 'Go away. All of you.' He whips out a revolver from behind his back. 'You're not wanted here.'

Michael whirls around. 'Oh God. Ariel! No!'

'Put the gun down, young man.' The sheriff raises his hands and moves towards him.

There's a loud crack. The bullet hits its target, and the sheriff topples over. Naomi screams, but the blood-chilling sound is quickly drowned in the cacophony that erupts from the crowd outside.

Dragging his nails down his cheek, the youth stumbles backwards but loses his balance and falls to the ground. He stares at the gun, as if he hadn't realised he was holding it. Throwing one last fretful look at Michael, he places the barrel beneath his chin.

Michael runs towards him. 'No, Ariel! No!'

The youth closes his eyes. Letting out a primal scream, he pulls the trigger a second time.

Donna gasps and covers her mouth with her hand. The last thing she sees before she turns away is the boy's brain matter flying in a bloody arc through the air behind him.

CHAPTER THIRTY-ONE

For the first time since I moved into Ascension House, nobody is guarding the door of Michael's wing. I peek out, a mole from a hole. Night is falling. The quadrangle is deserted, not a single Dominion about. But beyond the walls, a nerve-jangling hullabaloo has broken out. Sure sounds like the war has started. If only I *was* a mole, I'd burrow my way out of Edenville, away from this insanity.

Not without Jos, though. Not while he's still alive.

I close my eyes and pray for all I'm worth Raphael will save him, Michael will repent, and we can all carry on as usual.

But even as I do, I know it's impossible.

Raucous, angry voices force me to my senses. Keeping to the wall, I creep through the gate to the outer courtyard. The Powers, standing in a semi-circle, have their backs to me, but I can hear Michael beyond them, talking to what sounds like Otherworldlies who don't like what he has to say. Hidden in the shadows of the cloisters, I peer around a pillar for a better view.

A figure sprints past me in a blur of white, and I jump. He barges through the Powers and screams at the Otherworldlies to go away.

'Put the gun down,' a man says.

Gun? Through the gap I make out four strangers, two men – one tall, the other wearing a broad-brimmed hat – and two women, the younger of whom I vaguely recognise. Naomi? And Michael.

'Oh God. Ariel! No!' Michael shouts.

Bang.

I recoil, yelping. The man in the hat collapses, blood spurting from his belly. The youth keels over, but it's only when he hits the ground that I realise it's David. Clamping my hands over my ears, I watch helplessly as he jams the gun under his chin and, with a blood-curdling yell, pulls the trigger.

I fall to my knees. The last thing I see before I black out are tiny grey globules of his brain splattering in a puddle at my feet.

I come around, trembling violently from top to toe – even my teeth are shaking in my gums – and throw up. Still heaving, I crawl back to the cloisters. The gates are closed, the guard back in place, and Hepzibah, about ten feet from where I'm cowering, is crying softly and covering David's broken, bloody body with a sheet.

I bite my knuckles to stop myself screaming. It doesn't seem all that long ago he was showing me those dear little cygnets. We visited them on the canal every day for months, watched them turn from grey to brown. And on the momentous day they took to the sky, we held hands. Once, when we were out on Fisherman Cain's boat, David caught a giant catfish. He tried to pick it up, but the slippery monster wriggled and flopped about so hard, he lost his balance and toppled into the water still clutching it. He laughed so much I honestly thought he might drown.

David. Sweet, kind, gentle David who wouldn't hurt a soul. My friend. Dead.

Angry chants from the Guardians beyond the wall cut through my grief.

'Sod-o-mite! Sod-o-mite! Devil's filth!'

Are they talking about Michael? Do they know? I scan the courtyard, but there's no sign of my father, just Hepzibah, David's body, and a few Powers huddled together.

Oh my God, Jos.

I stagger to my feet and, keeping to the shadows, head back the way I've come. Without a backward glance, I dash inside, past the statues but, hearing raised voices in Michael's study, pull up outside the closed door.

'How could I have stopped him? I didn't see him. He came out of nowhere.'

'Was the sheriff alive when they left?' Raphael asks.

'I don't know. I think so.'

'He was an ally. He understood what you were trying to achieve. He even bought your horseshit about Daniel's body. But the FBI will come after you now. What was David thinking?'

'Ariel was trying to protect me.'

'He was sixteen, Michael. You have to stop this lunacy, for all our sakes.'

'I don't know what you mean?'

'You're out of control. First Daniel.'

'That was Abraham's doing.'

'For heaven's sake, man, you gave him the order. Kishi, too, with Joseph. And now this.'

'This has nothing to do with me.'

'It has everything to do with you. The poor boy was in love with you.'

Knife-like pain shoots through me; it's all I can do not to cry out. David. In love with Michael. So, it was him I'd seen. Oh God, it's so messed up.

'That's hardly my fault.'

'Then whose fault is it? Hmm? You encouraged him. Set the whole thing up. Dressed him in white. Gave him a key.'

'You seem to have all the answers. Why don't you tell me?'

'I've tried, but it's impossible to reason with a—'

'Be careful, Raphael. Or—'

'Or what? You'll have me killed, too? Joseph was innocent. He'd done nothing wrong.'

'Gabriel was possessed of the Devil. He tempted me. Of course he was guilty.'

My stomach somersaulting wildly, I grab my hair.

'My God, you really believe that. And I thought ... Oh, what does it matter anyway? It's over, Michael. The FBI will—'

'ENOUGH. Out of my way. I need to film the body.'

Sweet Jesus, Jos. Dead or alive? I don't know. I hare down the corridor into the chapel anyway. Jos is lying on the bed still wearing the mask. I whip it off and kick the ventilator under the altar cloth. Just in time because Michael marches into the room, followed by a distraught-looking Raphael. Seeing me standing over Jos and no sign of his equipment, Raphael steeples his fingers and bows his head.

'Where's the camera?' yells Michael from the adjoining studio. 'Never mind. I have it.' He sweeps back in and starts filming. It must only take him five minutes, but with Jos' life at stake, it feels like a lifetime.

Michael places the camera on the altar and flips out the tape. 'Leave no evidence. Burn the body. Now!' he screams when neither of us move. 'And you.' He glares in my direction. 'Come with me.'

I freeze. The things I've heard. The horrors I've seen. I shake my head.

'You will do as I say.' Eyes glinting, he grabs my arm.

I twist and squirm, but he's so mad right now, his grip is like iron. I peer over my shoulder as he drags me from the room.

'It'll be okay,' Raphael mouths and puts a finger to his lips.

We are in the large white room. Michael has said nothing to me. Not one word. I daren't ask him why we're here, not after Raphael signalled to keep quiet. Seems to me he's the only one who has the measure of this psycho. My heartbeat thunders in my ears. It's a wonder Michael can't hear it.

The door crashes open, and Ophaniel and Puriel march in with the mother of all surprises. Elijah. Jaw set, fists clenched, lips pressed in a thin line, he obviously means business. I didn't think it possible I could be more scared, but Elijah is one evil son-of-a-bitch when riled. I've suffered at his hands more times than I care to remember. Those nights he crept into my bed. The unbearable pain. It wasn't God's love we were sharing. What he did to me was as bad as what Michael tried to do to Jos. And right now I feel so sorry for myself I want to curl into a ball and cry my eyes out. But I mustn't. So I make myself as small as I can and try to stop my knees from quaking.

Michael shoves me in front of him and places his hands on my shoulders. 'Hello, Elijah.'

'A human shield. A new low, even by your standards.'

'You wanted to talk to me?' Michael says sweetly, as if Elijah has commented on the weather.

And now I'm so scared I know I'm gonna pee myself.

'Ascension House,' Elijah says, scanning the room. 'Edenville's ivory tower. My, my, you have done well for yourself. I suppose our money bought you all of this.'

Ophaniel throws Puriel a questioning look.

'Your time is up. We want you to hand yourself over to the authorities.'

Michael's grip tightens. 'We?'

'We've formed a delegation. I'm the spokesman. Ezra is handling the legal stuff. Leave now, otherwise we'll be forced to take action.'

'There is no need for talk like this. I'm busy doing God's work.'

Elijah leans in menacingly. 'I don't think so. He knows what you are. And take her with you when you go.' He stabs a finger in my chest. 'You and your kind are not wanted here.'

'ENOUGH. I WILL NOT BE SPOKEN TO LIKE THIS.'

I jump.

But Elijah doesn't flinch. 'Go now. Or suffer the consequences.' His point made, he spits in my face, turns and strides out of the room, Puriel and Ophaniel hot on his heels.

For what seems an eternity, Michael stands there, staring into space. Elijah's drool trickles down my cheek. I daren't flick it away. I hardly dare breathe. What in God's name will happen to me now? Will Michael leave and take me with him? And if he does, where will we go? And just as

I'm thinking I'd rather die than go anywhere with this deranged whacko who dares to call himself my father, he shoves me away.

'This is all your fault,' he mutters through clenched teeth. 'All of it. I wish I'd never set eyes on you. Go. Now. Get out of my sight before I do something I regret.'

It's been four hours since Raphael hooked Jos back up to the ventilator in his room. It's weird, but with all the madness going on, Raphael's collection of skulls, his pipes, the devil mask, and all those hundreds of bottles that struck the fear of God in me when I first set eyes on them, don't bother me anymore. Jos was sure he was drugging Michael, but I don't know. The way he's caring for Jos, seems to me Raphael is all about healing. And he's as good if not better at it than Doctor Seth and Doctor Luke. I'd like to know what all this stuff is. Where it came from and what it's for. But I'm too frightened about what's happening to Jos to ask. Raphael has promised me the painkillers he's injected will keep him comfortable. I'd never have thought it possible but I'm grateful I'm with him. I scuttled back the moment Michael told me to scoot. Not just because I've nowhere else to go. The fact that Raphael knows what to do all the time makes me feel a whole lot safer. Crazy, because right up until last night's supper, I couldn't stand to be in the same room.

Straight off, I told him what happened with Elijah, the angry threats he made.

'There's trouble ahead,' he says.

'What kind of trouble?'

'We'll know soon enough.'

'It's all my fault,' I whisper, but Raphael doesn't hear.

And actually, I'm relieved. I'd hate him to blame me, too. So, I stay holy-ghost quiet, confident that when the trouble kicks off, he'll have a plan.

Seems to me he's making a great effort to look after me, too. Not as a husband, though, because I get the feeling marrying me isn't top of his agenda either. But as a father. A real dad, the kind who protects and loves their kid no matter what. It strikes me he'd be good at that. And, now I've got my breath back and my galloping heart has slowed to a brisk trot, I'm itching to ask why he's determined to save Jos. These past few weeks he's done nothing but peer down his nose at him. Just goes to show there's truth in Mom's old saying, you can't judge a book by its cover.

The tannoy in the corner buzzes into life. My heart sinks. Seriously? In the middle of the night?

Raphael grits his teeth. 'Here we go.'

'Guardians. You have nothing to fear. You have seen the infidel is dead,' Michael says, his voice unnaturally high-pitched.

We wait, but Michael doesn't speak. Perhaps that's it. It's not as if he can explain Jos' death. It wouldn't show him in the best of lights. I gaze at Jos' lifeless body, his grey, sunken face. It's hard to believe he's still alive.

'It is the end of days!'

I press my hand to my heart. Bloody hell! What's wrong with him?

Nothing.

'Fear no evil!'

Sweet Jesus.

'Walk through the valley of death.'

Michael's voice is so quiet this time, I have to strain my ears to hear him. But apart from the rattle of his breathing, the room falls silent again. I bite my nails. Is that it? I glance at Raphael. If it wasn't for the muscle in his cheek working furiously, I'd think he wasn't listening.

'The sky TORN APART ...'

Oh, dear God.

'I see him. Eyes of burning bronze. Horns ... And snakes. Slithering out of the deep, dark chasm. The black, black sun ... TRUMPETS. Children, children everywhere. Sick and dying. And STARS. Bright, bright stars falling to Earth ... Angels. Flung into a LAKE OF FIRE beneath a blood-red moon.'

On and on Michael rambles. Shouting. Whispering. Speaking gibberish. Nonsense. Nothing like the Michael who's led us all these years.

Raphael shakes his head. A tear trickles down his cheek. Angrily, he wipes it away.

And then, Michael's voice again, barely a whisper. 'The Rapture. The Rapture.'

'Is it the end?' I ask.

But Raphael doesn't answer, he just sinks into a chair and cradles his head in his hands.

I must have fallen asleep at some point, because I'm shaken awake by Raphael.

'The courtyard is on fire. We need to wet the towels and block the gap under the door while we try and work out what to do. The whole place is made of timber, so we haven't got long.'

I take a towel and run to the basin, wondering if the sky has split apart and all the stars are crashing down to Earth. What will happen to us if it has? Will any of us be saved? And then I remember my mother, locked in the room across the square. Alone.

I drop the towel and grab Raphael's arm. 'Mom! You have to save her.'

'Hepzibah will do the right thing.'

'But what if she doesn't?'

'The people are firing flaming arrows at us, Lois. We need to concentrate on saving ourselves. Saving Joseph.' He tries to shake me off.

I cling to him, refusing to let go. 'Please, Raphael. We have to save her, too.'

His shoulders slump. Closing his eyes, he takes a few deep breaths. 'Yes, yes. Stay here and keep the door closed until I come back. If the smoke gets any worse, breathe through a wet towel, get on your hands and knees, and get the hell out of here.'

CHAPTER THIRTY-TWO

It's been a strange day. A day of considerable unrest. Unable to see out the small window, Esther has, nevertheless, heard the goings-on. Drums, chanting, and more alarming still, further gunfire. Judging by the screaming, people have been injured, possibly even killed. Are there executions in Edenville now?

It quietened down, and she slept for a while, but she's been startled awake by the tannoy. She thinks it's the middle of the night but, without her watch, can only guess. Like all Guardians, her knowledge of the Bible is forensic, and yet she can't make sense of Michael's ramblings. If pushed, she'd say he was talking about the Apocalypse, perhaps the opening of the sixth and seventh seals. But the garbled, incoherent language makes deciphering it impossible. He sounds deranged, like he's in the throes of a mental breakdown. Or high. But other than the psychedelic trips her fellow law students boasted about after eating magic mushrooms, Esther hasn't a clue about the effects of narcotics. Like Daniel, Lola is convinced Raphael is drugging Michael, but what if he's taking them out of choice?

His behaviour has been so erratic recently, it's plausible. She desperately wants to know what's going on, but the only person she has contact with is Hepzibah, and she must have been sworn to silence, because every one of Esther's questions thus far has been met with stony silence.

And now the smoke. Esther would have guessed they were cremating the bodies but for the smell of burning wood flooding the room. The wet towels under the door have helped, but the flames are licking at the walls. Esther hammers the door, but the red-hot wood scorches her hands. She springs back, screaming for Hepzibah. But if the wretched woman is there, she doesn't answer.

Overcome by a fit of coughing, Esther drops to her hands and knees. It's easier to breathe down here, but she must get out before she either chokes, or burns, to death. Wiping the sweat from her forehead, she scans the room. The stool. That should do it.

She crawls across the floor and clambers to her feet. Grimacing, she lifts it above her head and, with the last of her strength, hurls it at the door. The panels splinter. She kicks out a gap, covers her mouth with her skirt, and leaps through the flames. Eyes smarting, she runs outside, doubles over, and gasps for air. When her breathing has normalised, she hinges upright. The Olive and the Almond Trees are on fire, and large swathes of the building, but the quadrangle is empty. Not a single Dominion or Principality about. But where in the Lord's name is Lois?

Beyond the wall, the Guardians are baying for Michael's blood. Nearby, someone shouts. There's a blood-curdling scream, and a blazing ball of a man runs through the burning inner gate, throws himself on the grass, and thrashes about. But his body is black and, within seconds, he draws his last breath.

Esther glances frantically around, but the buildings around her are a roaring inferno. She is trapped.

Somebody yells her name. She turns to see a flaming arrow flying straight at her. She dives to the right and covers her head with her hands. When she dares look up, she sees the arrow has pierced the ground exactly where she'd been standing.

'Esther. Esther. Over here.' On the other side of the quadrangle, Raphael is beckoning anxiously.

'No, I must find Lois.'

'She's with me. Quick. We haven't got long.'

Esther hauls herself to her feet and, spluttering, stumbles through the smoke towards him. He ushers her into a room cluttered with exotic artefacts, books, and an array of coloured bottles filled with plant specimens. And, in the centre, a boy on a bed, an oxygen mask secured to his face.

'He's desperately ill and unable to move. I'm going to have to carry him,' Raphael says as Lola darts out of the gloom, flings her arms around Esther and jabbers in her ear.

'You're safe,' Esther whispers. 'Thank God, you're safe.' She clings to her daughter, tears streaming down her face.

'Hurry, please. We have to get out of here.' Raphael hoists the boy over his shoulder. 'Cover your mouth with wet towels and bring the equipment. We'll hide out in the teahouse.'

Esther prises Lola off her. 'Won't that be on fire, too?'

'I don't know. But even if we could get through the front gates, it won't be safe for any of us out there.'

Dear Lord, this should not be happening. Michael created a heaven on earth, and now, here she is, watching it go to hell.

Raphael lurches through the doorway, weighed down

by the boy and trailed by Lola, cradling what appears to be a portable ventilator.

'What happened to him?'

But Lola doesn't hear her. 'Bring Raphael's bag, Mom,' she says as she hurries after him.

The quadrangle is a fiery furnace, bodies scattered like charred logs on the scorched grass. There but for the grace of God, Esther thinks, weaving through them, past the burning trees, to the door to what must be Michael's wing. Two Dominions with blistered bodies and singed hair sprint from the building, screaming. They scurry around in search of an escape route before heading off in the other direction. Lola goes to follow them, but Esther reaches for her arm.

'Naneel and Hashmal,' Lola cries. 'We should help them.'

'Sweetheart, there's nothing we can do.'

Raphael puts his hand on Lola's shoulder. 'You must stay close. It's not safe.'

Lola wrinkles her nose but nods, and Esther sighs with relief.

But then she sees the flames ravaging the doorway. It would be madness even to attempt to go in there. She's about to protest when Raphael shoots inside, Lola hot on his heels. Fast running out of options, she presses the wet towel over her mouth and charges through the thick curtain of smoke, sidestepping the red-hot embers raining down, past life-size statues, the burning walls collapsing in her wake. They stop outside a closed door. Raphael gives it an almighty kick, and it swings open, but the ceiling caves in, missing Esther by inches.

'Quick,' he yells, motioning wildly with his free arm.

Esther turns to see a ball of fire racing towards her and flings herself flat on the floor. Flames lick the soles of her shoes. She closes her eyes and prays to her maker that her death be swift. But a hand is yanking her to her feet. There's an almighty blast, and the glass door on the far side of the room shatters into a million pieces. Quick as a flash, Lola crouches, and Esther does the same, covering her head as the fragments of glass rain down on them.

And now Lola is pulling her towards the yawning void where the door used to be. Out into the bright sunlight. Eyes stinging, Esther scrabbles blindly down the gravel path, gulping up the fresh air. Over the bridge. To the unharmed teahouse beside the pond.

Lola slumps on the veranda, heaving. There are scratches on her pale face, Esther notices, but otherwise she's unscathed. She drops down next to her. Too puffed to talk, she picks up Lola's hand, gives it a squeeze, and watches Raphael unhook the comatose young man from his shoulder. He lays him, gently, on the tatami inside the building and checks his pulse.

'Thank you for saving us, Raphael,' Esther says once she's caught her breath.

He releases a long, exhausted sigh. 'My name is John.'

'Thank you, John.'

'I fear we're a long way from being saved but we should be safe here for a time.'

'You'll think of something,' Lola whispers. 'I know you will.'

Esther draws Lola close, fighting back tears, determined to stay strong for her daughter. Determined to protect her. If only there was something she could do. But what that might be she has no idea? She feels so helpless.

'Michael asked me to come. We were friends, you see, many years ago.' John's voice breaks through her thoughts. She turns to look at him but he continues to speak without meeting her eye. 'We met in Colombia. I'd taken leave from Oxford University to study the indigenous medicinal plants of the Amazon for a book I was writing. Michael was travelling through. He was an exciting young man, an idealist with a thirst for knowledge, full of vitality. The local tribes were fascinated by him. There was nothing he wouldn't try. He had a lot to say, too. People were drawn to him.' He pauses, perhaps reliving the memory, before rolling back his shoulders and turning to look at her, his pain evident in the dark shadows beneath his eyes. 'Anyway, three years ago, he got in touch. He was at a crossroads and needed my help. I came at once, leaving behind the woman I loved because I believed in him.'

His regret is palpable. Esther wishes she could find the words to soothe him, but how can she when she'd been taken in, too?

'God's voice was fading. He was convinced yagé would help with the visions.'

She tilts her head. 'Yagé?'

'Ayahuasca, the Vine of the Soul. A sacred, hallucinogenic medicine prepared and used by shamans to enable them to return to the beginning of life. The Barasana Indians call it facing down the jaguar.'

So, Daniel had been right in a sense. She shivers, casting her gaze over Raphael's necklace. Jaguar teeth? she wonders as he fingers them.

'I only ever see colours when I take it, but Michael's visions were astonishingly vivid. He talked of a scarlet gash in the sky leading to another dimension, more colourful and more brilliant than Earth. His soul freed, he was able not only to talk with God again but walk with him, also.'

'So, what went wrong?'

'Drinking yagé isn't pleasant. It causes vomiting and diarrhoea, part of the purging process, which is why Michael begged me for other, less aggressive hallucinogens. Peyote, a cactus containing mescaline, a psychedelic compound. Dried and ground, it can be mixed with cannabis and smoked. But he didn't stop there. The Mazatec people believe Jesus speaks to them through the San Isidro mushroom, the Flesh of the Gods. Michael started taking them, along with mate de coca, a Peruvian tea he drinks from dawn to dusk.'

'He gave it to us,' Lola says quietly. 'Jos knew there was something odd about it.'

'The Inca's called it the Divine Leaf of Immortality. I warned him against it. The combination of chemicals was messing with his brain. The prolific and terrifying visions were making him paranoid and psychotic. He feared for his life and insisted he needed an army to protect him. But if you bring an unruly bunch of adolescents together, train them and arm them with guns, you're asking for trouble.

'It wasn't until he claimed God had ordered him to kill Daniel that I realised Michael was not the man I'd thought him to be. He seemed to lose all inhibitions at this time. Told me about his relationships with Daniel and Thomas. But then he started bragging about his affair with David, who visited him via the hidden door in this garden, disguised as the Dominion, Ariel. And how he planned to seduce young Joseph, here. I knew then God wasn't talking to Michael. He never had. Michael was delusional, a schizophrenic unable to distinguish his thoughts and ideas from reality.'

Esther touches her forehead, barely able to take it in. 'So, everything ... God talking to him. All this ... is a lie.'

'Yes and no. He believed God was talking to him because he heard his voice. But, of course, the voice was in his head. It wasn't real. Unfortunately, it reinforced his narcissism and enabled him to create this fictional world.'

Lola shrieks and covers her ears.

I did this, Esther thinks, and draws her trembling daughter to her chest. This is all my fault. An idiot, blinded by love. Unrequited love, at that. Will Lola ever recover, let alone understand? 'And yet he preached homosexuality was a sin.'

'Ah, but the rules, his rules, didn't apply to him. His people were in awe of him. Attractive, charming, powerful, he could have had anyone. And by providing hallucinogenic plants,' Raphael continues wearily, 'I compounded his illness. Turned him into a monster. Ultimately, I am culpable—'

'I told you to burn the body.'

The voice is menacing but instantly recognisable. Holding back a cry, Esther twists her stiff neck to see Michael, rising from the shadows of the teahouse like an apparition. There's no way he could've escaped through his wing. Has he been there all along?

Raphael rises slowly to his feet. 'He'll be burning soon enough. We all will.'

'You disobeyed me. I trusted you, but you're a liar.' Michael raises his arm and points the revolver Esther hasn't noticed until now, at Raphael.

Hearing Lola's screams, she springs up and raises her hands. 'No, Michael, don't. I beg you. Please.'

'It's okay, Esther,' Raphael says and turns away.

'No. You can't give up,' she yells.

Bang. Bang. Bang.

Esther reels backwards as Raphael's body judders violently with the blast of each bullet. Eyes wide, blood trickling down the corner of his mouth, he topples over, hitting the deck with a thud.

'You've killed him,' Lola shouts. 'Sweet Jesus!'

Esther reaches for her daughter and tries to push her behind her. Not that her body will save her. The bullet will go right through her. She can only hope Michael is not so insane he'd kill his only child.

But Michael is taking aim, his finger on the trigger.

It twitches.

'Hail Mary, Mother of God,' she mutters, 'pray for us sinners now and at the hour of our death.'

CHAPTER

THIRTY-THREE

The police car hammers down the highway, engulfed in clouds of dust. Donna wishes the driver would ease off the accelerator. She can't see the car in front. It would be just her luck if they piled into it.

But what if her death provides Jos with the incentive he needs to return home?

Ah, but the girls, how will they cope without her?

Rupert will have to step up and move back in. He'll have to tell them the truth about Naomi. About Ingrid. There'll be no skirting that issue anymore.

For goodness sake, she tells herself. You're being ridiculous. You're tired, that's all. Get a grip. You're not going to die. The police drive like this all the time.

It's not yet dawn, but it's a long while since they raced away from Edenville with Cameron Scott at the wheel, a whimpering Naomi in the seat beside him.

'Why did you leave Edenville, Naomi?' Cameron asked.

She shifted uncomfortably and said nothing for a while. But then she sniffed and, speaking in a low voice, said, 'I began to suspect Michael was making things up.'

'How so?' he pressed.

'Well, he claimed Jos was the angel Gabriel. It seemed ... it seemed so unlikely.'

'The man's insane,' muttered Cameron.

'I ... I didn't sleep with him, you know.' Naomi swivelled around to face Donna, tears streaming down her cheeks. 'Jos, I mean.'

But Donna's mind was frazzled. Unable to process Naomi's words, she'd stared at her blankly and Naomi, perhaps fearing another verbal onslaught, had quickly turned back.

In the back with the sheriff's head in her lap, Donna pressed her once-white T-shirt against the wound to his belly. It wasn't as clean as she would've liked and, as the car careered down the bumpy track, she found herself hoping that Hank Rivera wouldn't die of sepsis. Utterly ridiculous, because if she didn't pack the wound, he'd die anyway. Her T-shirt drenched with the sheriff's blood, she was struggling to see how she'd keep him alive. She was pretty sure it only took about eight minutes to bleed out.

They stopped, briefly, outside the gates where, on Cameron's instructions, Naomi got out and Steve got in, the reason for which became clear when the car skidded off again.

'I'm guessing you know how to use this thing.' Cameron pointed to the police radio. 'There's been a shooting. We need an ambulance and quick.'

Steve spun around. 'Donna!'

'Hank,' she mumbled.

Steve reached for her arm, gave it a reassuring squeeze, and picked up the receiver. Within seconds he was issuing instructions to whoever was on the other end. 'It's time you called in the Feds. Over and out.'

It was as if she'd stumbled into an episode of *Miami Vice*.

The ambulance intercepted them on the outskirts of Blythe. The sheriff was still alive. Donna hoped they could save him, but she supposed that depended on whether the bullet had ruptured any major organs.

It was only then she was able to process what had happened. The youth, who'd appeared from nowhere and who'd shot the sheriff, looked about the same age as Jos. She wasn't sure why that mattered. Jos would never shoot a man.

Ah, but the squirrels, her conscience nagged. You've no idea what he's capable of.

'You okay, Donna?' Steve asked.

She nodded and, biting her trembling lip as the ambulance sped away, slipped inside the car.

After that, they called in at the sheriff's station. One of the deputies, disillusioned with his boss's bullheadedness, had taken it upon himself to do some detecting of his own, and had unearthed the reason behind Hank Rivera's incomprehensible loyalty towards Michael. Ten years ago, word reached Michael that the sheriff's seven-year-old niece was dying of leukaemia. He called round at Hanks' house. With God's help, he told him, he could cure her. Conventional medicine had failed, and with nothing to lose, Hank agreed to let him try. Nine months later, the cancer was gone. In Hank's eyes, a miracle. Michael truly was God's servant. Forever indebted, whenever Michael asked for something, Hank obliged, including turning a blind eye to murder. It made twisted sense, but Donna found herself questioning why she'd worked so hard to keep the wretched man alive.

It was only after her adrenaline dipped that she became aware of the strange stares coming her way from the police staff. She'd been so busy trying to save the sheriff's life, she'd forgotten that, beneath her dungarees, she was shirtless. Arms wrapped around herself, she followed Steve into the sheriff's office.

'Try this,' he said, drawing a Rolling Stones T-shirt from a cardboard box. ''Fraid it's the best I can do.'

The T-shirt was a little on the large side and whiffed of male sweat – dead men's clothes, she thought with a shudder – but grateful, she slipped it on.

The police car escorting them back to the gates stops with a jerk, but it's not until the dust settles that Donna sees the dozens of vehicles, including four ambulances, parked haphazardly down the track.

Steve leaps out. 'Shit! Is that smoke?'

'Where?' asks Donna, fumbling with the door handle.

'Over there. Bloody hell, Angel Town is on fire.'

Dozens of worried bystanders are huddled together a few metres from the entrance, now cordoned off with police tape. She sees Cameron among them, comforting a harried-looking Lola.

'Oh, Donna,' Lola says and hurries over. 'Are you okay? Cam told me about the shooting. It must have been terrifying.'

'I'm fine. But the fire? The ambulances? What's going on?'

'I don't know. The guards won't tell us anything, and Rupert and I have spent the last hour trying to persuade them to let us through.'

'Michael must realise the FBI and the media are coming for him,' Steve says. 'The fire is probably some sick self-fulfilling prophecy. I told you the world is going to end. I may have got the date wrong but ... His back's against the wall. What else can he do?'

Cameron groans. 'Jesus, Steve. You're not helping.'

'Has anyone come out?' Donna asks.

'Not a soul. Oh, Cam, what is going on in there? Do you think Steve is right?'

'I honestly don't know, honey,' Cameron says, enveloping his wife in his bear-like arms. 'But the deputy is going in, and the FBI are on their way. They'll put an end to this.'

'You think?' mutters Steve.

Cameron glares at the journalist over his wife's head. 'Hey, Steve, what say you make sure they've called in the firefighters.'

'On to it.' Wagging his forefinger, Steve sets off towards the gate.

'Our darling girl,' Lola says, clinging to her husband. 'What if she can't escape? What if—'

But Donna doesn't have the stomach for what-ifs. Head down, she scuttles after Steve who has caught up with Todd and is listening, riveted, to what the younger journalist has to say.

'Apparently, a plane flies into Edenville once a fortnight with various supplies,' he reports, the moment Donna reaches them. 'And, every six months or so, John Messenger, a highly respected ethnobotanist Michael met in Colombia, heads to the Amazon to gather hallucinogenic plants.'

'What, like mushrooms, you mean?'

'Yup and ayahuasca, peyote, coca leaf, you name it. The Amerindians use them as medicines, but I suspect Terry Leech simply wants to get fried.'

'Jesus! Do you think John is the guy Thomas accused of poisoning Michael?'

'Must be. Weird, huh?'

Out of the corner of her eye, Donna spies Rupert by his car, beckoning to her to join him. Her mind all over the place, the last thing she needs is a conversation with him, but a question she longs to know the answer to continues to nag away. Gritting her teeth, she marches over.

'Be gentle,' Steve calls after her.

Rupert's face lights up as she approaches. 'Hey, Donna. How are you bearing up?'

But Naomi's admission is ringing in her ears and she's not in the mood for pleasantries. 'Naomi knew Jos was her half-brother, so why did she bring him here? She must have known you were a stranger to your son. What on earth could she have hoped to gain?'

Wincing, he appears to mull the question over. 'She was old enough to remember her mother.'

'And your point is?'

'Well, a couple of years ago, Vonnie decided to tell Ellie the truth about Ingrid and me.'

'You mean, she didn't know you'd run off with another woman when her mum was pregnant?'

He shifts awkwardly. 'Ellie rooted through my things and found some photos of Jos, Pauline had sent me. Did you know they kept in touch?'

Donna glowers at him, folds her arms, and taps her foot.

'Right, well, Ellie was angry,' Rupert continues, tugging his ear. 'She blamed me for Ingrid's death. She blamed you, too. I tried, but how can you explain the inexplicable? We fell out, she left and joined the cult. But then she came back, told me she loved me and wanted to try and work things out. Things were going well until I refused to join her. Seems it was the trigger she needed to seek the revenge she'd already plotted. The rest you know.'

No, thinks Donna, absently rubbing her arms, I don't. How could anyone in their right mind walk out on not one, but two wives without a word, let alone fail to understand the painful and destructive effect it would have on them both, not to mention the damage it would inflict on their children? Naomi had gained the father her kids missed out on, but it wasn't enough. How could it be when Naomi had worked out that the only person Rupert cared about was himself? The man lacked a moral compass. Okay, so he used to accompany her on the campaign trail, but that was probably because it suited him at the time. He must have become bored. Why else would he have gone to America, slipping skins to become an estate agent – the sort of career he claimed to despise – under the pretext of looking after the child he didn't know he had? He's an expert liar, a philanderer and egotist and, mug that she is, she'd been totally taken in. She'd been wrong to blame the child when the fault lay squarely with the father. Naomi was just as much a victim as she was. All those years she's wasted wishing him back. All the pain, self-doubt, and self-loathing she's suffered, wondering whether his leaving had somehow been her fault.

'I still love you, Donna.' He reaches out to touch her cheek.

The words trip off his tongue but slice through her like a knife. If he loved her, he would've explained all this years ago. They'd have fought, but who knows, she might have forgiven him. She might even have taken Naomi in. But he'd taken the coward's way out and run away without a word. She narrows her eyes and sloughs off his hand.

'I mean it. Seeing you again, I realise leaving you was the biggest mistake of my life. I love you and I want you back.'

Unable to contain it any longer, fifteen years of pent-up anger finally spill out of her. 'You're a mean, selfish bastard, Rupert. Frankly, I'm glad you left. When this is over, I promise I will never, ever speak to you again.'

And thrusting back her shoulders, she turns and walks away.

Donna is sitting beside Steve on the bonnet of his car, waiting for news. Her nerves are fraying by the second. It's been half an hour since the deputy drove into Edenville, and the fire shows little sign of abating. More perplexing still, nobody has fled the burning town, odd, given the hostile mood of the men protesting outside Ascension House. They'd been angry with Michael, furious about the allegations levelled against him. It seems unlikely they're staying to fight the flames. Had Michael enlisted the help of his guards and forced them to remain?

'So, what were your impressions of Terry Leech?' Steve asks. 'Madman or Messiah?'

Donna scratches her head. She'd been expecting a madman, and yet, face to face, he'd come across as perfectly sane. Charming, too, not to mention handsome. If she'd met Terry on the Aldermaston march, and not Rupert, who's to say he wouldn't have pulled the wool over her eyes as easily as Rupert had? 'He certainly looks the part.'

'Don't tell me you were tempted?'

'No, of course not, but now, at least, I understand why people are. Given the right circumstances, we're all susceptible.'

Steve smiles. 'You should talk to him, you know.'

'When I said ... oh, never mind.' What was the point? Steve was a man totally lacking in self-doubt.

'You should still talk to him.'

What is it with this guy? 'I just did. You saw me!'

Steve strokes an imaginary beard. 'Hmm. Not sure you can call that talking.'

'My husband's an idiot.'

'Yes, but he's a nice idiot. And he was once your idiot. I know you find this hard to accept, but he's going through hell, too.'

Donna clenches her jaw. Rupert's state of mind is of no interest to her. In life, you reap what you sow. And it's probably all an act anyway. How can he be concerned for someone he doesn't know? She wants nothing more to do with him. She's far too worried about what's going on in Edenville. Jos is in there. Are people burning to death? Are they being shot? She desperately wants answers. If only the FBI would hurry up.

'They shot the sheriff, but will they shoot the deputy?' mutters Steve.

Donna has a hellish vision of the sheriff's wound, spurting blood as she tries to staunch it. There's nothing remotely funny about that. Honestly, Steve can be a major pain in the arse sometimes.

'Sorry. Bad timing.'

Shielding her eyes from the sun rising above clouds of billowing, grey smoke, she glances down the track. Still no sign of the police car, but there is something. A dark speck in the distance. A tree? She strains her eyes. The speck is growing. A person? No, several figures, and they're advancing towards them. She leans forward. 'Look!'

Steve follows the line of her finger. 'Guardians?'

'I think so.'

'C'mon.' He leaps off the bonnet and sprints towards the gate.

The ninja guards are pointing their guns at four armed men who are dressed in what was once the same black uniform, but which are ragged and torn. Did they murder people before they fled? Donna wonders, as half a dozen deputies and assistants, clutching regulation pistols, home in on them.

'We'd better take cover,' Steve says and guides Donna behind a car a little way back. 'In case there's a shootout.'

Sweating profusely, Donna peers around the boot. The refugees have dropped their weapons. They raise their hands in surrender and the guards wave them through. Donna runs over, closely followed by Steve.

One of the deputies beats them to it. 'Keep back,' he says, attempting to steer them away.

'I just want to know what's going on.' Donna turns to an escapee, a young man of about nineteen with blistered skin and scorched hair. 'My son is in there. His name is Jos Prince. Do you know him?'

The man shakes his head and wipes the soot from his face with what's left of his headdress.

'But can you tell me what's happening?'

'Ascension House is on fire. People are trapped and burning to death.'

Donna clutches her throat. 'Oh my God.'

'Did Michael set it alight?' Steve asks.

'The Guardians did this.'

Steve's jaw drops. 'I thought they were devoted to Michael.'

'A young man with the Devil in him tried to seduce the Divine Protector. He's dead now, but the Guardians still turned on Michael. They are turning on each other. We were expecting a battle, but I never imagined it would be fought between ourselves.'

'Fuck!' exclaims Steve.

Donna fumbles for Jos' photo and shoves it under his nose. 'This is my son. Have you seen him?'

The man recoils.

'What is it? Tell me!'

But he has covered his ears and is moaning quietly.

Donna tugs his sleeve. 'He's dead, isn't he?'

'That's enough,' the deputy says and guides the injured man towards an ambulance.

'But my son,' she says, sobbing. 'My Jos.' All night she'd hoped they'd be together again. Now she finds herself praying he is still alive.

CHAPTER THIRTY-FOUR

I can't understand what's happened. Raphael is dead. Murdered by the Divine Protector. My own father, who any second now will kill my mother. Will kill me. Dear Lord, what kind of father kills his own daughter?

I think of the black wings on his back, his black moods and dark heart, his lies, and see him for what he really is. The Devil in disguise. Spots flash in front of my eyes. I'm going to faint. I know it. Maybe that's a good thing. Maybe that way I won't feel death's pain.

'Michael, please,' Mom says again. 'You don't want to do this.'

But I sense there are deep, dark holes in his jet-black brain that no words from Mom or me could ever hope to fill.

His right eye flickering, Michael cocks the gun.

No. He can't do this. He can't. I won't let him. But an alarm bell is blaring, warning me to keep my mouth firmly shut. If I say or do anything to upset him, we're dead.

His trigger finger twitches.

I squeeze my eyes shut.

Dear Lord. Seems any minute now, my life will be over. I

mustn't worry. Death is just the start. A new beginning. I am a true Guardian of God. I was born and bred in Edenville. I have never been of the Otherworld. And although this is nothing like how I pictured Armageddon, my soul will soon ascend to start my bigger, better eternal life in the Spiritual Realm.

Unless ... unless Michael lied about that, too? What if I don't ascend? What then? My chest is so heavy it feels like it might cave in. I don't want to die.

'WHAT SORCERY IS THIS?'

My eyes snap open and I gasp. Michael has lowered the gun and is pointing a trembling finger at the teahouse. At Jos, who was lying like a corpse on the floor, but is now sitting up and rubbing his eyes. I'm so relieved he's alive, it's all I can do not to scream.

Michael shrinks back. 'It is the Devil's work!'

'A miracle, surely,' Mom whispers. 'He who was dead, lives.'

I nod and play along. 'The work of God.'

Jos holds out an arm and inspects it as if he can't quite comprehend it's part of him. He raises his head and glares at Michael, anger simmering in his glassy, bloodshot eyes.

'A zombie. Risen from the dead. I told Raphael to burn the body. He should have burned the body. I knew it. I knew it. He was in league with Satan all along.' Snivelling, Michael swivels around and scampers over the bridge.

Tears trickling down my face, I rush over to Jos and fling my arms around him. 'I can't believe you're okay. You are okay, aren't you?' Blushing, I let go.

'I feel odd. Weak and stuff, but yeah.' He turns his hands over and stares at his palms.

'It must have been terrifying.

'It was. Like I was ... floating above my ... body.' He

pauses to catch his breath. 'I could see you all ... I could hear everything ... but I couldn't respond.'

'Raphael said you were locked in or something.'

'He saved my life.' He glances around fretfully. 'Where is he? I need to thank him.'

I clasp my trembling hands and tilt my head at Raphael's lifeless body. Blood has leaked from the bullet holes, surrounding him in a crimson aureole, his eyes staring blindly at the sky. Is his soul up there, watching over us? I wonder, as Mom kneels beside him and gently closes them?

'He was a good man,' she says. 'After all.'

And I'm thinking, no. He was more than that. So much more. He was the best man I ever knew. He helped me when no one else would. With him gone, how will I cope? How will I survive? How will any of us survive? A lump rises in my throat. I swallow it quickly. If I start crying, I will never stop.

'I got him wrong,' Jos says.

I shake my head, barely holding it all together. He isn't the only one.

Mom puts her arm around me. 'He saved all our lives. And now he's at peace. We should be thankful for that.' She peers over her shoulder. 'Are you able to walk, Jos? There's no way Michael can get back inside Ascension House. Once he's recovered his nerve, he'll come after us. We need to find a way out of here.'

The key, I think, patting my singed pockets. But there's nothing there. Oh God, in all the chaos it must have fallen out. My heart going like the clappers, I shove my hands inside and rummage around. And just as I'm thinking we're going to burn to death, my fingers settle on something solid. Dizzy with relief, I whip out the key and hold it up. 'He'll be searching for this.'

'You found it. Thank God. Help me support Jos, and we'll go now.'

Somehow, the three of us manage to hobble over the bridge and down the path to the living wall. Jos leans against it, panting. I take his hand and slowly, we sidestep down the narrow corridor. It's only once we reach the door that the panic I've conquered returns with a vengeance. 'What'll we do now? The Guardians are hardly gonna greet us with open arms.'

Mom draws herself up to her full height. 'We'll head for home.'

'It'll be the first place they go.'

'Samuel's barn, then. When night falls, we'll make our escape.'

'But—'

'We can't stay here,' Jos says.

I clamp my hands over my ears and squeeze my eyes shut. This can't be happening. It can't. Raphael dead. My father all-out crazy. Guardians baying for our blood.

Mom prizes my hands off my ears. 'You need to stay strong. Look at me, Lola.'

I open one eye.

She cradles my cheeks. 'We can do this, but you must have faith.'

I want to. But how can I when I know, deep down, she doesn't either, that she's being brave. For me. For Jos. Out of the frying pan into the fire, I think miserably. My hand shaking, I insert the key in the lock. I try but I can't shift it.

Mom takes over. Wincing, she lets go and blows on her hands.

I see the blisters. 'Jesus, Mom. What happened?'

'I burnt them on the door when I was trying to escape.'

'Oh God. We're trapped.'

'Let me have a go,' Jos says.

Mom shakes her head. 'You don't have the strength. I'll try again.'

Breathing deeply, I close my eyes and dismiss the negative thoughts charging around my brain. 'No. I'll do it.' Calmer now, I twist the key with all my might. I can feel the strain in my arms. My shoulders. My neck muscles. My face heats up with the effort. I will do this. I will not give up. I will not. Ugh.

I'm about to admit defeat when there's a clunk. Half laughing, half crying, I open the door.

Jos' arms around our shoulders once more, we stagger to the orchard, where we pause to catch our breath.

Mom plucks an orange, peels it, and hands it to Jos. 'Eat this. It might boost your strength.'

He does as he's told, and miraculously, it seems to me, some colour returns to his cheeks. Seconds later, we're off again. By the time we reach the edge of the alfalfa fields, we see that Ascension House is not the only building on fire. Edenville is burning brightly, the rows of identical houses glowing like torches. Fighting to extinguish the flames, a long line of men hurriedly pass buckets from the standpipe at the top end of Main Street. Will Farmer Samuel's barn still be standing? My chest tightens. There's no way out. We are going to die.

Someone screams.

I spin around and see Miriam, clutching her hair. Behind her, a small group of women are ogling us as if we're ghosts and not three people in fear of their lives. I spot Abi's mom, Susanna. Leah from The Mill. The witch, Keziah, her semi-bald scalp blistered and bleeding. Sarah and Dorcas with grime on their faces. Margaret, Rebecca, and Principality Judith, their clothes in shreds. Wailing, they drop to their knees and bow their heads.

I glance at Mom who shrugs. I inch nearer. The wails grow louder.

And then slowly, awkwardly, Keziah rises to her feet, hands clasped in prayer. 'He is come.'

I whirl round, fully expecting to see Michael, but no one is there.

She opens her arms and looks to the sky. 'The Lamb is risen.'

The Lamb? Where? I scour the landscape. Nothing.

'And his wife, Pistis Sophia.'

I stare at Mom questioningly.

'You,' she mutters.

'Me?'

'And Jos.'

'He has come to lead us to the light,' continues Keziah.

It's so ridiculous I want to laugh. But then I remember once upon a time I'd thought Jos was Christ. And Michael filmed Jos on the altar. They thought he was dead.

Goosebumps prickle my skin. I'm bone cold but I dare not move. Dare not give myself away. This isn't happening. It's a nightmare. A never-ending nightmare. In a minute I'll wake up. Only, thanks to the women's screams, the men have put down their buckets, and a crowd is gathering. I see Ben, his mouth hanging open. Farmer Samuel. Doctor Seth. Kushiel and Puriel, badly burned, and a Power without his headdress who I see is Jonah, Blacksmith Simeon's son. Miller Isaac and Fisherman Cain. Elijah, a dazed look on his mean face, and my sisters, Jemima and Isabel. Dozens more survivors, all of them spellbound. And as I am wondering what it is they're expecting us to do, their expressions change from ecstasy to anger.

They mean to kill us after all.

But no, they are pointing at something. I turn and see Michael, his face blackened, his clothes torn and charred.

And in his hand, the gun.

He holds it out to Mom. 'Shoot me, Zosia.'

'I am not going to shoot you,' she says quietly.

'Please.' Michael jerks his thumb at his people. 'They'll kill me anyway if you don't. Please, Zosia. Do this one last thing for me.'

'Nobody is going to kill you, Michael.'

'Fine. Then you've made your choice.' He raises his arm. Takes aim.

I lunge for Mom. 'NO!'

Too late. The gun explodes with a loud bang.

The bullet enters Mom's chest. Her body buckles.

Screams. So many screams. So much blood.

I cling to her. But she slips through my fingers, onto the road. A rag doll, not a person. I drop down next to her and reach for her hand.

'My name is Zosia. Don't ever forget it,' she breathes and her head falls limply to the side.

'No!' I yell. 'No. You can't die. Mom, please.'

Jos is helping me to my feet.

Someone cries out.

I glance up. The Guardians are moving in on Michael. His eyes wide with fright, he places the barrel in his mouth.

Another bang, and his brains burst through his skull. Silver slivers beneath a bright-blue sky.

'Look away,' Jos says.

And just as I'm thinking I've seen it all before, stars dance in front of my eyes and the world goes black.

CHAPTER
THIRTY-FIVE

The helicopter thrums as it swoops overhead. In the distance, a siren bleats and the firefighters set to work. Donna picks up a handful of dust and watches it run through her fingers. Vivid pictures are turning circles in her mind. A kaleidoscope of her life. The Aldermaston March and the anti-Vietnam demonstration. Storming the stage at the Miss World Protest. Gay Pride. Reclaiming the Night for Women's Lib. The Anti-Nazi League rally. Greenham Common. The inventory of a life lived banging a drum. The legacy of a social conscience. Cause after cause after cause. She'd turn her back on every one if it meant Jos could live. He was barely sixteen. A child. Her only son. Dead. And all for what? It was such a terrible, terrible waste.

Rupert passes her his handkerchief. 'Talk to me, Donna.'

She shudders. 'I can't cope with this. I really can't.'

'It'll be okay.' He puts his arm around her shoulders.

'Get your stinking, adulterous hands off me. It won't be okay. Okay? And I meant every word I said. So ...'

'Sorry. I'm sorry.'

'Jos is dead. My world is …' But she can't complete the sentence.

'Donna, I understand. He was my son, too.'

No, he was not your son. But she's too exhausted to argue anymore. She closes her eyes but, confronted by the hellish vision of Jos, precariously balanced on his window ledge, she quickly opens them again. Where had it all gone wrong? Bullying, Tess said. Billy and Tubs, his two best friends. And yet I didn't know. I was his mother, I should have been there when he needed me.

'It's an illness,' Chrissie said. 'A mental illness. And you're not a doctor.'

When had she grown so wise?

'Oh God. What'll I tell her?' she murmurs. 'She's about to have a baby?'

'What's that?' Rupert asks.

She holds her head in her hands. What is wrong with the man? I thought I'd seen the last of him. I all but told him I hate him. Why won't he take the hint and piss off? Go and support Naomi, the daughter I never knew he had, back at the station being grilled by the police.

'Donna! Donna! Get over here, quick. You, too, Rupert.'

What now? Tired and stiff, she hobbles over, to where Steve, Cameron, Lola, and almost all the other bystanders, journalists, and police have gathered, their eyes glued on Edenville.

Steve takes her hand and gives it a squeeze. 'You're gonna want to see this. Up here. Quick.' He springs onto the roof of a police car and hauls her up. 'See.'

Against the backdrop of a burning town, a young man with dark-blond hair, smuts on his face, and ragged clothes, staggers down the track, followed by a large group of equally dishevelled people, heads bowed, hands clasped.

In his arms he carries a teenage girl in a torn and blood-stained once-white dress, who clings to him like a limpet.

It could be a scene from *Jesus of Nazareth* but it isn't. It's real life. She has no idea why these people are following her son. She doesn't care. She thought he was dead, and yet here he is, alive.

Steve cups her face in her hands. 'It's him, isn't it, Donna? Can you believe it? Jos. He's alive.'

Yes, she thinks as he kisses her. Yes, it is.

And, holding her arms aloft, Donna tips her face to the sun and smiles.

CHAPTER
THIRTY-SIX

Once upon a time, I dreamt about running away from Edenville. Me and Mom together. Not Jemima. Not Isabel. Not Noah. Just the two of us. Mom and me. We'd go and find her family. Build a life together in a little house, away from here. Away from the Powers, The Meeting Room, the rules and regulations. Michael. There would be endless storybooks to read, champagne to drink. There would be hotels, dancing, and green lights at the end of wooden piers. Every day we'd laugh and smile. We'd run, we'd jump, we'd sing. We'd stay out all night if it took our fancy. We'd go wherever we liked. Take a holiday. Nobody would tell us what we could and couldn't do.

An exquisite dream. My dream. Lost in the dying embers of a fire.

Raised from the almost-dead, Jos is carrying me. I don't know how he has the strength. He is talking to me, too, in breathless bursts. Word after word after word. He means to soothe me with them. So I close my eyes and listen.

'My mother will take care of you. She's actually not that

bad. I mean, she can be a right pain, with all her campaigning and rallying. Honest to God, I used to think she cared more about her causes than she did about me. But she doesn't. Not really. She's just passionate about things. She always has been. I see that now. Me and my two sisters, we mean the world to her. She's always telling us we do. Always. It's been tough for her, without my dad. Well, I don't need to tell you that. Turns out he was married before. Naomi is his daughter. My half-sister. Did I tell you already? I really liked her at first but I reckon she's a liar, just like him. Anyway, what I mean is, you'll be safe with us in Brighton. It's by the sea and near the Downs. Cool place, Brighton. And our house isn't bad. You'll love it. And you'll love Tess and Chrissie, too. They're my sisters. Both older than me, but they're cool. Really cool. They're going to love you, too. And I'll be there, Lola. You mustn't worry about that. And I'll look after you, as well. And when you're old enough, who knows what we'll do. Of course, it's going to be new and different and you'll have a lot to get used to. I understand that, but I'll help you. And Mum will help you, too. And you'll go to school and make new friends. And when you've settled down and got the hang of things, you'll find it so much better than your life ever was in here. Everything will be okay, Lola. Trust me.'

I wonder if he knows the Guardians are following him. He's said nothing to them. Not a single word. He doesn't have to. He is born again. They believe in him. They will follow him to the ends of the earth. It's what they do.

Like me, it's all they know.

I have made it to the Otherworld. I never thought I would, but here I am. It looks the same as Edenville. Same mountains, same trees, same desert. But there are so many people, crowding us, talking all at once. Strange people. Loud people. I'm struggling to breathe. It's too much. Too much. I cling to Jos' hand as if my life depends on it. Well, it does depend on it. Without him, I'm alone.

A tall woman in a shirt with big red lips on it, flings her arms around him and hugs him so hard I'm worried she might squeeze the life out of him. I want to tell her to stop. Two times dead would be a death too far. But she is crying, so I don't, even though I know they're happy tears. A man with bushy blond hair and a huge grin stretched across his face pats her on the back, while a dark-haired man watches awkwardly from a little way off. At last she lets go of Jos and, together with the blond man, leads us to a pale-blue car parked a little way away.

'I'm Steve,' he says as the followers Jos has left behind begin to wail. 'You're safe now.'

I stare at him blankly.

'This is Donna. Jos' Mom.'

I glance at Jos. He's crying, too. 'Sorry, Mum. I'm sorry,' he says over and over.

'I'm sorry, too. For everything,' she says, and Jos lets go of my hand to hug her back. 'But it's okay. Everything is going to be okay.'

Cast adrift, I wrap my arms around myself. My eyes dart this way and that. What will happen to me now?

It's too much to take in. Too much.

Someone calls my name. 'Lola?'

I'm about to answer, but it's not me they're talking to. It's a lady in a large straw hat. She has steel-grey hair and hazel eyes. Sad eyes.

The deputy sheriff approaches her. 'Dolores Scott?'

I jolt. I know that name. I've read it often enough. Dolores 'Lola' Scott.

For Zosia.

Something twigs.

'Is it Zosia?' the woman asks. 'Is she ... dead.'

My mother's dying words leap out at me. *My name is Zosia*. I gasp.

The woman hears and turns to me. 'What is it, dear?'

I take a deep breath. 'My mother's name was Zosia.' My voice sounds odd – tiny and flimsy – as if it doesn't belong to me. 'She told me never to forget it.'

She eyes me curiously for a moment then crumples, as if I've punched her in the belly.

A tall man I'm sure I've seen somewhere, hurries to her side. 'Honey.'

She bats the air. 'No, no, Cam. I'm fine. I'm fine.' She places her hands on my arms and looks me square in the eye.

I see my mother in the orange flecks of her irises, in the slope of her slender nose and the curve of her rose-coloured lips. She smiles at me then, this woman whose heart is as broken as mine, and asks me my name.

'Lola.'

And as she repeats it over and over, tears streaming down her face, a tiny kernel of hope lodges itself in my heart.

The End

THANK YOU

A massive thank you for reading *Angel Town*.
If you enjoyed it please post a review on Amazon, or give it a rating, and help other readers discover the story.

If you'd like to hear my latest news, why not sign up to my mailing list on my website: www.fionacane.com

Or check out my author page: FionaCane@Amazon.com

ACKNOWLEDGMENTS

Angel Town is dedicated to my son, Sam. I started writing it shortly after he was diagnosed with clinical depression. His anxiety and low self-esteem had been building since childhood but it wasn't until his early twenties that he hit rock bottom. I cannot begin to describe how helpless I felt when I realised that, no matter how well-meaning my intentions, I could not make him better. I could only listen and empathise. It was the hardest, most painful thing I've ever had to do and I felt incapacitated and a failure. Thankfully, with the help and encouragement of family, friends, and an inspirational psychotherapist, he is on the road to recovery. I am immensely proud of the courage and bravery he showed during those dark times, and which he continues to draw on every day of his life. He is my brilliant, shiny bright star and I am so lucky to have him. Thank you for staying with us, Sam. I would be lost without you.

For your amazing feedback as my beta reader, Fran Kazamia, a million thanks. You have an editor's eye for plot detail and I cannot imagine writing a book without your input. Thank you, Ade, for another wonderful cover design. There simply isn't anyone better. To Damian Thornton, a, massive thank you for casting a forensic eye over the final draft. Your support means the absolute world to me, and I am over the moon that you think *Angel Town* is my best book yet. To my editor, Emmy Ellis, a round of applause for the speed with which you polished the manuscript. I'm dead chuffed *Angel Town* is one of your favourite books ever. And for all the hardworking bloggers out there, particularly Anne Williams, Anne Cater, John Fish, Sophie Hedley and Karen Hilton, I simply cannot thank you enough for your continued support. You are, quite simply, the best people in the publishing world.

Huge thanks to, Holly, for being the very best daughter a mother could wish for and for propping me up when no one else can. And to my husband, Simon, for your steadfast loyalty and your levelheadedness in a crisis.

AUTHOR'S NOTE

To gain an insight into cults – their obsessive lure, their charismatic leaders, rules and practices – these documentaries and books were invaluable: *Holy Hell; Children of God; Jonestown: Terror in the Jungle*; *Waco: The Rules of Engagement; Waco: Madman or Messiah; Wild, Wild Country; My Scientology Movie.* And the TV Mini Series, *Waco. My Life in Orange* by Tim Guest; *Not Without my Sister* by Kristina Jones, Celeste Jones and Juliana Buhring; *In the Days of Rain* by Rebecca Stott; *Stolen Innocence* by Elissa Wall; *Terror, Love and Brainwashing* by Alexandra Stein; *The Road to Jonestown: Jim Jones and People's Temple* by Jeff Guinn; *CULTS: In Too Deep From Jonestown To Scientology*, Lightning Guides. The effect of psychedelic plants: *One River: Exploration and Discoveries in the Amazon Rain Forest* by Wade Davis. Tetrodotoxin poisoning: *The Serpent and the Rainbow* by Wade Davis. Angels: *The Encyclopedia of Angels* by Constance Victoria Briggs. And the Apocalypse: *The Book of Revelations.*

ABOUT FIONA CANE

Fiona was born and educated in Sussex. After graduating from Exeter University with a degree in Philosophy, she worked in London in film, TV and entertainment PR. She moved back to Sussex with her husband and two children and coached tennis while scratching away at novels in her spare time.

Also by Fiona Cane

A SONG UNSUNG
THE OTHER SIDE OF THE MOUNTAIN
A PUSH TOO FAR
WHEN THE DOVE CRIED
KILLING FAME

Printed in Great Britain
by Amazon

81989051R00222